DANCING WITH VENGEANCE:
A Woman Reborn

*To Richard -
Wonderful meeting you in person! Keep practicing your songs without expectation and see what happens. ☺
Best!
Katherine*

DANCING WITH VENGEANCE:
A Woman Reborn

A Novel by

K. Gibson Newcomer

This work is fiction. With the exception of Attila the Hun, Prince Valamir and his brother, all characters are products of the author's imagination. Any resemblance to any persons living or deceased is entirely coincidental.

Copyright © 1994, 2000 by Katherine Gibson Newcomer
(as THE PHOENIX AND THE FALCON)

All rights reserved. No part of this book may be reproduced, stored in a retrieval system, or transmitted by any means, electronic, mechanical, photocopying, recording, or otherwise, without written permission from the author.

ISBN 1-58500-872-9

Front cover illustration by Irene Dunsavage
Front cover design by Gail Mardfin Starkey
Front cover portrait by John Santolo
Back cover design by Carlos Crosbie

1stBooks-rev.09/06/00

ACKNOWLEDGEMENTS

My special thanks to my husband and family, Karla Wiley, Betty David-Ross, and Christine Connell.

PROLOGUE

415 A.D.

Framed by the square courtyard, the open sky was bright. Noise from the city of Constantinople intruded, but the house's thick, stone walls muffled the din. Water danced in the large alabaster fountain, filling the inner sanctum with sparkling sounds.

A young child, no more than six, played quietly, almost secretively, in the shadows behind two tall pottery jars. Her dress was like a patch of indigo blue against the mosaic floor. Sunlight filtered through potted trees and glittered on the glazed urns. The jars, holding cooking oil, were decorated with painted birds, some on the threshold of flight, others already in the air. It was as if they were alive in the brilliant light.

The child, Helena, felt safe in her nest, hidden from her current nurse, a woman who always found fault with her. She was happy, engrossed in a world of make believe. Fiery white toy horses pulled Alexander the Great's chariot. Her five soldiers, by the magic of pretend, had become at least thirty; the tall urns were enormous mountains, blocking Alexander's passage to Persia. Her grandfather, a gifted storyteller, had brought the ancient conqueror to life during her lessons, but referred to him only as "Sikunder the Destroyer" because of the devastation he had wrought in Persia.

The miniatures, once her father's, had many nicks and scratches, having seen much in the way of "military" action. Helena remembered little about him, except his deep voice and the way his laughter filled a room. Though he had forgotten all of her birthdays, she treasured the toys because they had been his.

Her grandfather said that he would return for another visit someday, but Helena had stopped believing. The last letter from her father was well over three years old. Her mother was long dead, dying a few weeks after her birth. Soon after, her grieving father resumed his command in the Imperial Persian Army, leaving his infant daughter in his father's care.

Despite her grandfather's careful explanations, Helena felt sad when she thought of her father, not really understanding why he went away.

"Helena! Helena!" a woman's voice called. The nurse stood at the top of the central stone staircase, her middle-aged face creased, her lips pursed. The child edged back into the shadows, scarcely breathing, clutching her toys.

"Go away!" she thought.

Helena stared at her talisman: a large mosaic phoenix in the floor near the marble fountain. She thought it magical, almost believing that if she looked at nothing else, it would make her invisible. Family tradition maintained that anyone who crossed its flaming wings with joy would have good fortune for a full day and night. Of course, now that the Empire had become Christian, such beliefs remained within the family.

"Nurse! Have you lost your charge again?" Helena's grandfather asked in his baritone voice.

Startled, the woman screeched. When Grandfather willed it, he could move with the stealth of a cat.

"She-she ran off, master. Not wanting her lessons!"

"And what had you planned to teach today?"

"The usual things: how to dress the hair, the art of pedicure, showing a maiden's feet with perfection in her thongs..."

Helena's grandfather cut into the cooing recital.

"Enough! I never gave orders for such instruction! You are to keep her clean, freshly clothed, and well nourished!"

Miriam sobbed. "I-I must have misunderstood!"

"Perhaps you'll do better tomorrow," he said more gently. "Now be off!"

The nurse hurried down the stairs, around the fountain, and across the phoenix. Helena stared with quiet exultation at her rapid departure.

"Come out now," her grandfather said, looking down from over the urns. "It's time for your lesson."

She had not even heard his steps! He was a magician, she just knew it.

"Oh, Grandfather!" she said, laughing, running toward his open arms.

The rhythmic beat of a solitary horse, galloping hard across the wind-swept steppes intruded upon her dream. Her grandfather's face receded into shadow. Still half-asleep, Helena whispered, "No!"

Not breaking stride, the horse whinnied. It was deep, like a stallion's.

She opened her eyes.

She was cold, far from the warmth of that summer day in Constantinople. The chill wind rushed through the cracks of the mud and thatch house into the darkness crowded with sleeping women and children. She shut her eyes quickly, trying to go back to sleep, to her dream and to her childhood, where the safety of home and Grandfather waited.

CHAPTER ONE

427 A.D.

"Huns! A day's journey! In the name of the Gods, awake!" a man's voice ripped through the air, slicing through the last fragments of her dream.

Groggy from sleep, Helena rubbed her green eyes. Her ears strained, listening for another call. Her throat constricted as she inhaled the close odor of stale sweat and dirty clothes. Her son, only three, slept at her side. After all, at eighteen wasn't she a woman grown?

Blinking away tears, Helena remembered the hoof beats. They had awakened her, robbing her of Grandfather's embrace. She shivered, not from the cold night air, but from sudden fear.

The man's voice rang out. "Water for my horse!" he shouted outside in the chill autumn air.

She sat up, flinging long, dark hair from a wide brow, alarmed, yet obscurely disappointed. The horseman had not come for her. Marooned for five years in a small, primitive village, Helena had made a religion of hope. She prayed for rescue, yet continually speculated on avenues of escape. She waited and watched, and planned for the eventual day when Mikael would be old enough to survive the journey to Persia where her grandfather's family lived.

Brushing aside disappointment, she pulsed with curiosity about the night traveler. The women on the wives' side of the thatched house stirred, their whispers shrill with panic. Careful not to disturb her son, she quickly slid from their sleeping pad. Mikael dreamt with innocent abandon.

Her heart pounded. She stood, poised for action. The man spoke of Huns. Their very name inspired terror within the safety of the great walled city of Constantinople. Here on the open steppes, she could not begin to imagine the peril.

Her mind racing, Helena questioned who would travel at night in reckless defiance of the wolves. As winter approached, the animals ran in packs, hunger lending them desperate strength.

She glanced at the wooden back door. From the next room, Magga roused Kansbar, the aging leader of the village.

"Get up!" Magga whispered with a hiss.

He snorted, his sleep interrupted mid-snore.

Helena edged over to the woven partition separating the wives and children from Kansbar. She was not alone. Already other women were peering through the screen, busily elbowing each other aside for a better angle.

Helena was reluctant to spy on Kansbar and his mistress. But curiosity overwhelmed her sense of etiquette. Feeling self-conscious, she looked through the fraying tapestry. With his back to Magga, Kansbar sat inertly on their low bed. His large feet were motionless on the floor. A large fireplace was red with bright embers, warming their side of the mud and thatched house.

Helena burned with impatience.

"Go on!" Magga said, prodding him with her outstretched hand, mirroring Helena's frustration. "He said Huns!"

"The whore!" said the older wife at Helena's side.

Struck by her venomous tone, Helena stared at the graying woman. For the past three years, Magga had tormented Kansbar's wives, flagrantly exploiting her favored status with their husband. Tonight, Helena was glad that someone, anyone, even Magga, was able to prod Kansbar into action.

Outside, the horse jingled its bridle, its hoof pawed the ground.

Helena could wait no longer. First checking if Mikael still slept, she lithely stepped to the back door. Without a sound, she slipped outside.

As always, the wind from the steppes blew, buffeting her cheeks. The half moon was bright, casting long shadows. Hugging the wall, she walked lightly to the front edge of the house and peered around the corner.

Even mounted on a horse, Helena could see that the man was tall. His blond hair was tied back loosely. His metal breast plate gleamed in the moonlight. Over his shoulder, he carried a clutch of arrows, in his hand, a glistening blade. His horse was muscular, bred for speed.

Memory teased her. Years ago, in Constantinople, she had seen horsemen armed this way, but could not remember their tribe. A shaft of hope kindled in her heart. She held her breath. Exhaling slowly, she calmed the butterflies in her stomach and dared to consider if he could be a messenger from home. After all, she reasoned, why else would he be alone on the steppes? She studied him, watching his every move: the ease with which he sat upon his mount, the smooth, practiced manner with which he held his blade.

As if sensing her gaze, he looked in her direction. As he moved his roan horse toward her, she retreated into deeper shadow.

"You, there, come out. I see you," he said without menace.

Prudence forbade movement, but she stepped forward, away from darkness, into the moonlight.

"What's your name?" he asked.

Just then, Kansbar threw open the front door, announcing himself with a bang. Helena edged from view.

"You've disturbed our peace," Kansbar said in his most authoritative voice.

The stranger glanced once more in Helena's direction, but did not betray her presence. "I bring grave news," the blond man said.

"What is it?" Kansbar asked, his voice catching in his throat.

"Father!" Ivan bellowed from across the crude square. A young man emerged from his hut, blunt sword in hand.

The stranger assessed him with a glance, then returned his focus to Kansbar. "With my own eyes, I saw a large band of Huns, not a day's ride away."

"No," Kansbar gasped.

"I don't believe him," Ivan said, reaching his father's side. "I never heard of them riding this far." His light brown hair was lanky, obscuring a face which could have been handsome if not ruined by a perpetual sneer.

"No, son," Kansbar said, speaking slowly. "In my father's day, many bands passed through our lands. It was a time of terror. The stories were horrible..."

Kansbar looked at the stranger with considering eyes. "You say you saw them?"

"Yes."

"Come inside, we'll discuss this further."

The man leapt easily from his mount. He gave its neck a brisk pat, then allowed one rein to dangle to the ground. The horse lowered its head to the sparse grass, but did not move from its position.

Helena felt a stirring of foreboding. As Kansbar and Ivan escorted the stranger inside, she scanned the square for prying eyes. Keeping to the shadows, she stepped closer to the roan. It raised its neck and laid back its ears.

"Warrior-trained, are you? Well, I'll keep my distance," she murmured in a soft voice. Unafraid, she hummed the soft tune her grandfather had chanted to calm restive horses.

The animal pricked its ears forward, and watched her with alert eyes. Out of reach of striking hooves, Helena quickly noted that its breathing was smooth and its neck was dry.

"You're a beauty," she said.

As if in response, the animal nickered softly. His eyes still on her, he cropped grass again.

When she slipped through the back door, the women were in an uproar. Despite all the noise, Mikael had not awakened. Helena's face softened as she quickly smoothed the threadbare blanket over his slender shoulders.

Taking a position by the tapestry, Helena watched the stranger. At six feet, he towered over Kansbar, who was easily the tallest man in the village. Even Ivan's bulky build was no match for the visitor's muscular, though tapered, torso. The blond horseman moved with the grace of a panther: at ease, yet coiled for action. He radiated confidence.

Kansbar's expression grew cunning as he eyed the stranger's gear. Bile rose in her throat. She remembered that look all too well. Five years ago, he had gazed at her grandfather's caravan with the same light in his eyes. His words had dripped with obsequious courtesy as he had helped her grandfather, near death, from his white stallion. But Kansbar's face had been avid with greed as his eyes had lingered on the heavily laden camels and then Helena, as if she were a bundle of goods.

As Kansbar sheathed his weapon, a fine, Persian sword, she wanted to rip it from his coarse hands. The blade had belonged to her grandfather and his father before him.

Helena clenched her fists and forced herself to be still.

The blond man glanced at the sword with an expert's eye. She discerned no avarice in his expression, only surprise, tempered by curiosity.

Provocatively draped by blankets, Magga's pose was generous. Helena took an obscure satisfaction in the fact that the stranger looked at Magga once, then ignored her to warm his hands at the fire.

The flames burnished his blond hair with copper. His cheeks were clean-shaven, showing a strong jaw line; his nose was straight, if a bit long. His head carriage was erect, almost regal. Helena guessed that he had blue eyes, but the light was too dim for certainty.

He faced Kansbar. All at once, Helena knew in her bones that he was not a mere messenger from Constantinople, but a soldier, a hunter after prey. This man had seen others die in battle, many at the point of his own sword. His eyes scanned the room, checking his perimeters. Blood rushed to her face. Her breathing quickened. She felt fear.

Remembering her childhood training, she calmed herself by feeling her body as sensation, allowing its turmoil to pass without judgment. She sensed her grandfather's presence, almost as if she heard his voice, reminding her to listen not only to the outside world, but to her heart.

Her breathing became deeper, quieter. As she considered her impressions, Helena knew that something was terribly wrong. The horse had been fresh, not even lathered. The man's back was supple, with no signs of fatigue from hours in the saddle. His leather garb was sturdy, perfectly adapted for combat. His breastplate glistened, polished to a fine patina. He moved at one with the sword at his side without a trace of awkwardness.

He reminded her of a falcon, who watched dispassionately as the hare fled, just before swooping for the kill.

Helena retreated to Mikael, whispering him awake. She briskly dressed him in his warmest clothing and wrapped him in her old fur-lined coat. Firmly, she hushed his complaints. Pulling on a thick wool dress, she hid two small, sheathed daggers: one in her side pocket, the other strapped above her knee. Both weapons, finely made, were a tribute to her ingenuity. After her grandfather's death, she had managed to keep them, along with a few gold coins, from Kansbar by hiding them under her clothes. He had not thought to search her after she had given up her mother's ring without a word, mistaking her shocked grief as compliance.

As Helena prepared for the worst, the men spoke what seemed nonsense to her ears. Their voices were reasonable and moderate in pitch. Words about a band of Huns on the nearby silk route filtered through the partition. She believed none of it: this man had brought with him more than warnings.

Her ears roared, echoing her pounding heart. Anxiously, she combed fingers through her dark, flowing hair. Her heart whispered that Mikael was too young to survive a long journey. She dared not consider the wolves and roving, marauding bands.

But her instincts urged flight. Obeying the impulse, she picked up her old satchel, stocked for escape. In the leather bag, she had an old blanket, a few clothes, and most importantly, a bridle.

All that remained was to disappear through the back door.

"Let's go outside, Mikael," she whispered. "The night is clear. I'll let you look at the stars, just this once. Then we'll see if Grandfather's horse sleeps well."

Mikael's hand in hers, she quietly stepped to the door, closer to safety, the wolves pushed to the back of her mind. One danger at a time, she reasoned.

"Helena, Helena!" Ludmilla shouted, still the head wife despite Magga's attempts to subvert her authority. "What are you about, girl?"

Helena held her breath. In the dim light, she turned slowly, panicking, wondering if she had been seen.

"See to the men!" Ludmilla ordered. "Didn't you hear me call you? They asked for mead. Hurry and make yourself useful!"

Soundlessly, Helena placed her bag by the door. With Mikael at her side, she walked to Ludmilla's low pallet.

"Must I go in there? I'm afraid."

"You've nothing to fear, girl," Ludmilla reassured her. "But why have you wakened little Mikael? That's unlike you to disturb his sleep. Give him to me. I'll have Arianna put him back to bed."

"Ludmilla, something's wrong. There's more to the stranger than he's telling."

"Ridiculous! He's all alone. In trouble. Didn't you hear what happened to his caravan? Murdered by Huns! No one has heard of them since my father's time. You, of all people, should be sympathetic to his plight! Why, what if Kansbar had not taken you in, honored you as his bride? Think of what might have become of you!"

Helena became still. Like a torrent, words rose from her depths. "He broke his oath to my grandfather. You forget his promise to send word home. Instead, he paid off our guards so they wouldn't go back to Constantinople." She hesitated. "But Kansbar's greed lost him a fortune! Our steward would have rewarded him far beyond what he stole from our caravan!" she added with quiet vehemence.

"Have you no gratitude? We gave you a home! You disappoint me. Go. Serve the men!"

Helena collected herself. "You've treated me almost like a daughter, Ludmilla. For your kindness, I *am* grateful. I shall never say the same of Kansbar. Your Arianna is fifteen and not yet wed. I was thirteen when he forced me to be his bride."

"Enough, Helena. What's done is done. And remember that once Mikael was on the way, he left you alone. And Magga's been keeping him amused for over three years. Be thankful for your blessings, girl."

Helena lowered her voice. "I pray each night for her continued success."

Ludmilla laughed, a pleasant sound. Her eyes twinkled as they met Helena's. "Now hurry. We've no time for idle chatter. Go! The stranger won't bite you. My Ivan's there!"

At the mention of Ludmilla and Kansbar's eldest, Helena's shoulders stiffened. Yet, to his mother, she wisely offered no criticism. Before Ludmilla could prevent it, Helena whisked Mikael with her through the tapestry. The older wife sighed with exasperation.

Helena stepped quietly into the room, observing all the forms of modesty, eyes to the ground, head slightly bowed with her soft, brown hair obscuring her face. When Kansbar saw Mikael, his nostrils flared as his mouth twisted into a frown.

"By the gods, Helena," Ivan interjected. "Why did you bring the brat?"

Ignoring his eldest half-brother, Mikael flung himself into his father's arms. Even Kansbar could not resist the child's charm. He pushed him away gently, giving him an affectionate pat on the head.

"Had to see for yourself?" Kansbar asked, ignoring Ivan's sulky stare. "Well, just this once. Stay by the fire. If you don't say a word, I'll let you watch."

Mikael nodded solemnly, as if he had been allowed to participate in a secret ritual. He dashed back to his mother, his eyes dancing with excitement.

Her hands on his shoulders, Helena glanced at the dwindling supply of peat by the fire and immediately recognized a pretext for escape.

Kansbar clapped twice. "Helena, mead, bread, and meat for our guest."

As she stepped forward to obey, her eyes met those of the stranger's. For an instant, it was as if her heart beat with his. Her surroundings faded and she saw only the blond man. She breathed deeply, experiencing the unexpected rapport.

"Helena," the stranger said in a gentle voice. "Your name is not common in these parts."

His sympathetic tone assaulted her veneer of self-composure. Against all reason, she felt an impulse to ask his help. But she said nothing. Shaken to her core, she tore her gaze from his vivid, blue eyes and turned to prepare the simple meal.

CHAPTER TWO

The fire in the hearth burned low, permeating the room with the stench of smoldering cattle dung. Helena coughed, covering her mouth with her hand. Pulling it away, she stared at her slender fingers, now red and rough from chores, and remembered home where her tasks had been to study her lessons, sew a little, and practice her lyre. Clenching her fist, she resisted the poignancy of memory. Instead, she focused on placing breads and sliced viands on the table with smooth efficiency.

After pouring the mead, she waited near Mikael by the fire. She glanced at the nearly empty fuel basket and briefly smiled. Arianna, Ludmilla's youngest, had avoided her chores again. Ludmilla would scold her in the morning, but would not stay angry long. Almost everyone indulged Arianna, in one way or another. But Helena's expression grew somber as she wondered what the morning would bring.

Leaning against the stone hearth, Mikael rubbed his eyes. Suddenly, she decided to obey her heart and flee. Glancing at her hand in Mikael's, she reached for the worn, woven basket and started to rise. If questioned, she could say that she needed his help to fill the splintering bin with fuel.

"Come here, boy," Kansbar said, startling Helena.

She flinched. Mikael cheerfully ran to his father and crawled onto his lap. With a happy sigh, he rested his tousled curls on Kansbar's broad shoulder and closed his eyes. Helena's heart sank. As Mikael snuggled closer to his father, she became desperate. She considered telling Kansbar her suspicions, but discarded the idea. He would not listen to her, his youngest wife.

Ivan, Kansbar's heir, shoved food into his mouth. Four years older than Helena, he remained a petty bully, preying on the vulnerable. She could imagine his response to her vague, uncertain fears.

As the men ate, conversation halted in silent appreciation of the meal. Maintaining proper decorum, Helena kept her eyes lowered and checked her desire to study the stranger. With a slurp, Ivan drank the last of his mead and belched with a satisfied smirk. Kansbar stared intently at his plate as his thick fingers filled his mouth with food. Yet, he kept Mikael's head gently cushioned on his shoulder.

Remembering Kansbar's brutality toward her, Helena found this quiet display of his affection toward their son almost unbearable. For her, it was far easier to hate a monster than a man capable of love.

Ivan stole a quick look at his father who remained intent upon his food. In a heartbeat, the younger man winked at Helena and soundlessly mimed a kiss. Disgusted, she refused him the satisfaction of a response. She yawned, countering him with affected boredom. Had her circumstances been different, she would have laughed. He looked ridiculous with his lips twisted in an expression resembling a pout more than a kiss.

Despite her pretense of indifference, Ivan's unwanted flirtations revolted her. She felt no love for Kansbar, but she considered Ivan's behavior a betrayal of his father. Though younger than Ivan, she was, by relationship, his stepmother. But he was careful with his goading, making certain that Kansbar never saw, knowing all too well that his father would never believe her, a wife tolerated because of her rich dowry and the birth of a son.

Normally, she suppressed her hatred of Ivan. But tonight was different. Something about the stranger made her anxious. Already on edge, Helena found Ivan's behavior intolerable. Still, she remained cautious. Kansbar ruthlessly punished any hint of disobedience. A quick learner, she had countless times bitten back defiant words in her struggle to maintain a semblance of docility. In her heart, she held as a sacred treasure the belief that no one could bind her spirit and no matter the outer circumstances, within, she was free.

Tonight, she had risked Kansbar's anger by bringing Mikael with her. But she did not care. She would escape with Mikael or not at all.

Avoiding Ivan's bold stare, Helena inadvertently caught the stranger's eye. She blushed. Her physical reaction both confused and shamed her. When his eyes sparkled, she knew he had observed her quiet resistance to Ivan. His intelligence and perceptiveness did not fit her judgments of the man. The realization troubled her, making it harder to see him as the enemy.

Worse yet, something about him made her heart beat faster, giving her a fluttery sensation in the pit of her stomach. Examining him from the peripheral rim of her vision, she could not help but admit the barbarian was handsome. His blond hair, though long, was clean, glistening with red hues in the firelight. He was at ease with himself, calm and sure of his strength. She could not picture this man tormenting women to prove his manhood. Drawn to him, she wondered what happened to his blue eyes when he smiled.

Helena reproached herself. How could she think anything good about a man whose presence might be a threat to Mikael? She condemned herself as no better than Magga, reacting with her body, rather than her mind.

Resolving not to admire anything else about the stranger, she sat on the stool next to the fire, positioning herself at his back, hoping to make him uneasy. Kansbar remained at the other end of the table, drowsy after his meal. Ivan pushed away from the table and sauntered over to the large bed. He leaned against the wall near its head and exchanged significant looks with Magga. She smiled and hastily rearranged her covers, as if she had just noticed her ample display. The end result was the opposite, changing her presentation from immodest to flagrant.

When Ivan casually sat on the bed, Kansbar lost his lethargy. He rose from his low stool, still holding Mikael, and hissed at his eldest son. "Get away, Ivan! Sit with the men or leave!"

Magga was his next target. As his voice became progressively louder, Helena pictured the wives on the other side of the leather wall hugging themselves with laughter. Kansbar had never shouted at Magga with such outrage.

"You! Woman! Have you no shame? Cover yourself and join my wives!"

Mikael awakened at Kansbar's reverberating voice.

"Mama!"

Helena moved quickly to Kansbar, her arms outstretched for Mikael. Kansbar ignored her. Instead, he placed the boy on his bed and said, "Go to sleep, child. All is well."

At his gentleness, Helena felt her throat tighten with unexpected tears. She stared at the bed, her mind under siege by memories of her first night as his *bride*, and clenched her jaw.

"Get up, Magga!" Kansbar shouted.

When dominating his women, Kansbar was at his strongest. He understood his position in his home, and to a lesser extent, the village. He was the head of both, as had been his ancestors before him, tied to the cycles of planting and harvest. His father, her grandfather's friend, had been a man of vision, who reluctantly returned from his travels to assume leadership. In contrast, Kansbar never reached beyond the confines of his role. The village was his world, his protective shell.

As Kansbar turned from Magga to the stranger, Helena sensed his uncertainty. Traditions were mute on night travel. The formalities had taken him through the offerings of food and drink. Now he was on his own. He sat with a heavy sigh, his back to Magga and Ivan.

At last, he directed his full attention to the visitor.

"Once again, your name?" he asked.

"Valamir," the barbarian answered. His voice was pleasant, well-modulated.

Valamir was the picture of relaxation, his back warmed by the fire, his hand around a mug of mead. Helena experienced difficulty keeping vigilant against his magnetism. She thought with anger, he is as relaxed as a cat, ready to pounce on a mouse.

"But he's like the sun, warming me," a small voice whispered inside her heart. Despite her intentions, Helena became aware of his every move. Her heart beat with excitement. She denied it, feeling like a traitor to Mikael, now sound asleep on the large, soft bed.

Postponing her dismissal from the room, Magga sat up slowly, stroking her hand up the nape of her neck and lifted her rich, dark hair. A few paces from the bed, Ivan watched. She smiled at him, then at Valamir, displaying sharp, white teeth. But the light was poor, concealing most of Magga's show.

Staring at Helena, she flung off the heavy blankets. They dropped on Mikael and covered his face.

Helena cursed softly in Greek, a language unknown in the village. "Bitch!"

Valamir stared at her, his face alive with curiosity. Helena noted his interest, but spared him no thought. She ran to the bed, worried that Mikael might suffocate under the heavy furs and blankets.

Her thoughts were cold with hatred for Magga. In a few strides, she reached the bed and brought Mikael's head gently to her shoulder. His legs dangled to her thighs. He remained asleep, oblivious to the danger.

Unaware of Magga's intentional carelessness, Kansbar glared at Helena. "What are you doing?" he demanded.

Overwhelmed, she had no words. She tried to think quickly, shifting Mikael's weight to her hip. All the wives knew that speaking ill of Magga to Kansbar meant a slow, but certain death. The wives more than suspected that Magga was responsible for the demise of a rival the past year. The women whispered amongst themselves about her knowledge of poisons. Unfortunately, no one had any proof.

But Helena never ate anything that Magga had touched, nor would she allow her near Mikael's food.

Magga leaned over Kansbar's shoulder, causing her dress to open and exposed most of her breasts to Ivan and Valamir. At this display, Helena's confusion turned to mortification. In many ways, she was still an innocent. Magga's flagrant exhibition, using Kansbar as a stage prop, created a situation that was beyond her.

"Speak up, girl!" Kansbar shouted. "Do you need my hand to jog your memory?"

Helena could hardly breathe. Kansbar's next move would be to hit her hard, across the face. If anything, he was predictable.

Valamir cut the tension. "Do I have your leave to speak?"

Kansbar nodded, his face tight at the interruption.

Valamir persisted, but his tone was mild. "I noticed that the other woman covered the child's face with the blankets. Perhaps the mother was worried that he might be smothered."

Kansbar moved inward, becoming quite still. Helena had seen him go into an incoherent rage after such a withdrawal.

Valamir spoke again. "Of course, it is none of my affair. Please accept my apologies if I spoke out of turn. Your hospitality has been more than generous."

Shrugging his shoulders, Kansbar allowed himself a small smile.

"Women, you understand. Always a problem. But I thank you for your words. A good mother should be rewarded. Is that not so, Helena?" Kansbar added in a more bantering tone. "Perhaps the time has come for Mikael to share your attention with another little brother? We'll have to see to it soon!"

Her mouth sullen, Magga pulled away from Kansbar. She studied Helena with cold fury, calculating the next move in her deadly game.

Sickened by the thought of relations with Kansbar, Helena felt cornered and alone. Distressed, she retreated to the fireplace and crossed her arms in front of her slender frame. Suddenly, her eyes met Valamir's. For a moment, she found a refuge. He seemed to reach out to her, as if he were lending her strength. Again, she had an unexpected impulse to ask him for help. Her green eyes brightened with pain and the words died in her throat.

Ivan added to her turmoil. "Father, you joke! Look at your child-bride. Still like a skittish colt! What could she offer you after Magga?"

He laughed, but there was a hysterical edge to the sound.

Helena's confusion lifted. Ivan had no right to speak of her with such insolence, especially in front of his father. She took two deep breaths and went to Kansbar, her back straight with resolve.

"May I have your permission to join your wives? This talk dishonors you," Helena said.

Kansbar stared at her with shock, but then he chuckled.

"You are within your rights, Helena! Ludmilla could not have said it better. I see her hand in your training. I am pleased!" With a sidelong glance at Ivan, Kansbar continued, "Pray, wife, wait by my hearth. We may need more mead while I hear our guest's story more fully."

"Ivan!" Kansbar commanded. "Go outside and fetch more dung for the fire."

Ivan exploded, the veins on his thick neck grew large. "Me! That's women's work! Send her!" He pointed his strong, but stubby finger at Helena.

After a moment's silence, Kansbar replied quietly, but with authority. "You are a disobedient son. You disappoint me. Do as I say. I don't send my wives out to the dark winds."

Ivan whirled toward the door, cursing, but he obeyed.

"Now, Valamir," Kansbar said. "Tell me more about the Huns who attacked your caravan."

Helena leaned against the hearth, Mikael heavy in her arms. His eyes were open, but glazed with fatigue. She slid down to her knees, placing him on a mat and removed a small blanket from one of the shelves to cover him.

She stroked his hair gently. "Rest," she whispered, stifling a yawn.

While Helena struggled to keep awake, Valamir told his story. She listened, suspending judgment, wanting to believe him. He spoke of a large band of Huns who had attacked his caravan a scarce day's journey from the village. Magga, who had returned to Kansbar's side, gasped. The women in the other room were shrill with fear. Helena heard Ludmilla bring the group to order with a resounding "Hush!"

The noise awakened Mikael. He pulled on his mother's sleeve. "Why is everyone crying, Mama?"

"Because bad men are near. We must be quiet and listen."

Upon closer questioning, Valamir said he had one village to the east unharmed by the Huns because they had paid them bounty. No blood was lost on either side, he stressed, before describing his caravan, where nothing remained but the dead. He had been blessed by the gods to escape with his life, he said. But he blamed the caravan's guards. If they had not attacked, the terrible tradition of blood-price would not have been invoked, as he again emphasized that the cost of spilling Hunnic blood was annihilation.

Helena's distrust returned as she wondered how he had become such an expert.

Ivan returned toward the end of the tale. He slammed the door shut. The wind seemed to sigh. He dumped the fuel near the hearth, spraying Helena with fine granules of dried manure.

"You slut! You'll pay for this," he said in a low, vehement voice. "He talks of blood and prices. You'll know punishment when I've finished with you. My father shamed me with your work. I saw you looking at this landless night rider! Five years, and never once did you acknowledge me, my father's heir! But for him, your eyes grow soft! I'll teach you to look at another man. You've the rest of your life to learn respect!"

She hated him. Her passion broke through her veneer of caution. She spoke without thought of the consequences.

"Go away, Ivan! You sicken me! Your wife's alone. Maybe in the dark, you won't make her stomach retch!"

His mouth contorted into a snarl, then opened, as if to speak. The next instant, his fist found her face. Pain spread across her cheek and mouth. She fell. Her world became dark. The dreams came all at once. Grandfather! The phoenix! Alive, looking at her! Babbling voices, loud and insistent. More pain, but in her stomach. Ivan! Kicking her. Shouts from Kansbar.

"Stop! You're killing her!"

Mikael crying. Sharp bursts of agony. Then there was movement in the room and Ivan began to shout, "Leave me alone!"

Something in the room shifted, as if a breath of sweet air had come in. She heard the sound of a fist as it punched deep into Ivan's stomach, followed by a crack to his jaw. A tooth broke with a pop. Helena opened her eyes as Ivan fell to the dirt floor in a heap.

She hurt too much to feel the satisfaction of revenge. Instead, she whispered for Mikael. Kansbar spoke softly to the crying child and carried him toward the women's side. He motioned for Magga to follow, who for once obeyed without comment.

"Ludmilla! Attend to your son who clutters my floor. Arianna! Care for your little brother!"

Mikael clung to his half-sister, who held him close. Though Ivan's full sister, Arianna was Helena's friend.

Kansbar turned to Valamir and shook his head with puzzlement. His left eye was twitching. "Ivan wouldn't have killed the girl. But he doesn't discipline my wives. That's my place. We never needed a stranger's help in our quarrels. But for once, I'm glad of it. He wouldn't stop hitting her. I don't understand this."

Valamir, breathing audibly, said nothing. His expression was grim.

Kansbar spoke in the voice he reserved for the younger children. "Helena, sit up, girl. You've been hurt."

She tried to obey, but as she moved, the blood drained from her face. Her breathing shallow, she lay still.

Kansbar lifted her gently and carried her to his bed.

"No," she said. "Not here, please, Mikael needs me."

"You must rest. No one will touch you. Sleep."

Helena grabbed Kansbar's shirt with her fingers, all at once remembering something important. She tried to pull him closer so she could whisper in his ear.

"Please, Kansbar, listen."

"Ssh, child. Your head's been hurt. Lie still."

As Kansbar laid her down, she became desperate. "Please! This man, he's more than he seems..."

"Yes, he is. He's a wonderful fighter. I never saw anyone knock out Ivan with only two blows!"

With urgency, she whispered, "And more, Kansbar. I felt at the start that something was wrong, but didn't understand. Don't you see? Valamir is an Ostrogoth name!"

"What does that matter?"

"Remember my grandfather, Kansbar. He taught me about the world and its people."

At the mention of her grandfather, Kansbar backed away. A furtive expression played across his face.

"You babble, Helena. Enough of this. Sleep."

He moved to return to the low table and Helena panicked. She started softly, but ended in a shout. "Ostrogoths were conquered by Huns fifty years ago! They are pledged allies!"

Then the stranger's voice filled the small room as he shouted in an alien tongue.

Knowing the rudiments of Gothic, Helena understood the words. "Men! Come to me! To me!" ripped through her mind as she slipped back into a world of chaotic dreams.

CHAPTER THREE

Helena recovered consciousness. Men's voices reverberated in her head, but she felt too nauseous to care. Her head and stomach throbbed with pain. Fear remained, but it was someone else's, someone far away. Yet, her heart pounded, reminding her of danger. She opened her eyes and gasped. Huns milled around the room, fingering the pottery and touching everything. She did not see Valamir. Memory returned with betrayal. Despite herself, she had liked the Goth.

She pulled herself upright to a seated position. Though she moved slowly, the room spun. Helena breathed in deeply, trying not to faint. But blackness descended, capturing her again.

The dreams came anew, quick and incoherent, echoing with deep voices. She screamed, but only in her mind. The smell of many men, packed in a small space, assaulted her. She looked at the world again and saw Valamir beside her. To her shame, tears of relief came to her eyes.

He smiled at her, his blue eyes warm. "I'll keep you safe, Helena."

From the next room, the children cried with terror.

"Mikael!" she thought. At least ten Huns blocked her path. One man was on his small horse, hunched over its neck to avoid the lower members of the rafters. The animal was muscular, with no pretensions to beauty, yet still an innocent. Its rider, in contrast, was revolting. His cheeks were etched with small, triangular scars, his mouth was a slash in his face. His eyes were as cold as death.

She confronted Valamir, her throat dry. "Will you protect my son?" Without thinking, she had used Greek, the language of her youth.

He smiled. An eyebrow raised, he said nothing for a moment. In her bowels, Helena felt sick with fear. He leaned over to whisper in her ear, "For you, and you alone, I will guard him."

Her eyes widened. He had answered in Greek. His accent was northern, probably Thracian, but she understood him easily.

She stared at him with sudden hope. "Have you...do you...are you from Constantinople?"

"No, Helena, but news from the great city travels on the winds."

"My grandfather and I were from there..." The sound of Greek was poignant, bringing back home.

Valamir nodded, as if her statement confirmed what he already knew. She did not understand him. "May I join Mikael?"

Valamir glanced at the rider. "It would not be wise."

"You betrayed us to them." She spoke without considering whether her accusation was offensive.

"I know, but no lives need be lost this day."

She wondered at his words. A part of her yearned for morning, and wished that she could awaken from this horrible dream. Yet, in her heart, she knew no nightmare ever smelled so real. Valamir motioned to another blond Ostrogoth.

"Bevion, guard her," he said in Greek.

The man nodded. As he stepped near, his long hair glistened in the firelight. Unlike the Huns, he moved fluidly, at ease on the ground. His leather garments were supple from use; his right arm wore the scars of battle. He studied her with sparkling eyes.

Using Gothic, Valamir shouted, "Men! We've come to a place of wealth!"

The Huns grumbled with sounds that could have been pleasure, but the noise was guttural, warlike. Chills rushed down Helena's spine.

Her grandfather, Balusistriam, had been a gifted linguist. To please him, she had persevered in their lessons. Though fluent in Greek and Persian, she remembered only a smattering of Latin and Gothic. Helena wished that she had never had a use for the remnants of her skill.

To the civilized world, Huns were despicable, barely human. Beyond seeing them occasionally in Constantinople, her experiences had been limited to night terrors. Her nurse,

Miriam, would threaten her, telling her how Huns kidnapped bad little girls who would not go to bed. The tactic was so effective that Helena never told her grandfather, only realizing years later that he would have disapproved of the ruse.

Defying Helena's preconceptions, the Huns were varied in appearance. Some were true to type, being of the Mongol nation. Others were almost blond. Despite their differences, most had marked their cheeks with many tiny scars. Some had deformed skulls, the work of tight bands around their heads in childhood. Though they wore leather, many brightened the drab brown with colorful pieces of cloth. Armed with short swords, most had short bows and a pouch with arrows hanging behind their backs.

They were everywhere, moving incessantly. Some were eating the remains of the meal she had prepared a lifetime ago. Others nudged each other as they pointed to the partition. For the moment, it remained intact. The women's screams were high pitched, frantic with fear. The children simply wailed. Helena wanted to join the hysteria, but managed to keep it at bay.

Kansbar sat rigidly on a stool, unharmed, his mouth open. Ludmilla held Ivan in her arms, rocking him, as if he were still her young child. He looked pale, but his eyes glittered. Helena hoped malice would keep him lucid. Despite his strength, he could not overcome so many.

Valamir shouted, "Be still and obey!"

The men quieted immediately, a tribute to the Ostrogoth's authority. Valamir had loomed over Kansbar. Compared to the Huns, he was a giant. The courteous, reserved side of him was gone, all trace of gentleness vanished. Instead, a warrior stood ready for combat, with legs slightly spread, knees flexed, his weight poised on the balls of his feet.

He had emerged as a leader. When playing cat and mouse with Kansbar, Helena had glimpsed fragments of his personality. It was as if he had been sketched with charcoal: the lines had been drawn sharply and with definition, but the portrait had lacked depth. As a warrior, the picture became vibrant with menace. Valamir no longer restrained his dark side, but used it to control the men. In his own right, he appeared as ruthless as any of them.

He shouted, "Treasure is here for the seeking! We will bring Attila joy!"

The Huns greeted his announcement with a mixture of shouts and growling sounds. The noise was horrible, making Helena's stomach churn with bile. Fear for Mikael tore at her like a hungry wolf, shredding her heart. She needed to hold her child, both for his comfort and for her sanity.

"He waits for us many leagues to the North. We dare not tarry. When he sees our gifts, his pleasure will be deep! At daybreak, we'll fly to him!"

Despite her raw fear, Helena wondered at Valamir's words. He was describing her grandfather's property. But no one had given him any inkling of the wealth that was hidden behind the wooden shelves.

"There is someone here who will show us the treasure!"

Helena tensed for the final betrayal. Valamir called out in the dialect of the steppes:

"Magga! Come and join the men! Unless you'd prefer they came for you!"

Helena felt relief, anxiety, and curiosity, all jumbled together. With a fearless gesture, Magga threw open the curtain. Catcalls showered her. She ignored everyone except Valamir. Keeping her eyes on his face, she approached him with modesty.

Her voice was pitched low, full of promise. "How may I be of service to you, great Lord?"

"Our Lord awaits us to the north, woman. "Your lord," motioning toward Kansbar, "sits alone on that stool."

She blinked rapidly at his cool rejection, but did not slip from her role of the demure, yet accessible, maiden.

"Tell me where Kansbar keeps his wealth, and all might go well for you."

Magga pointed to the exact spot to the left of the fireplace. "Behind that shelf. Pull away the back panel and you'll be pleased, my Lord."

"You've been helpful, Magga. The tribe thanks you. Return to the women or remain with Kansbar, as you wish."

"Valamir, please let me stay with you," she said, opening her arms, palms up.

Despite the language barrier, Magga's gestures spoke to the Huns. They urged her on with raucous shouts. Unabashed, she looked deliberately at her tormentors and smiled. At her bravado, the Hun on horseback whistled with appreciation. She dismissed him with a toss of her dark hair and returned her attention to Valamir.

He frowned, his eyes cold. "Magga, you've no place by my side. Now go back to the women!"

She revealed her rage and hissed, "Helena should join me!"

"No, both she and her child are under my protection. She stays with me."

Her fists clenched, Magga's eyes were dark with malevolence. As she turned away, Valamir called after her:

"Touch Helena's son and you'll suffer."

She straightened her shoulders, but glanced at Valamir, momentarily unsure of herself. Elbowing her way through the Huns, she ignored Kansbar and Ivan completely. No one detained her, but several men laughed.

"Men, I warn you against that woman. Twice I saw her betray her husband, not just with me, a stranger, but with his own son. Such disloyalty is a menace," Valamir said. "Ishyite," he said to a Hun, "search behind that shelf."

The dark-haired man shuffled to the spot indicated. His hands moved nimbly as he knocked the crockery off with a few sweeps. After four hard blows with his fist, the back panel split, revealing Kansbar's cache. Carefully, he extracted several cloth bags, three small brass boxes, a few silk rugs, and an assortment of silver drinking cups. He handed each object to a comrade, who in turn placed them with reverence on the table.

As another spilled the gold and silver coins out of the bags, the raiders murmured with excitement. One by one, he opened the three boxes filled with jewels. The men's enthusiasm erupted into pandemonium. Many looked at Valamir with respect, bordering on adulation.

After all had seen the treasure, Valamir spoke. "Remember what we bring our Lord. His gratitude will be generous, as is his nature! Five shall carry the burdens of honor. Choose from amongst yourselves. Never forget, each jewel, each coin is deep in our memories."

Immediately, five men stepped to the table. Despite their physical differences, they moved in harmony, as if they were of one mind. In full view of the band, they separated the find into five piles. The others witnessed the packing, not hesitating to help with advice. Helena found the level of cooperation striking: she had expected them to fight to the death over the bounty.

Valamir bowed his head. "It is done. Attila will not forget the heavy burden that these five have accepted in his service."

That name again, Helena thought, trying to remember why it was familiar.

Valamir turned to Kansbar, at last acknowledging his presence. "We have done well here. So well, that your village shall suffer no further. But first, I need an answer to a question. I caution you to tell me the truth. Is there anything else?"

Kansbar raised his head slowly. Valamir's face was impassive, more like stone than living tissue. Kansbar unbuckled the Persian sword.

"Here, it is of good quality. Also, Magga has a ring made of Thracian gold. Like the rest, it was part of Helena's dowry." Accepting the blade, Valamir examined it quickly then handed it to Bevion. "Magga! The ring or life!" he called out.

Magga was silent behind the partition. Then she flung back the opening, spat at the floor, and hurled the ring in Valamir's direction. He reached and caught it neatly in his hand. She scowled, but did not return to the women's side. Instead, she made her way to Ivan and sat next to him, ignoring his mother at his side.

Everything was happening too quickly for Helena. With a furrowed brow, she watched Ivan and Magga whispering together. He was alert, fully recovered from his beating. Magga gloated, and glanced at Valamir with undisguised venom. Ivan looked oddly pleased. Ludmilla voiced her dissension by emphatically shaking her head. More than anything, the older woman's disagreement filled Helena with foreboding.

Valamir was oblivious to the conspirators on the ground. "Men! Bevion will carry the sword to Attila. I'll present the ring. May he be well pleased!"

Yells, combined with sounds that could have been cheers, resonated in the mud house. Bevion strapped on the sword, encased in a delicately etched sheath, so it hung down his back. The ring shone on Valamir's smallest finger. She thought fleetingly that to wear it, he must have narrow bones. Yet, Magga and Ivan continued to make her desperate with worry.

"Soon the sun will rise," Valamir said. "At the signal, all shall meet outside. The others will share our pride at what we found!"

"Greillia," he said to the horseman, "have all the houses been taken?"

In reply, the man threw back his head and moaned a macabre wolf cry. The sound was echoed by many identical calls from distinct locations in the village. Helena's back was swept with chills. Inside Kansbar's hut, the Huns murmured with satisfaction.

With slow insolence, Greillia spoke in Gothic. "Each house, as you told us. All is well with the tribe, even though you have made us into women, hiding in the dark!"

As he approached the Hun, Valamir's eyes glinted. Though Greillia was on horseback, the Ostrogoth had the advantage of height. As Valamir spoke, he could look down at him.

Locking eyes with Greillia, he announced to the men. "We have a prince's ransom from this place. In payment, we spare the village. Are we in agreement?"

After an initial silence, several unenthusiastic murmurs greeted Valamir's question. Into this pool of regret, Greillia threw his stone.

"I want my pleasure with the women. Starting with that one," he said, pointing at Magga.

Noise of agreement filled the room, battering Helena's ears.

Valamir raised his voice. "Still yourselves!"

Obedience was sudden.

"Who did our leader appoint as chief?" he asked Greillia.

The Hun kept his silence, but it was not a sign of respect.

"Who, Greillia?"

"You," he admitted like a curse.

Valamir's face was hard, cold. "This village has given us wealth. None of our blood has been lost. It does not owe us the blood-price."

"You do not let us follow the wind, killing and taking as we please," Greillia said, speaking to the others. "Your way is different. It is not ours. There are women here for the taking!"

The men muttered under their breath, agreeing, but unwilling to mutiny.

"Men!" Valamir shouted. "We've no time for play! Attila stands idle to the North waiting for us! If you have a horse to spare, persuade a woman to come. But I want no unwilling hostages. They'll only slow us. Already, we test our Lord's patience! And as for you, Greillia, perhaps the woman, Magga, fancies a change."

The Hun grinned with malice. "She's a beauty, ripe and ready, but would take too much watching. I don't need my throat slit in my sleep!"

The men laughed with enjoyment, mixed with relief, at his banter. Then he dropped his pretense of reconciliation.

"No, Valamir. I'll have the one who sits so still upon the bed!"

Helena's chest constricted. It hurt to breathe. Her legs needed to run, fast and hard. But escape was impossible. She endured in silence, drawing on a reserve of strength that she had never known. Compared to this man, Ivan was guileless.

"You'll not touch her. She's with me," Valamir said.

Greillia snarled. "I know! But you never keep any bitch long! Why bother with this one? She won't be good enough for you. You want a perfect woman. Maybe not even a woman. Perhaps you follow the ways of the old Greeks! Only satisfied by men!"

Laughing harshly, he pulled out his short sword. As he pointed it at Valamir's stomach, the Goth whirled away, unsheathing his weapon.

"You challenge me?" Valamir asked, his sword drawn. "Over a woman? Or because Attila gave me command?"

Greillia hesitated, then shrugged his shoulders. He put down his blade, resuming his relaxed slouch on his horse.

"I'll follow you, Valamir, for the sake of my cousin. But this is the last time."

"Good," Valamir said.

Looking at Magga, Greillia smiled. "Had enough of this miserable place, woman? Come with me. I'll take you far."

Magga rose slowly, dusting off her dress. She glanced at Valamir, then at Ivan, who was speechless on the dirt floor.

"I've no horse," she said, in the Gothic dialect, more proof of her varied background.

"I've more than one," Greillia said.

"Then I'll ride it for you."

"You speak one of our languages, but you must learn the mother tongue. I will teach it to you and much more."

"I've been longing for a teacher. The men here bore me," she said, staring at Ivan.

Magga's betrayal did not break through Kansbar's shock, but the veins in Ivan's face were purple with fury.

"Magga," he pleaded, "you cannot mean to leave me!"

"I'm already gone, Ivan. I was never here. Just passing the time, waiting for someone better. This Hun excites me. You never did."

Ivan jumped up quickly, pulling her to him.

"I forbid you to go, Magga. You'll not leave with him!"

"At least he's a man, not a young pup, stealing favors from his father's women!" Magga laughed viciously, then screamed, "Let me go, Ivan!"

He grabbed her waist, and clung to her, moaning with strange intensity. At his display, the men howled with ridicule.

Afraid of what Ivan would do if pushed farther, Helena shouted, "Magga! Stop! You're goading him! Calm him."

But Magga only struggled harder in Ivan's arms, slapping his face, and cursing him. Greillia edged his horse next to the intertwined couple, kicking Ivan in the stomach with a bestial snarl. When Helena saw a small knife in Ivan's hand, she despaired. It was Magga's dagger, the fruit of their conspiracy.

He aimed it toward Greillia's chest. With his forearm, the Hun brushed it aside, but allowed the dagger to plunge into his thigh. As Greillia's blood oozed from his leather leggings, he laughed, his teeth bared in a smile. Helena suddenly understood that Ivan, with the Hun's cooperation, had contrived the village's doom.

Greillia shouted to Ivan with delight, "Your blood will be the first to flow!"

With the dagger still embedded in his leg, he unsheathed his sword and raised it high. While the steel blade descended smoothly in a perfect arc, Ivan watched, his mouth open, as it struck his thick neck with a crunch. Blood spurted like a fountain, spraying Magga's hair.

As he fell with a thud, Helena slid off the bed and darted under the partition. On the other side, the roar through the thin wall deafened her ears. In moments, she knew the killing would begin. Her eyes found Mikael's frightened face. She was next to him, pulling him away from Arianna's terrified embrace.

She brought him to her heart and inhaled his boyish fragrance with a sob. In a heartbeat, she grabbed her satchel, still by the back door.

"Come, Arianna," she said. "Take your chance."

The girl cried hysterically, and began to rock from side to side. Helena spared her no more time and instead kissed Mikael's tear-stained face.

"We must be very quiet, Mica!"

She unfastened the back door, making not a sound. But it was guarded by a sentry, no more than ten feet away. Helena became immobile, thinking rapidly, then looked for something to throw. Finding a pottery plate, she opened the narrow door slightly, without making the wood creak. With a deep breath, she threw the plate as hard as she could. It landed with a clattering noise. As the Hun investigated, she slipped out with Mikael in her arms.

Running through the predawn darkness, she whistled for her grandfather's old stallion, Passial. He bellowed his deep whinny and Helena knew hope. Her heart sang as she saw the aging horse leap the low, stone pasture wall. The mare that had once been hers followed at his side. With the satchel bouncing against her back, Helena ran to meet them.

Their paths converged quickly. Out of breath, Helena murmured the white stallion's name. He halted, obedient to his old training. When she touched her foot to his near foreleg, he extended his leg, lowering his back at a slant. Having no time to bridle him, Helena prayed to her god the horse would still respond to voice and weight alone. She placed Mikael on Passial's back, pulling herself up behind him. As the stallion sprang to his full height, Helena almost fell off. It had been five years since she had last ridden. Her left arm circled Mikael and her right hand grabbed the mane.

She dug her heels into the horse's sides. Her voice was soft, but urgent. "Run, Passial, run."

The animal leapt into a gallop. The mare stayed with them, keeping pace. The stallion's strides lengthened into a run and Helena's heart soared. Moments passed. Dawn edged the horizon with red. Then she heard a sound that could have been hoof beats. She ignored it, praying to be wrong, and tightened her hold on Mikael. Despite his closeness, Helena felt utterly alone. As Passial pounded through the darkness and the wind, tears glistened across her cheeks and mingled with her streaming hair.

CHAPTER FOUR

In the cold morning air, Passial carried Helena and Mikael across the steppes. The chestnut mare galloped alongside, her tail raised high. The animals' thudding hooves reverberated within her heart, as if whispering, "Run, Helena, run."

She shivered.

"Mama! We go fast!" Mikael shouted, exhilarated, the thrill of the wild ride supplanting his memory of the raiders.

"Oh, Mica, I love you," she said, her arms holding him tightly.

In a low voice, she urged Passial on and pressed his sides with her heels. Instantly, he stretched out to a full run. Unburdened by a rider, the mare easily pulled ahead. A bird called, awakening in the early dawn. A small herd of antelope interrupted their grazing to watch the two horses racing the wind. Her muscles aching, Helena struggled to stay mounted.

Horrible screams, coming from the village, trailed after them. The awful clamor was punctuated by an eerie, masculine roar. Her skin crawled. Only the heat from Passial's body and her racing heart kept her teeth from chattering with terror.

"What's that, Mama?"

She kept her voice level, protecting him. "I don't know Mikael."

Helena scanned the horizon, searching for a place to hide. But the rolling steppes offered nothing, not even a gully. Though needing the cover of darkness, she longed for the sun. In the dim light, Passial could stumble into a fox hole, falling or even breaking a leg. She forced herself to trust his instincts, yet listened closely for any sound of a chase.

The beat of a galloping horse was unmistakable. She wanted to believe it was only an echo of Passial and the mare, but could not hide from the truth. Someone was gaining on them. Keeping a firm hold on Passial's mane, Helena turned to see a small, brown horse. Its rider was not tall, matching his mount's diminutive size: a Hun.

Her stomach contracted with fear. She kicked Passial, pushing him beyond his limits. In his youth, few horses could best him in a race. But he was eighteen, past his prime, and no longer in peak condition. His neck lathered with sweat, Helena knew from the roughness in his breathing he could not last. The pace would kill him.

The hoof beats were louder, closer.

She spied a clump of straggly bushes. "Mikael, I'll hide you and lead the horseman away!"

"No! Don't leave me!"

"I don't know what to do!" she whispered with panic to herself.

The bushes vanished behind them. Their pursuer's horse pounded a scant few strides away. Helena turned and saw Greillia, his face intense with animation. Horror steeled her resolve. Driving her left leg against Passial's side, she made him spring right. The Hun's mount easily duplicated the maneuver. Greillia laughed with raw glee.

Helena was aware of everything: the pressure of Mikael's body against her arm, the ache in her cheek from Ivan's fist, the smell of her own fear, even the colors in the sky as the sun emerged from its bed. Never before had she felt with such vividness what it meant to be alive.

Greillia's voice slashed at her essence, taunting her in Gothic.

"I've kept myself for you! The others will wait!"

Hate crystallized her courage. All at once, Helena visualized one of her knives deep in his stomach, the other in his throat. The image muted her panic. Suddenly, his horse was at her left, breathing hard. As she faced her attacker, his forearm cracked her shoulder.

The blow pushed her off-balance, making her lose her precarious seat on Passial. Desperately, she tried to stay on, but he was slick with sweat. With no saddle to anchor her, the combined weight of Helena and Mikael worked against them. They fell hard.

Impact was sudden, the ground uncompromising. Helena cushioned Mikael with her body, knocking the breath from her lungs. To recover, she needed to lie still for a few moments, but time had become a luxury.

A few feet away, Mikael lay on the ground, motionless. At a gallop, Greillia wheeled his horse in a tight circle, coming at her. Passial had just started to swing back. In her heart, she knew he would be too late. She inched toward her son, dragging her stunned body across the ground. Each movement was agony.

She whispered, "Mikael." But he lay still, eyes closed.

Then Greillia was upon them, his horse's hooves flashing, pounding hard. She saw death. Instead, the Hun leaned down, reaching for her son. As Greillia lifted him, love lent her strength. She leapt and clutched Mikael by the thigh. The Hun placed the boy across his saddle, stomach down, and her hand slipped to Mikael's ankle. He began to cry, high and piercing. Each frantic scream ripped at her heart. The brown horse pressed forward, dragging Helena, the soles of her feet bouncing on the ground.

Greillia fixed his eyes on her. "Let go, before you hurt him."

She held on, her whole being becoming the hand clinging to her son. But the Hun twisted her fingers, forcing them back and her hand fell away. She cried out. Her fist clenched at air, then nothing. The coarse, dry grass scraped her cheek and nose. She lay on the ground, incapacitated, feeling the earth rumble underneath with hoof beats, both near and far. Warm breath blew against her neck. Helena turned with frantic fear, only to see the white horse above her.

"Passial!"

Using the stallion's lowered neck, she pulled herself up. Her body was alive with pain, but she ignored it. Slippery with sweat, the horse steamed in the chill dawn air. A hundred paces away, Mikael screamed. With intense clarity, Helena saw him, struggling helplessly in Greillia's arms.

With all her heart, she shouted, "Mikael!"

The Hun spun his horse to a halt, raising dust. The sun shone at the steppes' horizon like a fiery ball.

She sobbed. "Down, Passial!"

He obeyed, but Helena, weakened by her injuries, could scarcely mount. Greillia jumped down, dragging Mikael, his small face contorted with terror.

"Bite him, Mikael!" she shouted astride Passial. She kicked her horse and he bolted forward, toward her son. Greillia's lips contorted into a smile. He lifted the child by the hair, raising his feet from the ground, negating resistance. Mikael's frantic screams became frenzied, striking his mother's heart.

Wild with desperation, she shouted in rough Gothic, "No! Don't hurt him! Take me, not him!"

Greillia made a horrible noise, a cross between a howl and a cackle. His arm before him, the Hun raised Mikael higher, stretching his curly hair, and drew his sword. Remembering Ivan and that same blade, Helena's mouth opened, but her throat was still, soundless.

Tears blurred her vision, but not enough to shield her from the sight of Mikael's face distorted by primal, animal fear. He whimpered. She rushed closer, uttering sounds like a roar. The Hun's laughter deepened.

As with Ivan, Greillia held up his weapon in readiness for its deadly descent.

Not believing what she saw, she begged, "Please, no!"

Mikael screamed, "Mama!"

With a hum, the sword whistled downward, cutting the air, meeting Mikael's neck with a grisly thump, snapping his spine.

The body dropped to the ground. Greillia elevated Mikael's head in triumph, his shout climatic. Sobbing, Helena continued her charge. The Hun stared at her, his smile welcoming. In an instant, he leapt to his horse, making it sidestep to the right. No match for the large pony's agility, Passial swept forward, running flat out and missing him.

In moments, Greillia was alongside, his arms reaching for her. Without thought, Helena sat back hard, giving Passial the command to halt. He obeyed, his back legs sliding. Outmaneuvered, the Hun ran on a few strides.

As Greillia wheeled back, he shouted, "Now for you!"

Helena had passed beyond fear. As the horses pounded across the steppes, she thought no further than her dagger in his throat. She refused to recognize Mikael's head as the trophy Greillia held up to the sun.

His horse neared, barely winded, in stark contrast to Passial, who labored for each breath. Though tears wet her cheeks, they were not for her. She did not care about her future, only the past, only Mikael. He stretched his arm and grabbed her long hair. As he pulled, her scalp burned with agony, but the pain was not hers.

She struggled, but her response came from the body's need to survive, not her mind. Again, she sat back on Passial, her weight telling him to stop. But Greillia was not fooled by the same ploy. Remaining abreast, he laughed and pulled her toward him, then dangled Mikael's head before her eyes, taunting her.

The white stallion snorted with fear from the odor of a fresh kill. As she gazed at Mikael's remains, fury transformed her. She screamed, not from helplessness, but rage. Reaching for the dagger at her knee, she pulled it from its sheath and plunged it deep into Greillia's forearm. With a howl, he released her. She extracted her knife with a sharp, downward thrust. The Hun grunted with pain. Shifting her weight to the left, Helena urged Passial away. But the Hun grasped her waist, dragging them down to the ground. He reeked of blood.

They landed together in a heap. Yet, off his horse, he was not as agile. At impact, he lost his grip on her torso. She rolled away, quickly pulling herself to a stand. She faced him, dagger glinting in hand, miraculously unwounded by her own blade during the fall. His luck had held as well. He rose to his feet, brushing himself off with deliberation.

"No more games, woman." He sneered rather than smiled. "Valamir will suffer when he discovers what is left of you."

His thigh oozed from Ivan's wound, his forearm bled bright red, but none of his movements betrayed pain. With silent desperation, Helena clenched her weapon. As he unsheathed his sword, the sound hurt her teeth. Then, quickly, with the flat of the blade, he struck her hand, hard. From the force of impact, her palm opened and the dagger dropped to the ground. She stared at it, golden in the sunlight.

Suddenly, the tip of Greillia's sword pricked under her chin. The Hun's eyes bored into her, alive with an intense, fanatical light. Useless, her right hand throbbed with pain. Without thought, she slipped the left one to her pocket, to the remaining knife, small and sharp. Locking eyes with her tormentor, she frantically worked to free her weapon from its wrappings.

At the same moment, her mind wondered if death would be sweet. With a smile, Greillia gloated, savoring his victory. Though her cheeks were gritty with dust smeared tears, her eyes were dry and watchful.

"Plead with me for mercy, bitch. Perhaps when I've finished with you, I'll grant you an easy death."

She stared, offering no reaction. He dug the point of his sword deeper, drawing more blood. Her eyes dropped to the silver blade. Unable to move, she stood still, barely breathing, her hand clutching her hidden knife.

Suddenly, she felt her grandfather's presence. But his source was not the gentle love which she had known so well as a child. It was different: dark, incomprehensible, and raw with menace. Words formed within her throat, words not of her volition, but from someplace else.

"I'll destroy you, Greillia," she said in a harsh voice not her own.

"What!" the Hun laughed, an ugly sound. "You threaten me!"

Then pounding hoof beats diverted his attention, lessening the pressure of his sword. Her right elbow jammed into his ribs as her heel slid down his shin and landed hard on the top of his foot. He swore with pain as she spun from his grasp.

She ran towards Passial, but a horse and rider intercepted her path. Hands lifted her up, sweeping her off the ground. Thinking of her knife, she looked at the new assailant. Instead, she saw Valamir.

She felt nothing: no gratitude, no anger, not even hatred - only deep fatigue. She trembled.

On horseback, Greillia raced after them. But Valamir halted his roan to wait for the adversary. He positioned her behind him.

"Hold on, Helena," he said. Her arms remained limp at her sides. Gently, he wrapped them around his waist, holding her wrists with his hand.

Greillia reined his horse down, forcing the animal's mouth to open from the pressure.

"I wasn't finished with her, Valamir!"

"Where's the boy?"

Greillia laughed. "In two pieces."

Valamir was silent for a few heartbeats. Helena whispered in Persian, the language of her cradle, "He's dead."

"You bastard! He was under my protection. If you weren't Attila's cousin, you'd die today," Valamir shouted.

"Fine talk! But who gave you the right to take the pick of the women!"

"Then come closer, Greillia. Fight for what you want!"

The Hun hesitated, shrugging his shoulders with a grimace.

"What's one woman in a village of so many?"

"Then you'd best hurry," Valamir said with a nasty edge to his voice. "I wonder how many have already covered Magga. She was the first to be naked. Maybe there's still some left for you!"

"The sons of whores! They knew she was mine!"

Creating a cloud of dust, he whirled his horse in a circle and galloped toward the village. Valamir watched him as he grew smaller in the distance. Satisfied that they were alone, the Goth dismounted, then lifted Helena down. Her mind reeled. She did not understand how she could be alive. It made no sense.

Valamir's face was shuttered, but his blue eyes were bright with compassion. The sun had risen, the blue sky promised a clear day. In the dips of the undulating plain, frost shaded the grass. Helena shivered.

The Goth touched her bruised face. "You shouldn't have run. I'd have kept you both safe."

Unable to speak, she sat. Her head lowered, she crossed her arms over her chest, and rocked herself as one would a child. She cried.

He sat beside her. "Tell me what happened, Helena."

In the distance, the screaming from the village continued. Nearby, Passial and his mare cropped grass peacefully, while Valamir's horse grazed, moving toward them, making a bid for company.

"What happened to your boy?"

Ignoring him, she searched with her eyes for the site of Mikael's execution. Unable to find it, she stood in an attempt to walk. Her legs buckled. She cradled her face in her hands.

Valamir spoke in careful Greek. "Please talk to me, Helena."

The sound of a childhood language beat against her inner sanctuary, weakening its walls. She needed to share the horror with anyone, even an enemy.

Her voice tight, she muttered in Greek, "He killed him. Cut off his head. For nothing. A little boy."

He put his arm around her. His touch was gentle, but she flinched.

"Are you hurt?"

She laughed harshly. The question was stupid. "Of course, I'm hurt! Your...confederate murdered my son!"

Steeling herself for his answering blow, Helena tensed. He dropped his arm from her side.

"You said you were from Constantinople."

She blinked with disbelief. In the village, thatched roofs flamed. Men on horses chased their victims like dogs. The women were dying, Helena was certain, slowly and with shame.

"Constantinople? What's Constantinople to me now? My son's dead. Over there, your people make a sport of killing. I've no time for this. Be done with me! Death would be sweet."

Valamir's eyes never left her face. His soft words were an assault. "I'm sorry for your loss."

Sympathy was the one weapon against which she had no defense. Looking away, she bit her lip. Her eyes brimmed with tears.

"I won't hurt you, Helena. I give you my word. Will you accept it?"

"No."

He smiled ruefully. "You're honest. I respect that."

Helena dismissed him with a shrug. The anguish after her grandfather's death was nothing compared to the black emptiness that obliterated her soul.

"Are you from Constantinople?" he asked again.

"Yes." It had become too much effort to resist his words.

"So. You're far from home."

Her voice was childish as she repeated, "Yes, far from home."

"Who was your guardian, Helena, when you lived at home?"

"My grandfather."

"His name?"

Her response was again adult, but belligerent. "What do you care about his name?"

"Please, Helena, tell me. I might have heard of him. I know people in Constantinople."

Her eyes widened as a deep moan escaped from her lips.

"His name was Balusistriam. They called him Balusistriam, the Persian."

Valamir exhaled deeply. His voice was solemn. "Helena, I came for you. In your father's name, your steward has offered a prince's ransom for information leading to your safe return. For two years, I've kept my eyes open, wherever we roamed. Though we don't travel near Constantinople soon, I'll find a way for you to go home."

She whispered to herself, "*You* were the messenger. Never, ever, did I imagine that it would happen like this. You've cost me everything; you've cost me Mikael!"

"Helena, we've much to do. You can't let your son journey to his god without preparation. Help me find him, so we can cleanse him for his final passage."

Her head jerked up, eyes blinking.

"Yes, you're right," she said, agitated. "I must tend to my son!"

Valamir whistled to his horse and the stallion trotted briskly to his master.

"Call your horses, Helena, or help me catch them. If not, you'll lose them forever."

"Passial!" she called with a desperate edge to her voice.

The white stallion lifted his head from the grass, then nickered softly. Still exhausted, he walked to her, the mare following. Standing beside her, she buried her face in his mane.

Valamir broke into her grief. "Are they of Arab blood?"

"Yes," she said, wishing he would stop his questions.

"Good. They'll keep the pace."

He rummaged in his saddle bag. "Help me halter them. We must keep them together."

As Valamir pressed ropes to her right hand, the light weight made her cry out. The cords fell with a whisper. Taking her wrist, he held it gently, examining her hand from all sides. Then he lowered his face to better inspect it and became vulnerable to Helena's remaining knife. But she did not draw it. Her call for revenge was specific. Only Greillia's blood would satisfy her need.

"Move your fingers."

Her voice was distant, her eyes fixed on nothing. "I cannot."

"It's broken. We must keep it still."

In no time, he had immobilized it with a piece of soft leather, preventing any movement of her fingers or wrist.

Turning from her, he haltered the horses.

"Your horse has no bridle? Remarkable...."

Before long, both horses were tied together, anchored securely to the roan's saddle.

"Come, we must find your son."

He placed her on his stallion, jumping lightly behind her. With his arm circling her waist, they began a methodical search through the long grass for Mikael's remains.

CHAPTER FIVE

Mounted, Valamir and Helena wove their way methodically across the steppes. Passial and the mare followed at a walk, snatching an occasional mouthful of the long grass. Except for the strident sounds from the village, the morning was tranquil. Warmer air blew from the south. Birds called; small animals foraged for food.

Helena felt twisted inside, her soul rancid. At her core, she could not understand how the land, her witness to Mikael's murder, could be so quiet. Someone, something, should share her pain. In the distance, the antelope continued to forage. The wind blew, buffeting the swaying grass, oblivious to the fact that her world had been torn asunder.

On the ground ahead of them, her dagger reflected the brilliant sunlight. As they approached, Helena saw Mikael's head. Sliding from the roan stallion, she rushed toward it.

"Wait," Valamir said, intervening, restraining her with his hand.

He strode ahead of her. As in a trance, she watched him wrap in leather what had been the essence of her son. His task complete, he placed the bundle in her hands, but kept possession of the dagger.

She did not care about the weapon. With Mikael's remains next to her heart, Helena spoke to him as if he were still alive, scarcely aware when Valamir placed her on the horse. He led the horse with easy strides, his long hair swaying as he glanced in different directions, searching for what was hers. In short order, he saw the small, leather satchel, brown against the wind-swept grass and changed course to retrieve it.

After a hasty examination of its contents, he extracted a coarse blanket from it and draped the woolen cloth over his shoulder. With methodical attention, he strapped Helena's nondescript pack to the mare, and leapt back on the roan. In the distance, black birds circled, silently, floating downward.

Valamir urged his horse to a gallop and Helena returned to the world. She saw the birds and moaned, understanding they came for Mikael.

"Hurry," she whispered to the earth, to the wind, but not to the man behind her.

As the horses approached the corpse, Helena's animals snorted with fear. The roan did not react. As Valamir went to retrieve the small body, Helena was beside him.

She sank to her knees, sobbing. In silence, he wrapped the remains in Helena's old blanket. Shrieking, the carrion birds flew off toward the village. As Valamir lifted the forlorn bundle, Helena reached for it.

"No, we must find a quiet place for him," he said.

She stared wordlessly.

"How should we prepare him for his journey?" he asked.

She spoke, in Persian, to herself. "No, how can this be? He sleeps. And I, I've lost my way out of a dream."

"Helena, you must attend to your son."

She stared, trapped in thought. When she finally spoke, her voice was hushed. "He'll need a fire to cleanse him. It must burn hot. But wood is hard to find on the steppes."

Valamir nodded, his eyes revealing relief. "I'll see to it. We must find him a quiet place. Give me what you hold. It's better that he be carried as one."

With reluctance, she relinquished her sad burden. When he approached Helena's mare, Sarelle danced away in fear, pulling hard on the lead line. Valamir spoke quietly to the animal, calming her. Using the straps that held the satchel, he fastened Mikael's remains to the mare's back. Sarelle snorted, but did not try to bolt. He stroked her neck, calming her, and efficiently checked her makeshift halter.

Lifting Helena to the horse, he mounted behind her with an easy leap. As they galloped north, away from the village, she didn't resist Valamir's arm circling her waist. Unable to keep her eyes open, sleep captured her. When the horses slowed to a trot, she awoke to the sight of at least three hundred tents. Far from abandoned, the area was a hub of domestic activity, with women and older men working at their chores.

Feelings of betrayal overwhelmed her. Without premeditation, she reached into her pocket for the remaining knife. Throwing her leg over the roan's neck, she tried to escape. Valamir held her tightly.

With anger, he demanded, "What are you doing?"

"You've taken me to your camp! This is no place for my son!"

The knife was in her hand, ready to stab his restraining arm. But she could not use it against him. She hesitated, then turned it to her stomach. Quietly, his hand covered hers, forcing her to release the weapon.

For the first time, his voice sounded weary. "You have a responsibility, Helena. This is not the time to be weak."

"Damn you!"

Ignoring her outburst, he pulled her to a more secure position on his horse. She wanted to bite him. His decency was an offense, compromising hatred. From the beginning, he had eluded being her enemy.

Yet, nothing mattered anymore. Her life was in ruins; her *rescue* was a bitter mockery. A long cherished hope had become a horrific nightmare. As they neared the encampment, grief swallowed her anger, leaving emptiness. Had choice been possible, Helena would have returned to the bleakness of the village if only to have Mikael again, alive in her arms.

Their entry at camp attracted attention. People looked at Valamir with respect, mingled with surprise. Evidently, no one had expected him to arrive before the others. A white-haired man, bright eyes lively in a creased face, hobbled with a pronounced limp toward the Goth. He bowed with deference, almost formality, then stood, awaiting orders. He showed no fear, only interest in Helena. As his blue eyes probed her face, she resented his curiosity.

Valamir spoke in cordial Greek. "You look for a story, old friend. We found Attila great wealth, losing none of his men."

"You look tired, Valamir."

"I am, Caratipian. A village fool attacked Greillia. You can imagine the rest."

The servant shook his head. "Remember, young master, worry about what you can change, leave the rest to your god."

Valamir laughed. "Young master! Only you, after all these years, think of me as young."

"To a man in his fifties, twenty-six *is* young." He pointed to Helena. "And who is she?"

"She's the one you told me about. There was a son, but Greillia killed him. She wants a great fire for the child's last journey."

His eyes widened in surprise. "A pyre! I heard that Balusistriam kept the old ways, defying the Magi's interdiction. Of course, most Zoroastrians now believe that to burn flesh is a contamination of the fire, the sacred light," he murmured more to himself than to them. He rubbed his forehead. "But in the end, who knows which belief is closer to Zarathushtra's word?"

"Caratipian...we'll talk about this later. The day has been long."

"Oh, of course, Valamir. My apologies. If she wishes, I could build a tower of silence, a Dakhma, instead of a pyre, and her child would replenish the earth through birds, wind and the sun." He paused. "May I speak with her?"

"Could I ever stop you from doing what you please?"

Caratipian shrugged noncommittally. As he spoke in Persian, his eyes were gentle. "You are with friends, Helena. I'll tend to your son as I would my own. Tell me what you need for him."

At the sound of her birth language, her face crumpled. "Build him a pyre."

Not understanding Persian, Valamir interrupted in Greek. "Do whatever she wants, just find a spot that's quiet, well out of sight of the camp."

Caratipian bowed again, hurrying away without further conversation, his limp more evident than before.

Valamir shouted after him. "Ride the packhorse, Caratipian!" With a smile, the servant turned and waved as he disappeared into the maze of tents.

Valamir clucked to his mount, cantering the stallion through the rows of tents. The other two horses fanned out to the right, forcing several people to jump out of the way as they passed. At the northern edge of the encampment, apart from the others, Valamir halted before a large, leather tent.

He slid from his horse. His movements were stiff, betraying his fatigue. He let the stallion's reins drop to the ground. The roan waited patiently, without being held, not even grazing. Reaching for Helena, he lifted her down, then stepped a pace.

"I must set your hand."

Her mouth twisted into a grimace. "It doesn't matter. Leave it as is."

His eyes glinted angrily. Exasperated, he said, "You have no choice! Sit in front of my tent and wait. I must see to these horses."

Without a word, she obeyed. Legs crossed under her long dress, she looked straight ahead and stared at nothing. She cried silently. The tears wet her cheeks, but did not touch her agony. She watched Valamir care for the horses because she did not have the energy to look away. He existed in her space and time, but was not real. When his hands unfastened Mikael's corpse, Helena buried her face in her arms.

Still upright, she fell asleep and dreamed. Huns, mounted on horses, pursued the villagers, running them down. Chaos surrounded her, but she could neither move nor speak. Ivan ran toward her, holding his own head in his hands, asking her to put it back on so he could see.

She screamed, waking from the nightmare. When she opened her eyes, Valamir was beside her. She wrung her hands and gasped from pain. Her right hand had begun to swell.

"Come inside with me, Helena."

She shook her head, overwhelmed by his closeness. He was a stranger, a man. Trust was inconceivable. The idea of being in the tent, alone with him, terrified her. Beyond her fear, she felt dreadful, every muscle tight with pain. Beyond exhaustion, her body shook.

Valamir picked her up and carried her inside. Its interior was gloomy, muted, illuminated from sunlight streaming in from the entrance and an opening in the sloping roof. The smell of well-used leather was pungent. He leaned her gently against a wooden pole, the tent's main support. Turning away, he rummaged through an oblong leather container. Her trembling increased, making sitting impossible. She slid to the grass floor, and crossed her arms over her chest in an attempt to regain self-control.

Again, his muscular arms were around her, moving her to his sleeping pad. In the back of her mind, Helena understood she should run, but she was too weary and weak to move. Covering them both with a warm blanket, he used his body to warm her. His hands did not wander. As she felt the heat emanating from him, her shaking lessened.

She slept, this time without dreams.

Upon awakening, Helena discovered that her hand had been re-bandaged in such a way as to render it immobile. Though still covered by the blanket, Valamir was no longer beside her. She heard him singing by the fire as he prepared a meal. The song was of ancient Thrace, in the days before Rome. The sound soothed her as she fell back to sleep.

Voices broke into her slumber. Opening her eyes, Helena understood from the shadows that the sun had shifted in the sky. Hours must have passed. Valamir and another man were talking outside, speaking Greek. As she listened, her left hand clutched the warm blanket, finding comfort in it.

"Bevion, what happened sickens me. Give me a fight with soldiers, not a slaughter of children and women! It's without honor."

"Valamir, you know the traditions. He gave you his trust. Such thoughts are disloyal."

Realizing that she held her breath, Helena exhaled deeply. In a different way than Greillia, she held Valamir responsible for Mikael. She looked at her surroundings, not wanting to hear his scruples. The tent was spartan, well-equipped with essentials, but without luxury. Using her left arm for support, she sat up. Though her body no longer shook, sleep had not diminished her physical agony.

Valamir had left her a wooden bowl filled with meat and water in a crude cup. Thoughtfully, he had remembered to leave an old bucket, obviously a slop pot. She forced herself to take care of the natural need, but weakness made the effort formidable.

Helena returned to the sleeping pad, breathing hard. She felt numb with inner cold and shivered. Trying to stop the shaking, she wrapped the blanket tightly around her shoulders and focused on slow, deep breathing. Calling upon her guardian spirit, she prayed for strength.

Often her grandfather had instructed her in times of trouble to call upon her Fravashi, the spirit who watched over her from birth to death. His keen blue eyes had twinkled with joy when he reminded her of Zarathushtra's sacred words: that within all humans dwells Sraosh, the ability to hear the divine voice.

Helena quieted her thoughts and tried to listen for guidance from Ahura Mazda, from the Creator. But she heard nothing save the beating of her heart, the noise of the camp outside, and the wind across the steppes. A twig snapped in the hearth and she sighed.

She thought about the ritual planned for Mikael and consoled herself that at least he would receive the proper death rites. Ignoring her protests, Kansbar had buried her grandfather in the ground, sacrilege to the ancient ways. Unlike the Medes, Balusistriam believed that the sacred fire would purify the remains.

Pulling the blanket tighter, like a shroud, she cried. But again, the tears brought no relief. As the men's conversation continued, she listened, running from grief.

"Valamir," Bevion said, "don't you see? The traditions are necessary. The tribe's very survival depends on them. People tremble with fear at the Huns' very name; their terror saps their strength."

"Empty words, Bevion. They don't change how my stomach feels when I see dead children, murdered for no reason!"

"Children grow up to be enemies, Valamir, just as Attila says."

"You can make yourself believe anything, if it suits you! I fight other men. A life taken in battle has honor. Killing women and children is not the same." He paused, before adding, "*Attila* knows how I feel."

Bevion was silent. Finally, he asked, "Was he angry?"

"No. He valued my honesty."

The name, Attila, continued to trouble Helena, but she could not remember why. Without thinking, she drank. As she swallowed the clear liquid, she was ashamed. It was not decent that she could drink, even breathe, with Mikael dead. Dropping the cup, she lay back on the thin pad.

"You didn't tell him about our mother, did you, Valamir?"

"Bevion, you forget. He was there, with us. It was before Rugliva sent him to Rome. But no, I didn't speak of her. What would he care? She's been dead more than fifteen years."

Bevion made a noise of exasperation.

"Her death festers in you to this day. You wouldn't worry about strange women and children but for her. Your memory makes you weak, keeping the blood tradition from your heart."

"Bevion, you don't know what they did to her. You didn't see our beautiful mother, after they had finished."

His brother's voice was compressed. "In truth, Valamir, I can't remember her face. You were twelve. I was only six."

Helena felt no pity, but an obscure exultation. The world had been cruel in its indifference, not pausing in its commotion for a heartbeat to acknowledge Mikael's loss. Except for her, no one cared. Bevion argued with his brother, the manservant smiled and waved, women washed their laundry, and, as always, the wind swept the steppes.

"When will you let me see the woman you kept?"

"I won't, little brother."

Bevion laughed, but with an edge.

"Come on, Valamir. I can't forget her. She was beautiful, so still on that bed. Her green eyes, enormous with fear, have stayed with me."

"Enough! She's not for you. She sleeps. Greillia killed her son. The bastard! And I'd promised to protect the boy."

"What's one brat less? You've grown soft."

Helena's heart beat with renewed vigor, outrage forcing her to feel again. She longed to punish Bevion's contempt with a dagger.

Bevion's voice became smooth, honeyed with persuasion. "Valamir, let me have her. You never keep foreign women. You've told me again and again that they can't be trusted. But something about this one touches me."

"She is with me. If you bother her, I'll beat you so that you can't sit on a horse."

Bevion laughed. "Do you think you could?"

"I know it."

"Well, when you tire of her, and you will, I won't mind being second. Unlike others I could name, you're not a spoiler of women. We could split the gold when we sell her. With her aristocratic air, she'd fetch a good price, more than a fine stallion!"

"Speak of other things or leave."

Bevion laughed again, but nervously.

"You like her! I don't understand. You never take women as hostages. Why this one? Did you notice her resemblance to our mother?"

"I thought that you'd forgotten how she looked, Bevion!"

"I lied. I remember what I wish. This woman's not Mother. Your little prize won't care for you. She's bounty, good for one thing."

"Go! I won't say it twice!"

"Put down your fist!" Bevion laughed harshly. "I'm off. But watch out, Attila may not be so easily put off. She has that delicate look he favors. He'll want her, with or without your permission. You know how he is about women. Get her pregnant. Then he might respect your rights to her, if you can keep her hidden until she shows!"

With a malicious chuckle, he mounted with a leap, making his horse grunt at the impact. When the horse struck off at a gallop, Helena breathed with involuntary relief. Bevion's words had forced her thoughts beyond the perimeters of sorrow.

Outside, Valamir muttered under his breath. "Damn him! He's right. Attila will plague me day and night until he gets what he wants."

Helena heard camp sounds, shouts, and horses approaching in the distance, but nothing from Valamir. Then he spoke with finality. "Well, he won't have her."

The words touched her heart.

He swept open the tent flap and strode inside, filling the space with his presence. Halting in mid-motion, he saw that she was awake. He sat across from her, at a loss. She pulled herself up to a sitting position; her movements were cautious from pain.

"How much did you hear?"

She tried to answer him, but could not speak. When Valamir was near, her fragile self-control crumbled.

"Talk to me, Helena."

Her eyes met his, but she could not hold his gaze. She stared at the ground, fighting for composure. "Most women would be grateful to you for saving their lives, but I'm not. I should have died today. But then you would be cheated of your reward."

"The ransom's not important. I've enough wealth."

"Then why did you bother to look for me?" She knew she was offensive, but did not care.

"The story was intriguing. Caratipian, being Persian, had heard it. I doubt that anyone else knows. When our leader, Attila, asked me to accompany him on his campaign, I agreed, but always kept my eyes open for a girl, about eighteen, answering to the name of Helena, with green eyes and soft brown hair, lost with her grandfather on the silk routes en route to Persia."

"Oh." She was quiet for a moment, then looked directly at him. "You brought Mikael's death. There's nothing left for me."

"You feel that way now," he said. "But life changes. It's never simple. You walk the earth, never knowing where your path will lead you. But don't doubt that you have a higher purpose."

"You're a philosopher. Yet, for one who thinks, your company is strange."

Valamir laughed wryly. "Your perception is astute."

"Yes, I've seen much."

His blue eyes assessed her, somberly. "I did not intend for your son to be killed."

"Then why do you ride with Huns? For five years, I dreamed of escape! You've turned my hopes into ashes, a mockery of what could have been."

"We're a conquered people. For fifty years, Ostrogoths have watched and waited, shaping the Huns in our ways. I do what I must. But for Ivan, the village would still stand. Greillia would have had no excuse for a massacre."

"Mikael's blood will be Greillia's death."

"Put it behind you, Helena. Even I think twice before challenging him. His expertise with arms is unique."

"I don't know how, or when, but he will die, settling his debt with me. And the earth herself will be cleaner when he no longer fouls the air with his breath."

"How is it that you, a well-born girl from Constantinople can pledge revenge with such ease?"

Helena was silent. When she did speak, it was to escape the void that had become her heart, not from a desire to share. "My father is Persian, but Mother was Thracian, descended from Celts. She died at my birth, but her blood sings for vengeance."

Valamir was silent, his face thoughtful. "My mother was Thracian."

His statement crept under her defenses, forcing her to see him as human, making it difficult to take pleasure in his ancient sorrow. Resisting their common bond, she winced, but spoke with gentleness. "In another life, under different circumstances, I would have sympathized with your loss. But now... you'd do better to send me to my son. I cannot bring good to anyone, least of all myself."

He moved closer, spicy with sweat. Yet, his smell did not revolt her. Placing his lips near her ear, he whispered, "You're wrong. Already you've renewed me."

She whispered, "No," but did not pull away. His earnest declaration only intensified her distress.

Confronting his eyes, so close to hers, she felt an unexpected affinity, as before, a lifetime ago in Kansbar's house. She held his gaze, experiencing the moment of rapport. With irony, Helena recognized that with Valamir, a barbarian, she had shed her protective, womanly mask. She looked away, breaking contact and ran from their connection with a volley of words.

"If Greillia is such a formidable opponent, why did you put yourself at risk for me?"

"He would have killed you."

Her inner turmoil increased. She changed the subject. "The sun is high. Did Caratipian find enough wood for the pyre?"

"All is arranged. You have but to set the flame."

She closed her eyes, feeling both relief and impatience. All of this talk had wasted precious time. Mikael waited.

"Thank you. For this, I'm grateful. Please take me to my son."

"After you eat something."

"It's better to fast."

Valamir frowned. "Had your son died peacefully, I'd agree. But you're not well, Helena. How can you ride, much less even walk in your condition? Eat. The food will lend you strength."

For a moment, Helena sat motionless, then picked up the meat with her uninjured hand. It was stringy. Forcing herself, she swallowed four or five bites, then put down the rest. Without a word, Valamir picked up the small cup she had dropped and replenished it from a leather flask.

"Drink," he said.

She drank it all. The meat had been salty. Feeling less lethargic, she stood slowly. "I must be clean. Is there a place where I can wash?"

"We'll cross a stream on our way."

Stepping forward with resolution, Helena's leg cramped with spasms. She felt cold all over, the air buzzed around her ears. Silently, Valamir gently took her in his arms and carried her outside. His horse was waiting, bridled and saddled.

"Valamir," Bevion said, mounted, his arms crossed, his animal occupied at the grass. His posture was relaxed, indicating a boring wait. He rode to them, at a leisurely walk, halting within an arm's length.

Valamir's face flushed with anger.

Ignoring his brother's reaction, Bevion spoke in crisp Greek. "I came to introduce myself. But to my regret, I don't speak her language. Unlike you, dear brother, I never had luck with foreign words. Will you translate for me?"

Though his speech was distinct, the smell of mead was heavy on his breath and clothes. He looked at Helena with lewd insolence. Her cheeks grew hot with indignation. She stared at him, enunciating her words clearly in Greek.

"Have you no respect for your brother? You gawk at his guest like a rude boor? Am I not in his presence?"

Bevion's mouth dropped with surprise. "She speaks Greek! Why didn't you tell me, Valamir? And how she speaks, like a noble born!"

"Some day I might tell you her story. But not now."

Turning from his brother, Valamir placed Helena on his horse, mounting behind her.

"Share it with me! You know that I can't stand a mystery!"

"Which explains why you have yet to be an initiate of Mithras!"

Bevion moved his horse in front of Valamir's, blocking the way.

His blue eyes were narrow, his head cocked to one side. "You won't dismiss me."

Helena felt Valamir tense behind her, preparing himself for a fight. She had no patience with their quarrel. Mikael was ready for his journey. "Your brother has arranged the final rites for my son. We go to him. Please understand that this is a private moment."

Bevion stopped blustering, nonplussed. Her words had been quiet, yet dignified. Backing his horse, he cleared the way for them. His smile was not pleasant.

He mock bowed. "My apologies."

Without further conversation, he cantered his bay in the opposite direction. Despite his inebriation, his back was straight and he sat his mount well.

Valamir headed north, the camp behind them. He made no comment about his brother's behavior, nor Helena's intervention.

Soon, they came to a small brook, bordered by a wide, sandy bed. Bringing his horse to a halt, he dismounted, lifting Helena off. "I'll wait while you wash."

The bright sun was past its zenith, well into the afternoon. Yet, even in October, it had the power to warm. The creek meandered toward the Aral Sea. Though the water was low, the current was steady. Kneeling beside it, Helena remembered other times. Before the birth of Mikael, she had found a secluded spot, downstream and made it her own.

Today, as the water glistened over the rocks, it could not lessen her misery. No matter where she went, darkness followed like a specter. She washed her face with the cold water until it was clean. With effort, she forced her body to stand.

"You're wet! The chill will drain your strength," Valamir said.

"It doesn't matter. I do what I must."

Remounting, Valamir allowed his horse to pick its way across the stream, avoiding the larger rocks. Then he urged the animal into a gallop. The wind tightened her wet cheeks with cold. She welcomed the discomfort as a proper observance of grief.

In the distance, she saw the pyre. She wanted to join Mikael, once the flames burned high. Her grandfather's voice seemed to whisper that suicide was immoral, giving ultimate victory to the Evil One. As a child, these words had made perfect sense. Now, they wearied her. Twice in five years, her life had been destroyed, shattering her will to begin anew. Though her need for revenge sustained her, it could not fill the void.

As they neared, Caratipian greeted them, waving a wooden torch. He had tethered his horse a hundred paces away, well out of reach of any sparks. Valamir took her by the hand, leading her to Mikael's body. It lay on a latticed litter, waiting for the pyre. As she stood over the remains, he stayed close, but stepped back a pace or two.

Someone had put the severed neck together, hiding the butchery with a wide scarf. Mikael's hair was combed, his face clean. His expression was dreadful, distended with rigidity. Helena touched his cheek gently, saddened that she had been unable to cleanse him. Stroking his hair, her tears dropped on his tunic. Careful not to disturb the fragile alignment of his body, she straightened his tunic and laid her hand on his torso. It was as cold as the wind around her.

She spoke to him softly in Persian. "My sweet Mikael, I'll miss you each day of my life. I long for you. You've been wrenched from me, leaving me bereft. You were all that was good, bringing the light back into my life. Without you, I'm in darkness. I say goodbye to your body, but not your spirit. As long as I walk the Earth, you'll be with me, at least in my heart. Remember me. Be with me, Mikael. My choice was death, but I am here, without you. I will love you, always."

She bent over him, kissing his forehead lightly, not disturbing the illusion of unity. Stepping back, she spoke to Valamir. "Let the flames take him."

Through a film of tears, she saw Valamir nod to Caratipian. They picked up the wooden stretcher and placed it on top of the mound. Mikael's head lolled to one side, breaking the mirage of entirety. She sobbed.

Caratipian handed the blazing torch to Helena, placing it securely in her left hand. She stared at it, transfixed, unable to move. The old man talked to her, quietly, in Persian, the sounds humming in her ears like musical notes. Though his accent was clumsy from disuse, his sincerity spoke to her heart.

"Child of Light, do not be deceived. Your son's death is a cruel trick by the Evil One. Do not allow him to turn you from your path. The Wise Lord did not call for the sacrifice of your child. Nay, it is his enemy, jealous of what is pure and good, who has brought you this desolation.

"Trust in the Goodness of the One God, Ahura Mazda, not his enemy, Angra Mainyu, the Liar. Though he could not save your son, he has given you a true friend in my master. Unknowingly, Valamir is in service to the Wise Lord, God of All Creation.

"Take this torch, pure with fire, and send your child to Ahura Mazda! Do it with joy in your heart, serene in the knowledge that you have given him a new life with the One God!"

Helena felt a glimmering of solace and bowed her head. "Thank you," she whispered in their common language.

She walked slowly around the pyre, touching the lit torch to it in many places. Once the fire had ignited, she tossed the stake into the inferno, wishing for the courage to follow it. Instead, she wept. For the first time, the tears brought relief.

Valamir pulled her from the intense heat, keeping his hands on her shoulders. Together, they watched the blaze burn brightly within the circle of stones, lingering as the sun streaked the sky with gold and blue. Keeping vigil, the three remained until Mikael's bones were covered with ash.

A few embers glistened. "It is done," Helena said. "Now the wind will take him to the corners of the earth and that is good."

Exhausted, she sank to the ground. When Valamir lifted her, she was deep in sleep.

CHAPTER SIX

Helena awoke to darkness. In the crude hearth, a small fire illuminated the tent with macabre shadows. The once familiar sounds of women and children were gone, replaced by wood singing in the hearth. Valamir slept, his arm wrapped around her, warming her body.

The image of Greillia, his sword above Mikael's head, flashed through her mind. Silently, she cried. Never again would she feel his hand in hers, his voice asking question after question, the fragrance that was him.

Despite Valamir's kindness, he remained a stranger, foreign, not Mikael. She didn't care that he had twice saved her life, first with Ivan, then Greillia. As Valamir pulled her closer, she stiffened, remembering to be afraid.

He whispered in her ear, "I won't hurt you."

Through his clothes, she felt his hardness. Her fists clenched, ready to strike. As time passed without event, her eyelids drooped. She slept.

Helena was roused by the morning light, streaming through the tent's entry flap which swayed gently in the wind. Once again, Valamir was gone, but had left her well-covered. She sat up slowly. Her body ached, but the pain had lost its intensity.

She noted the improvement in her condition, but dismissed it as irrelevant. She remained immobile, numbness her only feeling. From outside, Valamir's voice penetrated her grief.

"Caratipian. Half our men remain at that miserable village, drunk! And Attila expects us three days after the new moon. Already, it's the second day! Get Bevion. We must gather the men and be on our way."

In a rage, Valamir threw open the tent flap. When he saw Helena, he stilled himself.

Her lethargy vanished.

She did not hide from his hard stare, but said nothing, hiding her apprehension. Her heart raced. She wondered at her reaction. After Mikael, fear should have no power over her.

Moving with the grace of a tiger, Valamir sat across from her. He smiled, shrugging away his dark mood. "I've frightened you."

His perceptiveness disturbed her more than the anger he had disciplined with such ease. She resented his discernment: it was an intrusion, a violation of her inner world. As he edged closer, she was conscious of his every move. Filled with distrust, she tensed.

"Let me see your hand," he said.

She studied him before extending her bandaged hand. His answering smile was dazzling. With expert gentleness, he examined the injury.

"The swelling is down. Excellent. Does it hurt less?"

Her voice was rough from sleep. "Yes."

"You must drink." He offered her a small leather canteen. "Here, the water's fresh."

His eyes were compelling. Wanting to escape his scrutiny, she obliged him and drank.

He touched her cheek, barely brushing it. "It heals, but you will carry a bruise for at least a full moon."

His hand strayed to her shoulder, lingering, his eyes fixed. She wanted to run, somewhere, anywhere else, but the danger outside was far greater than inside.

Her mouth twisted. "You're scaring me."

Turning from her, he pulled his hand away and glared into the flames. His brow furrowed with a frown. His pensive, blue eyes glinted in a shaft of sunlight.

He cleared his throat. "Even with a scraped cheek and nose, you're a beautiful woman, Helena."

All at once, her cheeks grew hot.

His smile deepened. "When I saw you that night, you touched me. I could tell that you were afraid, but in a quiet way, you were very brave. Even before Kansbar called you by name, I knew you were the one. When that fool, Ivan, attacked you, I should have killed him."

She thought of Ivan and his ill-fated assault on Greillia. Her voice was tight. "Why?"

"Because he hurt you."

She considered his words, then spoke with quiet vehemence. "You brought Huns to the village."

"They would have come with or without me. I'd planned for a different outcome, but it was not to be."

Quickly, before she could stop herself, Helena asked in a small voice, "If I hadn't run, could you have kept Mikael safe?"

"I would have tried, but after Greillia killed Ivan, it was chaos. I thought that you were behind the curtain, unharmed. When the men tore it down, and I saw that you were gone....then Greillia, no where to be seen, I was desperate. Do you realize that I left my command to come after you? I've never done such a thing. But Greillia found you first."

Helena's reserve crumpled. She cried. His arm circled her, but she did not stiffen against his warmth.

"Your plan was good. But for Greillia, you would have been safe, until you met with wolves. But I would have found you. Two horses running leave deep tracks."

Leaning against him, she shivered, but not from fear. Rocking her gently, he stroked her hair.

"Why are you so good to me? A brother could not treat me with more respect."

He laughed with amusement. "My feelings are *not* brotherly. For you, I teach myself patience. If you were willing, I'd show myself. For now, I'll be content with this."

From outside, they heard Caratipian shouting, "No, Bevion! You can't go in!"

"You should have stayed home! You're too old to be on this campaign. Move aside! No? Then I'll change your mind."

"Put me down! How dare you pick me up!"

Bevion thrust his way into the tent, Caratipian at his heels, still protesting, his head shaking with disapproval.

"I'm sorry, Valamir," the Persian servant said.

"You're not to blame. Please, wait outside."

Valamir turned to Bevion. "You annoy him."

His brother smiled with satisfaction. With veiled contempt, he glanced at Helena, then spoke in Gothic, clearly assuming her ignorance of it. "You summoned me?"

Though his words were difficult for her to follow, she could comprehend him. Greek punctuated his accent, even in the Germanic language, making it easier for her to understand.

"Now that I've come, I need to know about this woman," he continued in a bantering voice. Where's she from? How did she come to be on the steppes? Gods, Valamir! She's lovelier than yesterday, even with that nasty bruise on her cheek. You should get her a pretty dress, one that does justice to her."

Bevion's resemblance to his brother stopped at the dark blond hair and blue eyes. Where Valamir was serious and introspective, Bevion's expression was cynical. Unlike his older brother, he was mercurial. His emotions played across his face at will.

Helena wished he would go away.

Glowering at his brother, Valamir kept his arm around her. "Why do you care?"

"She intrigues me."

Valamir switched to Greek. "Bevion, I've warned you. She's with me!"

His brother rolled his eyes and sighed with mock despair, putting his hand to his chest. When he laughed, the sound was harsh. "I'll live, perhaps, but you break my heart with your selfishness!"

Then his expression changed and became almost earnest. "If you want to keep her for yourself, hide her from Attila," he said, keeping to Gothic. "We both know his taste. By Mithras, his appetite wrecks my reputation. And this beauty would captivate his curiosity."

Attila again, Helena thought, the name's significance just beyond reach. She let her mind go blank and stared at the ground, thinking of nothing. Finally, she remembered. The story had swept Constantinople, creating much speculation. Attila, the nephew of the King Rugliva of the Huns, had been exchanged for Flavius Aetius, hostage for hostage. Flavius, a son of an Imperial General, had been a favorite of Rugliva and the Huns. In bitter contrast, the Romans had despised Attila. Clever, cruel verses had circulated about the taciturn Hun, mocking him. In Rome, away from his people, he had grown to manhood.

A few months before Helena and her grandfather had left Constantinople, Attila had returned to Rugliva's kingdom, vowing revenge. Romans laughed, but with apprehension. Something about the Hun made his promises terrifying. She shuddered, suddenly afraid.

Valamir spoke, reverting to Gothic, unaware of Helena's rudimentary skill. "What should I do, Bevion? If he tried to take her, I'd have to kill him."

"Would you, Valamir? You care about her! I don't believe it. You'd kill Attila? For a pretty girl? Oh, how the mighty have fallen! We may argue, but I don't want to lose my only brother. Who else could I tease? Caratipian just looks at me with disapproval, and Father...well, you know what he thinks of me."

He paused, considering Helena thoughtfully. "Force won't work. Think with your head, not your sword arm for once." He blew out with resignation. "If you must keep her, you'll have to marry her, with all the Hunnic ritual. Attila would never break with the law. Of course, he could find an excuse to kill you, then have his way without loss of honor. But he wouldn't. He likes you too much. Later, when you're tired of her, you could always repudiate her."

Valamir was silent. Helena held her breath. As she realized how much she had come to rely on his protection, the taste in her mouth was bitter.

"Well, Valamir? What do you think? Or do you have other plans for the girl? Perhaps I was wrong, you don't care enough to be bothered with the wedding rites. Let me have her. I'll keep her safe. When Attila asked for her, I'd be reluctant, driving up her value. He'd feel badly about depriving me, then double my price."

Valamir shook his head. "Enough! It's not what you think. She has another life. I promised to return her to it. I don't know if she'll agree to a wedding, even a Hunnic one, no matter the reason."

"You're such a...philosopher, Valamir. Always thinking about...things. Make her understand. If she won't listen, insist on a ceremony, promises be damned. It's for her own good. Otherwise, you'll lose her, then I'll have to keep you from Attila's throat." He paused. "Stay with her. Make her see it your way. I'll whip the men back to camp!"

Valamir laughed. "Many thanks, Bevion. Has Ishyite returned?"

"Yes. Can you imagine his wife's words if he had lingered?"

"Ask him to come with you. And Bevion, let him handle Greillia."

"You don't think I can manage him?"

"In truth, no. Look past your pride, Bevion. We may disagree about many things, but your blood is the same as mine. I won't risk you to a madman's sword."

He answered in Greek, "You worry too much! I'm off, but I'll be back for another visit. And remember, you owe me!"

Before Valamir could say another word, he was gone. From outside, they could hear him singing a bawdy tune. Valamir smiled to himself, once again shaking his head.

Not for the first time, she wondered if she were trapped in a nightmare, unable to open her eyes. Nothing made sense. Yesterday morning, she had watched Mikael die, helpless to prevent his murder. Today, Bevion undressed her with his eyes, all the while discussing Attila's taste in women.

She felt vulnerable and alone. Sweeping her hair from a wide brow, she hardened her resolve. Should Valamir relinquish her to Attila, death would be her last defense. As she remembered her grandfather's stern injunctions against suicide, Helena felt a moment's guilt. But it passed. He could not have understood what happened to the heart of a woman who was degraded, night after night.

Valamir hesitated. For Helena, his uncertainty made him more human. In a rugged way, he was handsome. He carried himself with innate athletic grace. His posture was relaxed, his movements effortless, but like a falcon, always ready for the kill. Yet, when he touched her, he was gentle.

He was a paradox, unlike any man she had ever known. Though physically strong, her grandfather had been no warrior. He had been a mystic, possessing both the earth wisdom and the essence of the Prophet Zarathushtra's teachings.

Despite Valamir's worries about honor, Helena considered him a man of action first, reflection second. Even his religion, the cult of Mithras, was the faith of soldiers, Roman and barbarian alike, cutting through the barriers of nationalities. Her grandfather had ridiculed the cult, repudiating its origins from Zoroasterism, hating that his only son had become an initiate: a military man instead of a priest.

As Helena watched Valamir's inner struggle, her feelings softened. He had accepted her without conditions, bruised and broken in spirit. Her heart ached, accepting what her mind would not acknowledge: a connection to this man.

"You must eat, Helena. Tomorrow, we break camp. If you wish, I'll take you to Mikael's funeral pyre this afternoon."

His approach to his dilemma was oblique, not simplistic as expected. She was surprised, then outraged by his use of Mikael as a ploy.

But she betrayed nothing. "That would be good."

"I'll wait outside." He left abruptly.

She sat quietly, calming her anger before joining him.

The day was clear. The sun shone brightly, but the wind was cold, sweeping hard across the steppes. Trying to keep warm, Helena hugged her chest. Valamir was busy with the horses, preparing them for the ride. In the distance, white clouds were edged with gray. Without the soldiers, the camp was quiet. Helena envisioned them at the village, and thought of the women. Her stomach recoiled at the image, nausea palpable. She prayed Arianna, her only friend, had found a quick death.

"Come, I've a saddle for your stallion," Valamir said. "And see how well Caratipian has cleaned your bridle. It looks better than new!"

His conversation was forced, at odds with his personality. Watching him bridle and saddle the horses with quiet expertise, she was silent. Passial did not resist his touch.

"He's a fine animal, Helena, worthy of a noble. But he's old. He'll have trouble keeping pace with the tribe."

She glared at him. "He's Arab. At age ten, they're in their prime!"

"Well, that may be, but he's weathered at least fifteen winters."

She flung her arms around Passial's long, white neck, her voice pitched high. "He's eighteen! My grandfather and father both had a hand in his training! He'll keep up."

"You don't understand. He'll do, but without a rider's weight. You should ride the mare when we travel. She's much younger."

Her arm dropped to her side. She fought back tears that choked her. The thought of another loss, even a horse, had brought panic. "Oh...I see."

"Let me give you a leg up."

She was curt. "No."

Before mounting, she checked Passial's legs and hooves, feeling his tendons for any sign of swelling after yesterday's desperate run. He was sound, but had a stone in his left fore hoof. She reached in her pocket for her small knife, then remembered that Valamir had kept it. With her fingers, she picked out the pebble. Her right hand, useless, throbbed. Compensating, she balanced Passial's bent leg on her knee.

Valamir broke into her preoccupation. "Your knowledge of horses surprises me."

Placing Passial's hoof on the ground, she straightened and confronted Valamir.

"Why?" she asked.

"It's unusual for a girl from Constantinople, with a gentle upbringing, to think to pick a horse's feet!"

She shrugged her shoulders and faced her horse's left shoulder. "Down, Passial." He obeyed. Mounted, she stared at Valamir.

He raised an eyebrow and smiled with self-deprecation. "You've reason to mock me, Helena. Your horse is schooled to perfection!"

"He's not mine. He only suffers me. He remains my grandfather's, then perhaps my father's. Compared to my grandfather's skill, I am a city-girl, bred soft and useless!"

"Why the anger?" Valamir asked in a hard voice.

Ignoring him, she urged Passial to a canter, heading toward Mikael's pyre. As the roan caught up effortlessly, Valamir's face was taut. She finally slowed her horse, but only to cross the creek, afraid to injure his hooves on the stones. Valamir grabbed one of her reins.

He shouted, "What are you doing? Why won't you answer me?"

"Because you're such a liar!"

"What do you mean?"

"You don't care about Mikael! You just want me to agree with Bevion's plan!"

His look was deadly. "You understood us. Yet, you said nothing, letting me worry myself about the best approach. And you sat there, listening, hugging your laughter in silence."

She swallowed quickly, realizing her temper had exposed her and made him feel like a fool.

"What would you have done in my place? I kept my knowledge to myself, little as it is." She spoke with less passion. "I wasn't mocking you. I've no laughter left."

His frown vanished. He was quiet for a moment. A smile transformed his face, piercing her heart. Unprepared for her feelings, she closed her eyes against him.

"Sit with me by the water," he said.

As he lifted her from Passial, her emotions were mixed: running from self-recrimination because she liked him, to raw grief, to obscure comfort in being in his arms.

While the horses grazed, they sat beside the clear stream. His arms no longer around her waist, Helena was relieved to be separated by a sliver of air. She stared at the rushing water. "I've heard of Attila."

"He's a mighty leader, Helena. I consider him my friend."

"He's a Hun."

"That's true, but beside Bevion, there's no one else I'd trust to guard my back in a battle. But Bevion speaks the truth about Attila and women. They are his obsession. At first, he'd try to buy you, and smile as he ignored my refusal. In the end, you'd be in his tent, not mine, no matter what I said. Then I'd have no choice, I'd have to kill him. No man steals my honor."

Her chest burned.

"With Attila, you would want for nothing," he said. "He'd shower you with luxuries. Your Greek would delight him. He'd pester you with questions about Constantinople. For a time, I know you'd be his favorite. Although his appearance is uncultivated, he is brilliant. His conversations can be lively. When the mood strikes him, he can make anyone laugh."

Her jaw quivered. "You want me to go with him, then."

"No! I'm forcing myself to be fair. Many women would want a share of his wealth. His fortune is immense, almost equaling his uncle's, King Rugliva."

Helena pressed her lips together tightly.

"Do you think so little of me?"

"I want you to understand your choice. In truth, the thought of you with him hurts me in a way I don't understand."

"You are honorable, Valamir, to praise a rival."

His smile was ripe with pleasure, but his eyes became serious. "Will you be my wife?"

Though anticipated, his question fell like a weight upon her heart. She drew away.

"I'm not ready to marry anyone!" she said, looking at the sky, the steppes, anywhere but his eyes.

"I can see no other way to protect you. If you wish, I'll wed you in name only."

"You mean that?" she asked, facing him.

"Yes. Don't you think that I see your grief? Your life cannot begin again until you've finished with the old. You need time."

She blinked. No one since her grandfather had been so kind, so tolerant. When he pulled her to him, she lay her head against his chest. His heart beat steadily against her ear. In silence, they sat listening to the water and the wind, watching the horses crop grass. Finally, the chill from the earth crept into them. Without a word, he extended his hand.

She took it, letting him pull her up, her thoughts pensive. "Do you have a wife?"

He laughed, but said distinctly, "No."

Her tone was neutral, almost indifferent, as if she were negotiating for a bolt of cloth rather than her own marriage. "Would a Hunnic ceremony be binding upon you, an Ostrogoth?"

"Only if the marriage was consummated, but that lies between us."

He played her game, his face schooled to seriousness, but Helena saw the laughter in his eyes. His relief had taken him to the edge of silliness, highlighting a resemblance to his brother.

"Bevion mentioned repudiation. Explain that."

He frowned. "The Huns have been known to cast off a wife, especially if the marriage was political in nature."

"And the Ostrogoths?"

"It's not common." He paused, then touched her cheek. "Upon my honor, Helena, I would never repudiate you."

Her eyes felt hot, but her voice was level, even harsh. "Would you have accepted Mikael into your tent?"

"Oh, Helena, I would have taken in your mother, had you wished."

She shouted, "Stop it! This is important!"

He folded his arms across his chest and chuckled. He breathed deeply, unable to keep the smile from his face. "Forgive me. I've been worried. Attila is our lord, and speaks for the law. Without your willing consent, the ceremony would be invalid. I'd have no way to shield you from him."

As he explained the essence of the situation, his laughter disappeared.

"Your law is just. I never, ever agreed to marry Kansbar. He said my words for me."

"How old were you?"

"Just thirteen."

"You were young. Surely, he waited to take you to the wedding bed."

"No, not one night."

"But you were still a child!"

She nodded her head, mute from pain. Overwhelmed by feelings of shame, she could not look at him.

"Was he gentle?"

Remembering, she spoke to herself rather than to him. "He was not gentle."

Valamir sat motionless, deep in thought. His hand touched the hilt of his sword.

"I never imagined the old man hurt you. If I had known, he would have died slowly, while I forced him to understand how he dishonored his young guest!"

Helena felt torn. She had detested Kansbar, but for the village's sake, rose to his defense. "He was good to Mikael. After my pregnancy showed, he left me alone. And then Magga came to the village and occupied his attention. For that, I remain grateful."

Valamir would have none of it. "Before you became pregnant, did he force you often?"

Her voice was tight. "Yes. It was his custom with a new bride."

Valamir spat on the ground. "What about the other men? Did he protect you?"

Helena's eyes flashed. "I watched out for myself. But no one, except Ivan, his own son, bothered other men's wives."

Valamir placed his hands on her shoulders. "You did well. Better than most. It didn't break you. You are without blame."

His words touched the rawness of her hidden shame. She slowly met his eyes. "If I agree to be your wife, in name only, will you keep to your bargain?"

"It won't be easy. I find you beautiful. But I give you my word."

She ignored his compliment. "What about your promise to take me home?"

His face shuttered, he looked away. "Do you want to go back?"

"I have a duty to my grandfather's house. Also, there's the question of your reward."

He laughed. "I told you, the money doesn't matter. I've more than enough. Caratipian's story demanded an ending. My duty's fulfilled."

Forcing herself, she persisted. "Will you be able to take me to Constantinople?"

"Yes, but not soon. We're not going that way."

She muttered under her breath, "Thank God for Constantinople."

He waited, his right fingers drumming his arm.

She dropped her eyes. "I accept the honor of being your wife." Then she looked directly at him. "But in name only."

He smiled and leaned to whisper in her ear, "We must seal the engagement with a kiss."

She pulled away.

"Please, Helena. You'll have to trust me, just a little."

Her throat pulsing, she nodded, all but imperceptibly. But his kiss was soft, almost fleeting on her lips. His hand caressed her neck, down her shoulder to her waist. All at once, she shivered.

He brought her close to his chest. "Your face is pale. We should go back."

"No! You said that you'd take me to Mikael!"

"You're trembling. You're in no condition to ride."

"Please."

He looked at the horizon. "If you must, but with me."

Valamir caught the horses and secured Passial's reins to the roan's saddle. He placed her on his horse and mounted behind. With Passial following, the roan stallion struck off at a canter. Ahead, Helena could see the remains of the great fire. Her eyes filled with tears, but she was glad to have come, needing to say goodbye one last time.

CHAPTER SEVEN

The roan galloped hard across the steppes, effortlessly carrying Valamir and Helena. Passial danced with the wind, straining against the reins tied to Valamir's saddle. As the white stallion lunged forward, his tail, held high, streamed behind him. The clouds billowed in the blue sky, the horses' hooves beat the ground.

As they approached the funeral pyre, the wind had blown away much ash, revealing Mikael's bones. Helena tried to console herself with her religion. Desperately, she wanted, needed, to believe that the earth would cleanse Mikael's body and his spirit would fly free to the Light of the One God. But Zarathushtra's teachings had become mere words.

Valamir reined his horse, halting him before the mound. Passial snorted at the smell of charred death, scorched by flames. The roan was unperturbed. Dismounting first, Valamir lifted Helena down, leaving a rein dangling on the ground, a signal for his stallion to stay. Both horses grazed.

Taking her hand, Valamir led Helena to the pyre, but stepped back, giving her the illusion of solitude. She bowed her head. After a moment, she looked up, her sight blurred from tears, and saw Mikael and her grandfather. From the far side of the pyre, they faced her. She gasped, but did not blink, afraid to lose the vision.

Her grandfather appeared no more than thirty, much younger than she remembered him, even as a small child. With radiance, he smiled at her. The love in his face was echoed by the warmth in Mikael's eyes. But her child's expression was shadowed by sorrow and she understood that he had not been ready for death. Her throat tightened with tears.

Golden light surrounded them, unlocking the chill within her heart. Though their lips were motionless, their voices spoke to her, softly, murmuring, encouraging her to walk in the Light of God. Her reaction was bitter. She felt abandoned, even betrayed. How dare they be at peace when she felt so wretched, so alone without them? She wanted to pour out her feelings, to share her agony, but could not.

They began to fade. She panicked, desperate to keep the connection, if only for another moment.

She entreated silently, "Please, don't go! Not yet!"

Responding, the figures solidified, dissipating the miasma gathering around them. "You must accept what is, Helena," her grandfather said.

She disagreed. "It's too much."

Her grandfather's answer was swift. "Your heart will show you the way, Helena. Listen to it."

Through a film of tears, she watched Mikael as he transformed, maturing into older childhood, then adolescence, until finally, he stood before her as a man.

She heard his deepened voice. "Mother, I want you to be happy. There's no death, only God. I am with Him."

Even as her heart opened to him, she wondered if madness stalked her mind. "It's too hard, Mikael!"

"We're with you. Always. We'll wait for you until you are called. But not by your hand. You can't come into the Light carrying the stains of your own blood."

Her grandfather's voice seemed farther away. "Find the strength, Helena. It is within you."

Now close in age, her son and grandfather linked arms. The light around them shifted, becoming brighter, more intense. She blinked her eyes, feeling oddly at peace, and they were gone. Only the wind, the steppes, and the ashes remained.

Deep in thought, she stared at the pyre one last time, then turned away. Valamir waited, leaning against his horse. All at once, she was dizzy, unable to move forward.

As he led the horses to her, Valamir's eyes reflected the blue sky. His face was somber. "It's time to go."

He put his arms around her, then lifted her onto the horse. With her body against his, they rode back to camp. No words broke the silence. They reached his tent, situated near the northern perimeter. The camp remained quiet, all but empty of men. Glad to be spared the sight of returning Huns, Helena was thankful.

In the afternoon sunlight, Caratipian prepared their meal. He looked at Helena with concern and then frowned at Valamir.

"Have you seen Bevion?" Valamir asked.

"No, not yet." He turned the meat cooking on a spit across a fire. "You've exhausted her. She's not well!"

Valamir dismounted, holding her in his arms, and glared at the servant with irritation. Remembering how Kansbar treated people under his control, she became afraid for Caratipian.

Without a word, the Goth took her inside the tent, placing her on the ground. "Rest. I must care for the horses. Tomorrow, we break camp. You'll need strength."

With her hand, she covered an inadvertent yawn.

As he smiled, his eyes were warm. "Make sure you eat what Caratipian offers. He can be fierce!"

"You aren't angry with him?"

"No, he's never shy with his opinions, but he's family. Try to sleep. I'll be back later."

Deep in thought, she stared at the fire. When Caratipian entered, carrying two bowls of food, she welcomed the interruption. The meat smelled savory, making her stomach growl. Placing a dish in her lap, he sat across from her.

"Eat. I made this especially for you." He spoke Persian, rusty from disuse. His dialect, graceful in its cadences, soothing to her soul, was the language of her cradle.

"May I see your hand?" he asked.

Her eyes did not leave his face, but she nodded. With gentle expertise, he examined the wrappings.

"Valamir did well by you. In time, you'll never know that any bones were broken."

"I'll never forget."

"How may I help you with your pain, Helena?"

Her eyes blinked with tears. The sympathy twisted in her heart. She stared at him, searching for hypocrisy, but saw only compassion.

"Valamir wants to wed me. I don't know what to do." She studied her the flickering fire.

"Why does he ask you this?"

"Attila. He wants to keep me safe from him."

"Attila," Caratipian repeated in a flat voice, his expression bleak. "Take Valamir's protection, Helena. He'll not hurt you."

"How did you come to be with him?"

Caratipian's smile was touched with bitterness. "I had the misfortune of traveling with a small caravan that was attacked by Rugliva's men. Having no one to ransom me, I've remained these twenty-five years."

"How awful!"

"The first months were hard. I tried to escape. They tracked me down on the second day, but did not kill me. Instead, they forced my face in the dirt and cut my right calf muscle, making me a cripple, cheating me of death. Years later, my situation improved. Vandalarius, Valamir's father, bought me to nursemaid his sons. They'd lost their mother and needed someone to watch over them."

"But why you, a man?"

"Bevion, at six, needed supervision. Valamir, just past twelve, was ready for a tutor. I had knowledge of history and the world. Vandalarius put me in charge of both, each at their level."

"Did you have family in Persia?"

"My family is Valamir and Bevion. At eighteen, when Valamir became a man, he bought me from his father. He gave me my freedom. It's my choice to stay."

Helena considered his words. Slavery was accepted, an institution intrinsic to the fabric of civilized society. But life with Kansbar had personalized her perspective, transforming it into repugnance.

She looked at Caratipian's dignified, lined face. "You found the strength to survive."

"Yes. In time, you'll find it, too. It's difficult for you to believe now, but the Lord has smiled on you by entrusting your life to Valamir's safekeeping."

She felt a shiver go up and down her spine, as if recognizing truth in his words. But she did not feel uplifted. Instead, her emotions and thoughts churned together in a frightening swirl, spiraling downward to despair. Everything closed in, trapping her. Dark feelings clouded her mind, making her question Caratipian's motives. He served Valamir, not her. Resenting how their common language had allayed her fears, she resisted its comfort.

Ignoring her suspicious stare, he began to eat.

Between mouthfuls, he spoke. "By reputation, I knew your grandfather."

"Why do you tell me this?"

He beamed at her. "Good. Don't give your trust so quickly. Listen to your inner voice, not words from the outside."

His advice, echoing her grandfather's, only made her feel more alone. She was too tired to be strong.

"While you eat, I'll tell you what I know of your grandfather."

"I'm not hungry."

"I heard your stomach growl. You've honored your loss, now attend to your body. Besides, don't you want to hear about him?"

She muttered under her breath, "You should have been a horse trader."

"Maybe I was, a lifetime ago. Please, share a meal with me. I don't like to eat alone."

Her mouth turned up into a sad smile and Caratipian's blue eyes twinkled. Using their fingers, they ate from the leather bowls. Though the meat had the pungent taste of wild antelope, it was cooked to perfection.

"Our religion has changed over the years, as you know," Caratipian said. "But unlike the Medes, who now control the Gathas, the very words of Zarathushtra, your grandfather remained true to the old ways, preserving them as best he could. He broke with the ruling priesthood, calling them corrupt, and chose voluntary banishment in Constantinople. Yet, the priests never tried to kill Balusistriam. Over the years, I heard many stories about his spiritual powers. Perhaps, they hoped one day, he would share his knowledge with them."

Eating her meal, Helena listened intently. Her grandfather had dismissed the Medes as impostors, not worthy of discussion. But at a deeper level, she was distressed by the juxtaposition of her memories of a kindly grandfather with Caratipian's description of a man renowned for mysterious abilities.

She spoke slowly, almost in a whisper. "Grandfather often told me that our line was descended from the Prophet himself."

"That would explain the Medes' interest!"

"Caratipian, no one could prove such a claim. The records have been long lost!"

"The Medes must have believed he carried the sacred bloodline. Constantinople is not beyond their reach. But Balusistriam grew old, free of an assassin's knife."

"Perhaps they didn't think that he was important enough to kill."

"You don't understand, Helena. His very existence was a threat to them."

Exhaustion found her. She yawned. "Well, his death has ended it. The Medes have nothing to fear from me."

Caratipian looked thoughtful. "It might be best if the Persians did not know about you. As Balusistriam's direct descendant, they'd have a use for you."

"Unless my father died in battle, he's in Persia somewhere. Why would anyone want me, a woman, when they could have the son?"

"That could be true. But now, more than anything, you need rest. I'll leave you to sleep." He paused. "I know someone with a bolt of beautiful fabric. I'd like to have a dress made from it. Would that please you?"

"Caratipian, what are clothes to me now?"

He did not try to soothe her with soft words. "I'm sorry for your loss, Helena. Do you need anything before you sleep?"

"No, but I thank you for your kindness."

He smiled, then quietly went outside. Helena curled up in a ball on Valamir's sleeping pad. She could hear the old servant outside, finishing his chores in the late afternoon sunlight. Before covering herself with blankets, she was asleep.

She awakened to Caratipian's voice shouting, "No! Bevion!"

Quickly, she sat up, confused. It was night. The fire flickered in the hearth and she did not know where she was. Her face was cold, numb with exhaustion. The tent seemed to spin. She leaned forward and rested her head on her knees, breathing deeply to ward away dizziness.

Her heart pounded, warning her of danger. She listened to the angry voices outside, but could not hear Valamir's. Bevion's words were slurred from drink as he shouted at Caratipian.

Her mind fully alert, she looked frantically for a weapon, but without success. Desperate, her thoughts were chaotic, ruled by fear. Then unbidden, her childhood lessons surfaced. As if her grandfather was beside her, she quieted. Panic swept through her body, but she released it to God. Her thinking cleared. She stood and saw her two knives hanging from the tent's intersecting poles, just out of reach.

Bevion pushed his way inside. Caratipian followed close behind. Remaining on her feet, Helena turned to face the intruder. With his body, he blocked the tent flap, barring escape. All at once, her hatred of Kansbar and Ivan erupted to include any man who would do her harm. She glared at Bevion with deep contempt.

He eyed her provocatively. Barely breathing, Helena locked eyes with him, hoping to keep him at bay.

Caratipian interrupted, "Bevion, please, come with me."

"No, I must speak with her. Alone," he said in a voice so like his brother's.

Protectively, Caratipian moved to her side. "Valamir speaks to the Shaman, negotiating his price for joining his hand with Helena's."

"No!" Bevion said. His lips a thin line, he switched to Gothic. "You must make him see sense. The plan is foolish. The bitch will cost him Attila's friendship. And for what? A woman?"

"Attila loves Valamir, Bevion. You underestimate his loyalty to his old friend. They played as children together before he went as a hostage to Rome."

With slow movements, Bevion slumped down, reeking of liquor. He put his head in his hands.

Caratipian was gentle. "What troubles you, Bevion?"

"Why should Valamir have her? He always gets what he wants. Beyond being the heir, he's Father's favorite. Even Attila respects him. And I need this woman. I've bedded two since I last saw her, but they did nothing for my pain. Her eyes, green like the sea, haunt me. Valamir doesn't have the imagination to appreciate her. If I had my lyre, I'd immortalize her face in song. And then, sing another for her body..."

"Bevion!" Caratipian said, pulling him up by the arm. "Come outside. I've cooked something special for you, hoping that you'd join me. We'll talk more, in private."

At the mention of food, Bevion became more cooperative, allowing Caratipian to lead him out. As they moved farther away, their conversation became indistinct. His voice was petulant, no longer aggressive.

Helena spared him no sympathy. He had violated her cocoon, shattering her fragile illusion of safety. Her heart pounded quickly. She trembled. She wanted to walk, fast and far, under the stars, and think. But that was impossible.

Trying to calm herself, she tidied her few possessions in the satchel. At the bottom, she found Mikael's spare clothing. Stroking the rough material, interwoven with strands of wool and flax, she was flooded with memories of him, laughing, in his red tunic and brown pants. She almost threw the garments on the fire, wanting the flames to burn away her pain. But the heavy material would only smother the small blaze. With a sigh, she refolded the clothing, letting it fall to her lap.

Gradually, she became aware of a soothing presence, diminishing her despondency. Sensing, rather than seeing, Helena felt Mikael was near. Her despair lifted, but her doubts returned. She wondered once more if imagination brought her close to madness.

When Valamir returned, Helena was relieved. Yet, she remained by the fire, staring into the flames. Ages ago, in Kansbar's house, Valamir had reminded her of a falcon, soaring in the air currents, untouched by the concerns of others. Beyond his remoteness, hardened by years of practice, Helena glimpsed his passion.

He joined her at the rudimentary hearth. "Caratipian told me about Bevion. I'm sorry for his rudeness," he said, his face hot with anger.

"I'm glad you're back."

His face softened, but he remained silent. Then he took her hand in his. "Your being here has made my tent a home."

As her eyes found his, the familiar sense of communion returned. The moment was quiet, yet vivid with intensity. When he placed his arm around her, she did not stiffen against him. Pulling her onto his lap, he held her. Her ear against his chest, she listened to his steady heartbeat, comforted by its rhythm.

"I've spoken to the Shaman. He's agreed to a ceremony."

Her body tensed involuntarily. The idea of marriage remained macabre, tarnished by nightmare memories of Kansbar.

"I promise that I won't force you, Helena."

She wanted to believe him, but her body remembered the past.

Yet, she did not withdraw from his embrace.

"Bevion thinks I'll cause trouble for you with Attila," Helena said to the ground.

Valamir laughed, but with a harsh edge.

"Did he? Is that how he convinced himself that raping you would be for my own good? He always finds a reason to justify taking what he wants, no matter the cost to me!" Valamir paused. "I'll have to beat him, just like when we were young."

"No," she said, to her surprise, "please don't. He was drunk. He didn't touch me."

"No thanks to his self-restraint! Caratipian spared me none of the details. But for him, tonight's outcome would have been different. A thorough thrashing will do Bevion good."

Helena fixed Valamir with her eyes. "Please let it be. He'll hate you because of me!"

His eyes sparked. "He must learn respect."

Deep within, she knew if Valamir humiliated Bevion, he'd be no different than a wounded animal, becoming vicious through hurt pride.

"I shall not come between you. Your blood bond is sacred," she said, persevering.

Valamir narrowed his eyes. "I've no plans to renounce him, but he will suffer enough to improve his memory. More than once, I told him to keep away from you."

"You asked me to marry you. Caratipian has arranged for a dress. If you beat Bevion, he won't be your witness to the ceremony. Have him stand by you and he'll leave me alone. As his brother's wife, I'd be forbidden."

Valamir was silent, withdrawn. Then he nodded abruptly. "Your reasoning is sound. But I'll miss seeing him on the ground, his hands clutching his stomach with pain."

His hand touched her face, softly. "Will you marry me, Helena? Tonight?"

"Yes." But without the brothers' crisis as a distraction, her heart felt heavy again.

"Caratipian has the dress ready. Do you want to see it?"

"Did he take it from a dead woman?"

"No, didn't he tell you he had a bolt of silk from a caravan? It was a gift of appreciation for their safe passage," he said.

"It's stolen, you mean."

"Don't let that ruin his gift."

Helena paused. "Because you ask for Caratipian's sake, I'll accept it."

Resting his hands on her shoulders, he kissed her softly on the forehead. He pulled away, reluctantly, his eyes alive. "You've made me happy, Helena," he said, embracing her again.

As he stood to leave, he stared at her and became very still. For a few seconds, Helena's world compressed into the moment and Valamir.

"I must see to the final preparations," he said. "Caratipian will bring the dress."

With white knuckles, he held the tall, supporting pole. As the entrance flap fell behind him, Helena blinked. Her heart drumming, she smiled. Valamir's blue eyes lingered in her mind.

CHAPTER EIGHT

Caratipian interrupted Helena's reverie. "May I enter?" he asked.

"Come in," she said, jolted back to the moment.

Along with a small bucket of water, he brought a simple dress, draped over his shoulder. Catching Helena's eye, its fabric shimmered blue and green. With unexpected poignancy, Helena was reminded of the Black Sea and the screeching cries of the gulls.

Caratipian's smile was quiet with satisfaction as he placed the garment on her lap. "Its color reminds me of your eyes. I hope it does justice to your beauty."

She shook her head with firm denial. In the village, she had felt awkward, out of place, and not pretty. Even in Constantinople, in her grandfather's loving home, she had considered herself lacking, and somehow inferior. From hushed servants' gossip, she had learned her bloodlines were not pure Persian like her grandfather's, but mixed.

Her mother had been Thracian, descended from the Celts. Though Balusistriam had often praised her intelligence, even as a young child she had sensed his disappointment that she looked more Celtic than Persian. His praise of her features had sounded hollow to her ears, especially as she grew older and more aware of his preferences. Yet, despite his bias, she had never doubted his love.

More than once Helena had wondered had her mother lived, would he have acknowledged her, his only grandchild. She had heard several versions of her father's courtship of her mother. All agreed that he had been wildly in love, to the point of being disowned. Her grandfather was fiercely proud of his ancestry, never speaking of Helena's Thracian heritage, damning it with silence. On the rare occasions when anyone spoke of her mother, they never called her by name, just Michilieh's wife.

Her father had added to her confusion during a rare sojourn in Constantinople. Though she had been only five, she could still picture his face as he whispered that she had her mother's eyes. He stroked her hair, then her body. When she whimpered with fear, he had pushed her from his lap, and stalked away. He left the next day, his farewell to her had been perfunctory, tainted by a cold, hard stare. When he visited again, a year later, he had avoided her. After that, she hated her resemblance to her mother. She wished for her grandfather's eyes, so blue that they rivaled the richness of the sky.

She came back to the moment. "Thank you, Caratipian. Your kindness is a gift."

His answering smile was warm. "I'll be outside, should you want anything."

Alone again, she stroked the dress and realized it was made of silk. With care, she placed it on the sleeping pad. Her motions were slow, even pensive, as she sponged herself clean and rinsed her hair. Shaking her head, she set aside her melancholy, spraying droplets from her wet hair.

As she dressed, the silk felt smooth and soft against her skin. The sensation brought her back to Constantinople, to when she shared her grandfather's evening meal. When they had guests, her dress would be fine, often made of silk. From the dining room, the sounds of the water, splashing in the fountain, would drift in from the courtyard. Through the open doors, she would watch the phoenix in the mosaic floor, its flaming wings glistening in the torch light, a mystical bird who found rebirth through a fiery death.

Her childhood memories were seductive: an indulgence and an escape from the grief that gnawed at her soul, hurting like an open wound. She turned from them and combed her hair methodically. As a girl, she had dreamed of love. But Kansbar had crushed her romantic illusions. Yet, Valamir's lips on her forehead had been gentle, though passionate with restraint.

He was a barbarian, riding with the vermin of the Empire: Huns. But she felt safe with him. Not since her grandfather's death, had she been so well protected. Smoothing the folds of her dress, she studied the flames in the small fire, knowing she would never be ready for what was to come.

She prayed, "Lord, be with me," then softly called for Caratipian.

His response was brisk. "Yes?"

"I've finished."

"May I enter?"

Her voice was dull. "Yes."

Looking up, she saw compassion in the old Persian's face. She gestured for him to sit beside her. Despite his mutilated calf, his body moved with inherent grace as he accepted her invitation. For making him a cripple, for stealing his poise, she hated the Huns even more.

"Does your leg give you much pain?" she asked in a whisper.

He smiled with irony. "Perhaps we'll speak of my difficulties one day. But dusk draws near. Soon the Shaman will wed you to Valamir." He paused. "May I help you, Helena, granddaughter of Balusistriam?"

Against sympathy, her defenses betrayed her, caving into nothingness. Her voice broke. "I've lost everything. My child, my grandfather, my life in Constantinople...all that I love is dead. This man, this Goth, seems to care for me. Maybe in another life, I could have felt something for him. But not now. Not with this emptiness. I look into the fire and wonder if I'm dead. And then...I think that I wander in Darkness and the Wise Lord has stopped looking for me."

Taking her hand, Caratipian patted it. "Helena, all is not lost. Valamir has pledged to bring you back to Constantinople. And you're not alone. I'm a compatriot, of sorts, and Valamir's heart is open to you."

She studied his wrinkled hand over hers. Caratipian's voice continued, persistently quiet and gentle.

"Two choices are before you. You may forge a new life, or retreat into the heartbreak of what once was. Surely, your grandfather, a descendant of Zarathushtra himself, must have taught you about the forces of dark and light. You must ask yourself, 'Which path takes me to the Wise Lord? Which path move me away from him? How shall I best follow the precepts in the five Gathas, the true teachings of our Prophet?' You've been denied death for a reason. You may not know why now, but one day it will become clear."

She shook her head. But his voice was kind, though insistent, wearing her down, as water over stone. "My words are not empty, child of the Light. Remember, once I walked through darkness, neither having nor wanting any hope."

Knowing he spoke the truth, she could not help resenting his tempered, philosophical words. So long as she grieved for Mikael, he was not gone. She sensed another possibility, a connection woven with light and joy. But misery was easier. The thought of embracing life again was too hard, requiring yet more stamina and courage. During her years in the village, these qualities had been transformed into a simple will to endure. But that strength, born of stubbornness, had vanished with Greillia's sword.

She looked at Caratipian's face. His blue eyes twinkled with wry intelligence.

"You've an inner light, Helena," he said.

"Caratipian, my world is ashes. Once, Constantinople was my home. Without my grandfather, it's just a pretty place with a fountain and a courtyard. The village was never a home, only Mikael. But he's bones, bleached by the sun and wind. Nothing's left, except revenge. Even Greillia's death won't bring back my only joy!" She looked at Caratipian with narrowed eyes, suddenly suspicious of his kindness. "Did Valamir ask you to talk to me?"

"No, Helena. I speak of my own will."

She searched for any sign of duplicity, but found none. Relief hit her hard, like a wave, and she realized how much she relied on his friendship. "Did Valamir speak the truth about Attila? Without this wedding, would I be in danger?"

Caratipian's lined face stiffened. "No one can foresee his reactions, Helena. But I know that he would be struck by you. Perhaps you don't realize it, but you have an air of elusive beauty, like a bird before flight. You are lovely. In this place, with this tribe, that puts you in jeopardy. Marry Valamir. He's far better than his compatriots. He has a heart."

At his words, she cringed. For five years, Helena had shielded herself from men as best she could. Without her consent, Kansbar had taught her one side of marriage. The idea of another joining made her afraid. She wished to be alone with Passial taking her somewhere, anywhere, across the windy steppes.

Caratipian squeezed her hand. "Come outside, Helena. The Shaman waits."

She did not want to move, but she followed him. As the tent flap swung shut behind her, she was buffeted by the wind. The sun, dropping to the horizon, made the shadows long. Her mind was silent, becoming the moment. Caratipian offered her his arm, leading her to where Valamir and the Shaman waited. Heading north, they walked only a long stone's throw from the tent, away from the camp.

Valamir stood, his hands behind his back, and watched her approach. He wore a robe the color of the sun, orange combined with yellow. As it moved with the wind, she realized he had shed his leather for silk. His hair was combed back, his face clean-shaven, animated with anticipation. Bevion was beside him, scowling, looking first at her then his brother. She did not acknowledge him, nor the men surrounding him in a semi-circle. They were irrelevant. Her eyes fixed on Valamir, her steps moved in rhythm with Caratipian's slow pace, each movement bringing her closer to the blond Goth.

As she reached him, her fears fell away. She was the drum beating slowly to the right, she was the fire in the circle of stones, she was the setting sun. She was nothing and everything at once. Valamir's blue eyes kept her anchored to the ground. In silence, she knew him.

Caratipian joined her hand to Valamir's. The physical contact felt warm, giving substance to the oneness she felt not just for Valamir, but the wind, the cold earth, even the faint sliver of moon. She stepped over the gray stones into the circle. Bevion left his brother's side, leaving Valamir and Helena alone with the Shaman. In his arms, the priest held a small bleating goat. She shivered, fearing for the white animal, not wanting more innocent blood to stain the earth.

The Shaman was a Hun, with all the barbaric insignia: the self-mutilated cheeks, the splashes of gaudy colors placed haphazardly over his leather clothes. Yet, unlike the others, he wore a long cape of pelts. His hat was unusual, made of furs and feathers, with the beak of a large bird at its brow. From the top of a ball on his tall staff, intertwined hair from horses' tails hung like tassels.

Despite all of his paraphernalia, Helena was not afraid of him. His expression was calm and reflective, as if he saw the outside world from afar. He pounded his staff twice to the earth. The drummer increased his beat.

He spoke in Gothic. "Woman, what is your name?"

She responded in the same language. "Helena, daughter of Michilieh, granddaughter of Balusistriam of Constantinople."

As she spoke one of the tribe's dialects, the drummer broke his rhythm, if only for a moment. Across from them, Bevion clenched his jaw with anger. He had not suspected her knowledge. Valamir squeezed her hand gently and smiled.

No longer seeming far away, the Shaman's eyes absorbed her. His intensity made her want to hide. But holding his gaze, she no longer felt alone. It was as if her grandfather and Mikael stood as witnesses in the Light of the One God.

The Shaman nodded at her gravely. "Helena, daughter of Michilieh, granddaughter of Balusistriam, do you take of your free will, Valamir, son of Vandalarius, grandson of Vinitharius, as your husband?"

Her voice was low. "Yes," she said.

The past impinged on the present. Her heart beating quickly, she remembered Kansbar as he officiated at their wedding ceremony. His kiss had been crushing, foreshadowing what would come later on his bed, with some of his wives watching from the other side of the screen.

As the Shaman placed his hand over theirs, Helena returned to the moment. "Valamir, son of Vandalarius, grandson of Vinitharius, do you of your free will, take this woman, Helena?"

His voice was deep. "Yes."

"Then I join you together as man and woman, husband and wife, through all time, until death takes you."

Letting go of their hands, the Shaman stepped back a pace.

"Do you, Valamir, have an offering of your love for your wife?"

"Yes, my mother's ring."

Bevion gasped, then muttered something under his breath. The ring was exquisite, delicately wrought Thracian gold, with a large, red ruby. Helena felt both overwhelmed and humbled. As Valamir placed it on her fourth finger, he whispered, "With my love."

Her eyes closed; the tears were hot under her lids. With the ring and his words, he was breaking her heart, forcing it to feel again. She had nothing to give in return.

"Do you, Helena, have an offering of your love for your husband?"

Valamir spoke urgently, his voice muted. "Holy one, the goat has been given in her name."

She became her essence and from its depths sprang her gift.

Disregarding Valamir, she spoke to the Shaman. "Yes, my grandfather's horse, Passial."

She whistled for the stallion. With his deep whinny, he answered. In moments, he appeared, a broken lead line dangling to the ground. A murmur of appreciation swept through the small crowd. Passial snorted nervously and tossed his head.

Valamir's eyes were bright. "You are generous, Helena."

As she looked at Passial, her heart was sore. All at once, she regretted her impulsive gesture.

The Shaman pronounced, "It is good."

He pulled a long knife from the folds of his sleeve. With a firm, steady motion, he drew it across the goat's neck. Remembering Greillia's sword, she began to shake. With a gurgle, the goat died. Helena whimpered. Valamir's arm comforted her, holding her tight. With his hand, the Shaman scattered drops of blood throughout the circle.

Smelling it, Passial snorted, his eyes showing white. Caratipian, now at his head, calmed the animal with soft words.

"You are wed," the Shaman said. "As the sun sets, to rest on its bed, Bevion, Ishyite, and these others will be the tribe's memory, remembering Helena and Valamir's vows." He placed his bloodied hands over theirs. With all of her strength, Helena kept the scream in her throat, her legs from running. "Your union is sealed with a sacred sacrifice. Be at peace with each other and the tribe." Then, without ceremony, he turned and walked away, silent and alone, the dead goat in his arms.

Valamir swept her up into his arms. He kissed her, briefly and softly. The men cheered. Helena did not listen. They seemed far away, someplace else. She studied Valamir's eyes, so serious, inhaling his spicy, masculine scent. He steadied her, causing her turmoil about the Shaman and his knife to fall away. As they left, the men clapped Valamir on the back, congratulating him. Bevion kept his distance, merely nodding as they passed. Looking anxiously for Passial, she relaxed as she saw Caratipian leading him toward Valamir's tent.

Still carrying her, Valamir strode through the twilight and took her to the stream. In silence, he put her down, then knelt, rinsing the goat's blood from his hands. Without hesitation, Helena followed his example, grateful for the opportunity to wash herself clean. He stood, extending his hand to hers. As she took it, he pulled her to him, holding her close.

He whispered, "Helena," and lifted her into his arms.

Inside his tent, he set her down. She waited, standing, uncertain of what would follow. But he turned away, almost as if he did not want to be too close. Taking a seat by the fire, he was preoccupied and self-absorbed. She sat across from him, at a loss by his withdrawal. Staring first at the ring, then his face, now so remote, she felt adrift.

His eyes met hers. "Are you hungry?" he asked.

The mention of food made her stomach rumble. The sound cut the tension and she smiled.

He touched her hand. "Passial belongs to you. Your smile is my gift."

Helena shook her head. "I did what was right. If you'll accept the return of your mother's ring, I'll take back Passial."

His eyes softened into sadness. "No, it's yours. She would have liked you very much."

"But Valamir, it's valuable! One day, when I return to Constantinople..."

"Then you'll always remember the man who was once your sworn husband."

His words shot like an arrow into her heart. She was silent, then spoke almost under her breath, "You, I'll never forget."

Moving with the grace of a giant cat, he sat beside her, his arm around her shoulders. Though he held her firmly, she did not feel trapped.

"We must eat," he said. "We break camp tomorrow. The day will be long." But his lips pressed hers, hungry with need. She did not stiffen against him. Still in his embrace, he lowered her to his bed. Her heart beat its panic. She felt like a wounded, wild bird, immobile and unable to fly.

He kissed her deeply, consuming her mouth, only stopping because she pulled away. His eyes were intent, but he did not speak, staying at her side.

Kansbar's abuse hung like an iron wall between them. Ashamed of her terror, she averted her face.

"Helena, I need you. As I speak, my hands want to know your body, my lips to bring you joy. Keeping my promise will be hard."

Words caught in her throat. Finally, she spoke. "I can't be a wife to you, Valamir. I'm only a shadow of myself, even that vanishes with the wind, leaving an empty shell."

He pulled her closer, stroking her hair, then her neck. "I want only you, Helena. Your troubles, I would share."

She tentatively touched his shoulder. His response was immediate. He kissed her again, long and hard.

She managed to whisper, "I can't."

He murmured, "I should go, Helena. Now."

Yet, when he pulled away, she felt alone. "Please stay," she said in a small, flat voice.

Wrapping his arms around her, he smiled. Without further intimacy, they lay together. Though the small fire in the hearth burned brightly, the shadows in the tent grew darker. The smell of meat, cooking outside, permeated the leather walls.

His breath brushed her ear. "Caratipian's made us dinner." He stroked her brown hair, then touched his lips to her forehead. With a laugh, he kissed the tip of her nose. His eyes became serious, turning inward to a private, remembered pain. "Just this once, Helena," he said, just before his mouth descended.

As his lips joined with hers, she felt engulfed. In her mind, she heard a wordless scream, the cry that had always come with Kansbar. But she did not feel the same revulsion. As Valamir pulled away, his eyes probed her face. He touched her cheek softly. "Will you forgive me if I don't take you to Constantinople?"

"I don't know. I can't think. Who knows? I only have this moment, none other. Let tomorrow take care of itself."

"You're all I ever wanted in a wife."

"How can you say that?" she asked. "How can you know me? I don't even know myself anymore."

He smiled. "Do you want words to explain what I felt when I first saw you? I don't have any. I only know that you have a home, for as long as you like, with me."

She lay motionless in his arms. Her voice was a whisper. "You've come into my life, bringing destruction, then salvation. If you hadn't been there, I wouldn't be alive, or would have been better off dead. When you're here, I can forget, if for a moment." She paused. "From the beginning, I felt that I'd known you before. Beyond that, I can't say, Valamir, except the tent feels empty when you're gone."

"You bring me joy."

"The Lord is cruel to bring you into my life on the day he took Mikael."

"Who can know God's plan? But He helped me find you, that I know." He briskly stood, his hands clasped behind his back. "Helena, how much of Kansbar's treasure was your grandfather's?"

Surprised by his abruptness, she blinked. "All of it."

"Why would he travel with so much wealth?"

"He was very rich. Most were to be gifts for relatives. But I don't think he planned to return. He was growing old. He wanted to find my father and see me safely married."

"Do you think your father is still alive, then?"

"We'd had no word of him for a long time. Although Grandfather would not admit it, my father's silence goaded him into making the journey. He wanted to find him."

"And you, do you want to see your father?"

"He's a stranger now. I was young when I last saw him."

"And the relatives?"

"None of them ever came to Constantinople. I don't know them."

"They are your family, after all."

"When Mikael was alive, I thought about escape day after day. I'd planned to make my way to Istakhr and find the relatives who still lived there. For my grandfather's sake, they would have welcomed me and Mikael as his great-grandson. Yet, in their hearts, they would have despised both of us."

"But why, Helena? How could they not value you?"

"Because my mother was Thracian. In their eyes, I'm an offense to their ancient lineage. Forgive my frankness, but they consider the Thracians no better than barbarians."

"Don't be ashamed of your mother's legacy, Helena. It is every bit as noble as any Persian's! As I told you, my mother was of Thrace. She yearned for home, never loving my father. He'd given her no choice but marriage. It comforted her to tell Bevion and me the Celtic legends, again and again. You've reason to be proud of your mother's family."

"Is that why you've been kind, for your mother's sake?"

Hunger played across his face. He returned to sit beside her. With fear, not passion, her heart beat quickly. He checked himself. "You look like her, I won't deny it. Even Bevion sees the resemblance. Her eyes were green, like yours, and you've the same high planes at your cheekbones. But you've more fire. She gave in to her heartbreak. You're a fighter, Helena. I've seen it with my eyes. I can respect your strength, but love your beauty. It was easy to marry you, Helena. You fill my heart."

She touched his cheek, then his muscular shoulder. "I don't want to go to Persia."

He smiled and kissed her gently. "Stay with me, Helena. Forever if you want. I'm happy when you're here."

Her face became hot. She blinked away tears. "I've never known anyone like you."

He laughed. "Good!" Then he sniffed the air. "The meat is done. I'm hungry. Caratipian!"

They waited by the fire. Caratipian came inside quickly, his keen eyes searched her face. His smile was soft. On a large leather plate, he carried meat and some flat bread. As he placed it before them, his expression turned serious. "Ishyite has sighted them. They return."

Valamir was casual. "Many captives?"

"He saw only one."

"Only one?"

Watching Valamir tear through his meal, Caratipian nodded. Helena's appetite had vanished with the news.

"Did anyone manage to kill Greillia?" Valamir asked.

"He survives."

"Too bad." Valamir turned to Helena and spoke with strong conviction. "You must not act against him. He's Attila's cousin. I couldn't protect you against the lawful revenge."

At the mention of Greillia, her throat tightened.

"You must promise to wait, Helena," Valamir said, "or I'll have to take measures for your own good."

She was vehement. "What do you mean?"

"I'd risk your hatred and keep you tied in my tent. Caratipian, tell her about the punishment for the theft of Greillia's blood."

"Even if you only wounded him, the Huns would cut off your nose, then your ears. If you somehow managed to kill him, your death would be hard, and very slow. First, they'd rape you until your insides were wet with your own blood. If you still lived, they'd take you apart, a piece at a time, first starting with a finger, then an eye, a breast, working their way through your skin, slice by slice. Because you are Valamir's responsibility, they'd tie him down to witness your dishonor. He'd go mad with the watching."

"They'd never take her alive, Caratipian."

"Then you'd suffer in her place, Valamir. Someone would have to pay the price."

Helena wanted to gag.

Caratipian continued, "With my own eyes, I've seen this and worse. Listen to Valamir for his sake, if not yours."

She was quiet for a moment. "I don't want to bring you pain, Valamir."

"Do you promise not to take your vengeance?"

"He deserves death, but it shall not be from my hand," she said in a quiet voice. In her heart, she knew that if anyone had survived, it would be Magga. With her knowledge of poisons, Magga would be able to exact revenge on Greillia, who would have not been gentle with his freshly captive prey.

Helena's expression was distant, as if far seeing, as she wished Magga success with their tormentor.

CHAPTER NINE

Sparking the flames, a stick dropped in the fire. In the orange light, Valamir's face was harsh and menacing: a warrior's mask. His passionate gentleness was gone, vanished as if it had never been. Once again, Helena felt adrift, lost in his strangeness, yet somehow not afraid.

He drew himself to his full height and frowned. "Helena, I'll come back after I inspect the men."

Her throat was choked. "Be careful."

A smile transformed his face. "I always watch my back!"

Without another word, he left. The knowledge of Greillia's return made her cold; the small fire, burning brightly, could not warm the chill in her bones.

"You made him happy," Caratipian said.

She did not follow his reasoning. "What?"

"Valamir. You bring a smile to his lips. Like when he was a boy."

She shook her head. "Seeing him just now, I wouldn't want him as an enemy."

He chuckled to himself, a rich sound. "That's as it should be. Else how could he keep us safe? Huns respect his strength."

"Yet, he's good to me," she whispered.

Caratipian smiled, his blue eyes lively. "His childhood training was excellent."

Helena teased him gently. "Nothing to do with you?"

"Everything! He has the best of my teaching."

"And Bevion? Wasn't he your charge at an even younger age?"

His lips became a thin line. He shook his head sadly. "I did what I could with him. He missed his mother terribly."

"I'm sorry," Helena said, ashamed to have upset him.

Caratipian shrugged. Waving his hand to dismiss her concern, he began his repairs on Valamir's bow. She watched him restring it, check its tension, then oil the wood. Later, as he aligned feathers on the arrows with painstaking attention, Helena wished for something to do. But her right hand still throbbed and when she breathed deeply, her chest was tight with pain.

Her life hung in Valamir's hands. He was a barbarian, a predator. Yet, he had penetrated the gray cocoon wrapped around her heart, bringing color back to her world. It hurt.

She sat in silence with Caratipian as he hummed over his work. By contrast, Helena felt useless. Sorrow stirred within her, but she turned from it. It was dangerous, the agony too intense to bear. She drifted to the past, to her grandfather and to Constantinople.

In the courtyard of their large, stone house, she had sat spellbound, listening as he made history come alive with tales of the ancients, and especially Alexander the Great. Of course, he would always call him Sikunder the Destroyer, the despoiler of Persia.

Her grandfather had sought her opinion about the current court gossip. In the process, he taught her to see past the intricate maze of the political game to the truth. He had been her world. Yet, he could not assuage her loneliness. Though she had never known her mother, dead since her birth, Helena's heart would ache at the sight of a woman bending down to her child with a smile.

Her father's visits were so rare as to be momentous events, but she could still picture him. He looked like his father, Balusistriam: tall, rather austere, dark hair, his eyes a startling blue, a voice that could boom with sudden laughter. Once when disagreeing with her grandfather, she saw him smile with pure mischief. He had filled the house with activity, always restless, seeming to chafe at the boundaries imposed by the stone walls. Helena knew he would never have survived as a woman in Kansbar's house, where women were expected to be docile, submissive, and always patient.

Helena wished that her father had settled down, remarried, or even sent messages home. If they had received word of him, her grandfather would not have set off on that journey. He might still be alive, her life intact in Constantinople. Though Mikael would not have been born, his spirit could have come to her through another child, spanning time, in its search for an old connection bound from love.

For the first time, she hated her father, blaming him for her heartbreak, for everything, not wanting to see him ever again. He was nothing to her but another soldier seeking oblivion in glory, neither caring for nor remembering his daughter.

Her inner voice whispered that her life had merged with Valamir's, step by step, with an inevitability set apart from time. But she rebelled against it, categorizing the Goth with her father: a self-centered soldier, thinking only of himself. The voice of her heart dissented. She was drawn to Valamir, as inexorably as a bird to the sky, but the price was too high and red with Mikael's blood. Tired and spent, she was afraid of sleep, of what her dreams would bring.

From the village, the wolves howled and Helena knew the Huns had finished their nightmare games, leaving behind corpses for carrion. She cringed, sickened by the images that crowded her mind. At least they won't have Mikael, she thought.

She watched Caratipian as he worked, allowing his attention to detail to soothe her. His hands checked feathers on each of the arrows, re-aligning this one or that until they were all perfect. Then he took out a small knife and began to whittle some new shafts for more arrows. He required nothing from her, not even conversation. With a friendly smile, Caratipian looked up, alert, yet serene. Grateful for his acceptance, her eyes filled with tears.

"Caratipian," she said, speaking against the grief that stalked her. "You're at peace with yourself."

His expression became serious, touched by old shadows. "I find happiness when it comes."

"Don't you long for more? Your own family, a son?" she asked, aware that in running from her sorrow, her questions were inconsiderate.

"What man does not wish for a son? But in this, the Wise Lord has been kind. He has given me Valamir to love as my own flesh, though he's not of my body. Just my heart."

His words stung her. Valamir had been Caratipian's bridge back from his abyss. Through a twelve year old boy, he had embraced life again and become reconciled to his fate. Helena resisted, wanting none of his peace. "I don't want to feel love again."

Caratipian's eyes were warm with sympathy, but his voice was sad. "I believe you, Helena. But your feet take you on your path to the One God, providing lessons along the way. You must learn them, else face them another time."

"Are you a mystic? Your words are my grandfather's, but their comfort is cold!"

"I'm no mystic, Helena," he said. "My wisdom is the fruit of my age. Hear my words or not. It's your choice."

Embarrassed by her outburst, Helena ran her hand through her hair. He did not deserve her abuse. Caratipian's words fell into silence.

"Why has Valamir been so good to me? He's with Huns, the filth of the Empire!"

"You're words are strong, if inaccurate. The Huns are many tribes, a confederacy bonded by language and custom. Valamir's people were conquered by them over fifty years ago. Over time, the Ostrogoths have molded their masters, assimilating them in gradual steps, changing from the vanquished to trusted allies."

"But why is Valamir so different? Even his own brother thinks nothing of rape!"

Caratipian withdrew into his thoughts, his face reflective. Helena waited as the moments passed. She became afraid that he would not answer. She despised herself for her curiosity, but much more for caring.

Looking his age, Caratipian met her eyes. "His mother was killed by a renegade band of Visigoths. She was pregnant, her belly deep with new life. She'd gone alone to a favorite spot, by a quiet pond, in the nearby woods. When Valamir's father, Vandalarius, returned from the hunt, both his wife and son were missing. We searched, only finding them as it grew dark.

"Valamir was holding his mother, cradling her head in his lap, singing to her. His father tried to pull him away from the corpse, but with each attempt the lad became more wild. Finally, I was able to separate him from her. We'd spent time together and I knew what needed to be said. After, Vandalarius bought me from King Rugliva, at a considerable price. He worried about Valamir and thought I could do some good. I've been with him ever since."

Helena looked at Caratipian's eyes, shining with tears.

She whispered, "Was her death quick?"

He stared at the flames. "No, she'd been raped so many times that her blood had spilled from her womb. As she lay in a pool of blood, they sliced open her belly and ripped out her child while she still breathed.

"Valamir had tried to cover her as best he could with his tunic and the fragments of her dress. When Vandalarius saw his wife, he cried. No one had seen him shed a tear since childhood, but he was not alone in his grieving.

"She'd been beautiful and it was terrible to see what had been done."

Helena's eyes were wet. Guilt gnawed at her. She was safe and protected. And Caratipian had said of the village, "Only one survivor."

She buried her face in her hands. "I can't bear it. There were children in that village, innocent children, old women who worked hard their whole lives and my friend, Arianna. Now they're gone, as if they'd never been, except as memories."

He was quiet for a moment. "Perhaps it was important, even necessary that you survived. Your destiny is before you, unknown, but you still breathe, whole, intact."

"You don't understand! It's wrong that I'm alive! Mikael is alone, without me."

"Nothing I say can change what has happened. But good can come from pain. You wonder at Valamir's kindness to you. Thank his memory of his mother."

"But he rides with Huns! How can I see past that?"

"No one chooses their families. Valamir is what he is: an Ostrogoth. Though he fights as one with the tribe, he takes pain not to make war on women and children. Be consoled by that difference. He's better than the Romans. Like Greillia, they kill children for sport."

Her bitterness remained. Suddenly, she remembered only Valamir and Caratipian had knowledge of her ransom. "How did you learn of my steward's reward?" she asked.

Caratipian smiled with deprecation. "I hear things that many do not."

"It might have been better had you not."

"Without Valamir's protection, you'd be dead. He decided to join Attila because he found your story intriguing."

Her voice was hard with accusation. "Why would he care?"

"Who can know what's in a man's heart?"

"The ransom is large," she stated.

"Valamir doesn't look for more wealth. He lives for adventure. The story I told him, I must admit, was worthy of a Persian. It fired his imagination."

"You think I was lucky to survive."

"Yes."

"I can't be thankful for my life. Its price was too dear."

Caratipian nodded, his expression pensive. Though he kept his eyes on her face, he was far away in thought. A stick fell in the fire with a thump. He blinked and began to gather his tools.

Helena glimpsed his pain. "Caratipian, I'm sorry."

His eyes met hers with surprise. "Why?"

She drew in a deep breath. "For all that *you* have lost."

His eyes softened. "I thank you for your sympathy."

She spoke from her heart. "And I, for yours."

The heaviness within her lightened, the feeling bittersweet. "Did Valamir tell you what happened to Mikael?"

"He was sick about it."

"Why would he bother about another man's son?"

His look was stern, but without rancor. "He cares for you, Helena. And because he cares, he's upset for your loss. Else he wouldn't spare it a thought. Valamir never lacks for a woman.

At home, the mothers hatch plots to wed their daughters to him. But he has never stayed long with anyone. None have slept in his tent. With you, though, he shows a gentleness that I haven't seen since he was a boy. If he gave you to Attila, his reward would be great. But instead, he protects you, making you his bride."

Helena did not know what to say, not wanting to acknowledge how her heart felt when Valamir's face lit up with a smile.

"You care for him, too, Helena."

She picked at her dress. "Do you think that he would have been good to Mikael?"

Caratipian nodded.

"Was I wrong to run?"

"You shouldn't torture yourself with what could have been. Your plan was sound. How could you know that Greillia would follow you?"

Her words tumbled out. "Valamir had promised he'd keep both of us safe. But after Greillia's sword... and Ivan fell, I trusted no one. If only I could change it and bring back Mikael."

"You need sleep, Helena. Lie down and rest. I'll keep watch for Valamir."

She followed his advice and was soon asleep under the warm blankets and fur-lined skins. A noise awakened her. She sat up, rigid with fear. The fire had died back, losing its battle with darkness.

Someone threw a piece of kindling on the fire. As it caught, the light illuminated Valamir's face. He looked tired and spent, betraying a weariness that had little to do with physical exhaustion. He carefully placed more brush and sticks on the pile.

His face chilled her heart. It was devoid of feeling and remote. Watching him, she lay still from terror. As his eyes adjusted to the brighter light, he saw that she was awake. A shadow passed across his features, but then he smiled. When he sat beside her, she forgot to be afraid.

CHAPTER TEN

The wind blew hard, pummeling the walls of the tent and driving the flames in the crude hearth upward. Helena shivered. As Valamir grasped one of her hands, his expression changed, becoming veiled. She felt oppressed by the pungent odor of his sweat and the steadiness of his breath. He was too close.

Her heart pounded, the blood coursed through the veins of her legs and she remembered Kansbar. The tent seemed to spin. She needed to hold onto something, anything, to stop her vertigo. But she would not reach out to Valamir. A vision of an old crone, saliva dribbling from her lips, flitted through her mind. As Helena recognized the face, she wanted to scream. It was her own, only much older. Through the force of will, she steadied herself, turning from the madness whispering in her ear.

From within, she heard her grandfather's voice gently reminding her to watch her breath, watch her body, without judgment, without concern. "It's a reflection of the One," he seemed to say. She breathed quietly, feeling her fear as sensations rippled through her body. It was as if the air vibrated, casting a shimmering blue tint. She felt a heaviness lift from her shoulders. Her heart quieted.

She looked at Valamir anew. He no longer seemed larger than life, only a man who was tired. His face was drawn with fatigue; his eyes were troubled. The tent was ordinary again, the drab brown colors obscured by the gloom. She felt refreshed and more alert, but could not understand why.

She set aside the puzzle. "You should sleep, Valamir."

As if to ward off his thoughts, he closed his eyes. Reopening them, his expression was fierce. "Are you well, Helena? Are you in less pain?"

Confused, she hesitated, then said, "Yes."

"That is good," he said, more to himself than to her. His blue eyes glinted in the firelight. With ease, he pulled her to his lap. His face against her hair, he rocked her like a child.

Comforted by the side to side motion, Helena was not frightened by his closeness.

Helena broke the spell. "Morning will come all too soon. We both need rest."

Not masking his desire, he stared at her. "I promised you, Helena," he said, his breath in her ear, "but it's hard."

Sick with panic, she shrank within herself. Her body retreated into immobility as a last defense. Her throat ached as she felt her fragile bridge of trust, so carefully constructed, crumble into dust.

Valamir smiled with self-deprecation and the air stopped beating against her ears. He whispered, "I've frightened you."

Still wary, she nodded slightly, feeling his hardness through his clothes. Anger rose within her and she lashed out, bitterness an unexpected ally. "What woman is safe with any man?"

"Why take by force, when by waiting, I can hope for joy?"

Steeled against his soft words, she stared at the ground.

His lips compressed into a frown. "Don't you believe me? Do you think I'm a twelve year old boy without self-control?"

She spoke evenly. "Trust is a gift. You are a man, with a man's needs."

He shrugged his shoulders with a smile. "There are more than enough willing camp followers to satisfy my *needs*, Helena."

The image of him, intertwined with another woman, tore at her. She despised herself for caring, realizing he would follow the way of men, sharing himself as he pleased.

She glared at him. He had a way of creeping under her barriers, subverting her resistance. His face was alive with mirth, tinged with impish satisfaction. She was reminded all at once of Bevion. As he chuckled to himself, she wanted to slap him.

"You're jealous!" he said, laughing.

He stood up, holding her in his arms, and twirled around within the confines of the tent, by sheer luck breaking nothing. When they were both dizzy, he stopped, then half sat, half fell down on his bed pad with her in his arms.

He looked more than a little pleased.

Pulling her down to the bed, he kissed her lightly on the mouth. Her body did not stiffen against him, but became still. With reluctance, he loosened his embrace, but remained beside her. His body was warm, his chuckle deep as he repeated, "You're jealous!"

She punched him hard in the arm. "Stop gloating," she said through her teeth.

"Shh, Helena, I'll stop," he said. "I'm happy that you care, even if a little."

He kissed her again, with tenderness, his hand stroking her hair. His embrace gave her a feeling of completeness, yet at the same time, made her angry. She pulled away from him, holding him at bay with her arm extended and her hand pressing against his chest.

"Next time, ask first."

"What if you say 'No?'"

"Accept it."

He smiled, but his eyes were speculative. "I could love a woman like you, Helena. You're strong."

With that, he turned from her and promptly fell asleep. She lay awake a long while, watching him, before joining him in his dreams.

It was dark, the light low in Kansbar's hearth. Ludmilla placed her hand on a man's throat, checking for a pulse. Helena edged closer to the bed, wondering why everything seemed enlarged. Then she saw her grandfather and understood that she was dreaming. His eyes blue opened, alive, despite his agony. He was dying again. Thirteen once more, she leaned over him and tried to hear his whispered words.

"It's time to remember, child. You're my heir, Helena. Not your father. Protect the Legacy."

"What do you mean, Grandfather?"

"Remember, Helena."

She awoke to morning, but felt uneasy. Valamir was outside in conversation with Caratipian. The background noise of the camp had become louder, like a steady drone.

Her thoughts drifted back to her dream. Her grandfather had exhorted her to "remember." Puzzled, she wondered if he meant the vision by the funeral pyre. Yet, the answer hid in the back of her mind, eluding her. She arranged her clothes and deftly brushed her hair. She smelled meat cooking and was hungry. All at once, she realized that she had lost her cocoon of numbness. She wanted to blame Valamir and his vitality, but could not: the change came from within.

The brush in her lap, she remembered her vision of the crazed crone. With a shudder, she understood that hate was no protection against despair. Its only gift was madness. But the journey back to life hurt like a foot that had fallen asleep: with sharp, prickling pain.

A blood-curdling shout startled her. It was joined by another, followed by roars of laughter. The Huns had returned: Greillia would not be far.

At the thought of him, she shook. Hugging her knees to her chest, she tried to regain her self-control, but could not. Her throat remembered the sting of his sword, her nose, his fetid breath as he pushed her to the ground. Valamir planned to break camp today, and the thought of being near Huns made her cringe. With all her heart, she wanted to stay sequestered in the tent, hidden.

When Valamir returned, she attempted to hide her distress. He paused at the doorway, then slowly sat down. His arms around her, he held her closely. She stopped shaking, his presence acting as a buffer against the harshness of reality. Yet, she was ashamed of her need.

Touching her chin lightly, he lifted it, raising her eyes to his. "What's frightened you?"

She could see that he was edgy and preoccupied. She felt awkward, hating to bother him with her fears.

"Tell me," he said.

With a deep breath, she forced herself to speak. "I'm afraid of Greillia."

He brushed a tendril of hair from her cheek. "I'll keep you safe."

She blurted out, "I feel like a child lost in the dark, with monsters chasing me."

"You're my wife. Any man who touches you is dead, as is my right under the law."

Her voice was small. "They wouldn't hurt you?"

He laughed. "No one would dare. I'm close to Attila."

"Even Greillia?"

"He's a mad dog, needing to be put out of its misery."

She nodded in agreement, but wondered aloud, "Why do you hate him?"

"He has no honor. The village...it was the worst I've ever seen. The people died...in agony. And it was Greillia, I know, who whipped the men into a frenzy. You and that woman, Magga, are the only ones left."

His final words reverberated in her mind. All at once, Helena understood her dream. She traveled back to the last night of her grandfather's life, locked deep in her memory, and remembered.

"Kansbar, do you promise that you'll send the message to my steward?" Balusistriam had asked, *his face ashen, his voice slurred with pain.*

"Yes," Kansbar answered. But he avoided her grandfather's eyes.

"Tell the guides that they shall be well rewarded."

"I will."

"I have your word?"

"I'll take good care of your granddaughter," Kansbar said. His eyes shifted to Helena, but his expression brought her no comfort, only a twisting dread, a need to be far away.

"Good, Kansbar. That is very good," Grandfather said with a gasp. He paused, regaining strength, and Helena realized then that he was dying.

"Did your father ever tell you about me?"

Kansbar looked down. "There were...stories, strange stories."

"They were true, Kansbar. We traveled a long way together, your father and I, exploring things that should have been left alone. In the end, we came back: he, to this village, I, to the Light. But I remember what I must. Helena! My dagger!"

Something in her grandfather's voice, in his eyes, made her bowels tighten with fear. But she obeyed, afraid of him for the first time in her life. She watched, unable to look away, as he opened the flesh of his palm in a straight line.

Balusistriam held up his bloodied hand so that Kansbar could see it. Then he clasped his palms together so that both would be red with blood. With his right hand, he inscribed a rune in the air, a focus of mystical power, then another, slightly different with his left. As he drew them, a nameless horror chilled Helena's heart.

"Should you, Kansbar, fail me, I curse your village. May all of your children die, so that your bloodline shrivels into nothingness. May all of your people be as dust, your village as if it had never been. But Helena will live, untouched by your ruin, safe and whole."

Kansbar turned pale. Ludmilla began to sob. Helena touched her grandfather's sleeve, whispering earnestly. "You've invoked darkness, Grandfather. I feel something strange, a presence. Send it away. Take back what you said. Nothing good can come of it."

He had only smiled sadly. "Helena, I'll be with you, always." Those were his last words. He died later in his sleep, with the smile of a child on his lips.

With an ache of despair, Helena returned to the present, to Valamir's impatience. He was distracted, ready to be outside. "All will be well, Helena."

She stood up, smoothing her dress, her heart taut with pain, and remembered precisely how her grandfather had drawn the runes.

"You don't look well," he said.

"He cursed the village. I'd forgotten."

His voice was tense. "Who cursed the village? What are you saying?"

"My grandfather. What have you heard about him? Caratipian seemed to know all about him." She added with bewilderment, "He was loved by everyone."

"I hadn't heard his name until Caratipian told me the tale of the lost heiress who vanished on the silk route. He was adamant that Balusistriam and his granddaughter should be found."

Her words a jumble, she repeated, "He cursed the village. Everyone but me, no exceptions, not even Mikael. He couldn't know that I'd have Kansbar's child. Magga hadn't come to the village yet. She was not a part of it. And we *are* the only survivors."

Valamir was silent, lost in thought. Finally, he spoke. "It's probably a coincidence. What were his words?"

She repeated the words verbatim, buried so long, yet so fresh in her mind that they could have been spoken yesterday.

He listened, looking troubled, restless with his discomfort. "Why would a curse take five years to be fulfilled?"

"I don't know. He did not place it within time; it stood by itself."

He shrugged, suddenly irritable. "We must hurry. We ride soon. We have to fold up the tent. Come outside."

She picked up her satchel and followed him, preoccupied with her thoughts, her panic about Greillia forgotten.

Beyond the snug confines of Valamir's tent, the world had changed. Pairs of men, with an occasional woman, were dismantling tents: first the walls, then the supporting wooden skeletons. Bulky wagons stood nearby for storage. Huns were everywhere, astride their small, hardy horses. Bevion was nowhere to be seen, but more importantly, neither was Greillia.

The fresh morning air was delicious, reviving her, sweeping away memories of her grandfather's curse. Caratipian placed his hand on her elbow and guided her to a safe place near Valamir's horses. When Passial saw her, he nickered. Helena smiled, happy to see him. Tersely, Caratipian told her to sit on the large rock. He placed a bowl of food in her hand. It smelled delicious: freshly cooked meat mixed with roasted grains.

"You'll not have more until nightfall. They don't stop for the noon meal, Helena, so eat what I've prepared." Without another word, Caratipian hurried off, taking her satchel to the waiting wagon.

She stared after him, suddenly reminded of Miriam, her old nurse from so long ago, who had been equally adamant. Shrugging her shoulders, she ate it all then wiped the bowl clean with some long grass before placing it on the rock. She touched her bandaged right hand and noted that the throbbing had lessened, becoming a dull ache.

Stretching, she stood. The two men had stripped the tent's outer wall and wrapped it in a neat bundle. Their speed was remarkable as they worked in unison.

Before turning to the next task, Caratipian glanced at her. "Put the bowl in the wagon, Helena, and take one of the flasks from the front."

The wagon was sturdy, made entirely of wood, without any decoration. Already, its interior was packed neatly. Meant to be pulled by a pair of horses, it had only two wheels. Some men had larger ones, able to stand alone on four. Valamir's had no roof, only rungs to hold down a tarp.

Absorbed in his work, Valamir had not spared her a moment. Feeling isolated, Helena sought comfort in Passial's company. As she untangled his mane with her left hand, she regretted sharing her memory of the curse with Valamir. It had disturbed him. Yet, as she thought of the runes, she felt a strong compulsion to draw them. As if outlined in fire, the images were etched in her mind. But she resisted the urge.

Ignoring the wave of macabre feelings, she checked Passial's legs and hooves with fierce concentration. When she heard a hollow laughter, her skin pricked with fright. She held onto the white stallion, as if he could exorcise her fear.

Angry at herself for being afraid of shadows, Helena shook her head. She pictured Light all around her and spoke in Persian, "In the name of the Wise Lord, be gone from me. I'll not have you!"

The beauty of the morning, with its white, fluffy clouds, returned to her, vanquishing the heaviness as if it had never been. She looked up and found Caratipian's troubled eyes. He had stopped his work with Valamir and watched her. She wanted to reassure him, but had no words. She felt cut adrift from humanity, connected only to Passial.

The tent pole came down with a thump. Caratipian, distracted by Helena, had broken the smooth rhythm of the teamwork. Her mare, Sarelle, spooked at the noise, snorted loudly. Passial looked with interest, but did not dance with fright.

"By Mithras!" Valamir shouted.

"I'm sorry. My mind wandered...," Caratipian said.

"Well, it's nothing that we can't fix," he answered, his anger downgraded to annoyance.

Helena tried to quiet the mare, bridled and saddled, ready for the day's journey. But with only one good hand, she found her hard to handle. As she led her away from the commotion, Helena knew that she would not be able to control her under saddle. These past years, Sarelle had only been used as a brood mare. Kansbar had not thought her much good for the plough, but even he could not bear to destroy her. The mare was beautiful, her brow wide, tapering down to a narrow nose. Instead, he had bred her for size, pushing her womb to its limits by using his workhorses as sires.

"Easy," she said. Her voice was firm, yet soothing. But she felt clumsy, handicapped by her injuries.

She felt someone's eyes. Looking quickly, she caught Valamir watching as she handled the mare. His expression was unreadable, even cold. Her heart sank. She felt the barrier between them and missed his warmth, wishing again that she had kept her disturbing memories to herself.

When he smiled, his stern expression was transformed. Her relief was tangible, but it brought a sudden shyness. He narrowed the distance between them in a few strides and took the reins from her. He jerked them down once. The mare jumped to the side, making an attempt to bolt. He let her play out a little, then snapped the reins again. Sarelle gave up and stood quietly, her eyes watchful.

Still holding the reins, but loosely, he stepped close to Helena. He leaned toward her, his breath whispering across her face. "Your story troubled me, Helena. Such things are known from the old days of Thrace."

Spontaneously drawn to him, she laid her head against his chest. Her left arm wrapped around his waist in a tentative embrace. She felt his hand touch her chin, raising it. With a kiss, he held her. She felt as if they were locked together, alone in their world. With reluctance, he broke the contact.

"I think I'm more than halfway in love with you, Helena. You're in my heart."

Her defenses were useless against him. "You've brought the colors back. I only wish that it didn't hurt so much."

He smiled, shaking his head. "You talk in riddles, but your voice is sweet."

As he looked over her shoulder, his tenderness vanished. Following his eyes, Helena saw Bevion. He was mounted, his entourage behind him: a male servant, an Ostrogoth woman, a large, black dog, and several horses.

His eyes fixed on her, Bevion sneered. "Seems I'm ready first, Valamir. But I see that you've been busy."

"Show respect. This is my wife."

Bevion's expression became a study in innocence. "You're packing is all but done. What else could I have meant, Valamir?"

"I don't like the way you look at her."

Bevion edged his horse closer and smiled down at the couple. "Hilja misses you, Valamir. I treat her well, but I know which one of us she has always preferred. After all, you were one of her favorite customers."

Overhearing, the woman flashed Valamir a smile. Though the look that she gave Helena was far from cordial, it was not venomous. Despite her veneer of sensuality, her posture was erect, her features open, quite different from Magga's dark brooding looks, so full of hate. Helena wondered why she had become a camp follower. Clearly, she was handsome enough to have found a husband.

Bevion jerked his thumb toward Helena. "Well, how was she last night?"

Valamir's answer was an incoherent roar. Moving with the grace of a dancer, he leapt at his brother, pulling him down from his horse. He threw him on his back, punching hard. Far from helpless, Bevion defended himself, hitting Valamir in the stomach. The answering blows did not stop Valamir; he kept the advantage, pinning Bevion to the ground. Helena felt confused. While she hated to see the brothers fighting, another part of her wanted Bevion to suffer.

Soon, the brawl lost its momentum. Valamir released him from his stranglehold and stood, looking down at him impassively. Bevion stared back, his nose bloody. Then they both started to laugh. Valamir offered Bevion his hand and hoisted him up. They grinned at each other like two boys. Caratipian shook his head with affectionate disapproval.

Helena exchanged a glance with Hilja. With a smile, the woman rolled her eyes at the men's antics. For the first time since her tragedy, Helena wanted to laugh, knowing that she would never understand men. As the feeling bubbled within her, it faded abruptly, crushed by the specter of grief. She tried to smile, to share in Hilja's amusement, but could not. For an instant, the woman's face softened.

Bevion pretended to punch Valamir's stomach, making him laugh. Helena was reminded of two puppies, teasing each other over a bone.

When Caratipian shouted to her in Persian, she was startled. "Helena! Danger! Greillia!"

Alarmed, she turned to see the Hun approaching on his brown horse. Quickly, she was by Passial, still without a saddle, signaling him to lower his leg so she could mount. She tried to warn Valamir, but the words died in her throat.

Seeing Greillia, Hilja scowled with disgust, then spat on the ground. Meanwhile, Caratipian shouted to the brothers in Greek. "Watch your backs!"

Valamir and Bevion moved as one, playfulness set aside, and faced Greillia. Each stride of his horse's even canter brought him closer. In an instant, the brothers were mounted.

Valamir positioned his roan between Passial and Greillia; Bevion flanked her side. The mare, unattended, arched her neck with excitement, but stayed near. Though Valamir's stallion showed the whites of his eyes at being near another male, he was too well-schooled to bite. Bevion's bay horse stamped its front leg and squealed. Passial countered the threat by laying back his ears, ready to take a mouthful of mane. Pride satisfied, the horses settled down.

Helena could not match their forbearance. Her heart throbbed with panic. She wanted to scream. Magga stumbled behind Greillia's horse, her hands bound tightly with a long rope tied to his saddle. Her face was swollen with bruises and the bodice of her dress was partially ripped.

Helena felt something shift within her, replacing her fear with an urgent call for revenge. She wanted the bastard dead, his entrails spilling from his abdomen, the smirk on his face transformed into a death scream. Her eyes danced at the gruesome image as her hand reached to where her dagger should have been.

When she looked at her empty hand, her very being pulsed with rage.

Valamir's eyes were on her, his expression serious. "Wait."

"For what?" she all but spat.

"For the gods' will, Helena."

"No," she said, but her voice was different, hardly her own. "I won't."

"It would be your death. You know that. But if Greillia moves against me," Valamir said, his smile dark, "then your patience will have its reward."

She nodded, accepting the intrinsic promise, but not because of his words. She believed his face: it had reminded her of her grandfather's when he had drawn the blood runes.

Greillia reined his horse to a halt, less than ten feet from them. As he looked at Valamir, his expression was sullen. Had he been a dog, he would have snarled. When his eyes met Helena's, she was reminded of a wolf ready to devour its kill.

She forgot everything: Valamir, Caratipian, the sky, and the earth. She concentrated only on Greillia and what he had done to Mikael. Her right leg brushed Passial's side and he moved to the left, giving her an unobstructed view of the Hun. Her body felt satiated with heaviness, a darkness that made her feel larger, more powerful then she had ever dreamed.

As she spoke, the words were ancient Persian. "Greillia," said a hollow voice, her voice. "I curse you. Each step that you take will lead you closer to the Dark Lord. You are his, marked by him, and he will give you his special reward. You and only you are cursed. Your death will be long and slow. You will linger, helpless, more like a woman than a man."

The Hun watched, transfixed, as her left hand quickly drew one symbol, then her right the other, the splint not impeding any detail of the intricate configuration. A shadow of fear passed across his face and for the first time, he looked vulnerable. If she had her dagger, Helena would have sealed the curse with her blood.

CHAPTER ELEVEN

The curse invoked, Helena stilled her voice. Her body no longer surged with power, but was quiet and debilitated. The raw sensation of omnipotence had vanished. She felt exposed. Her eyes on Greillia, she trembled with exhaustion. Seeing her weakness, he laughed and his mouth ripened into a vicious sneer.

Yet, behind his bravado, she sensed fear. Though her words had been Persian, she knew he had felt the full force of their malevolence. The curse had been woven, tightly, without a seam, lacking only her blood to secure it through time and space. How she understood this, Helena could not have said. The knowledge emanated from her flesh, her very bones.

Something of the power lingered: separate, alive, unwelcome. She could not give it a name, much less set it aside. She continued to stare at Greillia, undisturbed by the malice in his eyes. She knew darkness; she had been its instrument. His evil was puny and inconsequential compared to what had consumed her, what had fed upon her soul.

She wished it away. But unable to focus, her thoughts drifted. Time slowed, losing its continuity. Someone nudged her, but she ignored the prodding. Instead, with dispassion, she wondered why her hands had reversed the order of the runes, drawing first with the left then with the right. Oddly apathetic, she disregarded the mystery, staring at nothing in particular on the ground.

Again, there was an intrusion, someone squeezing her hand, shaking it. She stirred herself and saw Caratipian, his eyes intense with dread.

"Helena!" he whispered. "What have you done?"

She smiled with twisted exultation, cherishing the darkness. It was a cocoon, shielding her and keeping her safe. "Greillia will find his death hard."

"The Dark Lord doesn't do your bidding, you do his. If you don't stop this, he'll have you for all time."

"What's wrong with revenge?" she flung back. Caratipian persisted, his distress and affection creating ever-widening cracks in her shadow world, pushing through the miasma, forcing her to feel again.

"The price is too high, Helena. You'll pay with your soul, with your humanity. In the end, you'll be no better than he."

Hot with shame, she heard truth in his words. Still, the heaviness remained, its malevolence corrupting the very air she breathed. In despair, she struggled against its odious taint.

"You must do as I say, Helena."

Her voice was flat, monosyllabic. "Tell me what to do."

"Pray with me. Say, please Lord, return to me. Forgive me for I have invoked darkness. Without you, I am dust. Protect me. Guard me from all that is not You, and with Your sacred, golden light dispel any darkness from my soul!"

Helena repeated the first phrase with reluctance, forcing it from her throat. With each word, the resistance lessened, losing its hold. All at once, the corrosive presence was gone. The air smelled sweet once more; the sky was vivid blue.

"Now," Caratipian said, "draw this rune on Passial's neck."

He traced a small insignia with his finger through the horse's thickening winter coat. Helena watched him carefully. Unlike her grandfather's, the rune was simple. Drawing the sign, she felt refreshed, even renewed.

"In the old days, mothers would teach their children this rune as a ward against the Dark Lord. Can you remember it?"

Feeling an odd tingling, she nodded, unable to tell him that she recalled the symbol. Her grandfather had taught it to her years ago, when she'd been afraid of the dark. Speech had become a distant goal, requiring enormous effort.

"Helena! Do it again, quickly. This time draw the rune with your eyes as well, imagining it glowing with golden light."

She obeyed without hesitation. Her lethargy vanished, as if it had never been.

Caratipian let out his breath, audible in his relief. "Good. It's only a simple rune, but I don't know any others to protect you from that...thing you invoked."

Helena's heart opened to him. He was agitated and out of his depth. As she spoke, her voice was calm, quiet. She felt rooted to the Earth, yet part of the sky, the wind, the horse under her. "It will be enough, Caratipian. Have trust in the One. His Light alone vanquishes darkness."

For a moment, he looked bewildered, then elated. He smiled with a kind of pride. "You *are* of the old blood, Helena, as was your grandfather before you. Always remember that."

She shook her head, remembering last night's dream, wanting only the best of her grandfather, not this other memory that both compelled and frightened her.

Valamir interrupted them. "Caratipian! Helena!" he said in Greek. "Quiet! You distract me!"

His voice was harsh, but his eyes were troubled, almost afraid. He had sensed a part of the evil. Helena wondered how much time had passed. For her, it seemed a lifetime.

Caratipian bobbed his head with deference, but shot Helena a keen look. Feeling like a conspirator in a private joke, she checked the impulse to laugh by biting the inside of her cheek. Her self-control was tenuous: she did not dare catch his eye. Turning away, she saw Bevion staring intently, a witness to everything. But she did not care if he had seen the runes. They were not for him. For better or worse, they belonged to her and those of her grandfather's blood. She shrugged, dismissing him. He scowled.

"Helena," Valamir repeated.

Hearing his voice, she felt shy and apprehensive. She cared deeply what he thought of her. She edged Passial closer to him, but was conscious of the darkness that had enthralled her, that still craved Greillia's blood. It was unclean and foul. Valamir must not see it.

Shielding herself from the likelihood of his rejection, she took a deep breath before facing him. Her fear was not realized. Instead, she felt their connection, a communion between souls, as if it spanned a lifetime, not just two days.

Greillia severed their soundless harmony. "I've come to trade," he said in Ostrogothic, his accent nasal.

Helena and Valamir turned to face the enemy. Bevion moved to the right, positioning himself for combat. But Greillia did not attack. He had recovered his composure; his eyes darted everywhere, appraising first her face then her body.

Her reaction was immediate. Boiling with intensity, her hate resurfaced. The dark fire rose within her, her budding need for Valamir's approval forgotten. She wanted to see Greillia die, slowly, burning alive in the flames of her revenge. The hollow voice whispered, "Do it. I'll show you the way."

Caratipian put his hand on her arm, restraining her from drawing the runes. She turned to him with rage. "You dare?" she spat, rippling with power.

"Invoke the Light, Helena! Draw the sign!" he commanded.

She blinked, coming back to herself, and obeyed. As the compulsion dissipated, she heard a high-pitched scream from within her mind. Shuddering, she felt alone, outside humankind, but worst of all, vulnerable.

"Now again," Caratipian said, his fear apparent.

As she drew the symbol, Valamir said to Greillia, "You insult my wife. Show her respect or learn from my sword."

At the sound of Valamir's voice, Magga lost her stupor. Seeing Helena, her face showed surprise, followed quickly by a flash of hate. Immersed in her own struggle, Helena had lost her fear of Kansbar's favorite. Instead, she saw with a curious objectivity the profound changes in Magga. She was a travesty of her former self: her beauty degraded, her arrogance reduced to primal hatred, her greed transformed into the will to survive. Helena experienced a flash of pity for her, but was too drained to feel more.

"Your wife! You lie! You'd never marry outside your tribe, Prince Valamir! I come in good faith, offering this woman for that!" As he spoke, Greillia yanked the rope around Magga's wrists, wrenching her forward. "Look at her! Men dream of such perfection! And she's been broken! You'd have no trouble with this one!"

"First, you insult my wife. Now my word! Come to me. I'll give you my answer," Valamir said, drawing his sword.

"Unless you're afraid, Greillia," Bevion said, his voice a quiet taunt.

Helena visualized her dagger, deep in the Hun's throat, stopping his ugly words. Did he pause, just for a moment? she wondered. Caratipian remained at her side, his hand over hers. The title "Prince Valamir" reverberated in her mind, full of meaning, but she set it aside. Her fear of Greillia did not return: it had been supplanted by the whispering, hollow voice. Now that she had escaped its thrall, it terrified her.

"I've no argument with you, Valamir," Greillia said, his voice becoming wheedling. "I offer a bargain."

"You've made your offer. I reject it. Go!"

Bevion shouted, "You heard him!"

Greillia sat immobile on his horse, his eyes narrowed, his jaw moving as he ground his teeth. "You didn't let me finish what I started with her. I found her first. You've no right to take first pick. She's mine."

"I've made her my wife. Touch her and you die."

Greillia snarled, his face bestial.

"We understand each other," Valamir said, ignoring his rage. He added, almost as an afterthought, "You could get a good price for Magga, if you cleaned her up. Attila might want her. Think of the reward he'd give you."

Greillia grimaced, the expression resembling a smile, then kicked Magga in the back, pushing her face forward into the dirt.

"Son of a whore!" Helena muttered in Greek, the worst insult she knew.

Valamir shrugged, as if to say that what Greillia did with Magga was his own affair.

"Caratipian," he said, "saddle Passial."

Helena dismounted, watching helplessly as Magga struggled to her feet. Pitching her voice low, she called after her, speaking the language of the village.

"Anything you want, Magga. I'll help you. Anything!"

Magga jerked her head to look, her hate softening for an instant into gratitude. She glanced at Greillia, despite her appearance, unbroken. "I'll remember."

Speaking emphatically in the same language, Valamir interrupted their exchange. "You're not to interfere, Helena! It's not your concern. Do you understand? Mount up. We ride."

He watched her, his expression stern, unrelenting, as she got on Passial, now fully saddled.

"Give the signal!" he said to Bevion.

Bevion's throat opened, producing a low rumble, elevating into a roar. The sound was horrifying. As it was answered from all sides, Helena's skin crawled and chills swept up her spine.

Greillia shouted, his heels digging into his brown horse. As the animal broke into a canter, Magga tripped, falling again. Greillia did not slow his pace, until she'd been dragged at least ten strides. When he finally halted his horse, he leaned down and pulled her up by the hair. Placing her in front of him, he carried her face down, like a sack, until he reached his wagon, perhaps a hundred yards away. Without ceremony, he dumped her on the lumbering cart, tossing the rope to another woman.

As Helena watched, her face twisted with pain.

Valamir was curt. "You're wasting your sympathy. She deserves no better."

"No one deserves Greillia."

"*She* does. Consider this: who gave Ivan the knife? He didn't have one when Bevion searched him."

A picture of Magga and Ivan, whispering with significant looks, flashed through Helena's mind.

"She ruined everything," Valamir said. "My plan was perfect. Without her, the blood-price would not have been exacted. You'd be happy, your son in your arms. The woman poisons all that she touches. I know her kind. You shall have nothing to do with her!"

Shutting her eyes against his words, Helena knew Ludmilla and the other wives would have agreed. But her mind grew blank as she tried to understand that they were gone, that the village was no more. Despairing, she argued with herself, who could say what had doomed the village? Were Magga, Ivan, and Greillia instruments of her grandfather's curse or were they free agents, following their own free will? Could she have stopped it, by betraying Magga and Ivan to Valamir? Surely, she could have said something, anything to prevent what had happened?

Valamir had found his scapegoat, preferring Magga over a bizarre story involving curses and runes. Despite everything, Magga had Helena's sympathy: no woman should suffer at Greillia's hands.

As the Huns converged on Valamir, he grasped one of Passial's reins and pulled it, bringing Helena closer to his horse's side.

He spoke to her in a low, gentle voice. "Be strong. They'll do no more than look."

Remembering Greillia's devouring eyes, she cringed inwardly. "I don't want to be seen."

Valamir only smiled. "I can't hide you. All will see that you are with me. If I could, I'd cover you with veils, but it would only make everyone more curious. You *will* live through this day, Helena. That much I know."

She looked away, her eyes hot. To her surprise, she asked the question that came suddenly to mind. "Why did Greillia call you Prince Valamir? Was he mocking you?"

His eyes crinkled with amusement. "You didn't know, then? I wondered..." His smile faded. "Before the Huns came, the Ostrogoths were ruled by my grandfather, Vinitharius. Attila's uncle, King Rugliva, allows us our titles."

Helena mused, more to herself than him. "A prince...and I've brought you nothing, except curses from ancient days."

"Helena, not another word. You've given me happiness."

Her answering smile was spontaneous, without guilt. His hand touched her cheek with a light caress. All at once, they were surrounded by a small sea of Huns, rippling in ceaseless movement. With a slight nod of acknowledgment, Bevion flanked her mount with his horse. For once, she did not mind his sardonic company.

The Huns wore an assortment of clothing, ranging from the brightest to the most drab. The stench of their humanity was palpable. Their small, hardy horses snorted with impatience.

There were women, but they kept their distance. The focus of many eyes, Helena's stomach tightened. Looking down, she studied the texture of Passial's mane.

Valamir's roan was so close that the two horses' barrels touched, squeezing her left leg. The animals' ears were laid back, signaling their displeasure. Passial snorted loudly. Despite her anxiety, she marveled that the stallions did not fight.

Peripherally, she saw Valamir raise the hand that held Passial's rein. "Behold my wife! The Shaman has sealed our lives!"

Murmurs swept the crowd, mostly in Hunnic. Yet, none seemed surprised. News, especially gossip, traveled fast in any camp. Ishyite, Valamir's friend, pushed his horse through the crowd. "All husbands welcome you to our brotherhood! We'll drink tonight in celebration, and then in a year to commiserate!"

Affectionate, but cynical, laughter swept the ranks. Helena glanced at Valamir. By the set of his jaw, she knew that he was embarrassed and her heart warmed to him.

"May the gods bring you many sons!" The men roared jubilant comradeship. Ishyite inclined his head with greeting, his face sharp with intelligence. "Be at peace, little sister. You are at one with the tribe."

He clapped his hands hard, then looked up at the sky and laughed. The men cheered. But the words, "one with the tribe," stuck in Helena's heart like a dagger.

Valamir raised his voice so all could hear. "We ride to Attila. Already our Lord waits to the North, impatient. But when he sees the bounty we bring, he'll forgive us the delay!"

Again the men laughed, betraying no ill effects from yesterday's depravities. Helena began to feel ill, her stomach churning with queasiness. As the group began to disperse for the day's journey, Greillia thrust his horse through the crowd.

"I challenge Valamir's right to the woman!" His voice was hoarse with anger. "She's bounty...to be shared!"

"You've no right, Greillia," Ishyite said, blocking his way to Valamir. "The Shaman made them one. You desecrate the law."

Greillia's face was transformed by fury. His mouth contorted, as if his teeth were bared in the rictus of death. Ishyite stared back. He looked mildly amused and relaxed, though poised to fight. Intolerant of a poor loser, the crowd jeered Greillia.

"You're looking for more training, Greillia?" Ishyite asked. "I heard that Valamir offered you a lesson, but you refused. Were you afraid of his sword?"

The tribe's laugher beat the air. Greillia was trapped in a humiliating web of his own making. He made his horse rear, flashing its hooves near Ishyite's face. The other Hun, not impressed, crouched down, then wheeled his mount's rump hard into the other's raised belly. Ishyite's bay danced sideways. Deep in contact with its attacker, Greillia's mount had no where to go but down.

As the animal toppled backward, Greillia jumped off. Transfixed, the men watched the spectacle. The horse hit the ground with a crashing thud. The crowd erupted into pandemonium. The men held their sides, hugging their laughter. Valamir and Bevion joined the uproar. The felled horse stood up with a snort and shook itself. Greillia's face grew red with anger and shame.

Helena was quiet and watchful. Her enemy's public embarrassment did not satisfy one-hundredth of her revenge. It only made him more dangerous, more likely to try to catch Valamir off-guard and drive a knife in his back.

Ishyite offered his hand, but Greillia spat at it. Ishyite shrugged, a picture of nonchalance, answering the insult with indifference.

Valamir shouted, "We ride!" The horses leapt forward, even Greillia's, as its rider sprang to its back. To keep her seat, Helena grabbed Passial's mane. The earth rumbled under the horses' hooves; the birds circled to the north; the sun shone brightly in a clear autumn sky and Helena struggled to hang on.

CHAPTER TWELVE

The Huns, more than four hundred strong, pounded north in the direction of the village that had been Kansbar's pride. Each stride brought Helena closer to the birds, black against the blue sky: ravens, mixed with buzzards, shrieking with piercing cries. The ruined village was out of sight, blocked from view by a slight incline. Thin trails of smoke wavered in the wind: the aftermath of burning.

Helena saw the shape of a person abandoned near the ridge of the hill. Birds surrounded it, but at a distance, waiting for the safety of death. Her reaction was immediate. Closing the small gap between Passial and the roan stallion, she snapped her horse's rein from Valamir's hand.

His eyes were alert; his mouth was a frown. "What are you doing?"

She gestured toward the birds and reined Passial to a halt. "I'll be back!"

The horsemen thundered past. Valamir glared at her, his eyes impatient with anger. The wagons, following more slowly, offered Helena and Valamir a moment's solitude in the empty space between the two sections of the tribe.

She did not waste time on explanations, but urged Passial into a gallop toward the birds' prey.

He pursued her, shouting, "No!"

As Valamir reached for Passial's reins, Helena performed the same maneuver she used when Greillia had pursued her. Sitting back on the white stallion, she signaled him to halt, then pressed her right leg against his side, making him yield left. It worked: the roan ran ahead.

As Valamir wheeled his mount, he called to her, "Helena, most men would beat you for this!"

With an affectionate grin, she laughed quietly. Reining in Passial, she waited for Valamir. Trying not to smile, he shook his head. Still mounted, he pulled her from her horse, holding her tightly in his arms.

"Don't do that again," he said. His mouth on hers, she softened against him, not fighting the passionate embrace. He kissed her forehead and her hair, and whispered, "By the gods, I thought you were bolting."

Her hand touched his hair, then his cheek. "You're real and solid, speaking to something in me. But I don't know who I am or what I feel. Except...things make sense again when I'm with you."

He kissed her gently, then pulled away. "Why did you run off like that?" he demanded.

Her eyes did not flinch. "I told you!"

"You said nothing."

"I pointed to the birds. Someone's alive over there."

He looked troubled, then stubborn. "You may not see it."

"I'm going."

"You forget, Helena, that you're on my horse, in my arms."

"I won't beg, Valamir, but I must."

He stared toward the tribe. The horsemen were obscured by dust and the sun. The camp followers, several hundred feet off, had come abreast of their position. They both could see Caratipian, veering away, heading in their direction. The packhorses plodded behind the wagon. Sarelle, prancing to the side, was restive from the slow pace.

"He's like a mother to you!" Valamir stated with a wry shake of his head. His eyes narrowed and his lips pursed. "You said strange words to Greillia. Then Caratipian was at your arm, beside himself with worry. Why?"

Helena was silent for a moment, but risked judgment by answering. "I cursed Greillia."

Half to himself, he said, "I could feel it."

"I wondered if you could," she replied. "It was no more than what he deserves. But I didn't like what happened when I said the words. It frightened me." She paused and looked toward the distance. "Please let me see who the birds circle. I'll be haunted by not knowing."

He studied her with keen eyes, then shrugged and looked away. "If that's what you want. But you'll regret it."

He swung her behind him, then called to Caratipian, "Catch her stallion and wait. We'll be quick."

They set off at a canter toward the inert, pink shape. Hoofbeats followed them, and Helena turned to see Passial, reins flying in the wind. They soon reached a woman. The birds flew farther away: some waited out of reach, others headed to the village. She had been mutilated, almost beyond recognition, and left for dead.

But Helena knew her. Moaning softly, she slid from the horse and whispered, "Arianna."

Kneeling beside her only friend in the village, Helena cried. She whipped her coat from her back, shivering, not from the brisk fall morning, but from what had been done to the girl. There was a gaping hole where her nose had been. Her ears were severed. Arianna's large, gray eyes stared up at the sky with the pupils dilated. She blinked.

Helena touched her cheek, whispering, "Arianna," again. As she pulled her hand away, it was red with blood. Covering her friend's nakedness, Helena turned to Valamir with rage.

"Who...why? Who could do this?"

She shouted at him, holding nothing back. "How can you be with them, these...murderers? Is this what you do?"

His eyes were fixed. He dismounted and stood beside her. "Don't judge me. I change what I can and accept the rest. But no, I don't kill like this."

Tears were in her eyes. "I wish I could hate you, but I can't. You make my heart hurt, did you know that? Why did we have to meet this way? Why are you with the Huns?"

He knelt, his arm cradling her shoulders. "Who can question the gods? Accept what has happened. There's no other choice." He pulled her to him, gently away from Arianna. "We can do nothing for her. We must go."

"I won't abandon her to the birds!"

"She's dead, or good as dead, Helena. It won't matter if you watch her die."

She cried, moving back to her friend. "No! I can help her."

"She'd hate you if she lived. Look at her face. Come away."

"I can't leave her to die alone!"

"By Mithras, if I didn't care for you..."

"You'd do what, Valamir? Leave me with her, for the birds and the wolves?"

He smiled ruefully. "Don't be foolish."

She began to cry. "I don't understand what I feel for you. It's impossible. Nothing good could come from the way we met!"

"Do you think I have an answer, Helena? When I first saw you, I felt something. It hasn't changed, it's become... stronger. When I'm with you, no matter the words spoken, my heart is glad."

She closed her eyes and whispered, "Mine, too."

"I'll get the wagon for your friend."

His roan cantered back to Caratipian, but Passial stayed. Helena listened to the wind and the birds. On the other side of the ridge, a solitary wolf howled, signaling its pack.

"I love him, Arianna. I don't know why."

The girl clutched her hand.

Her eyes wide, Helena leaned closer. "Oh, I'm going to take care of you. You're safe now. You'll be all right."

But the girl moved her head, slightly from side to side, in mild disagreement.

"I'm so sorry, Arianna, so sorry."

Arianna's throat gurgled. "Be...well...Helena." Then she shuddered. Her eyes were open and unblinking, her body still.

Helena moaned. A wolf's cry pierced the chill air. She stared at nothing and buried her head in her hands.

Valamir returned quickly, ahead of Caratipian. His horse stopped a few feet from Passial, who laid back his ears and squealed, kicking out with a hind leg.

Valamir studied the remains. "It's for the best."

Helena was quiet, her voice soft. "I know."

She stood slowly. Her body felt heavy, suddenly old.

"Your coat," Valamir said.

"Arianna needs it. I've nothing else to give."

He shrugged, his nonchalance at odds with the scowl on his face. "I have one you can use."

"I can't stand to leave her like this."

"We're far behind the tribe."

He shouted, "Caratipian! Go back. We're coming!"

The servant waved and turned the wagon in a semi-circle.

Valamir glanced at the sky with exasperation. He dismounted and pulled Helena firmly away from the body. "It's better that she's in the open. It's cleaner. The birds will have her, but that's nature's way."

Without a word, he reached down to Arianna and closed her wide, open eyes. He hesitated, then pulled the small coat over the corpse's face, leaving the legs exposed.

Helena cried, grief coming from her heart. "What if there are more survivors? What if there are children? There were babies..."

"No one's left. This much I know. They burned it. It's gone, as if it had never been."

He lifted her to his horse, placing her near the withers. Catching Passial's reins, he mounted behind her and made a sound that was a cross between a hiss and a cluck. The roan sprang to a run. Passial stretched out beside him.

In no time, they reached Caratipian.

Valamir shouted to him, "Hurry!"

The packhorses broke into a canter. Despite his impatience, Valamir stayed alongside, rather than leaving Caratipian to fend for himself.

With Valamir's arm around her waist, Helena was lulled by the rocking motion of the canter. The air felt crisp against her face. The horizon was boundless: the rolling steppes a world apart from the bustle of civilization. The birds called; a hare showed a hesitant nose before darting away; a fox poked his head from his den.

It was morning and life continued, completely indifferent to Helena's sorrow. All at once, she felt hostile. The clouds should be black or at least gray. Instead, the sun shone and the sky was bright blue. She wanted to curse the perfect day.

But she did not. The memory of the hollow laughter, echoing in her mind, disturbed her. She tried not to dwell on it, understanding that even thought would bring it close. She concentrated on her breathing, seeking a narrow focus to dispel her dread. Missing the limited protection of her old coat, she felt the cold. Yet, she was glad that she had been able to give Arianna's corpse something, anything to cover it.

Soon they caught sight of the other wagons. Leaving Caratipian to join them, Valamir increased his pace, riding ahead toward the horsemen, wrapped in a distant cloud of dust.

Helena listened to Passial breathing hard. It worried her. In contrast, Valamir's roan ran easily, rushing to join the others. As they closed the gap, Helena tried not to think of Arianna. But the image of the mutilated body and the ruined face lingered, haunting her. Involuntarily, she trembled.

Valamir tightened his arm around her waist. "Don't be afraid."

She blinked back hot tears. A rider veered off from the group, galloping toward them.

As Bevion joined them, he laughed and shouted. "Catch your bride? Maybe you were too hard on her last night!"

Valamir ignored his teasing. "Has Hilja found someone else yet, Bevion? She seemed, dissatisfied when I saw her with you."

"Everything's fine between us!" he retorted, glancing at Helena. His blue eyes were curious.

"Helena," Bevion called. She turned, ready to lash out at him. She needed any excuse to escape the turmoil that escalated with each stride that brought them closer to the Huns.

His face was drawn from repressed feeling. "Don't worry. I'll help Valamir keep you safe."

"Thank you, Bevion," Valamir said. "You're good to your new sister."

Looking away quickly, Bevion could not meet his brother's eyes. Instantly, he reminded Helena of a guilty child, young and vulnerable. Valamir guided them left, away from the center of the band. The dust was thick, choking her.

From the right, Ishyite joined them. "Where do we break for camp?" he asked.

"There's a stream, many leagues to the north."

The Hun smiled. "Good, I'll spread the word."

Like Greillia, his face was marked with scars. Yet, for Helena, he was different; he seemed almost human. They rode for hours. The sun, still bright, was far past its mid-day peak, but Valamir's roan plunged forward. The only evidence of carrying a double load all day was his lathered neck.

Helena felt numb from exhaustion, but said in a loud voice, competing with the wind, "I should ride Passial. Your horse is tired."

He laughed. "You'd fall off. You're in no condition to ride. Maybe tomorrow."

In time, Helena's eyes drooped. Her dreams returned her to the village.

Alone with Ivan on his father's bed, she was terrified. With his hands and body, he pressed against her, pinning her down. She tried to scream, but her mouth wouldn't open. Her arms were useless, curiously immobile. Her heart thudded loudly, keeping time with her panic. Before her eyes, Ivan's face lengthened and transformed into the head of a wolf.

As he spoke to her, his breath was foul and reeked of death. "It's all your fault, bitch. My head's gone - stolen! This is all I have left."

His lips were on hers, drooling.

She awoke with a start. The sun was low in the sky, obscured by orange and purple clouds, stretching out the shadows of the horses and their riders.

"We stop soon," Valamir said.

Her voice was a murmur. "Thank God."

They rode in silence. Helena nearly fell asleep again, but fearing her dreams, forced her eyes to remain open.

As the sun set, Valamir reined his roan to a halt and raised his right hand. The horsemen created more dust as they stopped to listen. He pointed to a glistening stream at least two hundred horse lengths away.

"We camp. Tomorrow, we reach Attila. Sleep! Rest your horses. First light will come soon!"

The men roared their approval. Yet, they did not rush to the water. Instead, they made their horses walk, cooling them down before letting them drink. Helena hated to admit that they knew how to keep their overheated horses from water and protect their hooves from foundering.

From a distance, Helena saw Greillia. His eyes met hers. As she stared at him, a chill spread through her. Trembling, she pictured the Hun staked to the ground spread-eagled, with knives puncturing his hands and feet, and his blood spilling from his groin. He looked away.

She felt no victory, only grief, tightening her throat and soaking into her body. The satisfaction of Greillia's slow death would not bring back Mikael's laughter or even Arianna's shy smile. Though Valamir's horse had brought her far, he had not carried her any distance at all from the searing anguish. It lingered, catching her by surprise and stalking her through memories.

She struggled against hopelessness, refusing to be engulfed. Her hand clutched the roan's mane. "I've never heard you call your horse anything. Has he a name?"

She waited. Valamir's answer had become important far beyond its significance. The silence was killing her with a wordless scream. If only he would talk, it would go away, at least momentarily.

"I call him Hassan."

"But that's not Gothic!"

"It suits him. Caratipian used it first, and it's stayed with the brute ever since."

Behind his brusque words, Helena sensed affection in Valamir's voice. Somehow, it eased her pain.

At the stream, they dismounted. Valamir led her to a large, gray rock. With his hands on hers, he made her sit. "Rest. Caratipian will come soon."

She watched as he took off Hassan's saddle and rubbed down his coat, glistening with sweat. But soon Helena's exhaustion recaptured her. Resting her head against the rock, she fell asleep and saw nothing more.

CHAPTER THIRTEEN

Helena slept deeply, without dreams. When she awoke with a start, her back was stiff and her legs were sore from riding. Yet, her head was clear. As she sat up, her hands smoothed back her hair. She did not even remember being carried inside the tent. Though the sun had only begun to brighten the tent, Valamir was already busy. He was preoccupied, but she had come to realize that he often withdrew into his own thoughts and concerns.

She watched him repack the two leather bowls and cooking pot. Her stomach growled hungrily. He looked up at her and smiled. The pale sunlight shimmered on his long, blond hair and the brilliance of his blue eyes, so alive, caught her unawares. Her cheeks grew hot. Feeling a rush of shame, she turned quickly, hoping the shadows hid her blush.

"You slept like the dead last night," he said.

Her bitterness was immediate, almost reflexive. "I *live*."

"My words were unfortunate. Sometimes victory is surviving to fight another day."

"What difference does it make? Who misses Mikael, but me? Do the birds stop their song, does the Earth notice one less boy? I think not. We fade with the wind."

"It all matters! Somehow, some way. Did you ever think that I would have liked to have known your son? Children give me hope. Despite what Bevion says, at home I've seen him roll on the ground, playing with the boys. Caratipian would have been in his glory with a young charge. If you had died that day, I would have thought of you for years, regretting I hadn't saved you. It's time to stop feeling sorry for yourself. It changes nothing! You're alive. That's enough."

She whispered, "How can you be with the Huns?"

As he put his arms around her, she buried her face in his chest. She cried, clinging to him as if he were a raft in a turbulent sea. He stroked her hair softly, soothing her.

After she had quieted, he was brisk. "Now, I must see to your hand. It needs a fresh bandage." With a light touch, he examined it. "The swelling is less. Can you move any of your fingers?"

She wiggled her thumb, but nothing else.

As if it were a new toy, he held up a piece of wood, delicately carved. "Caratipian whittled a splint for you."

At this additional evidence of the Persian's kindness, Helena bit her lip. Not knowing what to say, she watched Valamir as he tended her hand, re-bandaging it with clean cloths tied securely around the smooth piece of wood.

Her voice was low. "You've both been good to me."

"I have my reasons," he said, kissing her mouth and pressing her back to the sleeping mat. As his hands stroked her body, she was excited, but in an unfamiliar way. She stiffened against him, feeling trapped and afraid.

He whispered in her ear, "I dream of you when I sleep."

She turned to him, searching for the truth in his eyes. When he kissed her again, she yielded to his embrace.

"Valamir!" Caratipian called. "It's time to break camp!"

"By Odin," Valamir softly swore under his breath. "See to something, Caratipian. I'll be out in a moment," he called. Cupping her face in his hands, he whispered, "If I stay any longer, I'll forget my promise."

He pulled away slowly, as if each movement hurt.

"Tonight, we see Attila."

"I don't want to."

He laughed. "I can't hide you, Helena."

"Give me back one of my daggers. I'd feel safer."

"I'll protect you. Besides, anyone would be able to take it from you."

"You could teach me how to keep it."

He smiled. "I would teach you many things, if you'd only let me."

She dropped her eyes. "You embarrass me."

He chuckled. Then his voice became serious and solemn. "I require your promise that you would only use it for defense."

"I give you my word."

He rummaged through a leather bag and extracted both knives, examining them with a professional eye. "The dagger is fine. How did you keep it from Kansbar?"

"I hid it."

"You kept little else, except a few gold coins and a knife only good for cutting meat."

"I saved what I could. I regretted losing my mother's ring and my grandfather's sword. The rest didn't matter."

"This ring?" He held up his hand, still wearing it on his fifth finger. "The one he gave to his whore?"

"Yes."

"I'll ask Attila for it. He'll not care about a plain, gold ring. The sword will be harder, but we'll see." Taking the ring off, he held it up to the light. "There's an inscription inside."

"It's in Greek," she said.

"I can't read, Helena. Can you?"

"It says, 'With all my love.'"

He smiled, his eyes twinkling as he put it back on. "I'll take your word!"

As he went out to join Caratipian, he laughed, holding both knives in one hand. She felt cheated. He had extracted her promise, then walked out and left her with nothing. But her anger was empty and hollow compared to the depth of her sorrow.

Finished with her preparations for the journey, she waited with her arms around her knees, trying to keep warm. The night had brought frost, but Valamir had allowed the fire to die so they could dismantle the tent. Shivering, she regretted her impulsive gesture to Arianna, but then felt guilty. Arianna had deserved much better than a thin, worn coat.

Valamir returned. "You're freezing!"

"You told me you would give me back my knives!"

He raised one eyebrow, then chuckled. "You'll keep me to my side of the bargain then?"

"Yes, or I'll take back my word."

Amused, he smiled. "I gave them to Caratipian to sharpen for you!"

She felt foolish. "Oh."

"See? You still don't trust me."

"It's hard for me."

His face softened for an instant. "No harm done. The camp stirs. I want my tent down. It's cold. We'll have to find you a blanket or something to wear."

Feeling uncomfortable and unsure of herself, she followed him. Caratipian was cooking meat over a fire. Her nose twitched at the agreeable aroma. Both men looked intensely pleased with themselves.

She felt annoyed at being left out of their secret. "Why are you both so happy?" she snapped.

"Look behind you," Valamir said.

She turned quickly. A leather coat was fastened to the side of the tent. It was her size, made of soft brown skins, with fur lining in its hood.

Her voice was hushed as she touched it. "It's beautiful. Who...? How did you...?"

Valamir's voice was gruff. "Caratipian. He saw to all the details, but not in one night. We had three women working on it."

"Your other coat was no protection against the wind," Caratipian said.

Valamir encouraged her, "Go ahead, put it on!"

As she slipped it on, Helena felt overwhelmed. "It's warm."

She stroked the material. "No one has been so kind to me since my grandfather died."

Valamir would not meet her eyes. "Well, it's no more than you deserve."

Caratipian rubbed his hands together, looking pleased. But his tone was brisk. "Time to eat. We don't have all morning."

"We should take the tent down first," Valamir said.

"Not on an empty stomach."

Valamir grumbled about servants who thought they knew everything, but acquiesced. As Helena caught his eye, they both laughed like children whose overly indulgent nurse had pretended to reprimand them.

Caratipian would have none of it. "Just as long as *both* of you eat."

They laughed even harder, his tone striking them as inordinately humorous.

Bevion's voice was like a bucket of cold water. "What's so funny?"

Valamir and Helena stopped for a second, then burst into laughter again.

"I'm no joke!" Bevion said.

"It's Caratipian..." Valamir said. "He orders us around like an old mother hen."

"Oh, that's nothing new. He's been doing that for years."

"Do you want something to eat?" Caratipian asked.

"It looks good," he said, sitting down.

They shared the meal together, but Helena and Valamir were careful not to catch each other's eyes. When they had finished, the three men took down Valamir's and Caratipian's tents. They worked easily together with the familiarity of a family.

Helena felt apart from them, like a stranger.

Valamir asked Bevion, "You're with us today?"

"Thought I might."

"Good." Valamir turned to Helena. "You'll have to ride the mare. Another day of carrying two won't be good for Hassan. I wish you could stay with Caratipian in the wagon, but it wouldn't be wise. My place is with the men. And, by law, Caratipian is forbidden to raise a hand against any Hun. If Greillia tried something..." He paused. "The mare won't give you trouble. I'll hold her reins."

She nodded. "I can ride."

Bevion spoke. "Valamir, I don't have command. I can stay with Caratipian. She'd be safe with me."

Valamir smiled warmly at his brother. "That would be perfect!"

For an instant, Helena thought Bevion looked haunted and uneasy, but the look vanished as quickly as it had come. Already busy with the horses, Valamir had seen nothing.

Troubled, Helena repeated her request. "I want to ride with you, Valamir."

"I'd like that," he said.

The day's journey began. Sarelle was frisky and impatient to be off, pulling the lead taut in Valamir's hand. The air was cold enough to see one's breath. Her hands like ice, Helena was thankful for the warmth of her new coat, but could not help but wish for gloves.

As the band answered Valamir's signal, Sarelle struck off at an easy canter. Unlike Hassan, the mare's gait was smooth, like a dancer's. As the other horses stretched out to a gallop, Sarelle wanted to run. Helena sat back using her weight to slow the mare. At the same time, Valamir shortened the lead. Sarelle stopped fighting the bit and was content to be at the roan's side.

Morning turned to afternoon. Occasionally, the pace slowed to a trot, but never for long. On and on they traveled, across the endless steppes, toward the North and Attila.

The camp followers, unable to keep pace, had dropped back almost out of sight. As the day lengthened, Helena ached from fatigue. Without any discussion, Valamir reversed their horses in the direction of Caratipian and the wagon. As they galloped through the dust, Bevion joined them.

From his seat on the wagon, Caratipian waved. Passial perked up his ears and whinnied to 'his' mare. But at their approach, the servant frowned.

"Why did you wait so long? Look at her! She's past exhaustion!"

Valamir turned to Bevion. "You see? He's just like when you were small."

Bevion chuckled. "He'd put me to bed if I came home wet from the creek, even in the summer!"

Bevion smiled. "Caratipian, don't be such a...mother. The woman's fine."

"No, she's not. She's about to faint! Help me get her in the wagon!"

Bevion and Valamir looked at each other, then quickly did as they were told. As Valamir lifted Helena from the mare, her ears rang. The steppes seemed to be spinning slowly in a circle. She rested her head on his shoulder and suddenly was loath to be parted from him.

Gently, he put her in the bay of the small, open wagon on top of the bed pads. Caratipian waved him away, then covered her with a warm, fur-lined blanket.

Helena kept her eyes on Valamir. "I'm sorry."

"Why?"

"I wanted to keep up."

His mouth twisted strangely. He shook his head. "You're not well. Caratipian knows about these things. Give yourself time. Soon you'll be laughing at day's end. I'll be back. Rest."

He took his horse's reins from Bevion. "You'll stay?"

"Yes."

"I owe you."

"I'll remember."

Valamir wheeled Hassan, then urged him into a run.

"He's such a show-off," Bevion said.

Helena looked at him sharply. "You're jealous."

"You speak the truth, woman," he said with a shrug. His smile was twisted. "I love him, of course, but I hate him, too."

"You're lucky to have family. He's good to you, Bevion, but perhaps it was not always easy to grow up in his shadow."

Bevion was quiet. "It was hard. He's perfect. The best at everything. No one ever understands that."

Covering her mouth with her hand, she yawned. "After all, he's six years older. Enjoy who you are and you'll find your way."

"Someone you could love?"

Caratipian interrupted, "Bevion, she needs to sleep. Enough of this foolishness."

Undeterred, Helena continued, "I could never trust you. But someday you'll find the one for you. But I thank you for staying."

Her eyes closed. Soon she dreamed.

They were alone, trapped in a ravine. As if by magic, Greillia appeared from behind a bend, laughing as he drew his bow. An arrow caught Caratipian in the eye and he crumpled to the ground. His sword unsheathed and shield fixed, Bevion charged. But Greillia's blade had begun its evil song. It sliced the air, taking with it Bevion's arm.

Helena screamed as blood gushed from his shoulder, from where his arm should have been. His face pale, Bevion held the gaping wound with his other hand.

Greillia shouted climatically, his sword blood red as he rode to her, "I've been waiting for you!"

Her scream was loud.

"Helena!" someone called. "Helena!"

Her eyes opened. Bevion was beside her, shaking her awake. "You were having a nightmare."

"Where's Greillia?"

"Who knows? Ahead someplace."

"He killed Caratipian, then cut off your arm."

"Go back to sleep. Look, we're close to the main camp. Greillia's a pig, but he's not mad. That's not his way. He'll complain to Attila and try to wheedle a favor out of his cousin. But between us, Attila can't stand him. He reminds him too much of his Uncle Rugliva. Now go back to sleep. You're safe with me."

But Helena did not want to chance her dreams. "You've been kind. Thank you."

Bevion scowled, then looked away. "You treat me like a brother."

"And that's what you are to me." She changed the subject. "How long was I asleep?"

"Look at the sun! It's been hours."

She sat up. "Do you think that I could ride Passial? My bones ache from this bumpy wagon."

Bevion laughed. "Caratipian! How about it?"

"Helena, are you sure?"

"Please, Caratipian."

"I'll have him ready in the time it takes a star to flash across the sky."

"Gods, Caratipian. Another poet in the family? I've had enough of Valamir's broody reflections to last a lifetime!" Bevion exclaimed.

Almost before she knew it, she was on Passial. Being with her old friend, her heart felt light.

"Can we catch up with Valamir?"

Bevion pursed his mouth. "Why? Don't you want to talk with me?"

Once again, Helena felt uncomfortable. His moods were mercurial. She was blunt. "I feel safe with my husband."

Bevion's cheeks turned crimson, his eyes narrowed as he looked over her shoulder. She turned, alarmed, but there was nothing. "I'll take you to him," he said.

"Bevion," Caratipian said, "I don't know if Valamir wants Attila to see her, at least not right away."

"Your point's well taken. Helena, we'll stay put." Then he added with mischief in his eyes, "Caratipian will be our chaperone."

Annoyed with him, she said nothing. From Passial's back, she had a better view of the crowd surrounding them. The majority were women, with a sprinkling of men. Some were driving the wagons; some were on horses, fully armed. She tried to count the lumbering carts, but gave up after one hundred. Wondering about Magga, Helena searched for her, but was unable to see her in the crowd. Then she heard a baby cry. Her eyes misted and she thought of Mikael.

The sun was a red ball in the sky, but they continued traveling. In the distance, Helena saw campfires with smoke rising in spirals. She thought that Attila did not hesitate to announce his presence to the world.

When Valamir galloped to meet them, Helena smiled, enjoying the way he sat on his horse and how his hair had become a burnished gold in the setting sun.

He reined Hassan to a halt. "Any trouble?" he asked Bevion. But his eyes were only for Helena. Her cheeks warm, she glanced at her hands.

"Gods, Valamir! Why don't you bed her right now? How you stare!" Bevion said with reproof.

Valamir studied his brother. "It's catching."

"What? What do you mean?"

"Just like Caratipian, you protect her. With him, she's a daughter. And in you, she's found a brother."

Bevion muttered under his breath, "Don't be too sure."

"I never am. No one bothered you?"

"No, of course not."

"Good."

"Helena," Valamir asked, "can you ride at a run? I want you with me when we enter the camp."

Her heart pounded, reminding her to be afraid. "Yes."

He took Passial's rein. "Caratipian! You'll find us with Attila. Bevion! We ride!"

The horses' hooves ate the ground, fast approaching the band of homecoming men. As they reached the others, Valamir and Bevion shouted. Their voices started low and gradually rose to a masculine roar. As the horsemen took up the cry, Helena gritted her teeth.

Faster and faster, the horses flew and the earth rumbled beneath them. As they neared the large encampment, other horsemen poured out from wide rows of tents, riding to meet them and answering them with horrifying yells.

As the two groups converged, they halted with only a horse length to spare. In front of Valamir, a space opened around a single horseman. He was broad, massive despite his short stature and dressed in plain leather clothes. Except for the jingling of the horses' bridles, all was quiet.

Valamir shouted, "We've come!" His band gave themselves a roaring accolade.

"We've found riches, Lord Attila."

The man looked at Helena intently. "So I see."

Valamir's voice was nonchalant. "The Shaman has made her my wife. She is called Helena."

Attila became still, then laughed. The sound was harsh.

"Well, who would have believed it? How many hearts did you break *this* year alone? How the women will cry when we go back, especially the mothers. Congratulations, old friend. May the gods make your union fruitful!"

Attila's brown eyes, sharp with intelligence, probed Helena and assessed her, belying his welcoming words. He was ugly. But despite his scarred cheeks and lank, black hair, he had an uncanny magnetism, radiating from within him. His features were Mongolian, as were Greillia's. Yet, Attila's face emanated strength instead of depravity.

Caught by his implacable stare, Helena felt like a bird about to be swallowed whole by a snake. When Greillia pushed his horse through the crowd, drawing Attila's attention, Helena was almost relieved to see her blood enemy, just to escape Attila's compelling eyes.

Greillia pointed at Helena. "Cousin, this woman is mine! Valamir stole her from me!"

Attila studied his cousin with quiet authority. "Valamir has married her. Would you give her the same protection?"

Greillia spat on the ground. "I saw her first. It doesn't matter if he married the bitch or not!"

"You question our law? You surprise me, Greillia. The Shaman has made their marriage sacred. Should either one repudiate the other, then you may come to me and ask for my decision. Until then, go in peace and find another woman."

Greillia pointed to Valamir. "You favor *him* over your own blood!"

Attila's face was impassive. "No, I uphold our law. Do not speak of this again."

Greillia scowled. "I'll see your bones rot, Valamir!"

Valamir laughed derisively. Cursing under his breath, Greillia rode on alone to camp.

"Lord Attila, if he harms my brother, I'll have my revenge, blood kin of yours or not," Bevion said.

Attila smiled. "And that would be *your* right under the law." His eyes rested on Helena once more. "Now, Valamir, tell me more about your new wife."

She was the bird again, held in thrall by the snake's beady stare.

"By your leave, Attila, I'd like to see my bride settled. May I join you later?"

"Of course, but bring her with you. We'll eat together in my quarters. You have much to tell me."

"As you wish, Attila. It would be an honor."

"I'm pleased we understand one another."

As the crowd dispersed toward the camp, Helena could not forget Attila's relentlessly probing eyes.

CHAPTER FOURTEEN

Helena and Valamir rode into camp side by side. The rows of tents were vivid and sharp against a deep, orange sky. As they passed the staring people, she shuddered. The moment became her breath, the rocking motion of Passial's canter, and most of all, the fear palpitating within her heart.

A tall, blond woman ran to Valamir, speaking Gothic, but too quickly for Helena to understand. Pointing at Helena, she shouted, her face raw with disappointment. Laughing, Valamir pushed her away from his horse with his boot.

She screamed after him, "Valamir!"

Looking straight ahead, he ignored her. Helena's stomach tightened. Again, she felt isolated and alone, wondering how she had come to trust this man, this stranger.

"Helena," he said.

Beside them, Bevion half-halted his horse, watching with curious eyes.

Valamir turned to his brother. "This doesn't concern you!"

He chuckled. "You're just embarrassed by Maude's little tantrum! What are you going to tell Helena? I'd love to hear."

"Enough, Bevion! Go bother someone else!"

As if to dismiss him, Valamir turned away. "Helena, look at me."

She kept her eyes on Passial's mane. Valamir reached over and brushed back her hair. "The woman was nothing to me, just a convenience."

She met his eyes. "What is any woman to a man?"

Bevion laughed.

"Be quiet, Bevion!" she shouted.

With a smile, he cocked his elbow, fist on his waist. "Who am I? Someone for you both to abuse? I think not! I'm going!"

As his horse cantered on, Helena's voice was terse. "What I said is true."

"My wife is not a convenience."

"I'm an investment to protect, not your wife."

His eyes narrowed. "You're wrong, Helena. I already told you the reward means nothing to me."

They stared, neither flinching from the other. But despite her intentions, her heart opened to him, dissipating her hostility. "Valamir, it's hard to stay angry with you."

He smiled. "May the gods continue to bless me."

In silence, he led her to the outer edge of the camp. Bevion was already busy tending his horse. A small creek ran brightly nearby. Helena dismounted and let Passial drop his muzzle to drink. Before he had his fill, she pulled his head away and walked him in a large circle. He was hot, his breathing was hard, and she did not want to founder his hooves from too much water.

Bevion watched her, his expression critical, clearly begrudging her credit for doing anything well. With quick expertise, the two brothers tended their horses. After rubbing them down with water, they let them go. The animals did not wander, but immediately lowered their heads to graze.

Helena tried to unfasten Passial's girth, but could not manage with her injured hand. Feeling a presence behind her, she whirled around with alarm.

But it was Valamir. "Rest, Helena. You've done enough."

Though needing his help, she wanted to brush aside his offer, too proud to accept. Her nod of agreement was reluctant, as if an admission of weakness. Avoiding Bevion, she went to the stream to wash the dust from her face and hands. The water was frigid. As she shivered, Bevion loomed over her. Frightened by his sudden appearance, she stood up quickly and was instantly defensive. He stepped close to her, his body almost touching. Helena turned away abruptly, her steps quick and angry as she walked to Valamir. Bevion grabbed her arm.

She winced with pain, pulling away. "Let go of me!"

He held on, unaware that he pressed a bruise. "Why won't you talk to me?"

"Because I have nothing to say!"

Instantly, Valamir was between them. "What are you doing? Leave her alone!"

Bevion released her, muttering to himself.

"What's wrong, Bevion? You look so strange," his brother asked.

"She won't talk to me."

Helena surprised herself with a gentle tone. "What do you want to say, Bevion?"

He gave her a look of devotion. But it vanished as quickly as it had come. "Anything."

She thought about her resemblance to their mother. In some ways, the proud, tall man was like a child, longing for what he had lost so young. "I'm not your mother, Bevion. She's been dead for many years."

His face flushed. "How?" he started.

Hesitantly, she touched his arm. "I think that she would have been happy to see you so well grown."

He blinked his eyes quickly, denying tears, then stalked toward his horse. Putting on its bridle, he spoke with his back to them. "I'm going to find the others."

They watched him, riding bareback, not glancing behind. Valamir was quiet and pensive.

In a small voice, Helena asked, "Did I say the wrong thing?"

"No, not at all. You spoke from your heart." He paused, then added, "Bevion never cried for her. He just forgot."

She hesitated, not wanting to be offensive, but had to speak her mind. "I can pity Bevion, but I cannot trust him, even if he is your brother."

Valamir frowned, but his eyes betrayed pain. "He was not always this way. As a child, before our mother died, he was happy and full of laughter. Afterward, he changed, becoming difficult, moody, and quick to anger. Maybe her death touched him differently than it did me."

"It made you kind."

"Sometimes, but not always."

A chill went up her spine, but she dismissed it, blaming the cold water, still damp on her cheeks.

Soon they saw Caratipian and his wagon approaching. Helena smiled and waved her hand, checking herself from running to met him.

Valamir's chuckle was rich with irony. "He's bewitched you, too!"

"What do you mean?"

"He says things that no servant would dare say. And I accept it. With a few words, he can make Bevion listen: a rare talent."

Caratipian, out of hearing range, waved back.

"I'm glad he's with you," Helena said.

Valamir put his arm around her waist and smiled.

After he had erected his tent, Helena lingered with him inside. Together in wordless companionship, they warmed themselves by a blazing fire. The aroma of Caratipian's cooking was delectable in the air. When a voice called from outside, Helena jumped.

"Prince Valamir!"

Valamir cursed. "The gods conspire!"

Helena whispered in Greek, "What's wrong?"

"Attila summons."

Her voice was small. "So soon?"

"You don't have to go."

She looked into the fire and spoke slowly. "Sometimes it's better to face things."

"Attila is always the exception."

"What do you mean?"

"It's impossible to say what he'll do. It would be best to keep you out of his way."

She shook her head. "Hiding would be a sign of weakness. I'll go. I won't allow him to see that I'm afraid."

"I honor your courage, Helena. But wait, I have something for you." Standing up, he reached behind him and pulled out her dagger, along with a new belt to hold the weapon at her side. She unsheathed it and saw that it was unblemished and its edge was razor sharp.

"Caratipian's an artist," she said with awe. "I can't believe it's the same blade."

"I want you to wear it for all to see. As my wife, you have the right."

Her voice was grave. "Thank you."

She wrapped the belt around her waist, but had difficulty fastening it with one hand. Valamir was quick to help, though his touch made her legs feel weak. She flushed.

"Prince Valamir!" the man repeated. "He waits!"

"In a moment! I won't be rushed!"

"Please! He's bellowing for you. And he'll blame me for making him impatient."

"I'll be there."

There was a pause. "Valamir," the man continued, "he asked that you bring the girl."

Valamir's face became still as a stone. "In those words, Ishyite? He said 'the girl,' not 'my wife?'"

"It must have been a slip of the tongue. He meant no disrespect."

Valamir turned to Helena, his hands at her waist. "You may change your mind about seeing Attila. I will defend your right."

Helena was frightened, yet inexorably drawn to the sparkle of menace in his face. "I want to be with you."

He kissed her on the lips, pulling her body close to his. Reluctantly, he disengaged from the embrace and took her hand, leading her into the night. Ishyite waited on his horse. Despite the long day, he was untouched by fatigue, just worry.

"Finally! Perhaps the gods watch over me after all," he said, staring at the couple. "We must hurry."

Valamir glowered at him. When he whistled for his horse, Caratipian led him from behind the tent, ready with saddle and bridle. Chewing the inside of his cheek, Caratipian fussed with Hassan's bridle.

In his peasant Persian, he said to Helena, "Be careful. Keep your thoughts to yourself."

Helena thought of her grandfather. From within, she heard a clear voice. "Trust, Helena. Let the Light guide you."

Her heart expanded and filled her with quiet bliss. Her mind questioned the experience, but she discarded her skepticism. The sense of oneness was too sweet. Seeing Caratipian's face pinched by fear, she smiled, wanting to share her euphoric sense of peace. His eyes blinked quickly and his chin moved awkwardly beneath his white beard, but he remained afraid.

Valamir lifted Helena to the horse and mounted lightly behind. With Ishyite leading the way, they rode through the maze of tents, illuminated by many campfires, into the heart of the Hunnic encampment.

Attila's headquarters stood within its center. Far larger than the others, his tent was surrounded by a circular expanse, filled with guards and slaves. A man with red hair, wearing rags, ran to take Valamir's horse. As he rushed to them, one leg moved stiffly. Like Caratipian, he had been crippled by Huns to prevent escape. Her stomach twisted as she remembered to be afraid.

Valamir tossed his reins to the slave, then lifted her down. "Be careful with my horse. He bites."

The slave nodded, holding Hassan with quiet expertise. Before turning away, Valamir watched with a critical eye. Helena's heart beat with desperation; her throat was dry. She tried to reclaim her moment of peace, but it had vanished. Valamir squeezed her hand. As she walked beside him to Attila's tent, her answering smile was forced.

At the entrance, a guard scrutinized them with implacable eyes. His face was crisscrossed with intricate scars, his skull deformed by a narrow, leather band. When Valamir nodded to him, he emitted a short greeting in Hunnic. The sound was guttural and harsh to Helena's ears.

He led them inside and announced, "Prince Valamir."

Attila was alone. As he turned to face them, Helena wanted to run away. His eyes were cold and unreadable. A dinner had been prepared, waiting uneaten on leather plates. "Outside," he ordered the guard.

Like Valamir's, the tent was spartan and utilitarian. An assortment of weapons was stacked neatly in two corners, a sleeping pad placed to the side of the fire. Attila sat on a plain, wooden chair. Yet, the way he filled it reminded Helena of a king on a throne. Several fine oriental rugs were on the ground. On one, well away from the fire, were a number of maps and rolled parchments.

"You're late. The dinner's cold," Attila said. "But come. Break bread with me."

Valamir sat across from him, keeping Helena on his right. To see her directly, Attila would have to turn his head.

"We came as soon as Ishyite called, Lord Attila."

"We're alone. No need to be formal, Valamir."

"As you wish, Attila."

The Hun's voice was pleasant. "Go on, eat. Tell me about your spoils."

Their food had been prepared with care, basted with a fine sauce. Attila's meal, however, was simple: plain meat in a leather bowl. As Valamir chewed, he answered, "We found you wealth, Attila. We were fortunate."

Attila's glance shifted to Helena, making it difficult for her to swallow. "I can see that. Please, tell me her name again."

Valamir's eyes glittered. "My wife's name is Helena."

"Why so tense, Valamir? Outside of battle, you are never so...irritated."

"She's tired and recovering from injuries. And your orders to Ishyite were to bring 'the girl.'"

"You're offended." He shrugged, a corner of his mouth turned down. "I meant no insult to your honor."

Valamir breathed out deeply. "Then all is well, Attila. We understand each other."

"Perhaps. But at least, answer my curiosity, Valamir. After all, I upheld your claim against my stubborn cousin."

Greillia, Helena thought, wishing him dead.

Valamir laughed. "What do you want to know? Your inquisitiveness could empty a well of knowledge."

Attila smiled, transforming his face from grotesque to magnetic. Helena found herself relaxing. Suddenly, it was an effort to remember Caratipian's warning.

"Where did you 'meet' Helena?"

"Two days' journey from here. At a small village. The same place where we found the fortune in jewels and gold."

"Clearly, she's not from the steppes."

"She was born in Constantinople."

"Constantinople! By the gods, a civilized woman. This explains why you've kept her. Does she speak Greek?"

"Better than I."

"May I ask her some questions? It would give me pleasure to hear Greek well spoken."

Valamir studied Attila, his blue eyes remote. "As you wish."

Attila switched from Gothic to Greek. To Helena's surprise, his accent was close to perfect, the intonation well-modulated. "May I call her by her first name, or would you prefer, for the sake of your honor, Helena, wife of Prince Valamir, son of Vandalarius, grandson of King Vinitharius?"

Valamir laughed. "Call her Helena. I trust your memory. You know whose wife she is."

For an instant, Attila scowled. Then his frown vanished.

"Well, we understand each other. But should you decide to set her aside, please keep my interest in mind."

Helena felt as if she were choking: each breath was a struggle.

"I'll not repudiate her, Attila. That is not the Ostrogothic way. Don't speak of it again, old friend."

Attila's eyes narrowed. "Have you told her of *our* custom? That a wife may leave a husband to take another?"

"There hasn't been time."

"Then by all means, Valamir, do so now."

Valamir turned to Helena, still holding her hand. "Helena, under Hunnic law, a man may repudiate his wife for any reason, but the woman has her rights. She may choose another man's tent if the first fails to provide food and shelter, beats her too much, making her life miserable, or because of an injury, not be able to give her children," he said in a quiet voice, allaying her fears.

"What say you to that, Helena?" Attila asked.

"I'm happy with my husband."

Attila was a study in silence. When he finally spoke, his eyes were grave, but veiled. "Your wife does you honor, Valamir. We will not speak of this again."

Relief swept Valamir's face. Helena's trust was not won so quickly. Attila seemed a man used to his own way.

He turned to her. "So, Helena, how did you find yourself in these parts? We're many months from Constantinople."

Helena felt each movement of her body: the tightness of skin on her knuckles, the flush in her face. Her heart whispered its terror. As she acknowledged it, the fear calmed sufficiently for her to speak.

"My grandfather and I were traveling to Persia to find his son, my father. We had word of his post as Commander in the Imperial Guard."

His tone was ironic. "All the way to Persia alone? These are perilous times!"

She flashed him a look of hate, not enjoying his pun.

"We had a bodyguard."

"Your wife has spirit, Valamir. A bodyguard. Interesting. Such luxuries cost much in gold."

"I didn't know the arrangements. I was thirteen."

"How old are you now? Seventeen, eighteen?"

"Eighteen." His eyes bored into hers, ruthless with cunning. She was tired of running from him. "And you, Lord Attila, what is your age?"

"Much older. I'm twenty-six."

"You don't look it."

"You took me for a younger man?"

"Older, actually."

He laughed, enjoying the banter. "Enough of me. For five years, you've been away from Constantinople. That's a long time for a girl to be away from the great city."

At his words, her heart ached. How dare he remind her of home? "It's been hard."

"Where's your grandfather now?"

"Dead."

"Recently?"

Behind his words, he mocked her. She hated him and his games. His presence on the steppes had cost dearly in lives.

"He died five years ago."

"That's good. Your grief for him has passed."

She felt her darkness, driving her to recklessness. "You know nothing! Your cousin, Greillia, murdered my son before my eyes. He was only three. My mourning has only begun."

"Helena! You may not be disrespectful to my Lord," Valamir interjected with a shout.

But Attila only smiled with delight. "She may speak her mind, so long as she uses Greek. Her diction becomes eloquent when she's angry. I enjoy a woman with spirit, at least to a point."

Helena seethed, hating to be spoken of as if she were not present. Belatedly remembering Caratipian's warning, she kept quiet.

Attila had not finished with her, but his questions became patient, taking her step by step through the death of her grandfather, her marriage to Kansbar, her relatives in Persia, and her father's service to the Persian Empire. Each query led smoothly into the other, even unraveling Kansbar's relationship with his son.

His interrogation exhausted her, allowing scant space to hide.

Almost as if he had saved it for last, he asked, "And what was your grandfather's name?"

"Balusistriam of Istakhr."

Attila nodded, his only reaction. "I know of this man."

She felt a rush of air, beating at her ears, and was upset that he had heard of her grandfather. In her heart, Helena did not want any confirmation of his darkness which had culminated in cursing Kansbar and all of his seed. For her sanity, she needed to remember him as kind and gentle. Her voice was hard. "What have you heard?"

Attila smiled, pleased to have captured her attention. "He followed the prophet Zarathushtra. But before that, there were stories - interesting stories involving magic."

His words resonated inside her, echoing what she already knew. "My grandfather was a good man."

"No doubt. But also a rich one. There is a large reward offered for Balusistriam's granddaughter. Valamir, have you heard of it? The amount is most satisfying."

"I've enough wealth, Attila. But should she want to go home, I'll take her."

"Last I heard, Goths weren't overly welcome in Constantinople. Please remember to say farewell if you go. I'd miss you."

With unexpected passion, she realized that she did not want Valamir captured or mistreated because of a promise to her. Her words came slowly, her voice subdued. "Nothing waits for me in Constantinople. My grandfather made our house a home, but he's gone. My father...I don't know where he is. Last we heard, he was in Persia. But he's a stranger. I would like to send word to our steward. He'd be glad of news of me."

Attila shrugged. "I lost my scribe and have only a small talent for writing. As we move west, we'll find one for your letter."

"Have you any way to send a message?"

"Every so often, I communicate with my Uncle Rugliva."

"Oh," she said, biting her lip in disappointment.

"We'll find a scribe eventually. I need one."

The thought of waiting a day longer distressed her. For five years, she had longed to send a message home. Now, the opportunity teased her, beckoning just out of reach. "I could write it," she said, even as she wondered how she would be able to make her letter legible with her left hand.

"You can? Most unusual."

"Why? It only takes time and practice."

"Of all the women that I've known, only a few had the knowledge. And they were Romans, noble born. He paused, his mind turned inward. "Who taught you?"

"My grandfather."

"He was a wise man."

Valamir interrupted. "Attila, Helena has asked for two things. First, her mother's wedding ring." He raised his hand and slid off the plain gold band, putting it down before Attila on the green and golden rug. It sparkled all alone against the rich texture. "Also, she'd like her grandfather's sword."

Attila picked up the ring, examining it with a professional eye. "Where's the sword?"

"Bevion holds it for you. It's good quality. The sheath is decorated with some semi-precious jewels. As my share, I'd be satisfied with the ring and the sword along with the two horses in my possession."

Attila shook his head. "You ask for too little, Valamir."

The Hun looked at Helena, his eyes bright with intelligence. "Helena, as my gift to you, I give you this ring, your grandfather's sword and one other thing that captures your fancy."

Helena tensed. As much as she wanted what he offered, she did not want to be in his debt. Sensing plans within plans, she rejected the opening gambit. "It would not be proper to receive valuable gifts from a man other than my husband. I am sorry, but I must decline your generosity."

Attila frowned and his eyes narrowed. Helena held her breath. Then he began to chuckle. "You've found a woman of honor, Valamir. Do you know how well the gods have favored you?"

Valamir was succinct. "Yes."

"Helena, I'll give Valamir this ring," he said, placing it back on the rug, "and the sword. He may do with them as he wishes."

Her smile was spontaneous. "Oh, thank you!"

"Your thanks is my payment, Helena. It pleases me to see you happy."

Embarrassed, she studied the rug. Valamir's hands were clenched; his knuckles were white.

"Is there anything else of your grandfather's you'd like?"

She contemplated the Hun, looking past the mutilated cheeks, the broad nose, and the corners of the mouth that hinted at cruelty. His eyes were lively and magnetic, far more than cunning. She sensed his brilliance and it frightened her.

"There is a small rug, mostly blue, with dark red. It's not new, but of fine craftsmanship. My grandfather used it in his prayers. I don't know if it's valuable."

"Nothing else? You don't ask for a pretty bracelet or a necklace to set off the green in your eyes? A beautiful woman should be adorned with jewelry."

The veins in Valamir's neck stood out at these words. Her reaction was immediate. She held up the Thracian ring that Valamir had given her.

"After this, what more could I want?"

Attila studied it, then glanced at Valamir. "Isn't that your mother's ring?" he asked quietly.

"You remember."

"Your wife wears it well."

Valamir picked up the plain band still on the rug. "Thank you, Attila." Without ceremony, he put it in her hand. She clutched it and brought it to her heart. Hindered by her bandaged hand, she tried to put it on, but was unsuccessful.

"What's wrong with her hand?" Attila asked.

"Greillia broke it."

Attila frowned. "His way with women is unfortunate. As an apology for my cousin, please allow me to give her a plain, gold necklace. That ring will only fit her fourth finger, already so well occupied by your mother's ring. As for the other hand, it needs time to heal."

"What do you say, Helena?" Valamir asked.

"With my husband's permission, I accept your gift, but not as apology. I can never forgive Greillia."

"Helena, you've insulted our host! You speak of his blood kin," Valamir said.

"I don't care! I want no offering in Greillia's name."

"I apologize for my wife's behavior, Attila. She does not understand our customs."

"No need, Valamir. Vengeance is something we Huns understand."

Helena trembled, sickened by the comparison.

"You are generous, Attila. I'll not forget," Valamir said.

"Think nothing of it." He snapped his fingers. In a moment, the guard entered with his head bowed. Attila spoke quickly in Hunnic and the man was gone.

Helena wondered if he had given orders for her death. She glanced at Valamir's face and was reassured by his lack of concern.

"Are we to break camp tomorrow?" Valamir asked.

"No, we'll have a ceremony. A celebration. Then we'll see if it's time to head back home."

"The men will enjoy the feast."

The guard returned, bending his knee, offering Attila the slender gold necklace, his hands outstretched with his palms up. Attila nodded, dismissing him.

"Valamir, I give this to you. Do as you wish with it. I'll see to the sword and the rug."

"My thanks, Attila." Casually, Valamir took Helena's ring from her hand and threaded the necklace through it. Attila watched, his stare avid, as the Goth fastened the gold chain around her neck.

"From time to time, Valamir, I may need to borrow your wife's services...as my scribe."

Valamir's jaw tightened, almost imperceptibly. "If Helena can be of help, it would be my honor. But with a broken hand, I can't see how she could write."

"While in Rome, I learned many things. Sometimes I have questions about spelling and grammar. Perhaps her training was more thorough than mine. I hated my tutor and didn't always listen."

"Surely King Rugliva would never notice if a word were misspelled here and there," Valamir said.

"Of course not, but his scribe would certainly point out any error. He knows how Rugliva loves to find fault with me."

Attila licked his lips, a distant look in his eye and added, "At least for now."

"As you wish. Though I trust you completely, Attila, I'd want to be with her. Your reputation with women is long standing and well-deserved."

Attila's smile was not pleasant. "Of course, Valamir. We wouldn't want her to fall prey to my charm."

Valamir only shrugged. "I'm not worried. Besides Bevion, who else could I trust so well?"

Attila inclined his head with dismissal.

"With your leave, we must go. I thank you for the excellent meal," Valamir said, standing.

"Come again and soon."

Turning to leave, Valamir took Helena's hand. From his chair, Attila murmured, "Valamir, had you heard about the ransom before we left?"

Helena's heart stopped.

Valamir faced him. "Yes."

"You are deep, my friend. Now I understand your strange strategies of attack. All this time, you've been looking for her, haven't you?"

"Yes."

"How can you collect the reward if she's your wife? Or perhaps your wedding is just an empty ruse."

"Don't insult me, Attila. I did not take this woman as my wife for a ransom! Can you accept that?"

"Our laws are binding on all of us. Your wedding is valid, but I had not expected to discover you so subtle."

Valamir laughed. "Have you forgotten so much? Didn't I help you when we were young to make Bleda look foolish?"

Attila glanced at the fire. "Perhaps we were too successful. In the end, Rugliva kept my brother home and sent me, the dangerous one, to Rome. He never wished to see me again, that much I know."

"You are my leader and my lord, Attila. If by chance, I receive the reward, it is yours."

"You'd not live to collect it, old friend. Keep away from big Christian cities. I need your crafty mind awhile longer."

Valamir laughed. "I've no intention of letting the Romans hang me on a cross!"

Attila's eyes bored into Helena. "She's worth more than the asking price. I wouldn't give her up."

"Good night, Attila. Your wives wait impatiently."

As they went outside, Helena heard him say to himself, "Perhaps."

The red-haired slave untethered Hassan and handed Valamir the reins. Placing Helena on the roan, Valamir acknowledged the Gaul. "You've done well."

The man bobbed his head with respect. Once mounted, Valamir tossed him a copper coin. The slave reached and caught it with the agility of an athlete. But his crippled leg marred his innate grace. Helena pitied him.

In silence, they returned to Valamir's tent. Bevion's tent was pitched nearby. In the cold, night air, Helena clearly heard the sounds of passionate lovemaking. Eagerly, a woman called, "Bevion, Bevion." Helena was reminded of Magga, who routinely pretended to orgasm. Embarrassed, she studied the stars.

His face pinched with worry, Caratipian emerged from his compact quarters, his expression clearing when he saw them. He closed his eyes for a moment, as if in a prayer of thanks.

He held Hassan's reins. "You're back."

Valamir burst out. "No thanks to Helena! Not only did she tell Attila that his cousin was a murdering brute, but she wouldn't accept Attila's apology on Greillia's behalf for breaking her hand!"

"Was Attila surprised to discover that Greillia had grievous character flaws?"

Valamir shouted, "It's not amusing!" He modulated his voice, speaking lower. "I've seen what happens to those who speak to him with less disrespect."

"What happened? Was he furious with her?"

Valamir was grim. "No, he was charmed."

"Which may turn out to be more dangerous."

Valamir glared at her. "Do you understand, Helena? You took a risk! It was foolish!"

Saying nothing in her defense, she shrank within herself and retreated to the tent. Inside, she sat by the fire with dry eyes and watched the flames.

Soon Valamir came inside, his face austere and his eyes cold. For a moment, they did not speak. When she looked at him, his face softened. He pulled her into his arms.

His lips were next to her hair. "You must never, ever speak in anger to Attila. Do you promise?"

"I'll try harder next time."

"You must do more than 'try.'"

Her voice was small. "I'll do my best."

His mouth descended on hers. His kiss was pressing and urgent, not gentle. He released her from his embrace. As he looked at her, desperation hid behind his eyes. "I couldn't bear for anything to happen to you. Don't be so reckless with my heart."

She rested her head against his chest. "I'm sorry. I won't do it again."

He carried her to the bed and lay down beside her, covering them with blankets.

Valamir whispered in her ear, sending shivers down her spine. "I dare not touch you again."

He turned his back to her and, fully clothed, fell into a deep sleep. Before long, Helena calmed her racing heart. Following his example, she found him in her dreams.

CHAPTER FIFTEEN

Helena awoke to the cold morning air. Shafts of sun streamed through an opening, which served as a primitive chimney and bathed the tent in pale light. As usual, Valamir was already gone, but had left food by the fire along with a bundle of kindling.

She tossed a few sticks on the embers. Watching the blaze re-ignite, Helena remembered the mosaic phoenix centered in the courtyard floor of her grandfather's house, its wings flaming with gold as it rose from the ashes of its own devastation. The mythical bird had been the family talisman, a symbol of good fortune. As a child, she had loved to watch the sunlight glinting on its outspread wings and had often wondered, in the stillness of night, when no one was awake to watch, if the phoenix became alive.

She shut her eyes against these memories. They hurt, reminding her of her loneliness, her lack of family to call her own. Pulling her legs to her chest, she rested her chin on her knees and listened, but heard no familiar voice, not even Caratipian muttering to himself at his chores. The silence worried her. But she refused to brood about it. Instead, she stood with a stretch, smoothing her dress, and brushed out her long brown hair.

Unsheathing her refurbished dagger, she admired it, reflecting shafts of sunlight from its sharp blade on the tent's leather walls. No longer as affected from her injuries, Helena felt restless. She ate without relish, only as a necessity. She stood, pacing back and forth, wanting to go outside. Absentmindedly, she began to tidy the tent and thought over her encounter with Attila.

He had interrogated her, plain and simple, and she had been unable to hide much from him. Usually, her mind could leap forward to safety. With him, it had been an effort to keep pace with his thoughts. Her mouth curved into a slight, self-deprecating smile, and she forgave herself. After all, she had kept the important secret safe: the dark, powerful presence that accompanied her inscription of the rune.

Finished with straightening the tent, she looked outside. The sun was bright and the air was fresh, but the camp was alive with people. Caution superseded her curiosity. She shut the tent flap and sat by the fire. Shortly, she heard Valamir's and Bevion's voices accompanied by the sounds of their horses' hooves slowing from a canter to a halt.

"Has all been well, Ishyite?" Valamir asked.

She had not even seen the Hun.

"Quiet. No trouble."

"I'm in your debt," Valamir replied.

"No. It is my pleasure to stand between Greillia and what he wants!"

"Watch your back, Ishyite," Bevion warned.

"You worry too much. Each day, Greillia sees my brothers and our cousins. He knows the price they would extract from his skin, his muscles and finally his bones for treachery against their kin."

At the image, Helena's stomach contracted.

"Will you share a meal with us?" Valamir asked. "My servant is ill, but Bevion and I have more than enough."

With thanks, Ishyite declined. Helena paced the tent, taut with worry about Caratipian. He was old, far too old for long days of travel. He should be home, warming himself by a fire, with a family to attend to his needs.

When Valamir came in, she rushed to greet him. "How is Caratipian? Should I go to him?"

He smiled. "We'll not be rid of him tonight if that's what you mean. His joints are stiff, especially his shoulders, that's all. It's not the first time. I ordered him to rest. Ishyite would not have understood my concern, so I stretched the truth, just a bit."

The constriction in her chest relaxed. Valamir stepped closer.

His lips near to hers, he asked, "How's your hand today?"

"Better. It doesn't hurt as much."

When his mouth touched hers, the sensations in her body were unexpected, making her cheeks flush.

"Would you hate me if I didn't take you back to Constantinople?"

"No," she replied without hesitation.

"Are you sure? I gave you my word."

"I release you from it. But I need to get word to John, our steward, that I'm alive." She hesitated. "Without my grandfather, Constantinople is an empty place, full of strangers."

He smiled. "But what of your father?"

"I have no father."

"The reward was offered in his name."

She shook her head. "It doesn't matter. For me, he's dead and died a stranger. My decision has nothing to do with him."

"He might have plans for your marriage."

"Where was he when Kansbar raped me, night after night? He abandoned me, forfeiting his rights!"

"You're angry with him, but nothing you say can change that your blood and his are the same. I'll arrange for you to send a message to Constantinople. Perhaps the steward will know where he is." He paused, before adding, "The thought of you, away from me in Constantinople, is... difficult."

"Valamir, I could stay with you forever. But I can't live with the Huns."

He looked into the fire, frowning, his forehead furrowed. Then his eyes met hers, hard and implacable. "I can't change what is. I can make you no promises, only that I love you."

She put her arms around him. "You've become my world."

They stood in silence, finding no way beyond their impasse.

Finally, Valamir said, "Come outside, Helena."

She followed him to the open sky. The mid-day sun was bright, but a pale yellow. As always, the wind blew. At the perimeter of the camp, she turned from it and faced the steppes, as if to deny the harsh reality of her situation.

"Does Caratipian need anything?" she asked.

"Just to be left with his concoctions and poultices."

"Where were you this morning?"

"With Attila. As commander of one of the four divisions, I made my report, bringing him all we found."

"What you stole, you mean."

"If that's how you want to see it! We took it because we were stronger. That is a warrior's way."

He stood, shoulders squared and firm in his convictions, his blue eyes dark and his mouth set. Helena both loved and hated him. She wanted to slap his face, but at the same time, throw her arms around him, never letting go.

His mouth became a radiant smile. "You're beautiful angry or crying, even when your eyes are red from tears. But Helena, this is my life. It's what I know. I offer no apology. I fight as a man, like all men before time. The strong defeat the weak. That is the natural order of things." He was quiet for a moment. "Do you judge Rome with the same harshness? Time and time again, they marched against the Northern tribes. Now it's their turn to suffer! Helena, we're apart from all that. We're just two people. We can't change the world, only what's between us."

"I hate your philosophical words! You'd do well enough in Sparta, if not Athens herself, with your convenient logic!"

He touched her shoulders lightly, looking down at her. "So you hate me?"

She blinked back the tears behind her eyes. "No, not always."

"Do you love me, just a little?"

Her cheeks grew warm. "Maybe just a little."

"Then that's enough," he said, sealing his words with a kiss.

She pulled away. "You're impossible, always working your way into my heart."

"That's because you like me, just a little."

"I could never explain it to you. I don't understand it myself."

"Try."

"I can't, the words won't come."

"Start at the beginning."

"I was happy as a child in Constantinople. My grandfather was a father, mother, and teacher to me. The house was beautiful: white stone reflecting the summer sun. But then my world vanished. It became Kansbar's hut and despair. Yet, after a time, I had Mikael. I gave him my heart. Because of him, I could wake each day and face what I had to. Then, you know the rest...but now, I can't imagine not seeing you tomorrow and the next day and the next."

"I want to give you children," he said.

She closed her eyes, feeling trapped and unready. "Please. I need time."

He pursed his lips and turned away. "It's hard to be with you, and not be close. It feels wrong, even unnatural."

"I'm sorry."

He shrugged. "I gave my word. Tonight, we celebrate. Attila has planned a feast. It will be good to drink wine and eat well."

"I'll wait for you."

"I wish you could. Attila asked that I bring you."

"And you agreed?"

His eyes were bleak. "I have no choice. He's within his rights."

She dug her toe into the grass. "When must we go?"

Valamir scowled. "We're late already. He wants you to help him with a message."

"He doesn't really need my help."

"You amuse him."

"You'll stay with me?"

"Yes."

As they rode together on Hassan, Helena was the target of curiosity. A boy, probably twelve or thirteen, ran his pony at their side, yelling. But he was friendly, hungry for Valamir's approval. She saw no sign of Greillia, nor of Magga, and was relieved. But too quickly, they reached the center of the encampment and Attila.

The area was guarded by men posted as if in four corners of a square. Women's voices came from inside another tent behind Attila's quarters. Helena assumed it belonged to his wives.

With her heart racing, she reminded herself that he was only a man, unable to read her mind. He lacked the perceptiveness of her grandfather, who had trained as a priest and learned sacred skills. Still, as another slave took Hassan's reins, cringing and bent over into a bow, Helena felt paralyzed. The air was fresh, the sky swept with clouds, and her stomach was in knots at the thought of Attila's eyes, boring into her mind, probing and devouring.

Valamir glowered at the slave, a slightly built, older man, perhaps a Breton. "Watch my horse well."

Shielded behind Valamir, Helena stepped into the tent. After the bright sky, she had trouble adjusting to the dim light. Attila sat by the roaring fire, poring over maps. With his thick, muscular arm, he motioned them to sit on the rug.

"Good, you've brought her. I've much work. You may come back later, Valamir. We'll be awhile."

Valamir's smile did not reach his eyes. "Your courtesy is thoughtful, but I hope to learn from watching."

Attila's face became still, revealing nothing. "As is your pleasure, Valamir."

As she became accustomed to the light, she noticed Bevion, standing in the shadows. He stepped forward, not looking his brother in the face, glancing at Attila as if for strength.

The stench of conspiracy hung between them.

"Bevion?" Valamir asked. "Why are you here?"

Bevion shifted his weight uncomfortably from side to side. Attila watched Helena. She met his stare, her mouth compressed into a frown, feeling obscurely betrayed. A torrent of angry words threatened to erupt from her lips. But she held them back, biting her tongue hard between molars and tasting blood.

From nowhere, a rhyming song the Romans had sung about Attila during his years as hostage ran through her mind. It had been childish, dwelling on his short stature and bulky torso, his silences twisted to suggest stupidity. As she remembered, her heart opened with sudden pity for him as an adolescent boy, enduring the Roman talent for ridicule.

Attila watched her face, his eyes keen. "You lost your fear."

"My stomach feels uneasy, but my thoughts are my own."

"You speak your mind. You are worthy of my friendship."

The compliment annoyed her. It felt patronizing. Attila's eyes continued to bore into her, like an assault. To escape, she studied the pattern on the rug.

He ignored her withdrawal. "Bevion, you've been useful. Go with my gratitude."

Valamir spoke after his brother left. "Why did he come here? Only moments ago, he was with me."

A smile challenged Attila's dour expression. "We were discussing strategy. New ideas interest me."

Helena looked at him sharply, certain in her suspicions. But he gave nothing away.

Valamir fingered his sword absentmindedly. "He was in a hurry to leave. Quiet, too. Unlike himself."

Attila's mouth turned into a frown; he raised a shoulder in a shrug. "Who can understand Bevion's moods? Perhaps he's thinking of tonight's celebration."

Something clicked in Helena's mind. Attila spoke the truth, but only a part. Whatever they had planned, it would happen this evening.

Valamir smiled. "He's my younger brother. It's my responsibility to look after him."

Attila's eyes clouded, and for an instant, he looked melancholy. "Valamir, may I ask your wife a question?" he asked, his expression veiled.

"If you wish."

Attila's voice was quiet. "Before you were angry. Then it faded into pity. Why?"

"Do you read minds?"

"Just faces."

She paused, thinking before speaking. "I remembered a Roman song about you. It wasn't kind. You were a boy, coming into manhood. It must have been hard for you."

As he considered Helena, Attila's face become more enigmatic than ever. His eyes were contemplative.

Finally, he spoke. "Valamir, though I accept your claim to Helena..."

Her mouth became dry. Blood rushed to her legs. Valamir said nothing, forcing Attila to continue without encouragement.

"If I gave you half of what you captured at the village, my entire share, after all, and my best stallion, would you be willing to set her free? I'd honor her as my wife."

Valamir stood, pulling Helena to him, not bothering to conceal his rage. "You, my oldest friend, insult me. What are trinkets and horseflesh to my feelings for my wife?"

"I'll offer you more."

"Damn you, Attila! Stop this. We go now."

"Valamir, stay. I couldn't help asking. Just now she spoke to my heart. My days in Rome were...trying. Her sympathy was a gift."

Poised to leave, Valamir said, "We had agreed to speak no more of this."

Attila grimaced. "I know, I know. But you understand me. I usually get what I want. It's become a habit. To make amends, I'll offer you a gift."

"What? Another horse?"

"You have reason to be angry. But listen. Last night, when Helena spoke about Greillia, you were afraid for her. This is my gift: Helena, alone in the tribe, may speak to me freely, without fear of punishment."

Valamir sat, motioning Helena to follow his example. "You are generous, Attila, more than generous."

"I place only one condition on my favor. She must continue to speak in Greek."

"Helena, do you understand?" Valamir explained. "Even I, though Attila's friend, choose my words with care out of respect."

She felt no joy at this boon. "Why, Attila?"

"Because it pleases me. But also, you represent civilization. I enjoy its outrage. Equally important, whenever you say anything that could offend me, Valamir looks ill. I need his competence and can't afford to have him compromised by worry for you." He smiled. "And I like the way your cheeks turn pink when you challenge me."

She wanted to spit at him.

He continued, "We've much work to do. Valamir, I hope you won't be bored. Please accept an offering of my finest mead."

They passed the afternoon. Attila wrote slowly with a quill on sheets of unrolled parchment and asked many questions about wording and spelling. Valamir drank. As soon as he drained his cup, a slave replaced it with another. Helena glanced at him, distress creasing her brow.

With a smile, Attila whispered, "A good cup of mead is his weakness."

"You mean to make him drunk!"

"Valamir? He could have five times more and still be himself. I like to see him happy."

She scowled at Attila. "The work is finished. It's time for us to leave."

"I'd be a poor host if I didn't offer refreshment first. What say you, Valamir?"

He shrugged. "Why not? My servant's sick. All that waits us is this morning's meal." His words were distinct, too distinct, requiring concentration. As she realized he was more than halfway drunk, her heart sank.

"Old Caratipian ill? Perhaps it's time for him to meet his maker. You'd be doing him a favor. Why should he suffer at the end?"

Valamir's lips compressed into a line. A red splotch appeared on each cheek. "He's part of my family."

Attila dismissed the subject with a wave of his hand. "Of course, of course."

Forgetful, Valamir sipped more mead. Helena seethed, not bothering to hide her exasperation as she watched Valamir empty another cup.

"And you, Helena. You don't approve," Attila said.

"Caratipian's been like a father to Valamir!"

Attila smiled. "He has a father, alive and well. Caratipian's a servant, nothing more."

"Servant or not, he has a right to his old age."

"Perhaps."

She hated him. He had intelligence, but its essence was twisted by something dark and malignant.

"What? No more arguments?" he asked.

"I won't be baited by you."

"You don't like me much."

"Perhaps."

He laughed. "But you're fond of Valamir, even half gone on drink."

"He's different."

"Do you really think so? Wait awhile. So far he's had ten full cups of mead. After another five or six, he'll be a changed man."

"You've kept track!" she said, enraged.

"Watch, you'll see he's no different than the rest of us."

"He doesn't make war on women and children!"

"He takes the smaller view. Mine is larger. I don't take pleasure in killing children. It's an unpleasant necessity. Unlike the Romans, I allow Valamir his fastidiousness. They would have his head, you know, and lose an able commander. I've learned from the strengths and flaws of the Roman beast. In time, when the world hears the name Attila, they'll feel terror. My rules are simple. Complete submission? We take few lives. Resistance? Then annihilation. The tactics are effective and proven over time."

"If your strategy is so clear, why would you confer with Bevion?"

His eyes twinkled with amusement. "As I said, I'm interested in new ideas."

She glanced at Valamir, brooding and looking into the fire. Then she whispered, "I think you're a liar! You use Bevion to conspire against his own brother!"

"Why would you say such a thing?"

"Perhaps like you, I read faces."

"But I'm accurate. You're not." He clapped his hands sharply, taking Helena by surprise. Attila smiled maliciously at her discomfort. A slave darted inside, groveling, his face to the ground.

"Yes, Lord of all Creation?"

"Food for me and my guests!"

Nodding, the man backed away on his knees. Helena looked away, hating to be a witness of his degradation. Valamir was whistling to himself, a sad song of old Thrace.

"Again, you judge me," Attila said.

"My opinion doesn't matter."

"But it interests me."

"You need a jester to amuse you. It won't be me."

"Please, tell me."

She sighed. "I think that you learned more from the Romans than you'll admit. Even now, you want your revenge from them. You'll make countless people pay because some Roman fools made you suffer. What will it serve? Nothing will erase your pain! You can't give it away!"

"You understand nothing. I'm just. My people are well-fed. In return, I expect obedience. The core of the Empire is rotten. To survive, the tree must be pruned, pared down to its stump. Rome, its fruit decaying on the ground and worms crawling from it, will be first, then Constantinople."

At the mention of Constantinople, Helena's eyes glinted, thinking of their greatest defense: the Greek fire, the ultimate weapon of terror. But she remained silent, refused to be provoked for his pleasure.

He mocked her. "You agree?"

She only shook her head. Two slaves carried in two wooden platters laden with meats and grain. Another followed close behind, bringing flasks and cups. Attila, as they ate their meal, kept his eyes on her as she encouraged Valamir to eat. With food in his stomach, the effects of the mead lessened. He regained his composure. Attila turned the conversation to the campaign, capturing Valamir's complete attention. Helena took the opportunity to fill his cup with water.

"I wonder if we should go back. Winter nips at our heels," Valamir mused, his voice nearly normal.

"We've been away a long time," Attila said. "Two years! Perhaps the men are ready. You could see if your father's new bride has provided him another son!"

At the mention of his stepmother, Valamir frowned.

Attila offered him more mead. At first he declined, but when Attila pressed the cup in his hand, he accepted.

"Valamir," Helena said. "Could we return to the tent?"

He smiled at her, his eyes warm.

Attila interrupted. "You're my guests at the festival tonight. I want you both at my side."

Helena bumped the cup of mead, spilling most of it.

"I'm so sorry, Valamir!"

"It's nothing." He paused, then laughed. "Too bad about your rug, Attila. It's turned red!"

"What are slaves for? Let me refill your cup."

Valamir waved away the flask. "I'll save room for later. We have a long night ahead of us. I want stay awake."

Attila's laugh was hollow.

Helena stood. "Valamir, we should go."

Attila's eyes were sharp with amusement. "The ceremonies draw near. We don't want to keep the men waiting."

Helena became motionless, a strange rage singing inside as she remembered the taste of power that came after drawing her grandfather's rune. Attila, watching her, wavered, his sleek confidence momentarily disturbed. Helena's fingers twitched, but she kept both hands at her sides.

Valamir extended his arm. As she touched him, her fury subsided. Outside, Hassan and Attila's black stallion waited, their ears laid back at one another despite being kept well apart by two Hunnic attendants. Torches had been lit against the darkness, creating a hazy light that gave off shafts of inky smoke. Even in the dull light, the black stallion's coat gleamed from careful grooming. Yet, its saddle and bridle were plain.

Valamir clumsily lifted her to horse, forcing her to grab Hassan's mane to stay on. When he leapt behind her, landing hard, his stallion grunted, unaccustomed to such abuse. Attila, completely sober, mounted with grace.

He smiled, confidence radiating from every pore. "To the festival!" he shouted.

The horses struck off at a brisk canter. Behind her, Valamir had no trouble with his seat, merging as one with Hassan. But to her shame, his drinking had loosened his inhibitions. His right hand caressed her thigh, and she felt his hardness through their clothes. His arm was around her waist and she felt trapped. Her throat closed with tears. Looking at the stars, twinkling against the black sky, she prayed for strength.

People stared as they passed through the camp, then chanted Attila's name like a prayer. As they approached the festival ground, Helena smelled the meat, roasting on the flames. It reminded her of the village after it burned. Torches had been lit. The dark, night sky was illuminated by many bonfires: the air was loud with voices raised in celebration. People tore at their food with relish, raising their cups of mead to Attila as he passed.

A Hun reared his large pony before them and shouted, "Attila!" Then he drew a knife across his forehead. The blood poured down his face. His cry was ecstatic, denying pain. Helena felt ill.

"Kaila honors you!" Valamir noted, his voice unnaturally loud.

Attila grunted.

The crowd was restive, buzzing as Attila's small party passed. He rode directly to the center, to the crest on a small mound. A chair waited for him, fanned by attendants. Slaves appeared at their horses' heads, trembling as Attila scowled. He made his face threatening, rolling his eyes, his teeth bared in a snarl.

Helena wondered why she was no longer afraid of him. Valamir lifted her from Hassan, grasping her in his arms. Smelling his breath pungent from mead, she ached with a disillusionment that hurt like an open wound.

She whispered, "Valamir, please put me down."

His look was warm and passionate, but his smile was a stranger's. "Ssh. I want you close."

Attila sat on his chair and glowered at the crowd. Men edged closer, wanting to be near. His voice was harsh, like iron gritting across stone. "The leaders of the war parties only!"

All but three stepped back ten paces. Valamir was the only Ostrogoth. At first, Helena saw no other women, but in the flickering torch light she noticed a few serving food, others at ease with their men. Beyond the fires, she saw shapes, prone on the ground, moving in the unmistakable rhythm of intercourse.

The night had become a macabre dream, intertwined with betrayal and conspiracy. Under the grandeur of the stars, she felt small and devastated. She longed for solitude and for the sanctuary of Valamir's tent.

Bevion hovered a few feet away, close to Attila's party. His long, blond hair shone in the firelight. His smile was forced. But as Greillia rode in an unswerving line toward Attila, Bevion frowned with annoyance. At the sight of the Hun's scarred face, Helena almost retched.

Greillia jerked his reins, forcing his brown horse to rear, dumping Magga on the grass before Attila. "I've brought you a woman. She'll please you."

Attila grimaced with disgust. "I like my women clean. You insult me with this ruin!"

Magga struggled desperately to sit upright. She used her most sensual voice, the one that had failed miserably on Valamir. "Please great lord, see past my bruises," she said in slurred Gothic.

One of her eyes was swollen into a slit, her lips were distorted from Greillia's fist, but Magga had not lost hope.

Helena found herself speaking to Attila in Greek, her voice earnest. "She was the most beautiful woman in the village."

For a moment, his eyes consumed her. He looked away. "I think not."

Greillia dismounted and prodded Magga with his foot. "I've trained her well, cousin. She'll do anything you ask."

Attila's face was impassive. "What do I need with another whore?"

"This one's *special*. You should have her at least once."

Attila shrugged. "Bathe her and stop beating her so much, then I'll look at her again."

Greillia nodded, his look exultant. He pointed the butt of his whip at Helena. "When are you going to give me that one? I'm the blood of your blood. She belongs to me."

The fire burned within Helena's chest, filling her heart with hate. She pictured him, burning alive in one of the bonfires and screaming in endless agony.

Valamir thrust Helena from his lap and stood, his legs wide and his hand on his sword. "I demand revenge for this outrage!"

Attila's voice was clear, hard, and absolute. "Not tonight. We have gathered in celebration. But Greillia - insult Valamir's wife again and you are no longer under my protection. It will be between you and Valamir."

Greillia's lip curled, showing one side of his teeth. "You've always liked him better than your own kin."

Attila stepped closer, drawing his sword slowly, then tapping the flat of it across his open palm. "You are disrespectful. Next time, I'll take your tongue."

Greillia gritted his teeth, then bowed his head. "Forgive me. I forgot myself. I'm yours to command."

"Your obedience pleases me, cousin. All is well with the tribe."

Darting one last venomous look at Valamir, Greillia prodded Magga with the stub of his whip. "Get up, bitch. We're finished here." He threw her on his horse, her stomach folded over the animal's back like a rolled rug. Mounted, he stared directly at Helena. His hand reached under Magga's skirt.

He fondled her. "Moan with pleasure or I'll teach you more pain," he said to Magga, his gaze locked on Helena's face.

When he wheeled his horse, Helena shuddered, deeply shaken. Valamir sat beside her, his eyes bright and focused.

"He'll never touch you."

She looked at him and felt comforted. Yet, as he drank again from a large cup, Helena glimpsed a stranger lurking behind his eyes.

CHAPTER SIXTEEN

Feeling distant, Helena watched Attila preside over the ritual of cup toasting. An assortment of men spoke, not at random, but in a loose order. The initial speakers were from the crowd. Each represented a small clan. The men took turns praising the tribe: some were brief, others were interminable. After each, they drained their cups of mead with one smooth motion. For Helena, the procedure seemed endless. After the first ten, she lost track. She sat beside Valamir, her lower back aching and her mind numb. Finally, the commanders of the four bands each gave a short speech. Three Hunnic leaders spoke in succession, their addresses sounding similar to Helena's ears. The speaker's voice began low, the words more like animal growls than human expression, and gradually increased to strident shouts.

As each concluded, the crowd erupted into a roar. The din grated on Helena, pounding at her head. She sat motionless and willed herself to keep from screaming.

Throughout the ceremonies, Attila's face was impassive. The crowd chanted his name ecstatically and repeatedly. When Valamir stood and bowed his head to their leader, the men fell silent. He raised his cup high in tribute, elbow straight, and spoke Hunnic in a clear, loud voice. Helena did not understand a word. The men began to beat their knees in rhythm to the speech, praising it with percussion. He downed the mead in a long, smooth flow, then held his cup above his head. The crowd erupted into pandemonium. The only discernible sound was the chanting of Attila's name.

Helena's terror was raw. She felt someone's eyes on her. Turning quickly, she saw Attila studying her. His smile sent chills up and down her spine. Instinctively, her hand gripped her dagger, which hung ready at her left side. His eyes followed her hand, and he nodded approvingly.

He waited as the chanting became a roar, beating the heavens with his name. He stood with two fists clenched in the air. The crowd groaned in ecstasy, then became quiet in hushed anticipation of his words. As he began, his tone was simple and clear. All listened, even Valamir, with an intensity that bordered on adoration. His voice grew louder, becoming more and more impassioned, freeing euphoric shouts from the Huns' hard hearts.

He was their god, Helena realized, and they would follow him anywhere, even to Hades and back. To be so well-loved, Theodosius the Younger, Emperor of the Eastern Roman Empire, would have groveled before the Christian cross.

With a respectful bow, a guard offered Attila a large club. Attila acknowledged him with a curt nod, then pounded the truncheon twice on the ground, terminating the formal proceedings.

While attendants unobtrusively cleared plates, others brought fresh platters heaped with slabs of meat. Drink flowed plentifully into quickly emptied cups.

Helena had no appetite. Valamir was stretched out on the ground and singing of Thrace. At his side, Bevion watched with calculating eyes. He had joined them, uninvited. With his expression nonchalant, he made sure that his brother's cup was kept well filled.

When Helena glared at him, Bevion's answering smile was smug. She wanted to slap him, but did not dare.

No other man had joined the select group congregated around Attila. Yet, the slaves served Bevion with the same careful attention as the others. Close to desperation, Helena stealthily kept vigil over Valamir. When she caught Attila's discreet signal to Bevion, her heart raced with anxiety. Moments after the Hun nodded his head, Bevion gestured to two women waiting in the shadows beyond the flames.

They came closer, their hips swaying, and arranged themselves around Valamir: one to the side and one behind. Helena recognized the Ostrogoth woman named Maude, but not the other blonde. Valamir smiled as Maude ran her fingers through his hair.

Cajoling them with soft words, Bevion encouraged them with laughter and smiles. The blonde wrapped her arms around Valamir's shoulders, then snickered as she whispered in his ear.

Without hesitation, Helena pulled her dagger from its sheath. Power, not born of darkness, surged through her veins, and she hummed an ancient marching song. Affecting indifference, she held her blade up to the light, studying it with narrowed eyes. She pointed it first at Maude, then the other. They looked at her, cautiously, and she smiled with cold confidence.

She spoke in rudimentary Gothic. "My blade is sharp." Without flinching, she pricked a finger, making it drip red. "Now, go!"

The women did not need a second hint. They retreated to Bevion. "You said that she wouldn't care!" Maude said, scolding him.

He shrugged his shoulders, put his arms around them both, and kissed Maude briefly on the lips. She giggled, then spoke quietly to the other woman. The three stood up together, linked as one, and walked toward the shadows.

Valamir forgot them. He turned to his equally drunken neighbor and began an earnest discussion. But shortly, it disintegrated into helpless laughter. Between gulps of mead, they took up singing, louder than before.

Attila watched Helena with icy eyes. "Perhaps I underestimated you."

Despite her still hammering heart, she did not flinch from him. "You broke your word to Valamir. I won't forget."

They locked wills, withdrawing from the outer world. Though surrounded by the celebration, they could have been alone in the flickering torchlight.

She set her shoulders. "You made him drunk. Your plan was crude, Attila, unworthy of your skill."

"You imagine things, Helena. I acted as a good host. Drink is all around me, but as you see, I am not in its thrall. If you want to assign blame, give it to its rightful owner."

"Then what of Bevion's ruse?"

"An amusing game."

She shook her head. "You wanted to separate us. I don't understand you! Valamir's your friend."

He looked away, studying the crowd. "Remember, Helena, I am no man's friend. Why aren't you afraid of me? You should be."

She did not answer.

"Perhaps you trust me."

"No. That's not the reason." She hesitated, thinking. "Before, when you spoke to the men, you terrified me. But when we talk, one to one, somehow, I know you."

She was silent, her better judgment demanding that she be still. In the throes of curiosity, she ignored her inner voice. "Does everyone open their hearts to you? I find myself wanting to tell you everything, though I do not."

He laughed quietly, pleased. "It's a talent. But why keep anything back?"

He stood over her, looking down, then smiled. "You are like a rose, fragile in its beauty. Perhaps it would be better if you stayed with my women tonight. Valamir is known, shall we say, for his excesses when he drinks. I'll keep you safe."

Blood rushed to her face and she shook her head; her eyes moved to Attila's leather boots laced with rawhide.

Suddenly, Valamir was between them, a head taller than Attila, glaring at him. His Greek was slurred. "She's not for you."

He stretched out his hand. "Come."

His arm loomed before her eyes, his fingers spread wide. She looked up to the familiar face, his breath stinking of mead, and once again saw a stranger. Her stomach tightened with fear. Behind Valamir's back, Attila shook his head slightly, in a veiled warning.

Valamir jerked his head toward Hassan. Helena grasped his hand, trying to pull him down beside her, hoping to sober him with food. "Eat, Valamir. The meat is good."

His eyes raked her body, sweeping up and down. "I am hungry."

She hated him for shaming her and tried to take back her hand. But he held it tightly, wrenching her into a clumsy embrace. From the shadows beyond the torches, a man moaned with pleasure and two women laughed. Bevion, Helena thought.

She closed her eyes against Valamir's betrayal. It had cast her adrift into dark despair, without a sail or an oar.

Attila whispered, "Stay with me."

Her body felt heavy, her skin taut across her cheeks, and she blinked away tears. She glanced at Valamir, his eyes crazed by drink, then at Attila. Her voice was tired. "Take me home, Valamir."

"Helena," he said, more to himself than to her. "You're sad." He looked away, lost to her again, ensnared by his drunken haze. "Attila, I'll be back later." He shouted, to no one in particular, "My horse!"

A slave scrambled toward Hassan, stumbling in his haste. Frowning, Valamir turned his empty cup upside down and shouted, "More!"

A woman appeared at his side, refilling it from a long leather flask. He smacked his lips, then drained the pottery mug. Helena wanted to hit him hard across the face, knocking the flagon from his hands. But her arms were heavy at her sides.

Attila's voice cut the air crisply. "You'd do better with my wives."

She met his large, compelling eyes, once more feeling like a mouse staring into a snake's open jaws. "And the next night? What would happen then?"

"Whatever you wished."

Valamir leaned against her, holding her shoulders tightly for support.

"My place is with my husband."

His mouth twisted, Attila shrugged. The man leading Hassan cried out with pain as the stallion stamped on his foot. Valamir turned with unexpected ease. Seeing his horse, he smiled broadly. Deftly, he placed Helena on Hassan. Her body remembered his sure touch, and for a moment, she was reassured. Then he swung up behind her and landed hard on the other side of the horse. Hassan snorted with surprise. Valamir laughed, the men joining him, until he had to clutch his sides.

Her heart sank.

The stallion pawed the grass impatiently, and Helena grabbed his reins. He tossed his head high, rearing against the pressure on his mouth. She tried to hold him with her one good hand, but the horse shook his head, fighting her.

Afraid, she cried out, "Valamir!"

He shouted, "Hassan!" But his usually firm voice came out as a giggle. Yet, he rose from the ground without difficulty, and took his horse in hand. "Beast!" he said, reprimanding him.

When Valamir mounted again, he was careful to stay on. His success was greeted by cheers, ragged from drink. He remained upright by grasping Helena's waist. Instead of the usual flying canter through the camp, the stallion, on a loose rein, took them home at a walk. He did not prance, or misbehave in any way, and Helena wondered at his obedience. As with any horse, he could sense his rider's vulnerability, but did not use it against him.

Valamir started to sing. His voice was melodic, clear, and perfectly pitched, but the song was bawdy: an insult to her ears. With each drunken breath, he crushed her hard-won trust.

As Hassan carried them through the camp, it was virtually deserted. Most of the tribe remained at the celebration. Her eyes hot with self-pity, Helena prayed that Greillia had not witnessed Valamir's vulnerability. She pictured them, both weaving from too much drink and fighting. The image made her feel worse and even more grim. Behind her, Valamir's lips touched her neck and his hand stroked her thigh. She grabbed it and wrenched her neck away.

She whispered to the sky, the indifferent stars, but most of all, to him, "I hate you."

He only said, "Ssh," as if they conspired together, then chuckled. Again, she wanted to hit him, but never considered using her blade.

The ride was interminable. If she had known the route, she would have run on alone. But in the dark, all the tents looked the same. Lost in his drunken stupor, Valamir did not guide them. She hoped Hassan remembered the way.

When they arrived, he slid off the horse and promptly fell asleep on the ground, leaving her mounted. Caratipian's tent was silent and shut. For a moment, Helena considered calling him; she was so desperate for help. But she could not. Valamir had said that he was ill, his joints sore with persistent aching.

She glanced at Valamir, stretched out on the grass, with his long hair tangled, and his chiseled face illuminated by moonlight. She dismounted with slow movements. Talking softly to Hassan, she fumbled clumsily with his girth, using her good hand. With effort, she eventually unfastened his saddle and placed it beside the tent. All that remained was the bridle, but she could not remember where Valamir kept Hassan's halter. Reluctant to let the animal loose without any restraints, she was more concerned about his reins becoming tangled in his legs. Seeing no better alternative, she undid his cheek-strap and tossed the bridle beside the saddle.

Still, the roan waited. She wondered what he wanted, but gave up with a shrug. She had more serious problems.

She shoved him with her shoulder, pushing him toward the other horses, and tapped his rump with the flat of her hand. "Go, Hassan! Find Passial. He's over there!"

The animal needed no further encouragement. Neighing, he set off at a smart trot. With soft whinnies, the other horses answered. Her task complete, Helena sighed with relief. Then she felt someone's eyes watching her. She spun round, her hand gripping her dagger, but saw nothing in the shadows.

She prodded Valamir with her foot, who was asleep where he had fallen and snoring. "Wake up!"

He came to slowly, shaking his head groggily, and allowed her to lead him inside. The fire was burned to embers. Despite his illness, Caratipian must have given it some care; otherwise, it would have died long ago.

Valamir slumped in front of the entrance, blocking it, adding to her apprehensions. The tent no longer felt like a safe haven, but a prison cell. Valamir's eyes were closed. A strange smile played on his lips. Hoping he would sleep, she was very quiet and resolved to keep watch against him.

With concentration, she fed the fire, hardly making a sound. The sticks flared. The play of the flames, the dance never the same, lulled her. She focused on adding a more substantial piece of wood and momentarily forgot her vigilance.

When Valamir grabbed her, she was caught off-guard. He pushed her to the ground, well away from the fire, and his mouth pressed hers so hard that it hurt. Then his hands were at her bodice, tearing away her dress. Helena retreated deep within herself. She became immobile and shut her eyes, not wanting to see his face. His fingers touched a nipple, then fondled her breast. His mouth descended, sucking passionately first one, then the other.

Finally, she was swept by outrage. "Valamir!" she screamed.

He ignored her.

She shouted, "You promised, you bastard!"

Relentlessly, he raised her dress, both hands tearing her undergarments. Her fists clenched, the right one sharp with pain. She considered using her dagger, but could not imagine driving it into his back.

Her body came alive, remembering her grandfather's training. With all her strength, she punched him hard in both kidneys. He cried out and pulled away, exposing his stomach. Her right hand burned in agony, but she ignored the pain and drove both fists deep into his solar plexus.

In the firelight, he looked like a demon. His face was raw with fury and his breathing was audible. As he raised his hand to hit her face, she cried out again, "Valamir!"

He gasped, suddenly recognizing her, but not in time to stop the momentum of his arm. Instead, he struck his fist hard into the ground, sparing her.

"Helena," he said, sitting back on his heels, away from her. He buried his face in his hands. "I could have killed you."

She edged farther away from him, trying to cover her nakedness. He raised his head and watched her with glittering eyes. His words were still slurred; he reeked of drink. "I've dishonored you...If I stay the night...I'll hurt you." His voice sounded strangled. "Helena, I'll be back."

"Valamir, someone's watching the tent!"

He stood unsteadily. "Attila has many eyes."

She was desperate: wanting him gone, but afraid to be alone. "I took off Hassan's saddle."

"Good...good," he said, staring at her, his eyes hungry with desire. Turning abruptly, he opened the entrance flap. His words were soft, like a caress. "I'm sorry."

Then he was gone. She pulled her knees to her chest, shivering. To the shadows, she mourned. "Oh, Valamir, Valamir." She whispered it over and over again, her eyes wet with tears.

Later, she roused herself and searched her satchel for her other plain dress. Her hand touched the soft silk of her wedding dress and she cried. She wiped her eyes on her sleeve and replaced her ruined traveling dress with one even more old and worn. Yet, she folded the torn garment neatly and buried it at the bottom of her satchel, as if to hide her shame.

Alone on the sleeping pad, her stomach pulsed with the aftermath of fear. Her right hand throbbed. The tent was quiet, the hearth was warm, and in time, she dreamed.

When morning came, the fire was dead. She awoke to the sun shining full on her face from above and shivered in the cold. The tent felt empty without Valamir.

Her stomach grumbled, but she ignored its need. More from habit than anything else, she tidied herself. When she had finished, she sat, immobile in the shadows, with a blanket drawn over her head and shoulders like a widow's cowl.

When she heard hoof beats outside, her heart raced.

"May I enter?" Attila asked.

Helena's disappointment was bitter, her voice hoarse. "Please, give me a moment. I'll join you outside."

She pulled on her coat, the gift that had given her such joy, and went to meet the day. She felt sick and devastated, but did not care if Attila noticed. He was irrelevant, unlike Valamir.

CHAPTER SEVENTEEN

The morning air was frigid; the sky was deep blue and crisp with clouds. Astride his black stallion, Attila waited for Helena to acknowledge his presence. His horse tossed its head, its mouth opening against the pressure the Hun applied to its bit.

She broke the tension. "Attila."

With his sharp eyes, he scrutinized her, searching for damage. He was not alone, but was surrounded by a semi-circle of Hunnic horsemen. Neither Valamir, Bevion, nor Caratipian were to be seen.

He spoke Greek. "I need your expertise with words, Helena. Come with me."

"No," she said, without pausing to consider whether she had the right to refuse. "I must wait for Valamir."

Attila scowled, then laughed. He said something in Hunnic to the men. Their scarred faces broke into knowing smiles. "He's busy, Helena. He might be awhile."

Inwardly, she winced with pain. But when she spoke, her voice was clear and unwavering. "I can't be with you in your tent, Attila. Without my husband, it would not be proper."

He was quiet; his face was a bland mask. Finally, he raised his eyebrow and smiled, but his expression was melancholy.

Again she spoke without considering the consequences, her throat dry. "Don't pity me."

His smile was sardonic. "He doesn't deserve your loyalty."

Her breath drew inward; his words breached her defenses to their innermost core. She reverted to silence, her only weapon, and stared at him with unflinching eyes.

"Enough," he said. "I'll have my things brought to you. We'll work together in Valamir's tent."

"We must be outside in plain view."

"But you're shivering with cold. You look tired, almost as if you've had a bad night."

Her eyes flashed, hot with tears. She blinked hard, keeping them at bay. "You want trouble between Valamir and me. Why?"

He looked pleased. "That should be evident!" He considered his words, speaking slowly. "It's good that you speak your mind with me. Never stop. It would be my loss."

The wind blew, lifting her hair from her shoulders. Attila's guards watched her, their eyes lively and amused. Though they could not understand Greek, the men knew an argument when they heard one.

She studied Attila: not as a Hun, but as a man. "You're an enigma, Attila. If you gave the command, your men wouldn't hesitate to cut me down. Your power is absolute. Even Greillia respects it. Yet, you bandy words with me, a woman, as if you really considered what I thought." She hesitated, uncertain whether to continue.

His eyes never left her face. When he spoke, his voice was rough. "Go on."

"I think you see me as a key to a door. Where it leads, you don't know, but you have to find out. Always, you have to know, your mind thirsting for more. I should be frightened of you. I see the cruelty in your face; you don't hide it. But your intellect, so quick to pounce, gives me pause. You have a brilliance that would scorch me if I got too close. If I were wise, I wouldn't talk to you, keeping safe in silence. But I can't." She smiled, suddenly surprised. "It's too much fun."

His face softened with delight, transforming his ugliness into charisma. "*You* are a treasure, Helena. If Valamir doesn't suit you, come to me. I'll speak to him."

As Attila said his name, Helena remembered Valamir's face blurred from drink, his lips hard on her mouth, and his hands ripping and taking.

Attila's voice was like a knife. "Did he hurt you?"

Stunned, she stared at him, hearing his sincerity, and shifted her weight back on her heels. He personified the barbarian ideal: violent and ruthless. Yet, he cared. Still, Helena could not allow him the intimacy of a confidant. "It's between Valamir and me."

"Again, you are loyal." His eyes hardened. "I'll make him appreciate it."

Caratipian hobbled toward them, his face white with pain. Without a qualm, Helena pushed her way through the Huns' horses and scolded him. "You should be in bed! You're not well!"

His pale blue eyes squinted against the sun, then swept the Huns. He spoke quietly in Persian. "We're not among friends."

Suddenly, Attila, his horse chewing its bit, was with them. As he looked down at the servant, his eyes were like black coals. Helena thought of thunder. "You never told us that you spoke Persian, Caratipian! Rugliva would never have sold you if he had known!"

Caratipian lowered his head. His hands clenched his trousers and Helena wondered what the Huns had done to make him so afraid.

Irritated, Attila waved his hand. "You may speak."

"I was born in Persia, Great Lord."

"Why didn't you tell us?"

"No one asked."

Attila gritted his teeth. "You...."

Frightened for her friend, Helena interrupted, "He's ill. Leave him alone!"

Caratipian's eyes pleaded with her, silently with warning. "Helena, show respect to Lord Attila."

Attila's mouth contorted into a snarl. "Go back to sleep, old man. Unlike Valamir, I have no patience with uselessness!"

His face expressionless, Caratipian bowed from the waist and edged backward to his tent.

"Why did you say that?" she asked.

"He's a rebel. We could never break him. His presence is an offense, a reminder of failure."

"You seem to value my spirit."

"You're a woman. If you were a man, you'd be dangerous and safer dead." His eyes appraised her. "Unless, of course, you'd swear to serve me, without question."

She flinched.

Attila smiled. He leaned closer to whisper and his tone was ingratiating. "Let's not speak of unpleasant matters, Helena. I need your help on my journal. I'll have someone bring my scroll and quill, another will make a warm bonfire."

"As you wish, Attila."

He clapped his hands loudly and spoke imperiously in Hunnic to one guard, and then another. They rode in two different directions, stretching their horses into a hard gallop. Filling the missing gaps, the remaining guards tightened their phalanx formation, partially blocking Helena's view of the camp.

In the distance, over their horses' backs, she saw a tall blond man walking toward them. His long legs brought him closer with easy strides. His head was lowered and his eyes studied the ground. When he looked up at the tent, crowded with Attila's guards, he stopped dead in his tracks.

Though Helena was unable to see his face clearly, she recognized Valamir. "He's come back," she whispered to herself.

Attila's voice was like a flask filled with rattling stones. "You love him."

She kept her focus on Valamir. His pace had become rapid as he approached. But when he neared, Helena averted her eyes and stared at the billowing clouds just above the flat horizon. Despite her display of nonchalance, her hand clutched the fabric of her dress.

Attila remained close. "Valamir! By the gods, you look spent! The men say that you covered three women last night!"

The words sped like arrows into her heart. She looked directly at Valamir and her face crumpled. For a moment, he held her eyes, then looked away, folding his arms across his chest.

Without hesitation, she fled to the solitude of the tent. She crouched by the ashes in the hearth, her head in her hands.

Through the leather walls, Helena heard Valamir's angry voice in Greek. "Why did you speak of the others in front of my wife?"

Attila's chuckle was malicious. "Maybe she'll look for solace elsewhere. Someone who will appreciate her and treat her gently."

Losing control, Valamir shouted, "The hell she will!"

Attila answered with silence. Afraid for Valamir, Helena held her breath. Attila laughed, the booming sound releasing the tension in her chest.

The Hun's next words were a hiss, shredding the air. "You've a right to be angry. After all, she's your wife. But never before has someone come between us."

"Attila," Valamir said. "I trust you with my very being. But by the gods, I wish that I could say the same about you with my wife! You keep coming at her, like a moth to the flame."

Attila paused. "You are my oldest friend. Next time, I'll try to remember. Helena doesn't seem to understand how it is for men. The last thing I need is a jealous woman!" He laughed. "Perhaps you should come with me for awhile. Your wife needs time to forgive you."

Valamir cleared his throat. "If you want me, send word."

Attila laughed again. "The gods be with you!"

Hoof beats punctuated Attila's departure, but Valamir did not join Helena inside. She forced herself to sit erectly, but her heart was sore with confusion. Time passed slowly. When Valamir entered, he said nothing. She could not meet his eyes.

He prepared a simple meal of bread and meat, dividing it into two. His hands shook slightly. Sitting across from Helena, he set one of the leather plates before her. She shrank from him.

"By Odin, Helena, I'm sorry."

His apology released her anger; her darkness called for revenge. But she would have none of it. Yet, she wanted to beat him, hating the fact that her will was trapped in a woman's body and lacked a man's strength. Having no appetite, she glanced at her plate with distaste. Equally indifferent to the meal, Valamir set his aside. Instead, he built a pyramid of sticks and dry mulch in the cold hearth. From a container behind him, he extracted flint and a small metal rod. Helena watched his finely shaped fingers as they worked with the flint, patiently creating a spark again and again. Finally, the flame caught, igniting the kindling. He smiled.

Her eyes grew hot, but she curbed the tears. Attila was at the edges of her thoughts, circling her and watching her like a predator. Valamir, her only protector, had betrayed her.

"Talk to me, Helena," he said, looking at her.

His eyes were soft, brilliant blue and his fingertips were pressed together. Her feelings for him lay just below the surface, waiting to snare her.

"No."

He withdrew into himself and became quiet and still. "I forgot myself," he said. His words hung between them.

"Come outside. We need water. Caratipian's not well enough to carry buckets back and forth to the stream."

"For Caratipian, then."

Valamir picked up two buckets and led the way outside. "Wait," he said.

In a moment, he emerged from Caratipian's tent with a leather container dangling from his wrist. "Can you manage this one?"

She nodded, wishing that the sunlight would not glisten in his hair, streaking it with gold. Side by side, they walked to the stream, noisy with women, washing clothes while they talked. More than one called Valamir by name.

He ignored them. "Come upstream with me. The water's cleaner."

Moving away from the camp, she followed him along the bank, studying his wide back and broad shoulders. His hair hung past his shoulders and swung gently with his easy gait. Thinking of last night, she studied the ground.

After the women's voices had faded in the distance, Valamir sat by the water and dropped his buckets. They rolled haphazardly toward the stream then came to a rest. Keeping more than an arm's length away from him, Helena remained standing.

"Sit, Helena. The sun feels good."

She shivered from the cold, but also from the turmoil that raced within her, spiraling with confusion. Finding a large stone, several feet away, she sat. As she hugged her knees to her chest, her long dress covered her legs.

The sound of rushing water soothed her, acting as a salve to her distress. Streams made the same music the world over, only the tempo varied: some rushed to find the ocean, others meandered, hushed in their steady flow.

Abruptly, Valamir stripped off his tunic, his boots and socks, and his weapons, leaving only his pants.

Helena was shocked. "What are you doing?"

He shrugged, but his smile was veiled, full of secret meaning. It eluded her, firing her anger, but most of all, her shame. "I feel dirty after last night," he simply said.

His eyes grave, he turned from her silently and waded into the stream to its deepest spot. He sat, splashing water everywhere. Dunking his head, he came up for air with a gasp, spraying water as he shook his hair. Helena thought of a large dog, shaking itself dry, but resisted the sudden urge to laugh.

Dripping, he returned to the bank, his skin prickled from the cold. He sat beside her, but not so close as to make her wet. He picked up one of his knives. His face was serious as he watched the sunlight reflect on its shining blade.

Not looking at her, he spoke quietly. "Did I hurt you last night?"

Words would not come. How could she explain the depth of his betrayal? "You shamed me."

"I know. But I don't remember. Did I...Did I..."

"Did you rape me? No, but only because I hit you as hard as I could, probably breaking my hand again."

"Thank you."

"For what?"

"Stopping me. Do you hate me?"

She shook her head, feeling trapped by his questions. "I don't know."

He put his knife in her left hand and gently closed her fingers around the hilt. "I owe you a blood-price. Mark me as you wish."

She dropped the weapon and it clattered on the stones. "My God, Valamir! If I'd wanted to cut you, I would have last night!"

His face was an opaque mask, revealing nothing of his feelings. He retrieved the dagger, balancing it delicately in his hand. She felt a chill, as if death walked near.

Her hand reached his wrist. "No, Valamir."

Without hesitation, he put the dagger's tip to his chest, over his heart, and sliced his flesh. She pulled at his wrist, trying to stop him, but, inexorably, he continued to draw some kind of rune, triangular in shape. Blood spilled, marking his progress, and still she did not let go.

"Don't do this, Valamir. Please. Again, you break my heart."

He stopped. "This way, I'll never forget what I did."

"It's enough. You're bleeding everywhere!"

He looked down, then shrugged. "Just scratches. They'll heal."

Again, the dagger's point was to his chest.

"Please stop, Valamir," she pleaded.

He hesitated. "It's not finished! It must be perfect. It's for you."

"No, not for me. It's for your conscience. I hate what you're doing. It's barbaric."

"And that's who I am, Helena. A barbarian. That will never change."

She released his wrist and turned away, hiding her face. Her tears were silent.

The knife idle in his hand, he touched her shoulder and lifted her chin so that her eyes met his. "Helena."

Her mouth twisted. His blue eyes were close, his brow crinkled in a frown, and she was shaking. "Forgive me," he said.

"I can't, not yet!"

"Take forever, just stay with me."

Her throat ached. "And at night, where will you be, Valamir?"

He kissed her brow. "With my wife."

Her hand touched his dagger, red with blood. "Will you put that away?"

He wiped it clean on the grass. "But the rune is only half done."

"It's like last night. You started, but in the end, you stopped. Drunk as you were, you did not hit me, but chose to strike the ground. Don't you remember?"

"I only remember waking and not seeing you."

His cut still oozed red. "We need a clean cloth to stop the bleeding," she said.

"The blood washes the wound. When it stops, we'll go back."

His arm wrapped around her, pulling her close. In the distance, a bird called. "Do you hate me, Helena?"

"No, but you've taught me fear."

He studied the horizon, his jaw pulsing and said nothing.

Later, they returned to camp, the buckets sloshing with water. Helena walked beside him, her thoughts in turmoil, but with a lighter heart.

CHAPTER EIGHTEEN

No one waited for Helena and Valamir. She was thankful for this small mercy, not wanting to see Bevion's teasing face, nor Attila's brooding stare. Valamir left his two buckets outside his tent. Helena's had splashed, darkening the hem of her dress.

"I'll give this to Caratipian," he said, reaching for her smaller container.

Her eyes followed him as he walked to the other tent, his step smooth and coiled. Drawn to him, emotion overwhelmed thought. She had lost everything: Mikael, her grandfather, her life in Constantinople, even the routine of Kansbar's world. Her trust in Valamir had been a lifeline - slender, but strong, keeping madness at bay.

Last night, his actions had severed the fragile cord.

He soundlessly placed the bucket inside Caratipian's tent and returned to her, his footsteps not even creating a whisper on the ground. "He's asleep," he said, taking her by the hand.

He led her inside, his gentle touch opening her heart to him. She thought she was a fool.

Confined in the tent, her fear returned. He stoked the fire, then contemplated her with warm eyes. She longed for the reassurance of his protective arms, but remained terrified by the memory of his weight grinding down on her and his hands snatching at her clothes.

She felt like a cornered bird with a broken wing, seeing its fate in a fox's glistening teeth. As her heart raced, something within her whispered that it was not normal to be so frightened by what men and women did together. But the thought only made her feel more alone.

Grimacing, Valamir took off his bloody tunic. His chest was unsightly: the mutilation was significant.

"I can't believe what you did to yourself," she said, assuaging her emptiness with words.

He pointed to scars on his shoulders and arms. "I've had worse cuts in battle."

Her hand reached for him, wanting to trace her fingers across his scars, as if her touch could eradicate the old pain. But she dropped it to her side. Despite her intentions, she stepped closer to him, needing to examine the still bleeding gash across his chest. His muscles were defined under finely textured skin; his scent spicy. In her heart, she understood that he had captured her anew, irrevocably, like a rabbit in a snare.

She kept her voice evenly pitched, trying to hide her confusion. "Valamir, you need bandaging. Can Caratipian help?"

He wrinkled his nose. "His poultices smell rotten. Worse, he'll insist I change the wrappings everyday."

"I'm going to wake him. He'd never forgive me if I didn't."

He held her by the arm. "I'll come with you. I don't like you going out alone."

"It's only a few steps away. I'll be fine."

His face was drawn and pale from the loss of blood. "Go, then," he said, waving her away.

In her rush, she ran into Bevion's arms, just outside the door.

"Helena! You've seen the light at last!" he said.

"Let go of me!" she said, pulling away.

Behind her, Valamir's voice rippled with anger. "Bevion!"

Bevion's eyes grew wide, looking at the blood on his brother's chest. "She knifed you!" He raised his arm to strike her face. "You bitch!"

Valamir grabbed him. "You ass! She had nothing to do with this. Go, Helena, get Caratipian. He may as well join the party."

Not needing Helena's summons, Caratipian came as fast as he could hobble. "What have you done to yourself?"

Valamir looked away.

The servant glanced at Helena once, then turned back to Valamir, his lips pursed. "There's a story here, but not a good one."

Seeing him, Helena wanted to cry. He was the same: the remaining glue which held together her fragile universe. "He needs something to bind it," she said.

His face sour with disapproval, Caratipian returned to his tent. He reappeared shortly, carrying various containers. Helena ran to him, offering to help. He only shook his head, thin-lipped with anger.

He was brusque, his eyes cold fire. "Sit, Valamir."

"Shouldn't we go inside?" Helena asked.

"The light's no good there; it's better in the sunlight." He bent over Valamir, muttering. "You're a damn fool." Then he extracted powders from his small leather bags, measuring them carefully before combining them in a small leather bowl. He continued to scold. "Any cut can fester."

Valamir waited, not bothering to hide his discomfort. Bevion observed with mocking amusement, until Caratipian glowered at him to shoo him away. He shrugged, but did not leave, intent on watching his brother's predicament.

As she watched Caratipian tend to his charge, Helena understood that Valamir had deflected her just anger with a self-inflicted wound. She seethed silently, realizing that his act was not a simple barbaric ritual, but the product of an intelligent, manipulative mind.

Caratipian poured a bitter smelling liquid on a clean cloth and abruptly ordered Valamir to lie down. As he cleaned the injury, the Goth's eyes widened, his only sign of pain. Thinking it served him right, Helena almost smiled.

Engrossed by his brother's ordeal, Bevion ignored her. Caratipian worked with quick expertise, covering the laceration with a poultice, wrapping it with an intricate bandage woven over Valamir's shoulder and back.

Caratipian glanced at Helena quizzically, then shook his head. "Sometimes, Valamir, it's better to trust that you will be forgiven, instead of forcing another's hand. Powerful gestures have a purpose, but rarely."

His face taut, he did not wait for a response. As he limped back to his quarters, his progress was slow. Without a word, Helena withdrew to Valamir's tent.

Bevion's voice was clear, easily piercing the leather walls. "By the gods, Valamir! I saw what you drew. Isn't it the rune of remembrance? And why? Because you pleased at least three women in one night? You did nothing wrong! When Maude told me of your strength, I was proud to be your brother!"

"You wouldn't understand, Bevion. The women weren't important; they answered a need. What matters is that I broke my word. Such a betrayal calls for blood."

"That's nonsense, Valamir! You treat Helena with the same respect as your brothers of Mithras. She's only a woman! Treat her well enough. And if once in a while, you cause her to hate you, too bad. Women learn to accept us as we are. They've no choice." He paused, then added, "How did you break your word, Valamir?"

"Leave it alone, Bevion. You're like a dog with a bone: always gnawing to find the marrow. When you fall in love someday, you'll understand."

"I fall in love every night, Valamir, usually twice."

"Is that why you look so tired, little brother? Maybe you're not quite up to it. You'd better check on Maude, she might be missing me."

Helena remembered the tall Gothic woman from the previous night and how she looked at Valamir. A fire exploded within her, reminding her of the words that had come unbidden to her lips as she cursed Greillia. "No," she whispered, denying the impulse. With fierce concentration, she drew the rune of Light.

The sensation passed. But the picture of Valamir and Maude, naked and intertwined, assaulted her, devastating her with jealousy. She paced the tent, needing to break free. She was unsure of what hurt the most: last night's attack or the fact that he had found solace elsewhere.

Shortly, Valamir joined her and she glared at him. "You went with Maude."

"I was with her when I woke up."

Helena stood next to him, looking into his eyes. Her left fist clenched, ready to strike.

He touched her arm, but she slapped his hand away. "Attila and Bevion had a plan, a simple one. You were to get drunk, leaving me exposed. And you obliged them. Did you know that Attila counted how many cups you drank? That he offered me his protection last night? 'Stay with my women,' he said, again and again. And that Bevion arranged for Maude and another woman to come and take you from me? Leaving me alone with Attila?"

His hands rested on her shoulders, but she did not spin away. "What did you do then, Helena?"

She smiled grimly. "I threatened them with my dagger and they went away."

"You did well, better than I. Helena, I can't undo last night. I wish I could." His hand stroked her face, lingering in her hair. "If I'd stayed, you couldn't have forgiven me. I'd have been no better than Kansbar."

Her face crumpled. He put his arms around her, and leaned down to her lips. "All I want is you, Helena."

"Last night was terrible," she whispered, lost in the varied blue of his eyes.

"I usually hold my drink well."

"Maybe they drugged it; I've heard of such things."

His brow furrowed. "It tasted all right, a little bitter perhaps. Attila wouldn't stoop so low."

"Perhaps, but he seems like a man used to getting his way."

"Well, he won't be having you."

His eyes searched hers, then his lips were pressed gently in a kiss. "Will you forgive me?" he whispered.

"Just this once, Valamir."

"Will you keep me company while I sleep?"

"I'll stay with you."

She lay beside him, warmed by his body. His hand stroked her hair until he fell into a deep slumber. She thought of the other women touching him, but did not care. He was her husband. For better or worse, she intended to keep him.

CHAPTER NINETEEN

As Valamir slept, Helena lay beside him listening to his steady breathing and the bustle of the camp outside. She shut her eyes against the afternoon sun, seeking the oblivion of sleep, but it eluded her.

Finally, she yielded to her restlessness and sat by the fire. Her muscles were stiff and her right hand throbbed with renewed vigor. She longed to be outside, away from this tent and this camp, astride Passial, riding nowhere and everywhere. She disciplined her thoughts. Many times in the past, she had found solace by reminding herself of the Living Words of the Prophet Zarathushtra. If she closed her eyes, she could pretend that her grandfather was beside her, patiently explaining the nuances behind the teachings. Something unwound in her, like a giant coil, and she relaxed.

Near dusk, Valamir's eyes opened, instantly alert. He turned toward her, inadvertently placing weight on his self-inflicted wound, and grimaced with pain.

Religious tenets set aside, she found obscure pleasure in his discomfort, wanting him to suffer for last night. But the memory of his knife slicing his flesh, blood trailing behind its point, was a torment that made her cringe inside.

"Does it hurt?" she asked, her voice muted.

As Valamir stood, he grimaced. "No more than I deserve," he said with a shrug.

Helena shook her head, annoyed and relieved at the same time. The man she now relied on had returned.

Through the walls of the tent, a voice called, "Valamir!"

The Goth frowned with irritation. "What do you want, Ishyite?"

"Attila requests that you and your *wife* join him for his evening meal. And Valamir, he reminded me twice to call Helena 'your wife.'"

"Did he? Good. He learns, if slowly," Valamir said with a satisfied smile. "We'll meet you."

"Sorry. Orders are to give you an escort."

Valamir's voice was a growl. "Why?"

"Why am I sorry?"

"Don't play games with me, Ishyite!"

"He said that he wants to see you sooner rather than later."

"Then you'll have to wait. I've been sleeping all day."

"I'll be here."

"Good." Valamir turned to Helena, his eyes brilliant in the late afternoon sunlight. But a frown wrinkled his brow. He spoke in a rush, his voice low. "Attila's like the wind about some things, a stone with others. For no reason, he changes his mind. Be careful what you say to him. It doesn't matter that he gave you certain liberties. If he becomes angry, he won't bother to remember his word. If you allow yourself to be provoked by him, he wins."

Regretfully, she remembered her conversation with Attila the previous night. "Do you find yourself wanting to tell him everything?"

He smiled, shaking his head once. "He has power over people. If your tongue wants to speak when your mind shouts for silence, look away from his eyes. Otherwise, he can compel you. And remember, never, ever tell him a lie. He'll know. He can smell your fear."

"Impossible. A dog perhaps, but not a human."

"He has the ability. I've witnessed it."

"Maybe he's just perceptive."

"Possibly, but more likely he has a gift, a talent for knowing." He took her hand in his, studying it, then looked at her directly. "You speak too easily from your heart, Helena. In Kansbar's house, you were careful, calling little attention to yourself. But you've changed and become reckless. I love your passion, but it puts you in danger. Sometimes I'm afraid where it might lead you."

She was quiet, considering his words and recognized truth. With a flash, Greillia's sword had obliterated her world. As she retrieved the fragments of her life, she had abandoned caution. With Kansbar, she had been passive, knowing submission was the best defense. That diffidence was dust, grit under her feet. The door to her past and her youth was sealed, the key buried. Dangerous or not, she endured in a more elemental form.

Thoughtfully, she ran her fingers through her hair. "I don't think Attila would harm me. He studies me, always provoking my opinion. The One God knows that I've been offensive. If he wanted me dead, he has not lacked excuses. I'll be more careful, not for him, but for you. I don't want you to worry." She straightened her dress, ran her eyes over Valamir's tunic, and frowned at a splotch of dried blood. "You should change."

He smiled, his eyes passionate. "Just remember: his temper has overridden his judgment more than once. If he hurt you, I'd have to punish him. Despite his flaws, he is my friend. I don't want to lose him." He pointed to his bloodied tunic with amusement. "If you think that I could hide this from him, you dream. His eyes and ears surround us all."

She was vehement. "I don't like being spied on!"

He frowned, then shrugged. "Some things I can alter, many I cannot. My people have survived the Huns' domination for fifty years. But as time passes, they become more like us, adapting to our traditions. Each change is a victory for the Goths. I believe that one day Attila will be King. Then the winds will blow more gently for my people."

Helena was silent. She felt rootless and alone, not wanting a future which included Attila. But Valamir was inexorably linked to him. And she could not imagine life without the tall Goth, without the sight of his slow smile, and without the warmth of his arms around her.

She wondered what her grandfather would think.

"We must go," she said, running from her quandary.

He stood, extending his hand. Without hesitation, she reached for him. As he pulled her close, the sense of oneness, of union, returned. His lips met hers, igniting her body. Her universe became small, allowing room only for his kiss and his hands on her body.

"Valamir," Ishyite called, his voice impatient. They went outside with Valamir's hand clasped over hers. Ishyite, flanked with an escort of four Huns, glared with irritation.

Valamir was unaffected. "I'll need my horse."

"He's behind the tent. Time passes, Valamir."

Hassan snorted and plunged forward, dragging a slightly built Hun in his wake. The stallion's ears were laid back, his foreleg pawed the ground.

Valamir laughed, enjoying the sight of the man's scrambling dance as he tried to keep clear of Hassan's hooves. "A moment, Ishyite, I'll get my tack," he said, darting back into his tent.

Ishyite regarded Helena speculatively, without overt sexuality. The other Huns shared his curiosity. Uncomfortable with their attention, she shifted her weight imperceptibly from side to side. Yet, she understood their interest: she was a novelty as the woman Valamir had married.

Unlike Attila, they were easy to ignore. In contrast, their leader wore at her defenses, reminding her of a wolf circling another's prey.

Valamir returned, carrying Hassan's saddle and bridle over his left arm. Without a word, he had the roan ready in moments. With a quick jerk of his head, he gestured to Helena to join him. Once mounted, she was careful not to put any pressure on his wound. She leaned slightly forward and balanced herself by gripping Hassan's mane with her left hand. Her right hand throbbed with renewed intensity. With half of their escort in front, setting a quick pace at a gallop, the rest pressed from the rear. The rows of tents flew by and the people's faces were a blur.

Too quickly for Helena, they reached Attila's quarters. As they arrived, the guards at the perimeter of the tent sprang to something resembling attention: those who stood, straightened their backs, the others on horseback took care that their mounts stood with their heads up and all four hooves square on the ground.

As Ishyite passed, the men bowed their heads.

Again thinking of his bandages, Helena dismounted first, forestalling Valamir's help. Instantly, he was beside her, his hand at the small of her back. The red-haired Gaul emerged from behind the large tent, ready for Hassan. With a curt nod, Valamir acknowledged him. The roan stallion swished his tail, then allowed the slave to lead him on a loose rein. With a small, wry smile, Helena contrasted Hassan's recent performance with the Hun.

Before Ishyite could announce them, Valamir led the way into the tent. Attila looked up from his study of maps, feigning surprise. But Helena was not deceived by his performance: he must have heard their horses' hoof beats. The treasure of the recent campaign was behind him: much of it had been her grandfather's. Valamir, silent, glowered at his leader.

Attila ignored his rudeness. "You've come. Good. Share food with me. We've much to discuss."

Valamir remained by the open doorway, his tacit insolence making Helena uneasy. Worried what Attila might do, she edged closer, as if to shield Valamir.

Attila's face was quizzical, but without humor. "What ails you, friend?"

"This is a meeting between men. The other war leaders leave their women in their tents. Why do you call for my wife?" Valamir asked, his voice calm, without fear.

"I need her."

"Her hand is useless. She can't write."

"That is a loss, but my interest reaches beyond her abilities as a scribe."

"What are saying, Attila?"

The Hun began to pace the tent, his hands clasped behind his back. "She's civilization. She observes, she thinks, she forms an opinion, and through her, I learn more of the Empire and its vulnerability. Valamir, the underbelly of the world is soft and ripe for our taking. In time, everyone will understand the lessons I shall exact!"

His words sent chills down her spine. She was afraid, not so much for herself, but for humanity. His appetite for power was unquenchable, inspired from revenge first, then ambition.

Valamir shrugged his shoulders, unperturbed. He guided Helena to a place near the fire. "We are happy to break bread with you."

Attila sat across from them and leaned closer. His glittering eyes fixed on Helena. His face was flushed. He tore into his meat with large, strong teeth like a wolf devouring its kill. "Are you pleased with my plan?" he asked.

Taking a moment to collect her thoughts, Helena studied the food. Attila's meal was different: his meat was almost raw, his drink was a thin milk, perhaps from a mare. "I don't know what you want, Attila," she replied. "Will you be another Alexander, spreading the best of Greece? Or will you bring ruin?"

He smiled with pleasure at the challenge in her questions. "I shall be the Scourge of God!"

"Why?"

"The world needs cleansing. Men are soft and decadent, seeking only pleasure. They have become women."

"What of Alaric? He was strong." Helena asked, thinking of the Visigoth King who had been intertwined with the Empire. He had aspired for high Roman command, then later advanced against Constantinople itself.

"The Visigoths will be worthy allies, coming to join their brothers in the fullness of time. No, it's Rome, succulent, rotting Rome, that calls for my special liberation."

Something within her whispered, "Kill him, kill him now. He's mine." She thought of her grandfather's rune, its image superimposed on Attila's face. Her fingers itched to draw the inscription. Her grandfather's final legacy, a darkness that she would not understand and would not believe in, rose within her, wanting Attila and his evil.

She resisted, watching the flames in the hearth become the Light. "And what of your Uncle Rugliva? Isn't he the King?" she asked in an unnaturally harsh voice.

Valamir interrupted, "No more questions!"

"Why?" Attila asked. "Don't you trust my pledge to her?"

"She doesn't understand about you and Rugliva. She should learn to control her tongue."

Helena clenched her teeth, hating Valamir for criticizing her in front of Attila, as if she were not there. Belatedly remembering Valamir's advice, she kept silent.

Beyond her anger, she was disappointed. In contrast to her grandfather's mind, Valamir's intellect had its limits, born of native caution and the soldier's instinct for survival. Her grandfather, a brilliant scholar, had encouraged her to explore and stretch the boundaries of her universe, even questioning its very reality. Sometimes Attila reminded her of Balusistriam, not in appearance, but in his passion for knowledge.

Though she had worshipped her grandfather, she had come to realize that his personality had ingrained flaws. He was a xenophobe, valuing only the Persian culture and loathing her Thracian descent. Still, he had loved her, transcending his prejudices, and had been a wise, even magical, guardian. Yet, at his end, he had unleashed a malevolence, dark with power, in a misguided attempt to protect her.

Her thoughts collapsed into bitterness as she judged herself and accepted her share of blame for Mikael's death. If she had trusted Valamir, he would have safeguarded her son. Instead, she had gambled and lost everything.

Mikael's image danced before her. Tears stung her eyes. She faced the unthinkable: her thirst for revenge was no different than Attila's, except in scale. Her blood called for Greillia's death. Attila's craving was the annihilation of the Empire.

She met the Hun's intrusive eyes.

"Tell me what clouds your face," he said.

"My thoughts are my own."

He laughed with raw pleasure, holding nothing back. "You see, Valamir? Your wife trusts my word!"

Helena realized his words were exact. With acrid poignancy, she wanted to turn the days back, to return to

Kansbar's house, and to rely on Valamir when it mattered: when he could have saved Mikael.

Attila had not finished. "As a favor, Helena, share your thoughts with me."

She studied him with clarity and a dispassionate composure, considering whether to speak. Her words came slowly, each a reflection of her soul. "I've no right to judge you. In my own way, I'm as much a monster as you. And like you, vengeance feeds me and keeps me alive. If I could cut out Greillia's heart, I would. But for Valamir's sake, I stay my hand. Attila, you want your price from the Romans. And why? Because they hurt you. They took something precious from you."

Valamir tugged at her arm, trying to stop the flow of words. But Attila held up his hand.

"Tell me what you think they stole."

"I don't know, Attila, but it must have been important, otherwise you wouldn't hate them with such passion."

"Think," he said. "Perhaps it will come to you."

Her words remained reflective. "I think they humiliated you. And you have never been humble. For your loss of dignity and for their disrespect, you cannot forgive them. I think that it would be better for you, and me as well, if we could both find our peace. But I, for one, am not ready to set aside my revenge. It defines me, and for now, gives me strength."

Attila's smile was warm. "You are a seer, Helena, though you know it not. You can teach me."

Acutely aware of Valamir at her side, Attila's presence filled her being, forcing all else into the background. Though she was physically repelled by the Hun, his intellect sparked her mind, crystallizing her perceptions and expanding thought. With Valamir, her heart felt alive, on the threshold of love. Like her grandfather, Attila prodded her thinking into fresh, sometimes uncomfortable, directions.

"I'm no seer, Attila," she said, denying the quiet, inner voice that had been with her for as long as she could remember - so different from the alien, reptilian feelings that followed the dark rune. When she moved in harmony with the calm sense of knowing, life flowed easily, at one with the fields and the sky. But it remained hard for her to listen and to have faith in her heart.

Anguish coiled within her, like a snake writhing with its head severed, as she realized her inner guidance had not urged flight with Mikael. Instead, fear had been her master. Guilt overwhelmed her. She prayed with her eyes open. The inside of the tent came into sharper focus: her breathing was quiet and deep. She heard a subtle resonance, like many voices, humming. Her perceptions made no sense to her, but they were liberating and helped to calm her turmoil.

His attention directed to Valamir, Attila discussed his plans for the return to the Danube and Rugliva's kingdom. In his voice, Helena heard longing to be home and also metallic harshness when he mentioned his uncle by name. His tone became crisp, void of emotion, as the conversation shifted to the division of the spoils.

Helena tried not to listen, hating the impending desecration of her grandfather's possessions. Her flash of peace dissipated and she felt its loss with an ache in her throat. But her heart opened, silent testimony to the strength of spirit; no one could sever her connection to God. Uplifted by this belief, she set aside her qualms and paid heed to the men's conversation.

Attila glanced at her, his eyes seeking a breach in her defenses. But he soon became engrossed in analyzing the merits of each war party and left her alone. He paced the room again with deliberate strides, using the motion of his body to clarify his thinking.

Finally, he stopped before Valamir. "You have asked for too little: a mare, an old stallion, a plain gold ring, a rather fine sword, and an excellent prayer rug. These are nothing compared to the quality of your find."

Helena frowned, annoyed at Attila's description of Passial, who was her only living connection to her grandfather. She loved the horse as a dear friend, not as an animal. After Mikael's loss, her bond with the white stallion was intensified by desperation. With effort, she kept a fiery retort to herself.

"I am pleased to bring you wealth," Valamir said with evident sincerity.

Helena was proud of Valamir's lack of greed. Almost daily, Kansbar had fondled her grandfather's gold, crooning to the precious stones.

Attila studied Valamir with detachment, then shook his head. "Why don't you want more? I don't understand you, Valamir! Wealth is power. If I don't give you a fair share, the men will be unhappy, thinking I cheated you. Morale will suffer and they won't search so effectively for me next time. Then I'll be the loser."

Valamir frowned. "Give me what you wish. Just so long as it's light and easy to pack."

Helena smiled, finding Valamir's practicality both endearing and funny. He turned to her, his blue eyes questioning. "Do you want anything else?" he asked.

Feeling the strength of their connection anew, Helena wondered why it was so easy to become lost in his eyes. Her heart beat quickly and she had an urge to touch his cheek. But she kept her hand at her side. Attila stopped pacing. Helena could feel his stare.

As she pulled her gaze from Valamir's, exhilaration surged through her veins. Attila did not bother to mask himself: his expression was avid and fascinated as he studied a rare creature.

"May I show Valamir the better stones?" Helena asked.

"As you wish."

From a small pile of jewels displayed on a plain, woolen cloth, she picked up a diamond. It was not overly large, but she remembered that her grandfather had been impressed with its clarity. Then she chose a specific ruby and an emerald, leaving the rest to one side.

"Those three are worth more than all the rest. How did you know?" Attila asked, his voice barbed.

"My grandfather. Each gem was to be given to a relative. These were for his brothers."

"Your family in Persia is large."

"Perhaps. They are strangers to me."

"Valamir, pick one of the three."

Helena's rebuttal was sudden. "Why shouldn't he have two?" She did not care about the gems, but felt an obligation to negotiate the best trade for Valamir. Despite his lack of interest, she considered it a point of honor.

Attila chuckled with pleasure, enjoying the barter. "And why should I give Valamir two of three, when he has married the jewel of the collection?"

Blushing, Helena forced herself to persevere. "Without him, your men would have found nothing, burning the village instead."

The Hun shrugged. "Perhaps. But we have our ways of finding things."

Involuntarily, she shuddered. His tone, more than his words, invoked within her tortured images of people screaming, people she had lived with for the last five years.

Seizing the advantage, Attila continued, "Besides, Valamir has you. The reward offered for your safe return is worth far more than these baubles."

"He'd have to live to collect it!" Helena blurted out, cringing at the thought of him in Constantinople, being dragged away in chains, a proud lion roaring.

"What fool would take you home when ransom can easily be brought to our domain?" Attila asked, his aggressive tone changing their game of barter into something else, something dangerous. His eyes were empty, expressionless and dead. Shaken, she felt cold fear. Blinking back tears, she bit her lip, unable to hide her distress.

"Attila!" Valamir said.

The Hun breathed deeply, regaining a semblance of control. He smiled with self-deprecation. "I've frightened you, Helena. That was not my intention. As an apology, Valamir may have two of the stones."

Helena could not fathom why he cared. But her confidence in him eroded and her tongue was still.

Valamir interrupted, "No, Attila. One is more than enough. But I could use another servant. Caratipian's not well and I need help with my horses. Let me have your red-haired Gaul."

Attila was silent, then grimaced, showing his teeth in something resembling a smile. "Rhys is not to be trusted. He's useful with horses, but needs a firm hand. He's stubborn, willful, and only understands a whip. I cannot guarantee his behavior."

"I need help and he's not afraid of Hassan. If he's more trouble than he's worth, I'll give him back."

"My patience with him is finished. The next time he defies me, I'll kill him. Keep him, if you want, but watch your back. Take your pick of the stones. Though Helena's beauty needs no ornament, it should have its tribute."

Valamir smiled. "You must remember that one, old friend. Few women could resist its eloquence."

With a slight grin, Attila met Valamir's eyes. "Helena is impervious to my charm."

"As she should be! May she choose the gem?"

"Well, I don't know, Valamir. She has the talent of a horse trader."

Nonetheless, Attila pushed the three sparkling stones closer to her, his eyes lively with curiosity. Untouched by the gems' lure, Helena felt at a loss. Kansbar had handled the precious jewels so often that she felt his imprint lingering, sticky with his greed. But the smaller diamond had not interested him. Oblivious to quality, he had preferred the larger stones.

"Choose, Helena," Attila said, his eyes compounding her hesitation, making her chest tighten with desperation.

Her voice was low, almost a whisper. "The diamond," she said, not picking it up.

"You're not happy," Attila said.

"These things have only brought me pain." She thought of Kansbar's face when he had first sorted through her grandfather's possessions: his lips pursed, almost bloated, his eyes narrowed as he fingered each item with a sensual caress. He had never believed that anyone could have more wealth.

From the beginning, he was unwilling to risk his newfound riches for the promise of a greater reward.

As he placed the stones in a small pouch, Attila's expression was bland. "If you don't mind, Valamir, I'll have the Thracian goldsmith make a necklace for this diamond. Memories can change, Helena. Nothing stays the same. Remember that."

She did not know if his words were meant as a threat or as comfort. Where once she might have asked, now she remained quiet, and unobtrusively finished her meal. Though more relaxed than before, Valamir remained watchful. Ignoring the cup of mead, he drank only from his own water flask. Both relieved and grateful, Helena edged close enough to him for her shoulder to touch his arm. The contact helped her to feel safe.

Shortly afterward, Attila clapped his hands twice. An attendant entered and cleared the remains of the meal. Next, Attila shouted, "Ishyite!" The Hun lifted the tent flap, strode smoothly, and stood before his leader, waiting respectfully. Attila was curt. "Have the drummer beat the gathering."

Ishyite nodded before vanishing to the open sky. In moments, Helena heard a drum, its percussion syncopated, beating three counts, over and over. The camp erupted into commotion. Men presented themselves to Attila for orders. He pointed to the pile of goods. "Take the spoils to the ceremony."

As Attila's commands were obeyed, Valamir stood, not concealing his wish to be gone. His hand reached for Helena. She rose to her feet, stiff from sitting. The rug had offered minimal protection from the cold ground.

"Valamir," Attila said. "You will ride with me." He stood across from them, taller than Helena, but not by much. Valamir loomed over both of them. The Hun's quick glance swept them, leaving Helena chilled. Then he smiled broadly. "I'm pleased that all is well between you and your bride."

Her body became taut, sensing an attack. She could not anticipate Attila's next move: his maneuvering was too quick, too shrewd for her to counter, every conversation an exercise in tactics. Trusting her instincts, she could only keep alert. It would have to be enough.

Valamir was succinct. "We are as we seem."

Attila looked rather pointedly at Valamir's tunic, still splotched with blood. The Goth did not reply. Attila preceded them outside, holding the tent flap open for them to follow. He waited for Helena to pass, then smiled broadly at her, suddenly pleased. His mood swings confused her. She would never understand him.

Their horses pawed the ground, restive to be off. A young boy, no more than five, streaked past her, squealing with laughter as his mother gave chase and almost ran into Attila's arms. The woman's eyes grew wide as she backed away, stammering. She screamed something in Hunnic. The child stopped his game. Helena thought of Mikael and her face tightened as melancholy captured her heart again.

CHAPTER TWENTY

Under a sky tinted red by the setting sun, Attila's servants rushed to load a horse-drawn cart with spoils of the campaign. Scowling, the Hun watched as the wagon lumbered toward the ceremony grounds. As Helena and Valamir mounted, the red-haired Gaul was nowhere to be seen. She wondered at his absence, but soon forgot with the effort to remain astride. Attila set the pace at a hard gallop, shouting with excitement. With ease, Valamir's roan followed the Hun's deft maneuvering through the multitude of tents.

At the edge of camp, they entered the ceremony grounds, their horses stretched out in a pounding run. The sea of horses and men made way for them, opening, then closing behind. A deafening roar beat Helena's ears. The men chanted, "Attila! Attila!"

It was as if they worshipped him.

Attila guided them to the same spot as the previous night. He dismounted with a flourish and flung his reins to an attendant. A solitary chair waited for him, surrounded by a variety of pillaged goods. In the distance, Helena noticed the cart with her grandfather's possessions making steady progress as the driver skirted the crowd.

Several horse lengths behind Attila's chair, animals, including a few oxen, were tethered. Near the animals, Rhys was manacled with chains on his wrists and ankles. Despite the humiliation of being grouped with animals as chattel, he held his head high. She honored his pride. With a chill, she understood that, if not for Valamir, her circumstances would have been at least as ignominious.

As Valamir lifted her from Hassan, her eyes remained on Rhys.

Following her gaze, the Goth gently touched her chin, turning her face toward him. His expression was intense and his mouth compressed. "Say nothing to Attila in front of the men. Nothing. Do you understand?"

"I won't," she said.

"Good," Valamir said. He gave Hassan's neck a brief pat, then relinquished the reins to a servant. Holding her hand, he took his position at Attila's right.

The Hun stood, his hands at his waist, surveying the gathering. He waited, glaring, until the crowd's drone abated. He strode forward and addressed them in Hunnic. Cheers greeted his rousing words, measured in succinct phrases. The men did not quiet until he raised his arms, with head bowed, for silence. In crisp Gothic, he commanded the other war leaders to join him. Not for the first time, Helena was struck by the regular intermixture of the two languages, sometimes in the same sentence, evidence of the growing symbiosis of the nations.

With the exception of Bevion, last night's select group gathered around Attila. For Helena, his absence only underscored his complicity in the plot against Valamir. Not a commander, he had no right to take a seat within the inner circle. Yesterday, Attila had allowed him that privilege.

"Valamir's band has brought me wealth!" Attila said, pointing to the wagon behind him. "Behold the gold and gems! He has asked for little, giving up his share. But he must have his reward!" The men roared their approval. Valamir stood reluctantly. Attila paused, again demanding silence. When he spoke, his voice was low and rich with drama. "Valamir! From this day, you are my second in command. I honor your cunning, your patience in strategy. These are virtues worthy of a Hun!"

Cheers erupted from the men, but not just for Valamir. More than anything, they celebrated their nature: they were Huns. Not wanting to consider the consequences of Valamir's promotion, Helena retreated to cynicism, wondering if the men's reaction would be the same mindless outburst whenever the words "Attila" or "Hun" were mentioned.

Attila snapped his fingers, then pointed to Valamir. With alacrity, attendants presented the Goth with the sword and rug. A soldier, dragging Rhys, hit the back of his head, forcing him to grovel at Valamir's feet.

He flashed his sword, pointing the tip to the soldier's neck. "Be careful with my property!"

The Hun's foot was raised for another blow, but he dropped it to the ground, almost losing his balance, as he obeyed. When Helena heard Passial's whinny, her heart leapt. From horseback, another Hun led both the stallion and the mare. She hated that they had been brought here. But time began to hurry, moving too quickly for thought.

Attila reached for her hand, pulling her up. As he looked at her, his eyes were smoldering. Her lungs felt on fire, parched with fear.

"This woman is Valamir's!" he said, joining her hand with the Goth's. "The Shaman has bound them!" Again, he paused, waiting for the clamor to cease. "I bestow upon him one gem, a ring, and many gold coins." With the exception of the ring, already strung on a necklace around Helena's neck, Attila held up the diamond and each gold coin before placing them, one by one, in Valamir's hands.

Then his voice was low, the communication private: "Enjoy the fruits of your labors, Valamir."

Finished, Attila raised his arms, palms outward. As the men clapped rhythmically, their approval edged toward pandemonium. Leaving Helena and Valamir behind, he stepped closer to the crowd, his hands at his waist, and spoke again in Hunnic. Her hands in his, Valamir guided Helena to a rug on the ground.

As evening ebbed into night, torches were lit. For Helena, the ceremony was endless. She watched as each man came forward, eager for his prize, until her eyes glazed with fatigue. She wondered how Attila kept from becoming hoarse.

Behind her, Passial nickered, restless to be away from this noisy place. Worried that he was being mishandled, she turned to him, but the Hun was gone, leaving his charges to their own devices, though safely hobbled. Then her eyes found Rhys. He was still on his knees, but he had raised his head. His red beard did nothing to hide the fatigue in his face. Yet, as his eyes flashed with hostility, she understood him. Hate sustained him, delivering him from shame. She hoped that Valamir had not made a deadly error in judgment, that the Gaul would not murder them one night while they slept.

With bitter irony, Helena understood that, in Attila's mind, her difference from Rhys was only a matter of degree. Both of them had been labeled and designated as property. Helena wanted to tell Rhys that no one could subdue his spirit, no one could truly own him. But she had no words to express what was etched in her heart. Eyes fixed on the ground, he retreated once more into himself.

She hoped that he already knew.

Time passed. Helena did not pay much attention to the distribution of spoils, the most valuable portion being her grandfather's possessions. Many Huns received a gold or silver coin, or some an inferior jewel.

The back of her neck prickled, and she looked up to see Greillia. He stood before Attila, staring at her. By his side, Magga was bound at the wrists with a heavy cord, the end held loosely in his large hands. Helena's blood rushed to her legs, urging flight. To avoid seeing him, she dropped her eyes and noticed her grandfather's prayer rug, partly open. The torchlight glistened on the silken pattern, highlighting the blood rune, hidden in plain view by being intermixed with another pattern.

Without realizing it, she reached for her knife, snared by an acute craving to seal the curse against Greillia with blood. But a hand closed over hers. With desperate rage, she turned to see Valamir's implacable eyes staring at her, seeing the darkness that had become her soul. She shrank from his judgment. As if it were hot, she released her knife. Valamir kept hold of her hand, putting it safely in his lap.

Greillia bowed to Attila. "Cousin, tell me how I have shamed you. Tell me of my dishonor." He pointed to Valamir. "Else why would you put this *Goth* above your own *clan!*"

Attila's gaze swept him mercilessly. In his hard eyes, Helena saw Greillia's death. The crowd was hushed, expectant.

Incapable of a modicum of self-control, Greillia stepped closer to Valamir, but well beyond a sword's length. "He cheated me! He stole from me!"

The tribe remained silent, waiting for Attila's lead.

Into the void, Attila spoke, his voice barely above a whisper, but projected so that all could hear. "Who saw the woman first?"

Greillia hesitated. "Valamir, but I found her after she ran."

Attila turned to those who had followed Valamir and were grouped together for the ceremony. "Men! My cousin gnaws at my patience! Give me your counsel. Was Valamir's claim to his woman clear?"

Speaking for the band, Ishyite stood. "Only a blind man or someone truly stupid would not have known!"

The men laughed, not caring if Attila saw their antipathy. Greillia's persistent complaints and grievances had not made him popular. They had tolerated and suffered him for Attila's sake.

"Why do you trouble me with this nonsense?" Attila said, his voice moderate, escalating with each word like a martial song drawing to a finale. "Have you lost all respect for our traditions, for our laws, and most of all, for me that you come before the tribe whining like a spoiled child? Weren't you once my cousin? I do not know you. You are a stranger, though still of my tribe. Perhaps the day will come when you deserve the honor of belonging to my family, but that remains to be seen."

Greillia threw himself to the ground, groveling at Attila's feet. "Forgive me, Lord Attila. My selfishness blinded me. But see? I brought you my woman. I give her to you, as is your right, unlike Valamir, who denies you!"

Attila ran his appraising eye over Magga, who had been made more presentable. She wore a different dress, though not new, it was in one piece, not ripped to shreds. Her face, still bruised, was less swollen and clean. Even her hair had been combed.

But her beauty was a shadow of its former glory.

Attila's nose twitched, almost disdainfully, but then he looked at her again. "You insult Valamir. His wife is not a whore to be passed from man to man. Perhaps you cannot understand that. Most would. But I'll accept this woman for one night. Then we'll see if I know you again."

Greillia, his forehead on the ground, reached for Attila's felt boots. "You honor me."

Stepping back a pace, Attila avoided his touch, unsheathing his sword. "Rise and accept my gift to you."

Greillia sat back on his heels, immobile as the point of the sword hovered in front of his right eye. "Ishyite told us that even a blind man could have seen Valamir's claim to the woman," Attila said. "Perhaps you'll see better without one of your eyes."

Not blinking, Greillia became a statue, betraying no weakness and no fear.

Attila grunted with approval. "At least your courage is worthy of a Hun. In this, you are one with the tribe. But you've offended my honor. Only a gift, a gift of your blood, will appease it." His eyes narrowed and his voice became flat, without inflection. "Will you make me an offering?"

Greillia nodded once. The sword remained poised before his eye, then floated down to his cheek, piercing flesh until it met bone. Attila's smile glittered. No sound issued from Greillia's throat, even as his cousin, his leader, wrenched the sword away with a downward thrust, ripping open his cheek.

Blood flowed from the wound, wetting Greillia's tunic. Helena stared, forgetting everything but the blood, running in thin rivulets down his cheek. Even Attila was lost to the shadows and the darkness that was her mind. A voice hummed in her head, whispering like the wind on a starless night, "Do it. Do it now." As if it had its own will, her hand withdrew from Valamir's loosened grasp and quickly inscribed in the air her grandfather's rune, summoning the ancient force.

Closing her eyes, she surrendered to the ecstasy, not caring that it was pernicious and deadly to her soul. It filled her, lending her strength. Yet, part of her, crushed into silence, was crying.

Her voice was like dry leaves, swept across stone by the wind; her words were archaic Persian. "Greillia, may the earth drink your blood, may she eat your bones, quenching her appetite on your bloated carcass. May your death be slow, lingering. I'll rejoice on the day that your shadow no longer walks beside you. Because then all women, all mothers will have reason to smile. I give you to the darkness, to do with as it pleases."

Once more, she resonated with power, as if her body had grown in stature, able to dominate. But the exhilaration soon faded into exhaustion, leaving her cold and shaken. Still the dark presence persisted, though outside of her body. She remembered that she should be afraid of it, that it was profane, but she ignored the danger. She had the right to a just revenge.

An inner voice, coming from her heart, thrust through her rationalizations as a clear tone, tolling, "This is evil, an abomination: forcing nature, bending her to its malevolent will." The words seared her conscience, scorching her belief that she was a decent, good person.

Not for the first time, she wondered at these voices, afraid that she had taken the first steps down the path to the wizened, crazy crone, to that horrible vision of what could be.

She pictured the rune that Caratipian had shown her, understanding that she should use it. He had worried that it lacked strength to negate the darkness. But Grandfather had taught it to her, describing it as potent through its simplicity. Oddly reluctant, she focused on her heart, feeling it expand with light. Slowly, she put her finger to the earth and forced it to inscribe the counter sign. Instantly, the malevolence was gone. She shook her head, resisting the temptation to lie on the ground and sleep and denying exhaustion by rubbing her eyes.

Not trusting her self-control, she turned to Valamir to keep her eyes from Greillia. The man who had become her husband watched her, his expression apprehensive, as if he held his breath and waited. Trying to smile reassuredly, Helena almost began to cry. His methods of retribution were honorable, but he had the luxury of being a man, a soldier who could kill.

She averted her face, only to be ensnared by Attila's compelling stare. He had seen everything. His interest was avid and voracious. His probing eyes were spellbinding, and Helena shuddered, reminded of the presence that followed her inscription of the dark rune. His thirst for knowledge was palpable and devouring. She could not move or even blink. Panicking, Helena thought of her grandfather's rune, knowing it would help.

But she felt a shift within her heart. Suddenly, she smiled and called on the Wise Lord to help her, his misguided servant, and knew she would not have to pay with her soul. Suddenly, Attila's eyes became as any other man's.

Her smile broadened at his look of consternation. She felt proud, even vindicated by her trust in God's Light. Attila raised an eyebrow, then nodded his head once, as if to acknowledge her brief victory.

Greillia lingered, still at Attila's feet, the blood flowing more slowly down his cheek. Standing to the side, Magga kept desperate eyes fixed on Attila, as if he were her only hope.

Despite herself, Helena began to worry. What if Magga wormed her way into his confidence? The whispered words about poison floated through her mind, but she tried to put them aside, telling herself that the wives had been unable to prove Magga's guilt. She thought of Illyas, Kansbar's last wife, writhing on the ground, clutching her stomach, her pale eyes fixed on Magga. Helena knew what she had to do.

Yet, she resisted. She had no allegiance to Attila. He was not her friend, but the enemy of the civilized world. She owed him nothing. Magga would have no need to poison him: she would covet his power, wanting to feed on it. But deep within, Helena understood that Magga's arrogance was perverse and twisted, allowing her to justify her actions, even if ruin followed in its wake. She remembered Ivan and Magga whispering on the ground, Ludmilla shaking her head in emphatic disagreement, and the knife in Ivan's hand. Magga would do anything to survive: even betraying those who loved her without thinking twice. In the end, she had cast her lot with Greillia, forsaking both Ivan and Kansbar.

Helena felt prompted to tell Attila about the rumors. Still, she hesitated, trying to believe it was for Valamir's sake. After all, if Attila died, Greillia would contest the band's leadership through blood. The taste in her mouth became bitter as she admitted her worry had nothing to do with Valamir. It was personal. Attila was dangerous and ruthless, but vibrant and so alive. His intellect, a constant challenge to her will, continued to captivate her mind.

If he died, she would miss him.

As Attila pointed to Greillia, his stance was regal. "Has this stranger satisfied my honor?" he asked the tribe. "Or does he owe me more?"

The crowd's answer was mixed. Though they shouted in Hunnic, the language was no barrier to Helena's understanding. Some touched their knives to their throats, graphically delineating their opinions; others turned their thumbs up, imitating the Romans. Magga edged closer to Attila, distancing herself from Greillia. Her head was bowed, but her cheeks were flushed with excitement. Her tongue flicked across her lips, as if tasting Greillia's blood.

"Valamir," Helena whispered.

"Ssh, later."

"I've something important to tell Attila."

"Can it wait until after the ceremony?" he asked, his concern for his leader superseding protocol.

"Yes, but he must know before tonight."

Valamir nodded. "I'll see to it."

He wrapped his arm around her, providing a shelter from exhaustion. With a contemptuous wave of his hand, Attila dismissed Greillia and signaled for Magga to be taken away. The proceedings wore on. Helena's eyes grew heavy and she fell into darkness, not waking until the ceremony drew to its end.

Valamir nudged her. "It's over!"

She opened her eyes, confused, and did not immediately recognize her whereabouts. Memory returned with torment. Torn by indecision, Helena grappled with her quandary. If Magga pleased Attila, why should she resort to poison? After all, hadn't all of the wives heard her weave her magic with Kansbar, night after night? Helena deliberated and wondered if her motives arose from dislike of Magga rather than sincere concern for Attila's well-being. As Kansbar's favorite, she had harassed the other women and taunted them with her elevated position. Forcing herself to be honest, Helena acknowledged that the sight of Magga humbled and helpless had its appeal.

Attila spoke his closing words. The answering roar was deafening. Helena clenched her teeth and endured the sound. She forced her hands to stay at her sides, not allowing them to shield her ears. The crowd started to disperse. Easily half of the spoils remained with Attila. Magga was already gone. Detached, Helena watched as his attendants carefully placed them in the waiting wagon. A slave brought the Attila's black stallion; another led Hassan.

Attila motioned for Valamir and Helena to approach. "The men were pleased." He seemed restless and ready to go. "Until tomorrow morning."

"Attila," Valamir said. "Helena wishes to tell you something."

The Hun turned to her. "Can it wait?"

She shook her head, uncertain of what to do. She tried to hear her inner voice, but it was silent.

"Helena, talk to me." Attila's voice was brusque, but not unkind. In it, she heard affection.

Her heart beating fast, she met his eyes. "It's for Valamir and you alone."

Attila shouted to the accumulation of soldiers and servants who surrounded them. "Be gone!" Obedience was instant: at a discreet distance, all waited to finish the tasks left undone.

"Now, Helena. Step closer and tell me in Greek, but softly."

Keeping her hand in Valamir's, she approached the Hun. Attila looked pointedly at their intertwined fingers and smiled, shaking his head. "Always thinking, aren't you?"

"It keeps me alive," she said.

He laughed. "First, I must know something. Has this to do with Greillia?"

"No."

"Tell me what you said to him tonight. The language was strange, but it reminded me of Persian. What did you say? You drew a symbol with your hand. Explain it," Attila said.

"I can't, not now," she said, feeling ashamed and not wanting to expose her darkness.

He narrowed his eyes. "You will tell me, but I'll wait until tomorrow. Now, give me the information you wish to share."

Her doubts set aside, she faced him. "It's about the woman, Magga."

"Greillia's new whore?" Attila laughed incredulously. "What can she matter?"

Concisely, Helena described Magga's position in the village, the mystery of her background, and her character. Attila nodded impatiently, not impressed. Helena paused, gathering the will to continue. Feeling guilty, she believed her next words would destroy Magga's chances and hated for any woman to be at Greillia's mercy.

Valamir interrupted. "The bitch betrayed the old chief with his own son. Their relationship was old and ripe with contempt for many months. She even tried to attach herself to me. When all else failed, she flung herself at Greillia. She's not to be trusted."

Attila shrugged. "Is this all?"

"No," Helena said. "There's something else. All the women suspected that Magga was a poisoner. We watched her rival die painfully, her stomach cramped, but none of us dared speak against her. I've no proof, but you should know that I never let her near my son's food, nor mine."

"Why warn me, Helena? You could have let me take my chances," Attila said.

Helena felt miserable. "I don't know. Maybe we were wrong, maybe Illyas just died of natural causes."

"Did anyone else fall sick that night?"

"No."

His eyes were magnetic, his face close to hers. "You didn't want to denounce Greillia's woman. That much I could tell. Why did you speak?"

She looked down: trying to escape and wanting to hide the tears wetting her lashes. "I don't want you to die," she whispered.

"But you don't approve of my ambitions."

"Valamir needs you."

Attila chuckled, but shook his head. "You've another reason. Don't the Christians believe that truth is good for the soul? Tell me."

She faced him, her eyes dark with anger. "Maybe I'd miss arguing with you!"

He grinned. "You undervalue yourself. You are loyal, Helena, a true friend. And I thank you."

"We never proved Magga's guilt," she said, still feeling troubled and wanting to be fair.

"Don't worry. I'll not harm her, at least not tonight. But I'll enlighten her about what we do with poisoners. And then she'll teach me her secrets."

"You'd work with poison?"

His eyes were blank; his face was a mask. "No, it's a woman's weapon."

As he turned away from them, she sensed his lie. With troubled eyes, she watched him mount and ride off. Despite his words of friendship, she silently vowed to keep Valamir's food safe from his hands. Worried, she touched Valamir's arm. "Did I do right? I wanted her to kill Greillia, but now Attila will warn him."

"I'm proud of you! You protected a friend! Attila is connected to me; our destinies are intertwined. If he died, it would be my loss."

Her stomach turned. In choosing Attila's well-being over Magga's, she had become an ally of the heir apparent to the most hated barbarians in the Empire.

"What's wrong?" Valamir asked. "Are you sick?"

She shook her head. "I care for you, but you ride with Huns."

"I am who I am, Helena. But you have my heart."

She was silent. "I've never known anyone like you. You came into my life, changing everything, and I'm afraid. Yet, when I'm with you, I feel alive."

They were not alone. Attila's attendants finished packing his share of the plunder in the waiting cart. Others cleared the debris from the ceremony. Valamir's breath caressed her ear, arousing her body with unexpected sensations. "Some day, with your consent, I *will* marry you with my body and not just my heart."

He cupped her face in his strong hands, his eyes passionate, and she blushed. He smiled, amused by her reaction. "I treasure that you're shy, at least about this." He released her, but his hand retained a light pressure on her back.

Then he noticed Rhys, still in chains, waiting next to the rug, the sword and the two horses. Valamir frowned and tightened his hold on Helena, as if to protect her. Rhys ignored her, locking eyes with Valamir, as if daring him.

"Attila has warned me against you, Rhys," Valamir said, speaking in Gothic. "He tells me that you're trouble, that you'd be better off dead. But his needs are different than mine. He requires the souls of his slaves and unquestioning obedience. I need someone to help me with my horses. Are you interested?"

Rhys's face was shuttered, his nod grudging.

"How well do you speak our language?"

"Enough to be useful," Rhys said, his accent inflecting his words up, then down, as in a musical phrase.

"Good." As one of Attila's house servants passed, Valamir grabbed him by the shoulders. "I need a smith, now! Bring me one with the tools to remove my slave's chains."

The man bowed. "Prince Valamir, that one's a runner, even with a cut tendon. You must reconsider unchaining him. He only understands the whip. Then he's obedient, at least for a while."

Valamir's expression was terrible; his voice was a roar. "Are you deaf? I asked for a smith, not your opinion! Go!"

Without an argument, the servant ran. Scowling, Valamir pointed to the Hun who had brought Passial and Sarelle. "You! Take those horses back where you found them!"

The man followed orders without a word. Valamir grunted with approval. "At least a soldier knows enough to obey, unlike certain servants who think that they know what's best for everyone."

"Why are you so angry at Attila's man?" Helena asked.

"Because he dares to disagree with me!"

"But Caratipian does all the time."

"*He* has wisdom. That one," he said, inclining his head toward the servant running toward the interior of the camp, "is no more than a petty fool. Always complaining!"

Rhys snorted with laughter, but immediately suppressed it.

Helena and Valamir quickly turned to look, but the man's face had again become as blank as stone. Valamir pursed his lips and studied the Gaul. "Rhys, would you like to be your own man?"

Keeping his features rigid, Rhys tried not to betray his interest, but his eyes blazed.

"Well?" Valamir asked, not continuing without an answer.

"May I speak the truth?"

"I wait for it," Valamir said.

"The gods willing, I would be my own master once again."

"Then listen. I don't keep slaves. They are a nuisance. But a good servant, that's another matter. Do well by my horses, make yourself useful to Caratipian, guard my wife on the journey home, and I'll set you free. I'll have a scribe give you papers and money for your trip to Gaul as your wages."

Helena's throat felt tight, her eyes hot with emotion at Valamir's generosity. When she was six, her grandfather had given Miriam, the nursemaid, her freedom. The woman's middle-aged face, usually pinched with worry, had been transformed with joy, obliterating years.

Rhys bowed from the waist to Valamir. "You'll never find a better servant. When I heard that you had asked for me, my heart was glad. All of the slaves know you are just. But I've no one left in Gaul. My village is dust - razed by the Romans."

Helena's heart constricted.

"Once we've crossed the Danube and reached home," Valamir said. "You can decide. Stay with me if you like. I'll pay you for your time."

Rhys radiated happiness: his posture was erect and proud without defiance. "You are truly noble. I thank you."

Valamir nodded, almost curtly. "Then we understand each other."

"Yes, Greillia will never come near your wife, so long as I have breath in my body!"

"What do you know of this?" Valamir asked, his voice instantly vehement and suspicious.

"Only what my eyes and ears tell me."

"Then you have done well. Look," he said, pointing to the smith, hurrying toward them with two horses: one for himself, the other for his equipment. "We'll get this iron off you."

"You've work for me, Prince Valamir?" the Hun asked, bringing his horses to an abrupt halt.

"Yes," Valamir said, pulling out a silver coin and holding it before the smith's eyes. "Do you see this?"

He nodded, his face alight.

"It's yours if you take off these manacles without causing my slave pain. Hurt him, and you get nothing. Do you agree?"

The smith did not hesitate. "I can do it."

He turned to his job. First, he carefully wrapped cloths between Rhys's skin and the metal bands. As the smith worked, Valamir watched intently. When the last manacle dropped to the ground with a thud, the Hun's face was wet with perspiration.

"You did well, smith," Valamir said. "As a reward, you'll have not one, but two, of these coins."

The Hun examined the money in his hand, then looked at Valamir with child-like delight. "I'm at your service, Prince. Ask for me again, and I'll come like the wind!"

Valamir, laughing, waved him away. He turned to Rhys. "You'll have to walk."

With deft motions, Valamir strapped the Persian sword to his side, then placed the prayer rug in Rhys's arms. As they returned to the tents, Valamir kept Hassan's pace slow, much to the animal's chagrin.

CHAPTER TWENTY-ONE

Caratipian waited outside his tent. As he watched Rhys hobbling behind Hassan, he did not bother to hide his hostility. When Valamir leapt down to greet him, the old servant scowled in silence. The Goth turned from the implacable stare and became suddenly engrossed with helping Helena dismount. No longer able to postpone the inevitable, he faced Caratipian.

Veins stood out on either side of the old Persian's neck. "Who's that?" he shouted, finally speaking, pointing at the red-haired man.

"Rhys. He was one of Attila's slaves."

Caratipian folded his arms across his chest. His upper lip twitched. "I don't need help!" Abruptly, he stalked inside his quarters.

Valamir stared after him. "See to my horse. His halter is hanging by my tent," he said to Rhys, handing him Hassan's reins. He gestured toward the other horses. "Leave him with the white stallion and the mare. Then come back and wait."

As Rhys untacked the roan, Valamir observed with a critical eye. Though pleased that one of Attila's servants had returned Passial and Sarelle, Helena stepped closer to examine them for any sign of injury.

"You'd better come with me, Helena," Valamir said, interrupting her. "This may be more delicate than I'd imagined."

She nodded and gave Passial a quick pat on his neck. But her heart was light. Caratipian's act had not fooled her. He just hated to admit he was no longer able to do everything.

Uninvited, they followed Caratipian into his tent. He was grumbling to himself as he stirred food in a pot over a fire. "Rhys, indeed!"

With a graceful hand motion, Valamir signaled Helena to sit beside him. She ignored his suggestion and knelt behind Caratipian, rubbing his back and shoulders with her one good hand. "Rhys has a way with horses, but needs direction. Should you accept him, he'd be fortunate. If Valamir sends him back,

Attila will surely kill him. Apparently, he's not easily cowed, even after repeated beatings," she murmured.

"You're very clever," he said, softening against her touch. "Giving me his particulars so I have to accept him out of guilt."

Helena winked at Valamir. "No more than you're a stubborn, old man!"

Caratipian sighed with contentment as her fingers rubbed the back of his skull. "I capitulate, Helena. I'll see what I can do with this man, Rhys. But I make no promises. If he won't listen to me, I don't care what Attila does to him!"

When she pressed her thumb where his neck met his skull, he exhaled deeply. She stood, absentmindedly touching her fingertips together, careful not to exert too much pressure on her injured hand.

"Tell me about this Rhys," Caratipian said. "I imagine that Attila sent him here with nothing but the clothes on his back."

"Clothes? Rags would be more apt!" Valamir said, laughing. Then he shared with his oldest confidant what he knew about the Gaul, including his offer of freedom.

"You're too easy," Caratipian said.

"No, he's been a soldier. He deserves respect."

"Well, at least I won't have to worry about having my throat slit when I sleep."

"Exactly. Come outside and I'll introduce you properly."

Caratipian followed Helena and Valamir, complaining to himself about having to break in servants who only knew how to kill. But when he saw Hassan already at grass, content with the other horses, he relented. "Oh, very well. He'll do."

"Good," Valamir said. Rhys squatted by Valamir's tent, waiting and staring at the stars. Quickly responding to Valamir's wave, he bowed as the Goth introduced him to Caratipian. The chore complete, Valamir turned away from them, hiding his smile. "Good night! Sleep well!"

Once inside their tent, Helena and Valamir laughed like mischievous children, afraid of being overheard by their elders. "You should have seen Caratipian's face when he realized you were leaving him alone with Rhys!" Helena said.

"He'll be fine. He just hates change. He'll complain for awhile. Later, he'll insist that Rhys was his idea!"

Valamir pulled her to him, his eyes bright. A smile hovered on his lips. He stroked her hair. "I knew you the moment I set my eyes on you. I don't understand what's happened, but it doesn't matter. I'm just glad that you're here, with me."

"I wish I'd trusted you. Then I'd have everything," she said, thinking of Mikael. "My mind doubted what my heart already knew."

"Don't look back. You don't have the past. You can only mark the present."

She lingered in his arms, absorbing the tangy smell of his leather clothing and enjoyed the sensations coursing through her body. Both shocked and stimulated by her desire, she showed none of it. The sexual act still frightened her in a way that transcended words.

His eyes devoured her. "We must sleep. Tomorrow will be hard."

As they lay together, he did not touch her. She wanted to be closer, but was paralyzed by chaotic fears. Yet, she could not imagine being anywhere else.

The morning was bright, but cold. For once, Helena was awake before Valamir. As she looked outside, the camp was asleep: hardly anyone was stirring. She moved about the tent quietly, not wanting to disturb him. Shivering, she put on her coat and sat by the fire, feeding its dying flames with two slender sticks. With her hands inside her coat, she stared at the embers spurting upward as the kindling ignited.

Yet, the image of Valamir's face during the assault persisted in her mind. He had been a stranger, almost indifferent, and cold in pursuit of his need. She forced the memory forward to the next morning, when he had mutilated his chest with a rune.

His barbarism repelled her. But with painful honesty, she considered how the darkness compelled her and wondered who was more civilized. Mikael's face floated in her mind. She turned from grief by readying for the day's journey.

Finished with her packing, she sat beside the small blaze. Valamir stirred, but did not awaken. Restless, Helena pulled out her dagger, examining Caratipian's expert restoration. Running her fingers over the smooth ivory handle, she wondered where Valamir had put her grandfather's sword. Her brow furrowed, she scanned the tent, to no avail. Disappointed, she realized he must have left it with Caratipian for repairs.

Almost as if it were a talisman, she wanted to hold it, believing it would act as a ward against the darkness. Feeling certain Caratipian would be awake, she went outside. The dawn's light edged the horizon, promising the sun. Helena listened outside the servants' tent, but heard no rustling, only an intermittent snore.

Enjoying the solitude, she walked the short distance to visit Passial. He greeted her with a deep whinny. As she combed his mane with her fingers, she talked to him about Valamir. Contact with horses, especially Passial, brought her peace.

Startled, the stallion snorted, breaking her reverie. Helena's heart pumped with alarm. Turning quickly, she saw Greillia, bearing down on his mount, less than three lengths away.

Her left hand on her knife, she shouted, "Valamir!"

With no time to mount, she ducked under Passial's neck, using him to shield her. She held her dagger low and out of sight. Greillia halted his horse with a bestial snarl. Her skin crawled. She screamed again for Valamir, but kept her eyes on Greillia, afraid to look away.

Instantly, her fear was gone. Words came unbidden from her throat, in slow, distinct Gothic. She felt implacable and remorseless. "I see before me a dead man."

The Hun laughed, but she could sense uneasiness emanating from his very pores. His distress fed her, increasing the darkness churning within her. "Your death was slow. And without honor," she said.

Greillia, his face pale, yanked his horse's mouth hard, forcing the animal back two paces. "What are you saying, bitch?"

With her knife, she sliced her bandage, the splint falling to the ground. "I've cursed you twice already. Last night, the Dark One took your blood, but now he calls for mine."

Greillia watched her, spellbound, as she slit her palm, opening it with a straight line. Her blood dripped on the earth and she let the dagger follow. It landed with a small thud. She rubbed her hands together, gently, but thoroughly, so that both palms were red. As if from a distance, she heard Valamir shouting, "Helena! No!" but she ignored the sound. It was irrelevant: a distraction.

Her hands bloodied, she drew the rune. The power filled her, making her feel beyond judgment, even time. As her eyes fixed on his face, Greillia stared aghast. She spoke in Gothic. "The earth herself joins me in my curse. She thirsts for your blood, longs for your bones. You are the last of your line. No children will follow you to your Creator. Now, go! Find your destiny!"

She heard Valamir's footsteps, running toward her. Not pausing, not releasing Greillia from her eyes, she repeated the words in ancient Persian. Finished, she heard Valamir breathing at her side.

Stricken, Greillia spoke to Valamir. "She's a sorceress! You should have warned me!"

Helena's answering smile was filled with malevolence. As Greillia urged his horse into a gallop, she stared at the blood on her hands.

"Helena, what have you done?" Valamir demanded.

She looked up into his blue eyes, bright with worry, and broke. "I don't know!" She stared at her red hands and sobbed. Valamir put his arm around her shoulders, but she pulled away. With despair, she lowered her head and felt contaminated and unclean.

He touched her chin, lifting her face to his. Shame swept her, but it was parried by the remnants of her exultation. Again she heard her inner voice. "No more, Helena. You've called on the Dark One. Each time he comes, his hold on you grows stronger."

"When I heard your cry, my heart was in my throat," Valamir said. "But you didn't need me. Never before have I seen Greillia so afraid. I felt something strange in the air, like a roaring stream, pulsating with currents. I don't understand what happened, Helena, but Caratipian can see to your hand."

She felt drained of her life force. Resolving never to release the darkness again, she squared her shoulders. But from deep within, she heard the laughter, heavy with malice, and knew in her bones that good intentions alone would never suffice. Valamir bent down to retrieve her dagger and splint. With a sigh, she drew the light rune, knowing that it would help, but wishing it could affect a total cure. He stood beside her quietly, waiting for her to speak.

"Something's very wrong with me," she said.

"What do you mean?" he asked in a gentle voice.

"When I see Greillia," she said, her words hesitant, "I feel a presence. It used to be outside of me, but now I feel it within. I say terrible things and mean them with every fiber in my body. When it's over, I feel utterly empty. It makes me afraid."

"Maybe Greillia just brings out the worst in you," Valamir said. "I know that he does in me."

She shook her head, disappointed in him.

Valamir took a deep breath, as if to try again. "I don't know about these things. But the Shaman would. His world is different, more at one with the earth and all of its forces. We could ask for help."

Feeling renewed hope, Helena nodded. Her heart lighter, she heard the soft calling of the birds as they greeted the day. "We could ask the Shaman," she repeated, as if it were a prayer.

As they returned, Valamir's arm was around her shoulders. Caratipian, outside with Rhys, walked toward them. "What happened? Did Greillia hurt her? She doesn't look well."

With bitter irony, she thought his question should have been reversed. She stared stolidly ahead.

"She re-injured her hand. Talk to her while you tend to it," Valamir said.

Despite his arthritis, Caratipian met them quickly. When he studied her hand, his eyes widened. "What have you done to yourself?"

She forced herself to look at him. "When I saw Greillia, I drew the rune."

Needing no other explanation, Caratipian only nodded. His mouth was set in a grim line. "I'll need my kit before we pack up."

"Rhys and I will take care of everything. You see to Helena," Valamir said.

Caratipian protested. "You'll never get it all into the wagon!"

Helena touched his arm. "Stay with me."

Glancing at her face, he blinked his eyes quickly. "Come sit by the wagon, so I can make sure they do it right. I'm not so old that I can't do two things at once!"

Dawn had come, sweeping the sky with glory. The camp was alive with activity. While Caratipian fussed over her hand, Valamir and Rhys tended to the tents. Helena felt numb inside, trapped by an emptiness she could not understand. Unlike the misery after Mikael's death, this feeling was pernicious. It was as if the darkness stole her soul, bit by bit, leaving her shaken and defiled.

Helena thought of her small victory over Attila when he had sought to compel her with his eyes. The Light had been potent and effective against him. But she did not trust it to protect her against physical danger. Though deeply frightened, she vacillated about asking the Shaman for help, unwilling to relinquish her only weapon against Greillia.

As Caratipian cleansed her wound, she bit her lip, not from pain, but from an acknowledgment that she was not ready to renounce the power. She had savored the spectacle of Greillia's face transformed by fear.

A taste of exultation lingered in her mouth.

In soft Persian, she described these feelings to Caratipian. He listened without interruption, and more importantly, without judgment.

Finally, he spoke. "The Shaman will help you find a better way to be strong."

She swallowed, not wanting more tears, and studied Caratipian's expert work on her hand. He had bandaged it neatly, an extra layer between her cut and the splint. Mortified by what she had done to herself, she looked at him.

Caratipian's eyes twinkled. "Valamir's injury was worse!"

Helena laughed. At the sound, Valamir looked up from his work, his face reflecting relief.

"He'd be better off with a woman of his own tribe," Helena said, not for the first time.

"Stop feeling sorry for yourself," Caratipian said. "Nothing good ever came of self-pity."

An impish grin touched the corners of her mouth. Keeping her voice neutral, she looked him in the eye. "I guess it's a good thing I didn't wound my good hand. Then I wouldn't be able to bring you to your senses with a decent back rub!"

Staring at each other, their laughter was sudden and mutual, not stopping until Valamir interrupted his work, demanding to know the joke. Yet, they had no words for an explanation.

Valamir shrugged his shoulders, but looked pleased at Helena's changed mood. "Since you're both feeling so much better, come and help." But the tents were already dismantled and the wagon was all but loaded.

"I'm impressed, Valamir. Clearly, you don't need my assistance! Besides, Helena and I are hungry for breakfast!" Caratipian said.

"By Mithras! I'll never understand why I put up with you," Valamir said, shaking his head, not hiding the affection in his eyes.

Caratipian watched him rejoin Rhys. "In some ways, he's like Bevion, hating to be left out."

Helena's defense was immediate. "He's a good man, better than most."

Caratipian chided her. "I love him, too, but that doesn't mean he has no failings. None of us walk in perfection. Now let's eat quickly, while we can."

With a wave of his arm, Caratipian gestured to Valamir and Rhys. After hurrying through the meal, the men made the final preparations for the journey.

"Do you want to ride on the mare or in the wagon?" Valamir asked Helena.

She thought for a moment. "Sarelle. I want to be with you."

His smile radiated in her heart. Nothing else mattered but the way his eyes lit up as they met hers. Reaching for him, she touched his cheek. Immediately, he cradled her in an embrace. Already, the bulk of the tribe was mounted, ready for the day's journey.

"We must ride," he said reluctantly, gently disengaging himself. "Rhys! Saddle the mare!"

The Gaul efficiently readied Sarelle. Valamir helped her up and she was astride the restive mare. When Sarelle laid back her ears in irritation at Hassan, the stallion responded with a soft neigh. Hoping her horse would not fuss all day, Helena wondered if the mare was in season and able to be bred. When Valamir attached a lead line to her bridle, Helena did not protest, accepting that Sarelle would be too much for her to handle with only one good hand.

Leaving Caratipian and Rhys with the wagon and other horses, Valamir and Helena rode toward headquarters. Attila sat astride his black stallion at the center of activity, impassively watching the smooth flow of operations. In a covered wagon, Helena could hear his women talking and laughing amongst themselves.

His greeting was brusque. "You've come. Good. Stay with me." As he inclined his head to Helena, his eyes narrowed. "You've much to tell me. We've time enough to talk, time for me to hear what you were reluctant to say last night."

She avoided the issue. "Where's Magga?" she asked, not out of curiosity, but out of concern that she had survived the night.

"Over there," he said, gesturing behind the wagon.

"Greillia won't be pleased," she said.

Magga raised her head and stared with malevolence at Helena.

"He will when he receives the payment for her services," he said, abruptly ending the discussion. "Now, Helena, tell me what you said to him last night."

Her throat tightened, but not from Attila's question. Greillia had come to fetch Magga. He yanked her to her feet by the hair. Following Helena's gaze, Attila grunted with disapproval as Greillia struck Magga to the ground.

"He's a fool," Attila muttered to Valamir. "The woman's worth money, but not after he's finished with her." He called out, "Greillia! Here!"

The Hun looked up, his face wild, and kicked Magga one last time. Trying to protect her face, she covered it with her hands, moaning. He spat on her, then swung on his horse and galloped the few strides to his cousin.

You called me by name!" he said, his face jubilant. Seeing Helena, he became rigid, as if bound by an invisible cord. He stared, unable to turn away.

Helena felt the darkness hovering, craving expression, but she controlled it, refusing the compulsion. Not wanting to risk more of herself, she averted her eyes, releasing him. With his mouth open, his breathing was shallow and fast. As if to find safety in Attila's hard stare, Greillia concentrated on his cousin.

She heard the laughter, baleful and seductive, luring her with its song. With discipline, she called on the One God to protect her from unclean presences: both spiritual and physical, she added with a quixotic flash of humor.

As if by accident, Valamir backed up his horse just enough to obstruct most of her view of the two Huns. His eyebrow raised, he smiled at her, but his nostrils were pinched.

"Yes, Greillia," Attila said. "I know you now. Here is your reward for the favor of your woman."

Helena craned her neck, wanting to see. Probably remembering the "gift" from last night, the puncture that was now an oozing sore, Greillia seemed rooted, yet waited patiently to receive more pain.

Attila held up a large gem, yellow and translucent. His mouth agape, Greillia stared at it with awe. As the sunlight glinted off the stone, Helena recognized one of the least valuable in her grandfather's collection: a gem destined for a relative lacking in discernment. She choked back the impulse to laugh with a hard cough.

The stone in his hand, Greillia turned it over, studying it from all sides. "It's magnificent," he said, his voice a reverent whisper. He glanced at Magga, who remained by Attila's wagon. She had pulled herself from the ground, her face in her hands. "She told me that you'd sent her back. You've given me riches. I don't understand, cousin."

Attila cleared his throat. "I may require her company from time to time. She's all that you promised. Keep her clean and in good condition. And Greillia, I'll not be interested in her services if you pass her around the tribe. I'll compensate you well, to make up for the lost profit."

Greillia bowed his head. "I don't deserve your generosity."

"That is true," Attila said.

Greillia frowned, then looked him straight in the eye. "Cousin, Valamir's woman cursed me with the Earth power! She said I was a dead man."

Hearing a tremor in his voice, Helena curbed the macabre elation bubbling within her. She stroked Sarelle's neck and prayed.

Greillia's voice became hoarse. "She used her own blood!"

Attila raised his eyebrows and whistled. "Did she? Interesting."

"Didn't you hear me? She told me I was dead!"

"Do you believe her?"

"Yes."

"Then you are marked. You'd best ask the Shaman. He'll tell you what to do."

Greillia nodded like a wayward child. "I'll trust your wisdom, Exalted One." He wheeled his horse and galloped toward Magga. Without breaking his horse's stride, he twisted sideways in the saddle, lifting her in front of him.

Attila kept his eyes on Greillia, not bothering to veil his disgust. He motioned for Helena and Valamir to come closer. "Last night, you cursed him. But you don't want to talk about it."

Belying his mild voice, Helena sensed his boiling rage. She had the impulse to plead for his mercy and confess everything. Yet, she kept silent by holding steady and expanding the Light in her heart. Drawing strength from her essence, she told Attila what had happened. Her voice was quiet; her thoughts were clear.

Attila listened intently, oblivious to the commotion of the camp's dismantling. When she had finished, his questions flew at her like a volley of arrows. "Why only Greillia? Why not me? Why not all of us?"

"He stole my son's life." She paused. "Valamir thinks that I, too, should ask the Shaman for help."

"Perhaps, Helena, but wait and see what happens with Greillia."

"Why?"

He laughed, a short, brief sound, like a stick cracking in a blazing fire. "To see how the curse works!"

She shook her head with disbelief. "But he's your cousin. Because of you, Valamir won't touch him, unless he attacks first."

"And Greillia knows that. He has not challenged Valamir to an honest fight, preferring to hide behind his kinship tie to me. But our law is silent about words."

Helena's eyes narrowed. "You learned many things from the Romans I think, including the talent to prevaricate like an orator."

He smiled broadly, showing his large white teeth. "A Hun survives, learning much from his enemies." His laugh rang out, a peal of triumph.

Valamir's voice was a bucket of cold water. "I'm going to take her to the Shaman, Attila. Each struggle with the force weakens her."

Attila frowned, shrugging his shoulders. "Just be certain that Greillia's not there, looking at the problem from the other side!"

Valamir chuckled. Pleased with his witticism, Attila squared his shoulders and surveyed the camp's activities with fierce concentration.

Helena felt disheartened. They did not understand. If the darkness won, the price would be her soul. She looked to the west, yearning for her old home in Constantinople, where life had been defined by her grandfather's kindly presence. She sighed, realizing that the past was gone and closed forever.

When Attila threw back his head, he howled. Startled, Helena flinched. "To me!" he shouted, his face transfixed with jubilance as horsemen converged upon them.

With dust and uproar, the day's journey began.

CHAPTER TWENTY-TWO

At least two thousand horsemen undulated across the steppes, inexorable as an ocean wave, ceaseless and steady. The sweet fragrance of crushed grass mingled with the pungent odor of sweat in the air. Helena held fast to Sarelle's mane, afraid of being trampled by the flashing hooves. Riding alongside, Valamir was preoccupied: his face was austere. She passed the morning in silence. Her thoughts sustained her, cloaking her fear.

Most of the women, along with servants and slaves, followed with the pack animals. Except for an occasional curious glance, no one paid her much attention. She was relieved that the novelty of Valamir's marriage was becoming old news. As she glanced at Attila astride his black stallion, he effortlessly dominated the men, drawing all eyes and casting the rest of his world into shadow. She was grateful to be obscured by his presence.

He shouted a terse command, signaling a halt, and gathered his war leaders around him. With a wave of his arm, Attila motioned Ishyite to join the select group. Encircled by this select company, she stared at the ground, hoping to escape notice. The earnest discussion was in Hunnic. She did not understand a word. When finished, the men broke apart with guttural shouts. The sound sent chills up her back.

As the tribe resumed its journey, Helena studied the sun. Attila had altered their course to a more southwesterly direction, skirting Persia's borders. Helena wondered if he planned to avoid the southern tip of the Ural Mountains. The range folded gradually into the plains. The terrain was hilly, with narrow valleys perfect for ambush, which would diminish Attila's advantage in size. In the open, the only threat to the Huns would be an Imperial command.

Curious, she asked Valamir about it. He looked at her coolly with his eyebrows raised and apparently surprised by her grasp of strategy. His answer was an abrupt nod.

"Where's Bevion?" she asked, realizing she had yet to see him.

"Somewhere, who knows?" Valamir said, unconcerned.

"Doesn't he usually ride with you?"

"Yes, but he's not good at sharing my regard."

This news brought her no comfort. Seeing her face, Valamir laughed. "Don't worry, he'll be back when he wants something."

Attila overheard the last part of their conversation. "Bevion, you mean?"

"Who else?"

"At least you're fond of him. I can't say the same for mine."

"Bleda...," Valamir said, his words trailing away to nothingness.

"Exactly! An idiot! So of course, Rugliva keeps him close, listening to his drivel, while he sends me first to Rome then to the East, hoping I'll never come back."

Helena listened, remembering the rumors about Attila's brother. He was said to be a simpleton.

"Perhaps Rugliva wanted your eyes and ears in Rome," Valamir said.

Attila laughed with malice. "No, friend. He wants me far away, preferring the advice of fools. Meanwhile, against tradition, he allows our people to become Roman mercenaries! I promise you, Valamir, one way or another, that will change."

Believing him, Helena shivered.

She retreated to the sanctuary of her own thoughts. The two men ceased raising their voices against the dust, the wind, and the rumble of pounding hooves. As the sun passed mid-day, Valamir asked her if she wanted to rest in the wagon. She shook her head.

At last, the setting sun transformed the sky into a quiet spectacle of orange and purple. Attila raised his arm and his throat reverberated with a deep roar. The cry passed through the tribe, bringing the army to a halt in moments. Valamir took his leave of Attila, impatient to find Caratipian and Rhys.

As they turned away, Attila said, "Break bread with me when you're settled."

"As you wish. Helena will not join us."

Attila frowned, not masking his irritation. "Why?"

"See for yourself. She's exhausted."

Feeling Attila's eyes on her, Helena was too numb to care.

"Very well," Attila said. "Come to me when you can."

Then Valamir's arms were around her, lifting her from Sarelle to Hassan. Leaning against him, she struggled to stay awake.

Valamir whispered in her ear, "You're stubborn, Helena, but you did well."

A smile played across her lips, but vanished as she surrendered to sleep. When she awoke, it was night. The fire burned brightly in a small hearth, casting eerie shadows on the walls of the tent. She was alone. Ravenous with hunger, she sat up quickly and found food left for her near the fire.

As she ate, Helena listened, hearing the occasional whinny of a horse, a few men laughing in the distance, but mostly the wind. The sound reminded her of Kansbar's village, where she had spent hours letting her thoughts and dreams mingle with the steady breeze, as if it could take her home.

Cupping her chin in her hands, she stared at the fire, and inadvertently stirred her pool of memories. With intense clarity, she remembered a summer's day in Constantinople. She had been eleven, sitting with her grandfather by their marble fountain in the courtyard of the spacious, stone house, laughing when a gust of wind coated them with fine droplets of spray.

"Our Spirits are as drops of water, Helena. Separate, yet part of the whole," he had said.

"What do you mean, Grandfather?"

He took her hands in his, smiling with his blue eyes. "Someday I'll become the Light. I won't be with you anymore."

Tears stung her eyes. "You'll never die."

He laughed. "Our bodies die, but not our Spirits. They are immortal. When the day comes that I am gone, don't deny my birthright by grieving too long. We are Eternal, one with God.

In time, we must shed our bodies and go home to Him, until we return for the next lessons on the earthly plane. Though you'll miss me, I'll be with you always, watching over you and loving you as my own."

For all these years, she had forgotten, her eleven-year-old mind not comprehending his words.

But now she did. Mourning would not bring back Mikael or her grandfather. Only the passage of years would diminish the fierce pain. With a sharp intake of breath, she accepted that their spirits had not died, only their bodies, their shells. She accepted the possibility of remembering them with joy, unblemished by sadness, and felt a quiet oneness that transcended words.

Time passed, stretching deeper into night. Restless, she stood and wondered why Valamir was taking so long. She wanted to look outside, but hesitated, remembering that morning and Greillia. She busied herself around the tent, trying to be useful. When Valamir finally returned, her heart leapt. Yet, her relief was offset by irritability.

"You're awake!" he said.

"Where have you been?" she asked, hating herself for sounding like a shrew, but unable to stop. She knew he had been with Attila, but the thought of him with three other women lingered, fouling her with jealousy.

"With Attila," he said, his face tightening into a frown.

He filled the tent with his presence. She found herself beside him, surrendering to a need to be close. "I missed you," she said, but did not reach for him.

His smile warmed her heart. "It is a joy to return to my tent and find you waiting."

His kiss was tender on her lips, drawing her into him. But she fled from it, from the feelings that it invoked, by pulling her mouth away. Though wanting his embrace, she was rigid with fear. The wind whispered to her, beckoning her out into the night. A longing to see the stars filled her, a sight usually denied the women in the cloistered life of Kansbar's house.

"Are the stars bright tonight?" she asked, not looking at him.

"See for yourself, Helena." Taking her by the hand, he led her outside. The sky was black and free of clouds. The stars blazed in the fall air. The moon was a white sliver, radiantly shining.

"It's beautiful!" she said in a hushed voice.

He put his arm around her shoulders, sharing the moment in silence.

A horse whinnied. Helena remembered her mare. "How's Sarelle? She's not used to working all day."

"She's quiet," he said, chuckling. "Finally tired!"

"And you, Valamir, are you tired after being with Attila?"

"No one can match his energy. He kept talking and pacing. And I was impatient to be gone and to be with you."

"I could be with you always," she said, wanting to tell him more, but the words would not come.

He hugged her, but she took care not to press against his wound.

"Valamir," she said, then hesitated. "What does the symbol mean that you cut in your chest?"

"You don't know?"

"Only what I heard Bevion say."

"It's the insignia of remembrance, but also loyalty, prized above all others by the brotherhood of Mithras. When I see it, I'll think of you."

"I don't think you did it for me, but to bypass my anger. If you'd given me time, I would have forgiven you."

His laugh was quiet. "Perhaps I didn't want to leave it to chance."

Inside, they lay on the bed pad in each other's arms. But, Helena felt restless, her longing for him superseded by fear.

He kissed her, his hand cradling her face. "Until my wound heals, I won't press you to be my true wife. By then, you'll know what you want," he said, speaking as if he could read her mind.

In the darkness, her eyes filled with tears. She needed him as much as she yearned for the night sky, the stars, and the sight of a horse at play. He had become intrinsic to her being and to her heart.

Her voice was a whisper, barely audible, the words wrung from her soul. "I want to be your wife, Valamir. I can't imagine life without you, but I'm afraid. Before, with Kansbar, it was so painful. I want to forget and put it in the past, but I can't. It stays with me like a curse, spoiling my love."

"Helena," he said, stroking her hair and kissing her brow. "I'd never give you pain. But should we become one, the Shaman's words would bind us for life."

"What are you saying?" she asked.

"The Shaman has brought our spirits together. We've but to complete the ceremony. Should we complete the union, our destinies are joined. I could never take you home."

Her breath was a sigh. "You *are* my home, all that I ever wanted in a husband, but living with Huns... I don't know."

He smiled. "Well, once we return, we'd be with my people. Ostrogoths are fighters, a strong nation. But we do have houses with roofs overhead!"

She laughed, holding him tight, unwilling to let him go.

"Will you marry me, Helena? This time with your heart?"

As she started to speak, he laid his finger across her mouth. "Ssh. Wait. Tell me when I can come to you whole, unblemished by a wound."

His lips brushed her brow once again, then he fell into a deep and immediate sleep. Wide awake, Helena watched him in the firelight. His blond hair was burnished gold by the flames, his profile definite. With a timid kiss, she touched his mouth. Though his eyes did not open, his arms embraced her.

Yet, he slept.

In the morning, the camp readied for the day's journey. Helena studied Valamir covertly. She searched for flaws, needing them to counter the impulses of her heart. But it was hopeless. Her grievances seemed petty and contrived, useless against the fabric of her incipient love. She tried to help while Valamir, Caratipian, and Rhys packed away the tents.

Caratipian shooed her away. Feeling in the way, her thoughts turned inward. Since childhood, a sadness had ached within her, silent, and always waiting. Even in Constantinople, she had felt different, unworthy of her grandfather's love. He had cherished her and provided every material comfort. But he had never acknowledged her Thracian mother, not once mentioning her by name and denying half of Helena as if it were unclean.

Through servants' gossip, she knew that her father had loved her mother, defying Balusistriam by taking her as his bride. After her death from childbirth, Helena's father had left Constantinople, seeking distraction from his loss, committing himself to service in the Persian Imperial Guard.

Helena agreed with her grandfather's philosophy that each lifetime contained many lessons. But this belief was a hard master, demanding consistent moral strength and a willingness to shoulder ultimate responsibility. She looked for something to do, anything to escape her unrelenting thoughts. Valamir, Caratipian, and Rhys had been efficient: they were all but finished with the morning's packing. She walked to the horses, still tethered, but fully ready for the day.

Passial whinnied, eager for a treat. As always, he lightened her heart. She smiled and scratched his neck, wishing he were young enough to carry her the entire day.

Surprised by tears, she buried her face in his mane. She had tried to accept her grandfather's message in her dream: finding joy in her memories and releasing the pain. But it was hard. For the second time, her life had been turned upside down and her reality ripped to shreds.

Sometimes, when she awoke, it was hard to remember where she was.

She thought of Constantinople and her grandfather's house, filled with colorful mosaic floors and the cheerful sound of the fountain. Without her grandfather's lively presence, it was only a building, its walls made of solid stone: cold and unfeeling.

Her father's face, so like her grandfather's, floated in her mind. He was a stranger. She wondered if he even knew that she was missing. She assumed her reward had been offered by John, the steward of the house, in her father's name. At the thought of John, she smiled. He had always been kind to her. Somehow, she vowed to herself, she would find a way to send word of her *rescue*.

As she combed Passial's mane, the image of Kansbar's village haunted her. She studied the sky, not wanting to visualize the houses, charred beyond recognition and the bodies left for the birds. Her eyes drifted downward, back to earth, and she saw the multitude of Huns. Their talent for cruelty hung over her head like the descending point of a sword.

Ludmilla, Kansbar's first wife, would have told her to make the best of a bad lot. Her sensible advice had been unstinting and constant: a woman must accept and be obedient to her place in the world. For Helena, docility had been a mask, worn as a dress but one size too small, stifling and constraining. In the past, she had tried to follow Ludmilla's example to make her lot bearable. But she had never been able to quiet her inner voice, screaming in silence against acceptance of a life she had so bitterly despised.

With a spark of malice, Helena noted that Ludmilla's methods had not helped her in the end. But she was shamed by the thought. She shook her head, knowing she'd never qualify as a *good* wife, one who is compliant and tractable. Suddenly, she laughed out loud, savoring her freedom from spending her days forever playing a role.

Valamir accepted her, allowing her the liberty to be herself. But his price was high: to be with him, she had to live with Huns. Yet, in either the Roman or Persian Empire, she would have had no voice in her marriage. Without her grandfather to intercede, his eldest male relative had the right to inter her in a mausoleum of loveless matrimony, her very body to be put into the service of her father's line.

Her choice was clear. She gave Passial one last pat, and untied Sarelle. Thinking of Valamir, she hummed a lilting tune. The mare breathed gently on Helena's face, making her smile.

She stroked the animal's muzzle, then scratched behind her pointed ears.

"Your touch looks sweet," a man's voice said, startling her.

Her hand on her knife, Helena reeled to face the intruder. It was only Bevion, looking hesitant despite his comment. His large bay horse, sturdy enough to carry a man his size, was restive and eager to set off.

She ignored his disconcerting words. "Good morning, Bevion."

"And to you, fair sister-in-law."

With deliberate speed, Valamir joined them, greeting his brother with a playful tap on the bay's rump, making the horse jump. The ploy was unsuccessful: Bevion's seat was unshakable, immune to the unexpected. He brought his horse under control and grinned at his brother.

Valamir's eyes twinkled. "You ride with us today?"

Bevion shrugged. "Might as well."

"Good," said Valamir. "Helena, Caratipian wants to see your hand."

Helena wondered about the dressing covering Valamir's wound, but was reluctant to mention it in front of Bevion. As Caratipian examined her hand, she felt foolish. Under the bright sun, her anxieties about curses and dark forces seemed remote and implausible. But even in full daylight, she felt chilled at the thought of her words to Greillia, how they had erupted from her soul with the force of a dark, coursing river.

Distressed, she sought Caratipian's eyes. As if for protection, she hastily drew the sign of the Light across her heart. "Valamir thinks that I should speak to the Shaman. Could he help me?"

Caratipian looked at the horizon, then back at her. "The Shaman understands the earth and its magic, seeing the invisible threads of our relationships to it and each other. He'll not betray any trust you place in him, but I don't know if he'll be able to help you. This...legacy from your grandfather, it's old, beyond time. But see what he can offer."

Her disappointment was keen. She wanted Caratipian to tell her that everything would be fine, that she should stop worrying and that the Shaman would have the answer. But he had not. Watching him fasten a fresh bandage around her hand, she felt despair.

She prayed, focusing her attention within her heart. In silence, her inner voice reverberated within her Being, speaking quietly within the pool that was her Essence. "Helena, the darkness hides behind shadows. Once you see it truly, its power is lost. Compared to the Light, it is nothing. Do not be afraid."

Comforted, Helena inadvertently sighed. Caratipian smiled at her, his wise eyes full of affection. "Next!" he said to Valamir.

As the Goth turned, Helena could have sworn she saw a moment's fear cloud his face. In a stern voice, she whispered to Caratipian, "You be gentle with him."

Caratipian laughed. "I always am. He just hates being poked and prodded. Songs have been sung about his bravery in battle. But afterwards, when his body takes its due, he reconsiders his rashness."

Struck by the image of Valamir fighting, sword to sword, Helena's throat became dry. "Does he get hurt often?"

"Just a scratch, here and there," Valamir said, overhearing the end of their conversation.

She whirled around. "You and Bevion walk like cats!"

He smiled tenderly. "A light step is a weapon." As he sat beside Caratipian, his face hardened with resignation. "Do your worst."

Helena looked away.

Afterward, Valamir and Helena mounted, ready to leave Caratipian and Rhys with the wagon. Rhys wore sturdy, leather clothing, his once bare feet encased by old, but patched boots. With a wry smile, Helena acknowledged Caratipian's talent for procurement. As if by magic, he acquired whatever was needed.

They struck off at a canter, with Bevion alongside his brother, uncharacteristically silent.

When they reached the center of the multitude, Attila greeted them with a shout. "We ride, Valamir!"

His arm rose with his fist clenched, signaling his men. They chanted his name, beating the sky with their frenzy. Keeping their horses to a trot, they cleared the wagons before allowing their mounts to spring forward into a gallop. Singing, the men repeated Attila's name, punctuating their cries with macabre howls. Sensing the tribe's hunger for battle, Helena prayed that no one would cross their path that day.

The next few days passed without incident. The steppes were desolate, more suited to nomadic sheep herders than military patrols. But the Huns met no inhabitants. The low rumble of many horses' hooves would act as a warning for anyone to hide. The wind blew more chill, announcing the threshold of winter. Their progress was significant: already they were less than two days' journey from the Caspian Sea. In under a week, they had covered the distance that had taken her grandfather's caravan more than two.

As usual, Attila invited Valamir and Helena to share his meal. She was tired of his probing eyes, his sharp questions and his need to know everything.

But tonight, Attila settled down to business. "The men are restive, Valamir. They need action."

Helena could not help but think that the last few days had been nothing but incessant movement.

"What do you plan?" Valamir asked.

Attila was nonchalant. "We're close to the northern silk route."

Helena cringed inwardly. She remembered traveling on the same track with her grandfather. Though their bodyguards were strong, close to sixty men, they would have been nothing against a force Attila's size. Not for the first time, Helena wondered why her grandfather had undertaken the risky journey. But once he had set his mind to a task, his will had been indomitable, thwarted only by death.

"The men would be happy to bring home more bounty," Valamir said. "But I've no interest in innocent blood."

"What do you mean?"

"Let any men or soldiers take their chance with us. But leave the women and children alone."

Helena's throat pulsed.

"And you, Helena? What do you think?" Attila asked, his voice smooth as a coiled snake's skin.

Her voice betrayed her, cracking with emotion. "Anyone who takes a child's life is a murderer, cursed by God for all time!"

Attila laughed at her outburst. "I'd begun to wonder if you'd lost your tongue, the gods forbid. But to my relief, I see that my concern was misplaced."

"I meant what I said," Helena said, her voice low with fervor.

"And do you think that your friends, the Romans, spare children when they travel north into our lands?"

"The Romans are no one's friend," Helena retorted. "You of all people should know that!"

Valamir placed his hand on her wrist, cautioning her.

But Attila persisted, undeterred by Valamir's concern. "Why should I spare an enemy's children, leaving them to grow into men?"

She wanted to snarl. "Because people on the silk routes aren't your enemies. They're your prey! Rome's your adversary, not some poor merchant who has the misfortune to be in your way."

Attila's mouth twisted up with repressed laughter. "Your eloquence has moved me."

She shook her head. "I've amused you. That's all."

"Well, that's true. But should the caravan spill none of our blood, their lives will be spared. That is my custom."

"What if one hot head plays the fool? What then, Attila?" she asked, thinking of Ivan.

"Who could say, Helena?"

Sickened, she was silent. Later, returning with Valamir to their tent, Helena said, "I hate him. He's a monster."

"Most people are deep inside."

"But not everyone has to prove it every day!"

"Ssh," he said, holding her close. "Attila likes to tease you. He enjoys your passion. Let tomorrow wait. We'll see soon enough what it brings."

As they lay side by side, he stared at her. Restraining himself, he only kissed her cheek, abruptly turned away, and promptly fell asleep.

Helena's dreams took her back to the village and to the women's screams. Red with blood, children cried. The stench of decaying flesh was palpable. Suddenly, Greillia bore down on her, sword in hand. She awoke with a start. Shivering, she edged closer to Valamir and his warmth.

She closed her eyes, searching for sleep, but it eluded her. Her terror remained, growing in the silence of the night. To escape it, she wanted to rouse Valamir. But he slumbered deeply and she did not have the heart to wake him.

She thought of her father and wondered what he would say to the discovery of his eldest daughter riding with Huns. Would he care? Did he even remember her face? In truth, when she thought of him, she saw her grandfather, only younger, with blue eyes, framed by dark curly hair. Was her father any different than the Romans or any fighting man? His creed was a soldier's; his standard was the Persian Empire.

Yet, she missed belonging to a family, even her father's. Struggling against the unexpected longing, she cried silently until her eyes were dry, until her father was as dead as her past. The smoke from the fire spiraled to the opening above. As she looked upwards, she saw the approach of dawn, streaking the sky with pink.

She thought of rising, but was too comfortable and warm to move. Moments later it seemed, Valamir touched her shoulder. "Wake up! The tent must come down!"

Opening her eyes, she saw his face and smiled.

He laughed. "You're beautiful, Helena."

Disagreeing, she shook her head, unable to meet his eyes. He caressed her cheek and her hair, and kissed her gently on the lips. "Hurry! Get dressed. I'll be back. I should have woken you earlier, but you looked too spent to disturb."

When he left her, the tent felt empty and abandoned. Wanting to join him outside, Helena briskly prepared to meet the day.

CHAPTER TWENTY-THREE

Enveloped by sunlight, Helena stepped out into a boisterous, yet organized chaos. Involuntarily, her body recoiled from the throngs of men engrossed in multiple tasks. One was tending to his horse's hooves by anointing them with rare oils. Another carefully polished a glistening shield. A young man raced by them on his bay horse, which was, by Roman standards, hardly larger than a pony. His face was intent and focused on his goal. Women's voices were raised in a lively song as they washed and gathered water for the day. As each verse was completed, more than one woman laughed. Helena surmised that it was probably a bawdy tune, but she could not know for certain as it was in Hunnic.

Though she was safe, protected by Valamir, she could not deny the truth of her situation. She rode with Huns: the vermin of the Empire. Somehow the women did not affect her. But the sight of the Hunnic warriors, with their myriad of facial tattoos and unnaturally shaped skulls, filled her with a visceral horror. Beyond her loathing, she was afraid, not for herself, but for Valamir. The image of him in battle, sword glinting and singing as he fought, flashed through her mind. She shivered at the thought of an enemy's blade finding his heart.

Seeing Caratipian, Helena went to him and sought solace from his company.

He acknowledged her with a smile. "I've something for you."

Hobbling to the wagon, he extracted a pair of warm gloves. They covered a small leather square, folded neatly into a long triangle. Placing his presents in her hands, he was careful not to put much weight on her healing bones. She touched the gloves gently, admiring them.

"They're beautiful," she said.
Caratipian shrugged, but looked pleased. "Open your gift, Helena."

She gingerly unwrapped the leather and saw her other knife, the small, plain one. Freshly sharpened and retooled, its blade glistened in the sharp, morning light.

"You remembered," she said, tears in her eyes.

"What troubles you, Helena, that a little kindness can make you cry?"

She looked away. "I thought you'd forgotten."

"Of course I didn't, but that's not what worries you."

She hesitated. "I love a man who rides with killers and thieves."

"Valamir has his own destiny," Caratipian said. "He'll be King of his tribe one day. I won't live to see the changes, but I sense them in the air. Attila, as mighty as he is, reaches for the stars, but they will burn him."

"I love you, Caratipian," Helena said, not understanding how the phrase could come so easily from her heart.

"And I, you. In Valamir, I've a son, and in you, a daughter."

"What of Bevion?"

"He struggles hard to be a man. Though I love him, he tries my patience. When we return, he'll not be happy to see that his father has a new child."

"How do you know? I thought their father was old."

"As old as I, but with eyes only for his new bride. She was pregnant when we left, but Valamir and Thiudimir did not know."

"Thiudimir? Whom do you mean?"

"I'm sorry. Bevion. He doesn't like his first given name, so he uses his second. I don't know why. Thiudimir has a noble sound."

"Poor Bevion, he doesn't even like his name." She paused. "But who knows if the child is still alive?" she wondered aloud. "At the village, many babies died young."

At the thought, Helena pictured Mikael. Her heart became a void, dark and imponderable. She squared her shoulders and studied the sky.

"How's your hand?" Caratipian asked, changing the subject.

"It doesn't hurt like before. I can move my fingers a little."

"Let me see it."

With quiet efficiency, she slipped the knife under her belt, holding the gloves with her good hand. Caratipian unwrapped her bandages with expert gentleness, setting aside the splint.

"Wiggle your fingers."

Wincing, she obeyed.

"Your cut is all but healed, but its scab still holds tight. Your bones will need at least another ten days. I'll save the splint, but we'll do without it for now. Slight, slow movements will be good. But be careful not to strain it."

Her hand dressed, Helena found that she could move it tentatively, without pain. She watched Valamir as he smoothly dismantled the tents with Rhys. Feeling her eyes, he looked up with a smile.

Her heart expanded with love, poignant, yet bittersweet. But her fear remained, like ice, wintry and brisk. "He wants me to bear his children, Caratipian," she said, her cheeks warm.

"They'd be beautiful," he said.

"I wonder what my grandfather would say?"

"I'd hope he would ask you to listen to your heart."

His words eased her anxiety, softening the walls of her protective shell. "I love him. My eyes drink in his presence, and I long for more. But I remain afraid."

"Be his wife, Helena, and find the happiness you deserve."

Her voice was husky. "You're my friend, Caratipian," she said, unable to say more.

Shortly afterward, Valamir joined the silent duo. But with embarrassment and renewed shyness, Helena could not meet his eyes. He touched her cheek, encouraging her to look at him. As she blushed, his smile grew wide. His arms embraced her and she softened at his touch, cherishing his warmth. He chuckled.

"Why do you laugh, Valamir?"

"Nothing. It's just that with you here, my day is sweet."

"I could be with you for all time," she whispered.

Behind his eyes, she glimpsed a flash of pain, gone so quickly she wondered if she had imagined it. In its place was

Valamir, adult and fully grown, with any ancient grief well-hidden.

"You have my heart, Helena," he murmured in her ear.

In the distance, men shouted. Valamir surveyed the camp with a professional glance. "We're headed to the mountains," he said. "The day will be short, as Attila commands."

"He rules the sun in the sky?" Helena said with sarcasm, angry about the planned foray.

Valamir narrowed his blue eyes. "You've no right to judge him."

"Perhaps not, but his methods are not honorable."

He flinched, as if she had struck him. He looked away. "I am what I am."

She met his eyes, crying. "I just don't want you to be killed." He pulled her to his chest. "I couldn't bear it," she added quietly.

"No one will touch me."

"Watch out for Greillia."

"Bevion rides with me. In combat, he is loyal."

"Good," Helena said, feeling slightly relieved. "I'm sorry to be a shrew on the day you could face a sword."

Lifting her hair away from her face, he smiled. The twinkle in his eyes faded. "But you're right. I find no honor in innocent blood. It gives me no pleasure, only disgust."

"You fulfill your obligations to Attila. But be careful, Valamir. You carry my heart."

"I will always come back to you," he said. "I promise."

Her stomach drummed with excitement, but her eyes studied the ground. He kissed her forehead, then her lips.

"Today you stay with Caratipian and Rhys. They'll take care of you."

She nodded, checking tears. "Until tonight, then."

He hugged her, almost fiercely. "Yes, my wife."

As he leapt upon Hassan, she watched, not taking her eyes from him until he was lost in the crowd of converging men. He did not look back, which was just as well. She was crying again and did not want him to see it.

She joined Caratipian a few horse lengths away. "I'm riding Passial today."

"Good," he said. "Then I'll not have to ask Rhys to change his tack!"

Helena shook her head incredulously. "How do you know my mind?"

Looking mysterious, he shrugged.

"Well?" she asked, needing to know.

With mock exasperation, he looked up at the sky, then relented. "I listen to my heart, my Sraosh. It tells me what to do. It's never wrong, though sometimes thoughts muffle my hearing."

"But how do you know if it's from your spirit, and not something else?" she asked, thinking of the darkness that overwhelmed her whenever she saw Greillia.

"I watch my body," Caratipian said. "When I hear my heart, I feel calm and connected to all. But if I feel tense, impatient, or insistent on convincing others of my rightness, then the voice is from fear. It's not a mystery, just common sense."

She nodded, but despaired, certain she would be unable to hold fast to the Light when in Greillia's presence. Feeling hopeless, she began to believe that the curse was too potent for her to master alone. "I'll never have your wisdom, Caratipian."

"Give yourself another forty years!" he said, laughing. "Now stop worrying and enjoy the day. Winter comes, chilling the earth, but the sun shines brightly. Reflect on how its light glorifies the One God, instead of your imperfections!"

"Yes, Caratipian." Her tone was meek, like a child's, but her lips curved into a slight smile.

His eyes sparkled at the shift in her mood.

As the wagons headed north, guarded by at least five hundred soldiers, the main body of the horsemen veered southwest. Riding alongside the wagon, Helena attempted to locate Valamir in the teeming attack force, but without success. Rhys rode beside her, his seat on the horse firm, reflecting years of experience. But he was taciturn, not once glancing in her direction. She respected his privacy.

As they reached the foothills of the Urals, there was a subtle, fragrant aroma of trees in the air. Fallen leaves rustled under the horses' feet, reminding Helena that it was autumn. Blocked by the sloping mountain ridge, the wind blew in sudden gusts, but not as strongly as on the open steppes. The sun was bright; the air was brisk.

A scouting party, perhaps thirty horsemen, rode toward the wagons, shouting in Hunnic. The commander of the escort answered in an enthusiastic bellow, waving his arm to quicken the pace. Relieved, Helena recognized Ishyite. Valamir's friend led the wagons deeper into the hills and into a valley, alongside a stream meandering through its center. Helena noticed immediately that it was wide, open at both ends, and not conducive to ambush.

When Caratipian and Rhys set up the tents, it was well past mid-day. As the three shared a meal, Helena fretted in silence. She longed to see Valamir and thought of how his serious face lit up with a smile. As best she could with one hand, she helped Caratipian wash the dishes and was grateful for the distraction.

Then there was nothing else to do. Because of her injury, she could not sew or even write. "Could you tell us a story, Caratipian?" she asked. "Something about times past?"

Rhys moved away, but looked surprised when Caratipian gestured for him to return. "You could learn a thing or two, young man. Listen and hear about the great King Xerxes, who has been much maligned by certain Greek historians."

Her knees to her chest, Helena heard about the ancient Persian King from a man who had remained loyal to his heritage, despite years spent with barbarians. Caratipian's strong partisanship of the Persian viewpoint, so reminiscent of her grandfather, brought a smile to her lips.

After Caratipian had finished his tale, Helena could not resist teasing him. "But if the Greeks were so pitiful and weak, how were they able to defeat this great son of Darius?"

Caratipian grimaced with irritation, aptly suspecting that she provoked him. His answer was succinct. "Luck! Plain and simple!"

Laughing, Helena went inside. Once in the tent, she felt restless; she was tired of the limits imposed by her incapacitated hand. The hours passed slowly. Still, there was no sign of the men. Helena had been in and out of the tent, at least a hundred times, scanning the horizon for a glimpse of them. Night fell with no Valamir. Inside the servants' tent, Helena shared a meal with Caratipian and Rhys. They were quiet, preoccupied with their own concerns. Each was dependent upon the Ostrogoth's survival.

Finally, Helena broke the silence. "Caratipian, why do you think they've been so long?"

"Attila," he said. "He likes to play as he stalks his prey."

Helena lost her appetite. The meal finished, Caratipian ordered Rhys to walk Helena to her tent.

"Do you think I need an escort for twenty paces?"

"Yes."

"Oh," she said, suddenly afraid of sleeping alone.

"Inside, you'll be safe. The traditions are strict about entering a tent uninvited. But here, take this," Caratipian said, handing her grandfather's sword. "Valamir wanted you to have it."

Aloof as ever, Rhys walked beside her. She held the sheathed sword tightly, as if it were a magical talisman. At the entrance, he turned to her. "I'll not sleep until Valamir returns. If you cry out, I'll hear."

"Thank you, Rhys," she said. But in the moonlight, his face looked macabre and almost menacing. She wasted no time going inside.

After tending to the fire, Helena rested, planning to await Valamir's return. Instead, she fell asleep, swept into roaring dreams. When a blast of frigid air rushed into the tent, Helena awoke. She sat up, her mind immediately clear, and saw Valamir.

He looked tired and worn, his face haggard. In an instant, she was beside him, searching him for signs of injury. He stank of blood.

"Where are you hurt?" she asked.

"Just a few scratches, here and there," he said, slowly setting down his shield and sword.

"I'll get Caratipian."

"No need, Helena."

"What about Hassan? Did Rhys take care of him?"

Valamir nodded, then gingerly took off his tunic. Except for his right shoulder, his woolen undergarment was free of blood. Feeling ill, Helena realized that the rest had not been his. Yet, concern suppressed her revulsion.

"Let me see your shoulder," she said.

He gave her a small smile, as if too tired to resist her will.

"Sit down and rest," she told him, angry as she realized that his *scratch* was significant. "It needs Caratipian's poultices. Don't you know that?" Her voice grew louder, edging toward hysteria.

"Ssh, Helena. I've had much worse." He held her wrists and gently pulled her down to his lap. Close to him, her agitation dissipated, transforming into an unexpected excitement. Her world contracted, becoming his face and the warmth of his body.

"I was so worried about you," she whispered.

"See, I came back, as I promised." He paused, as if considering whether to speak. His words, when they came, were slow, each costing him dear. "If I could arrange safe passage for you to Constantinople, would that make a difference?"

She was startled by his question. "What do you mean?"

"I've an uncle who is in the Imperial Roman Service. I might not be welcome in Constantinople, but he could guarantee your safety."

"Why do you ask me this?" Helena asked, shaken by the thought that he wanted to rid himself of her.

"I don't want you to think that you have no other choice but me. I want your commitment from freedom, not fear."

"Are you sure that's the reason?"

"What else could it be?"

She looked away, ashamed.

"What are you thinking?" he asked.

"That you're tired of me."

He laughed, shaking his head. "Sometimes you're a foolish girl, Helena." He held her tightly. "Don't you know that if you went back, you'd break my heart?"

"Well, I'm not going," she said, flinging back her hair.

His eyes were soft, echoing his smile. "Will you be my bride?"

"Yes," she whispered, her throat tight.

He kissed her hard, then pulled away. "Wait. I can't come to you with the stench of battle on me. I should be clean."

She held his arm. "Don't leave, Valamir," she said, suddenly afraid that if he left her to bathe in the creek he would never return. "Stay and let me sponge the dirt from you."

His eyes were serious, studying her face, as if he saw her for the first time. "I'd like that, Helena, very much."

She filled a leather bowl from a bucket of water, spilling some of it, clumsy with only one hand. But she didn't care. Nothing mattered except being close to him. Finding a clean cloth from her satchel, she dipped it into the water and began to wash his face, starting with his forehead, working her way down to his mouth and chin. The cloth turned brown with dust and grime. Opening the tent flap, she tossed out the old water, then refilled the bowl. With the rinsed rag, she stroked his neck and drifted down to his shoulders, careful to avoid the cut across his upper arm. The injury was not deep, she realized, relaxing her concern. It could wait until morning for proper bandaging.

As she massaged his shoulders, bathing them with water, Helena explored the way his muscles merged together and how the fire illuminated the fine texture of his skin. She took her time, sponging him clean.

When she moved to his front, her shyness returned. Touching his chest, even through the barrier of a wet cloth, her cheeks were warm. The wound over his heart had all but healed, although some of the scab had torn away during the day, revealing a red scar.

He followed the direction of her eyes. "I'm not yet whole."

Her voice was hoarse, barely a whisper. "It doesn't matter."

She retreated to his back and loosened the grit from his hair with the wet cloth. She ran her fingers through it, untangling the thick, blond strands. He sat quietly, giving himself to her care. With another cloth, she patted him dry, leaving his hair damp, but not dripping.

She stood before him, feeling awkward, not knowing what to do. He watched her, his bright eyes alive in the firelight. "Would you put on the dress that you wore for our wedding?"

Her cheeks grew hot. "Only if you don't watch."

Pointedly, he turned his back and faced the wall. As she searched her satchel, her hands were trembling, nervous from old fears. Despite her intentions, her heart beat with panic. Finding the dress, she smoothed it with her hands, finding comfort in its soft texture. It reminded her of home, of Constantinople.

She took off her traveling clothes and pulled on the dress. "I'm ready," she said, but knew she lied.

Standing, he turned with the grace of a cat. His smile was deep and possessive, yet he did not approach her.

"You're beautiful," he said, extending his hand, stepping closer, not moving until she reached for him. "You're shaking." He pulled her to his bare chest, and stroked her neck, then her face. "I won't hurt you," he whispered.

She wanted to believe him, but her body remembered the past and tensed. He lifted her in his arms, carrying her to his bed. They lay side by side, but he did no more than hold her. Wrapped in the familiar comfort of his arms, she began to relax.

His hand lifted her hair away and he kissed her neck. Chills of excitement swept her spine. As his lips found hers, she churned with elation. Her trembling ceased, replaced by inner urgency. His hands and mouth explored her: she was too overwhelmed to feel self-conscious. She had no time for her thoughts or doubts, only the present.

Valamir removed her dress, leaving her chemise. His fingers loosened the ribbons in her bodice and caressed her breasts, making the tips harden. Sliding down her undergarments, he unbuckled his belt. Naked next to her bare skin, he kissed her, his lips pressing hers and his hand stroked between her thighs. She moaned with pleasure.

"I love you, Helena," he whispered into her ear.

She clung to him, wanting to be his. The pain of her past was forgotten, as if it had never been. Then he was inside her, their hips moving rhythmically as one. Her body was inundated by sweet intensity. She whimpered his name, barely able to speak. As he consummated his passion, she was swept once more with pulsing, exquisite sensations.

When it was over, she felt shy. He smiled, his eyes enormous, close to hers. "You are my wife, Helena, for all time."

She touched his face. "When I first saw you, I loved you, but did not know it. So much has happened, but you are my heart, my love, and my life."

His embrace was fierce. "Helena, will you give yourself to me again?"

"Yes," she said, laughing.

Afterward, as they lay together, she felt so drowsy that she could not move. He covered them with a blanket. Intertwined, they fell into dreamless sleep.

CHAPTER TWENTY-FOUR

Helena awoke to Valamir's eyes watching her. As he kissed her, his hands gently explored her body. Her mouth yielded to his tongue as they merged, moving as one, in the timeless dance of love. In giving herself to him, she felt complete, no longer rudderless and drifting without purpose. She clung to him, returning his fervent embrace, and shared his ecstasy. When their passion was exhausted, Valamir raised himself on one elbow and smiled. Embarrassed, she blushed.

He leaned over, allowing her no place to hide her eyes. "I love you, Helena. As my wife. I wish that we could stay together all day, alone, like this, but we must rise and face the morning."

His lips met hers, but did not linger. Yet, his arms did not release her, holding her against his chest. Alarmed, she remembered yesterday's wound. "I have to look at your cut."

"Only if you'll give me one more kiss."

"I don't negotiate kisses, Valamir," she said, laughing.

Without a pause, his lips merged with hers, sweet with emotion. Under his caressing hands, she moaned.

"Attila can wait," Valamir said.

Their bodies reunited in harmony, as if they had known each other a lifetime. Between waves of euphoria, Helena whispered, "I love you, Valamir."

"And I, you." But his body answered her more completely than his words ever could.

Afterward, they disengaged, almost as if they were afraid to linger in each other's arms.

"Now let me see your wound," Helena demanded again, smiling.

As she touched him, her heart raced. With discipline, she concentrated on the laceration. It had bled clean, but needed the protection of a bandage. She inhaled his scent, wanting to be with him in their private place, and dared not to meet his eyes. "Caratipian will have herbs to help it heal," she said.

Valamir reached for her. "Please, don't," she said. "I've no resistance to you."

"Just one more kiss, Helena."

"No!" she said with a laugh. "That's what you said last time! And here we are, still in bed, with the camp awake all around us!"

A corner of his mouth turned down. "I don't care."

Her heart opened as she understood his desire for her had superseded his call to duty. "Just hold me a little while longer," she said. "Then we'll greet the day."

He pulled her to his lap. Helena broke their silence, not from discomfort, but because she wanted him to know her mind. "I never thought that being with a man could be like that."

His eyes twinkled mischievously. "Like what?"

Again, she blushed self-consciously, but persevered, not wanting to be susceptible to his teasing. "So pleasurable," she whispered to the ground.

He answered her with an ardent kiss.

But she continued, needing to resolve a lingering shame. "I wish I'd come to you a virgin, Valamir."

"Don't say that! I was the first man you gave yourself to freely, of your own will. Who are we to argue with how the gods joined our lives? Had Kansbar sent you back to Constantinople, I never would have known you. I only wish you hadn't suffered. Know that if anyone tries to hurt you again, Helena, I promise you their life will be forfeited to me."

She answered him with a passionate kiss.

When Ishyite called from outside, Helena jumped. "Valamir? Are you there?" he shouted.

"Yes!" came the retort.

"Oh," Ishyite said, pausing to collect his thoughts. "Attila wants you. He requests your wife. He needs her to translate."

Helena looked at Valamir with agitation.

"Don't wait, Ishyite. We'll be along soon."

"As you wish, but you know how he is when he has an idea."

Valamir chuckled. "Off with you!"

Her throat tight with distress, she searched Valamir's face with her eyes.

"Helena," he said slowly, considering his words. "We took two prisoners. A woman and a child. They are Persian. Besides Caratipian, you're the only one who speaks the language. But Attila delights in goading him. If Caratipian reacts badly, Attila could punish him for disrespect, even to the point of ordering his death. And I could do nothing to prevent it. Though I'd prefer to keep you from Attila's sight, you are safe with him. In his peculiar way, he cares for you." He stood and offered his hand.

She did not want to go. But she reached for him, modestly covering herself with a blanket. Valamir caught her in his arms. "Until tonight, Helena."

His arms enveloped her and she relaxed. "I want to stay here with you."

He stroked her hair. "Before you know it, we'll be alone again."

Breaking away, he dressed. He held up his bloody tunic, as if deciding whether to wear it. He glanced at her with a raised eyebrow. She shook her head once, firmly. "I'll wash it for you, Valamir."

With a private smile, he chose another garment. When they were both presentable, Valamir guided her into the cold sunlight. The aroma of meat across a fire greeted them, drifting in the wind. As they ate, Caratipian chastised them about not seeing to Valamir's injuries, but not harshly, and smiled at what he saw in their faces. He tended Valamir's wound unobtrusively and bandaged it securely with clean cloths.

"Ride with me, Helena," Valamir said, but all she wanted was his lips pressed on her mouth, his body one with hers.

Once Rhys led Hassan to Valamir, he relinquished the reins. Rather pointedly, Rhys's eyes were cast down. He would not look at them. Unlike Caratipian, Rhys struck a discordant chord, like a sour note in a perfect song. But her quiet joy was not easily dampened. Effortlessly, she overlooked his sullen mood.

Nodding curtly, Valamir dismissed the Gaul.

"I'll ride behind you," Helena said. "I don't want any pressure on your shoulder."

He whispered in her ear, his breath caressing her neck, "It's only a scratch, Helena. I'll miss you in my arms."

"But I'll be able to hold you," she said, her eyes meeting his, her cheeks warm.

He moved closer and touched her brow, brushing her hair back with his hand. "Until later."

She breathed in the aroma of his skin. His blue eyes were so close to hers; as she studied the way his straight nose met his eyebrows, the camp seemed far away. He broke the moment by placing her astride Hassan, then mounting lithely in front.

She clasped her arms around his waist, holding him. The stallion carried them through the camp at a gallop. Helena felt elated, in rhythm to the beat of the horse's gait, in harmony with its master.

When they reached Attila's quarters, a Hun reached for the roan's reins. He was bulky and his torso was wide. His glance at Valamir was mingled with awe.

Dismounting, the Goth turned to the man. "Be careful of his hooves. He uses them as a weapon."

The man eyed Hassan warily, with a creased brow. As Valamir lifted her down, he spoke in Greek. "Hassan doesn't suffer fools gladly. Most people know that. He'll be treated with respect, which is all I want."

Arms linked, they walked briskly toward the large, main tent. Helena glanced at his face, her heart full, and smiled. Attila emerged from his quarters, glowering with impatience. His greeting was a frown.

His foul humor did not affect Helena's exhilaration. Her joy was like a bird with wings, soaring in the air currents. She broadened her smile to include the Hun.

He scowled, turning his back on them, walking inside. "Now I see what took you two so long!"

They followed him. But Helena felt awkward, not wanting the world to know her private happiness. Confronted by Attila, sitting erectly on his chair, she had no time to regain her composure. He was withdrawn and pensive. Helena felt tongue-tied, deserted by wit when she needed it the most.

Valamir got straight to the point. "You needed an interpreter?"

"Yes," Attila said. His eyes narrowed, never leaving her face. He relented with a smile. "So, Helena, I think I'll abandon hope of having you as a wife."

She held his gaze, but her fear dissipated, like rain falling on hot stones. Attila watched her, almost speaking to himself. "It's for the best, I think. Despite my intentions, I'd have broken you. I've no talent with sensitive women. Never have, never will."

Valamir interrupted his soliloquy. "Attila, your insights are intriguing, but you speak to my wife. Enough of this. What about the woman? I brought Helena to translate."

Attila stood, his expression stern, but Valamir did not flinch from his glare. "You are within your rights. I saw you together, so clearly in love, and felt sad. The gods are kind to you."

"And I'm grateful," Valamir said. "But we're no closer to discovering why the woman was so far from Persia."

Attila clasped his hands behind his back, and drew himself to his full height, as if closing that part of himself that had been awakened. When he spoke, his tone was pragmatic.

"Helena, I need your help. We captured a caravan. In my care, I have a mother and child."

At his words, Helena felt as if a knife was at her throat, making breathing difficult. Her heart pounded, echoing her internal torment.

"Don't look at me like that! I haven't hurt them," Attila said. "Considering the number of guards that she had, she's worth a large ransom." He laughed. "Notice that I said 'had.' Fifty trained Persian soldiers are nothing to us!" He paused, full of himself, before remembering his present requirements. "Unfortunately, she speaks only Persian."

"Why didn't you ask for Caratipian?" Helena asked.

"He's a peasant, not cultured. You are the correct choice. Perhaps the Persian bitch will have heard of your grandfather and condescend to speak. I'm beginning to tire of her. She's beautiful, but her arrogance curdles what should be sweet. I've treated her kindly, but she has no gratitude. When she looks at us, she doesn't hide her scorn."

"What of the child?" Helena asked.

"The little girl? She's of no account. Who needs another brat? Speak to this Persian...woman, Helena. Find out her name and, more important, who will pay her ransom. If she won't cooperate, tell her that I'll rape her until she learns to enjoy it. It will take a long time, because every time she sees me, she scowls with disgust. You tell her that when she begins to bore me, and that won't take long, I'll sell her to the highest bidder, either here or in Rugliva's domain."

"And what of her child? What you do plan with her?" Helena asked, her heart in her throat.

"Tell the mother that I'll sell the girl to a cheap brothel, to be raised as a well-trained whore."

Helena's voice was a rasp. "You'd do that?"

"Yes, but this child is brave, despite her fear. If the mother doesn't cooperate, I'll let you have her." He gave Valamir a look of pure mischief. "Haven't you always said, old friend, you want no part of killing innocents? Well, accept the responsibility that goes with fine principles!"

Attila's charge weighed heavily on her soul, pushing her joy to the past. "I understand," Helena said. "I'll do my best."

"I knew that you would, once you understood how things were."

Valamir interrupted. "Helena, don't worry. I don't think Attila has any plans to sell the woman."

Attila shouted, not hiding his chagrin, "Valamir!"

"It's true enough, isn't it? I saw how you looked at her. You may have plans for this Persian, but none of them include any other man. I won't have Helena upset."

Attila folded his arms across his chest, his face brooding. "I wanted her to be convincing."

"I won't allow anyone to frighten her."

The situation overwhelmed her. She sat on the blue and red rug in front of Attila's chair, her head in her hands, staring at nothing. Breathing was an effort. Attila had offered her another child, as if she were a puppy, too charming to destroy. But she thought only of Mikael, remembering his shining face.

If she had been alone, her grief would have found release with a long, keening cry. Instead, she was silent, her body immobile as stone.

Valamir and Attila stopped arguing.

"Come, Helena," Valamir said, offering his hand.

As if it were a lifeline extending across a rocky chasm, she studied it, wanting to grab it, and go home. But she was reluctant, tired of hiding, and filled with a need to face life as it was.

"Stay," Attila said. "Break bread with me. We'll speak of other things."

Helena made the journey back to herself. "That would be good, Attila. I'll meet the woman after you tell me what you want to know," she said with measured tones.

Surprised, Attila beamed at her like a teacher with a particularly apt student. His glance to Valamir was smug and full of self-congratulation. He clapped his hands loudly and a slave appeared, bowing obsequiously. Attila barked orders in Hunnic. In moments, they were served a hot beverage, bread, and meat.

"I need your counsel," Attila said to Valamir.

The Goth took a seat beside Helena, so close that they touched. Before when they had been alone, his proximity brought her intense, almost succulent, excitement. Now she felt numb. She picked at her food listlessly, oblivious to the men's discussion about routes and provisions for the tribe.

Despite her intentions, the image of a vulnerable, Persian woman with a child haunted her, echoing the immediate past. She delved into bitterness and condemned her love for Valamir. Her inner judge whispered insidiously that he rode with Huns, and that he shared in the blame for Mikael.

But she could not lie to herself anymore. She began to accept her burden of the responsibility for her tragedy. Had she relied on Valamir's promise of protection, Mikael might well be alive. When Kansbar's house had been transformed into hell, she had trusted her instinct first, forgetting all else. For too long, she had been on her own, dependent on her slender resources to survive, unable to believe in any man's word.

As Valamir spoke earnestly to Attila, she watched him, enjoying the way the shafts of sunlight caught the planes of his face, his eyes, so blue and clear, and loved him. What she felt for him was clean, beyond thought and words, and separate from her grief for Mikael.

He glanced at her and smiled. His eyes filled her face. Her lips softened into a wry grin and the heaviness around her heart lifted. He was her talisman, keeping darkness at bay. Comforted, she reached up and touched his cheek.

Attila's voice was harsh. "Shall I leave you alone?"

Embarrassed, she blushed and studied the ground. Valamir's rebuttal was a short laugh, as if Attila had made a poor joke. She leaned on him, wanting to be away from this Hun with the probing, unsettling eyes.

Valamir was blunt. "What of the Persian woman, Attila? What do you want Helena to ask?"

Attila's eyes were bright and alert as a carnivore in pursuit. "I need information. Who is she? Where is she from? Why was she on the silk route away from the safety of her husband's harem? We found many fine things, but I think she's worth far more. Helena, you must tell her that resistance is useless, she will be much better off cooperating while she still has skin on her face."

Helena gagged, but stilled her reaction. She looked Attila in the eye and resolved to protect this woman and her child from his abuse. "Where is she?"

"Close. With my women. Are you ready?"

"Yes."

He clapped his hands loudly. A slave, the sinewy Breton, answered the summons, his head touching the ground. Attila barked an order in Hunnic and the Breton darted outside. Helena's fears settled in her stomach, twisting it.

She was afraid for the woman. The logistics of negotiating ransom with the Persians would be difficult, if not impossible. Attila would have to send word to the woman's husband or father, then wait. If the woman was noble and well-connected at court, the Persians would send an army large enough to engulf Attila's command. Though his force was strong, close to two thousand men, they were far from home. In contrast, the Persians would have the resources of a nearby Empire.

Yet, when the prisoner and child were ushered inside, Helena felt chilled and repelled by the woman, hating the way she held the little girl's hand. She squeezed it tightly, oblivious to the child's look of pain. The Persian held her head high, almost regally. Her hair was dark, her eyes deep blue, and her profile was fine and well-proportioned. As she looked first at Attila, then Valamir, her lips retracted into an arrogant sneer. The glance that she gave Helena was potent with contempt.

Yet, the child, no more than six, her hair a mass of dark curls, her eyes brimming with tears, pulled at Helena's heart, sparking her maternal hunger. Helena folded her arms across her chest and decided to help the woman for the child's sake.

In his cultured Greek, Attila initiated the conversation. "Sit with us," he said, motioning to the floor.

The women stared at him, making no effort to understand even his gesture.

Helena translated. Hearing Persian, the woman's patina of arrogance vanished, revealing fear. Mystified by the reaction, Helena raised her eyebrows. But suspicion quickly followed bewilderment. She wondered what the woman had left behind in Persia.

The prisoner regained her composure with a toss of her hair. "You speak Persian," she said.

"That much is true. Please sit," Helena said, smiling with encouragement at the little girl.

The child's face brightened. As the woman acquiesced, she pulled the girl into her lap. Her knuckles were white as she grasped the small shoulders. "What is your name?" Helena asked.

"Rhoddinia."

"And the child?"

"Her name is of no interest to *you*. Why do you travel with these...savages? Your accent hints at better times!"

Helena wanted to slap her face, hard enough to bring tears to those cold, blue eyes. She resisted the impulse and clenched her fists at her sides. "This is my husband, a Prince of the Ostrogoth nation, and the other is Attila, nephew of King Rugliva of the Huns. Perhaps you have heard of their people."

"Barbarians! Who can remember their names? They all look the same."

"Rhoddinia, you're in great danger. Is there someone who will ransom you?"

The woman was silent.

Helena pressed her, wanting to know more, deciding to breach her defenses through her pride. "Why are you so far from your husband's home? Did you run away or take a lover, perhaps?"

Rhoddinia spat on the ground. "How dare you! You bitch... no better than a whore. I am of royal blood and need not discuss my life with *you*!"

With a supple movement, Helena stood, staring down at Rhoddinia. She was silent, with her lips compressed. Yet, when she spoke, her voice was even, not betraying the anger running through her body like a fresh, cleansing river. "You *will* beg my pardon this moment, then apologize to my husband and Attila for your disrespect. If not, I'll hand you over to Attila, and tell him that you refused to cooperate. Already, he has described his plans to peel the skin off your face, one layer at a time, slowly, with fine expertise."

"I will not," Rhoddinia said, gritting her teeth.

Helena turned her back to the woman. "May you die well."

Except for the child's rapid breathing, the tent was silent. Then Rhoddinia whispered, "I am sorry."

Helena faced her. "Say it in Greek so they can understand."

The woman bowed her head, attempting to hide the flush spreading across her cheeks. "I don't know the words!"

"Then I'll teach you," Helena said.

As the woman repeated the phrase slowly, Helena's eyes did not leave her face. "Good. We can proceed, Rhoddinia," she said, resuming her place near Valamir.

Attila watched, not masking his avid interest, but Helena did not acknowledge his curious eyes. She gestured toward him with her head. "He has guaranteed the safety of the child. He's promised her to me should you fail to cooperate. It's your choice."

Rhoddinia's eyed darkened with hate. "Bitch! You can't adopt her! She's a direct descendant of Darius, in line to the throne."

Helena's laugh was curt and mocking. "You can't be serious! Even if she is of royal blood, many others stand before her."

"That doesn't matter! She is who she is. No one lives forever."

"And you, are you her mother?"

"Are you blind? Can't you see the resemblance?"

"No. Not at all. Perhaps she takes after her father."

Again, Rhoddinia spat. "Cyrillic? I think not!"

"You're lying. I can see it in your face. I can even smell your fear. Who are you running from, Rhoddinia? And whose child is this?"

The woman's answer was an aggrieved silence, punctuated by venomous eyes. But Helena ignored her, and instead spoke to the child in a gentle voice. "Little one, I'm going to have Rhoddinia leave for awhile so that we can talk quietly together. Nothing will happen to her. But I don't think she wants to be my friend."

Rhoddinia interrupted. "I will not leave her!"

But Helena dismissed her protest. "Attila, have this woman removed. For the child's sake, treat her gently. But watch her. Keep her from your women. She may be dangerous."

Hands behind his back, Attila raised one eyebrow and smiled. "As is your command."

Determined to unravel the mystery surrounding the little girl, Helena was in no mood for his teasing. Silently, she watched as Attila clapped his hands, summoning the guards.

Rhoddinia would not let go of the child. The guards had to pry her fingers from her arms. As they led her out, screaming, Helena touched the girl's hand. The child's eyes were wet and her chin quivered.

Helena offered her some bread. "Would you like some?"

The child shook her head, but eyed the food with interest.

"You're probably used to better," Helena said, her voice neutral. "What's your name?"

"Altiere."

"What a pretty name! Did Rhoddinia give it to you?"

"No, my mother did!"

"And where is she?"

"Died in the fighting."

"Yesterday?" Helena asked, her heart in her throat.

"No, when Rhoddinia came with the soldiers."

"Why did they kill your mother?"

Altiere cried. "I don't know!"

"You must miss her very much," Helena said, pulling her close, holding her in her arms.

The child sobbed. As Helena rocked her side to side, she quieted.

"Altiere, where were you when the soldiers came?"

"Istakhr."

Helena's voice was a hoarse whisper. "Istakhr," she repeated, stunned to hear the name of the religious center of Persia, the city her grandfather had called home. She cleared her throat, trying to speak with a normal voice. "I've heard of it. My grandfather had family there."

"We do, too. We had a message from Mother's father that he was very sick and close to dying. She was very worried and asked for permission to visit him."

"What happened?"

"When we got there, the house was empty: no servants, no grandfather, just Cousin Rhoddinia and the soldiers. They killed our guards." Altiere began to sob. "And they hurt Mama before she died. She kept telling me not to watch. When Cousin Rhoddinia saw, she....slashed at the man's back with a knife and tried to make him get off Mother. He was bleeding everywhere, kneeling over Mama, and he took out his sword, and put it in her stomach. Then she stopped moving, and her eyes just stared at me."

"Oh, Altiere," Helena said, joining her tears.

The child continued, her voice high pitched. "Rhoddinia screamed at the soldiers and made them take away the men who did those things to my mother. She told me that she was sad about what had happened, but she was lying. She didn't really care. I hate her! My mother didn't like her and said that she was jealous because my father didn't take her as a wife." The child paused, then pulled her head back so that she could look at Helena's face. "You can let that bad man hurt her," she said, glancing at Attila. "I wouldn't mind."

The child's anguish grated like shards of pottery across Helena's heart. She whispered, "I'm so sorry, Altiere, so very sorry. A bad man killed my little boy. It still hurts."

"Was it that one?" Altiere asked, gesturing slightly with her head toward Attila.

"No, another Hun. And I hate him for what he did."

"You understand. You're nice. I want to stay with you."

"I like you, too. But don't you think that your father might be looking for you?"

"I don't know him well. Mother was not his only wife."

"Who is your father?"

Altiere took a deep breath. "He's the Emperor's brother."

Suddenly, Helena understood the rationale for the child's abduction. "Altiere, someone will come for you. Soon you'll be home, safe and sound."

"You didn't tell me your name."

"Helena."

"But that's not a Persian name."

"I know, but it's a good one."

"I'm tired. I miss my mother."

"Rest your head on my lap and try to sleep."

"Can I stay with you?"

"For a little while, Altiere. I'll make sure that Rhoddinia isn't near. Close your eyes while I talk with the men."

As Helena related what she had learned to Attila, Altiere drifted into sleep. Concluding, she leaned forward and spoke earnestly. "Look for an Imperial Force of at least fifteen hundred men. With this outrage, Rhoddinia has struck at the heart of the Empire. They will want vengeance."

Attila's face was veiled, masked behind his thoughts. "You've done well, remarkably well, Helena."

"It wasn't hard. If you take the time to listen, children are usually straightforward." She smiled mischievously at Attila. "In Altiere's mind, you're the 'bad man.'"

"I've been called worse. And what about you, do you agree?"

Helena shook her head, not willing to be so easily baited.

"You have no sympathy for the Persian? After all, she's a woman," Attila asked.

Helena raised her head, looking him in the eyes. "She betrayed her family. She lured her cousin to a hard death. Rhoddinia deserves whatever she gets!"

Attila's smile was rich with amusement. "Spoken like a Hun!"

Valamir interrupted. "Enough of this. If I'd known, I'd have insisted that Caratipian take care of the questioning. It's been too much for Helena. But I tell you Attila, that woman, Rhoddinia, is a viper. And like all poisonous snakes, she should pay with her head."

Attila stood. "Don't attempt to shelter Helena from the world, Valamir. It can't be done. Before we finish with Rhoddinia, we need to know what was in her mind. Was her plan to ransom the child? There is a story here, one that intrigues me."

Helena was thoughtful. "I don't understand the whole of it. I suspect a plot against the Emperor, treachery from within the palace walls. Someone has spun a fine web, but I don't think it's Rhoddinia. She's a player, to be moved this way or that. No, we haven't seen the master of this plan."

"She'll tell us what she knows. Don't worry."

"Not with Helena's help!" Valamir said. "I will lend you Caratipian, but only if you promise that he'll be treated with respect!"

Helena continued on the same tangent as before. "The Persians will reward you well for finding her. After they've finished with her, they'll know everything she has to tell. They have methods of torture that you could not even imagine."

Attila shook his head, as if disappointed in his ablest pupil. "Don't underestimate our inventiveness, Helena."

She disagreed, but politely. "They've had more than a millennium to perfect their 'art.'"

"Search the woman again," Valamir said. "She's not frightened enough. She probably managed to keep a weapon."

"I'll personally oversee it. We did not make her strip. Now we should see her, before her body is ruined by the Persians' knives." He paused. "Yes, she will learn more intimately about our hospitality."

Uncomfortable with the far away look in his eyes, Helena forced herself to speak. "I'd check her..." She hesitated, deeply embarrassed.

"Go on," Attila said.

Her face warm, she whispered, "Make certain that she has nothing in her private parts, Attila. With a woman of her kind, anything's possible."

"I admire the thoroughness of your thinking, Helena."

She ignored the compliment. "And Attila, don't tell her why you're keeping her apart from the child. The uncertainty will prey on her, making it easier to discover the truth."

Attila smiled with agreement.

She felt bone-weary and unable to cope. She glanced at Altiere and wanted to touch the child's smooth cheek, unblemished by time. "Attila, did any of your wives bring children on this journey?"

"No, I only brought my younger wives."

"That's too bad for Altiere. Being with other children might help her to forget. She wants to stay with me, but you have the guards to protect her more adequately."

"It will be done," Attila said.

"Would you allow Caratipian to visit her in your women's quarters?" Helena asked.

Attila was silent while thinking. "Perhaps, but only if you came with him."

Helena cradled Altiere in her arms. "I'd be glad to accompany him, but for the child's sake, it would be better for her to have two visits instead of one. She speaks only Persian, as you know. It would help her if we came at different times. You can't imagine that Caratipian, at his age, is any danger to your wives' reputations?"

Attila cleared his throat. "He may come alone, but must meet with the girl outside, in full view of the world," he said, smirking, teasing her with her own rules of decorum.

"Then it will be as you wish, Attila. May I take her to your wives now?"

"I'll introduce you," he said, motioning for them to follow him through a smaller entrance at the back of the tent.

As Helena stood, Altiere awoke and began to cry. Helena soothed her with a soft lullaby in Persian, and the child held her tightly. At the thought of leaving her, Helena's throat caught, but could not help being relieved. She did not want to become too close to the little girl, to care too much, only to lose her.

Valamir waited outside while Helena followed Attila into his wives' tent. Its interior was luxurious, strewn with brightly colored rugs and soft fabrics. His wives were young, none older than Helena, and very pretty. Yet, as they listened to his instructions in Hunnic, they betrayed little curiosity about Helena or the child. Instead, they accepted his words with passive docility. Helena wondered if their unquestioning obedience bored him, like a bland diet.

Rhoddinia was no where to be seen. Helena quietly explained the plans to Altiere.

"I want to stay with you!" the child said.

Patiently, Helena told her that the women would be kind and if she needed her to ask for her by name. One of the wives, a dark-haired girl with clear brown eyes, came closer to Altiere and smiled. From behind her back, she shyly pulled out a small doll.

Tears in her eyes, Altiere's face glowed as she clutched the small bundle of rags and wood to her heart. In Gothic, Helena stammered her thanks. She watched as the woman brought the child some warm food with a smile.

When Helena joined Valamir outside, Caratipian had arrived, his face pinched with worry. In Attila's presence, he kept his eyes down and his hands at his sides, betraying not a hint of pride.

The Hun regarded the Persian with bleak contempt.

"Remember, Attila," Valamir said, unafraid. "Treat him with respect. He's my servant and a free man."

Attila frowned, then put his fists on his waist. "Does he understand what I require?"

"I've explained the situation. He's eager to help."

"That is good."

As Helena and Valamir rode away on Hassan, Helena looked back at Caratipian walking behind Attila toward the main tent.

"Will he be all right?" she asked.

"He'd better be," Valamir said, more like a growl.

As day faded into dusk, Caratipian had yet to return. Valamir kept Rhys busy, tending the horses, checking the wagon's harness, but did not let him touch any weapons.

The stars came out, glittering in the sky.

"Should you go for Caratipian, Valamir?" Helena asked over their evening meal.

"No, my place is with you. Attila will send him back when he's discovered what he needs from the woman."

Thinking of Attila's methods, Helena felt chills up and down her arms. After their meal, they lay together. Helena was afraid, not of Valamir, but of what future the Persian girl might bring.

As they made love, Helena held nothing back, giving herself to him as if it were the last time.

CHAPTER TWENTY-FIVE

Early in the morning, Attila's scouts roused the entire camp. Their voices were loud shouts as they galloped toward headquarters, trumpeting the news that a Persian Imperial force marched toward them less than half a day away. The prospect of battle enervated the men. Small bands charged through the rows of tents, yelling and igniting the others into ecstatic tumult.

Reared on stories of Persian invincibility, Helena was sick with fear. She pictured their chariots lined in rows, pulled by black horses, slicing through the Hunnic ranks to her heart, to Valamir. She could not imagine how the Huns, little more than a rabble, could hold against a disciplined Imperial line.

Before leaving, Valamir kissed her hard on the lips, then rode off at a hard gallop to meet Attila. Outside, Helena sat motionless, watching the camp's uproar. Caratipian and Rhys worked together with smooth efficiency, sharpening an extra sword and checking bows and arrows. But Caratipian's face looked drawn and haggard. He would not meet Helena's eyes.

Her stomach in a hard knot, she visited Passial, hoping to soothe her dread. She groomed the white stallion, talking to him in a soft voice, not forgetting to be vigilant against Greillia. The wind blew in gusts from the northeast, making the walls of the tents billow like sails. Helena looked at the gray sky, overcast with clouds that promised colder weather, and realized suddenly that no one need die today.

Risking the onset of winter, the Persians had not come to exact justice from Attila, but to rescue the honor of the Royal house. After all, his raids had been well outside their borders. Any interest in him would be incidental to his possession of Altiere. She was their prize, their mission.

Helena glanced at Caratipian and Rhys, busy with Valamir's weapons, and knew she had to intervene. Yet, the thought of facing Persians, even as a translator, filled Helena with a desperate foreboding. She avoided her feelings, and concentrated on the puzzle of Altiere's abduction. So many stood in line to the Persian throne before the child that the kidnapping appeared pointless. As she remembered her grandfather's stories about the Royal Court, her eyes widened. Poisoning was an art form and a necessary convenience. Still, Helena could not imagine it being unleashed with such widespread devastation.

In the Persian Court, anything was possible, even the death of an entire Royal Family. When she had been young, she had wanted to live there with her father in a grand house. But Balusistriam had been adamantly opposed to her dream, wanting nothing to do with the Empire. Only when he had grown old, too close to death to be a threat to anyone, had he decided it was safe to return. Yet, he had planned to live in Istakhr, center of Zoroasterism, away from the power struggles near the throne.

At the sound of a horse cantering toward them, Helena and Passial both looked up. Involuntarily, her body remembered Greillia: her heart leapt to her throat. When she recognized Bevion, she almost welcomed him as a diversion from her troubling thoughts.

He reined his horse to a halt. "Attila needs to speak with you. Valamir told me to come."

"Hello, Bevion," Helena said, obliquely rebuking him for his abruptness. "You seem well."

He looked off into the distance, shaking his head. "You're a strange girl, Helena, but you've made my brother happy. Come, ride behind me. It will be faster than waiting for Caratipian to saddle and bridle your horse."

She shook her head, not wanting physical contact with him. "We can go. Down, Passial."

The stallion lowered his leg, allowing her to mount easily, without any pressure on her hand.

Bevion's eyes narrowed critically as she sat the horse without bridle or saddle, only a halter. "You can't keep your animal under control that way!"

"Perhaps. Lead the way, we'll follow."

Bevion wheeled his horse in a tight circle and then urged it into a hard gallop. Passial lunged forward with a leap, making

Helena grab his mane. Bevion glanced back with a condescending smile. As he saw that she and her horse rode as one, his superior expression faded. He pointedly ignored her until they reached Attila's quarters.

A murmur of approval at Helena's bold entrance swept the crowd of Huns waiting for Attila. She shifted her weight backward, giving the white stallion the signal to halt. He collected himself and stood, all four hooves square on the ground, as if at attention.

With a sidelong glance, Bevion spoke in Greek, "Show-off."

But she only laughed - a short, sparkling sound. As he averted his face, Helena glimpsed a grin.

Valamir strode out of Attila's tent, his face bleak. When he saw Helena, his frown disappeared. He preemptively snapped his fingers at one of Attila's slaves. "Take her horse to Hassan, but treat him well!" His arms wrapped around Helena, lifting her down. Feeling his body close, she wished that they were alone.

As the slave reached for Passial's halter, the stallion snorted, throwing his head away from the grasping hand. "Passial!" Helena said. "Find Hassan. Go!"

Her horse laid back his ears at the slave and whinnied. Hassan answered with a deep bellow and Passial struck off at a smart trot to join him. The man, left behind, scratched his ear in surprise.

Helena started to explain. "He's not used to strangers," but realized she had spoken in Greek. Not understanding, the slave opened his palms. She repeated her statement in Gothic and the man nodded with relief, glad not to be blamed for an animal's misbehavior.

Catching Helena's eye, Bevion laughed derisively. "And I thought the horse was well-trained!" But his words trailed into nothingness as he focused his attention behind her. Following his stare, Helena saw Greillia approaching, his bay horse running at a hard gallop.

Her ears roared, but her breathing was slow and disciplined. As she felt her hate, time and space were suspended, moving at a languid tempo. Oblivious to all but Greillia's advance, she watched with her eyes narrowed. From within, she felt darkness needing release and solace through a final revenge. Her hand slowly reached for her dagger, but Valamir grasped her by the wrist, firmly restraining it. She turned on him, cold with rage. When she saw the concern in his face, her heart softened.

Assaulted by a multitude of sensations, she forced herself to gaze into his cool, blue eyes. As if confessing to a Christian priest, Helena whispered, "When I see him, I lose myself. Almost as if I'm mad! I don't know how to stop it!"

"Don't look at him. Just at me."

She stared at him, drawing strength from his will, allaying the chaos of her upheaval. With a smile, Valamir brushed her hair from her cheek. "Come inside, Helena. Attila wants to speak with you."

He clasped her uninjured hand and ushered her inside the large tent. Attila brooded over a fire, his arms folded across his chest, his drab leather tunic muted against the blue and red carpet thrown on the ground.

He raised his head; his mouth was compressed into a thin line. "Sit, we've important matters to consider."

Imitating Valamir, Helena took a place on the rug, her thoughts tumultuous from fear, and wondered how Attila planned to parley.

"We'll need an interpreter when we meet the Persians," Attila said bluntly.

"I'll go with Caratipian," Valamir said.

Attila's head shook once, slowly. "No, old friend. It must be Helena."

Valamir shouted, "Why would you think of risking her?"

"When they see a female, they'll be curious and hold their arrows. Remember, they search for Rhoddinia and the child. As you near, they'll realize their mistake, but few men will shoot through a beautiful woman's heart before hearing her speak."

Valamir began to protest, but Helena interrupted him, her hand gripping his shoulder. Her voice was even, belying the dread curdling her stomach. "Who else meets the Persians?"

Pleased by her tacit acceptance, Attila smiled. "Valamir, of course, Ishyite, and two others who are of no significance except for their skill with swords. If they try to take you, they'll pay the price with their blood."

Helena ignored the unpleasant inference. "Why Valamir?"

"His presence is imposing. After all, he is the son of a King. The Persian commander will recognize him for what he is."

"And Ishyite? Why him?"

"He's one of my best men. I trust him with my life."

She stared at Attila. "But our lives will be in jeopardy, not yours. Will he give Valamir the same loyalty?"

"Helena," Valamir said. "Ishyite is my friend. Don't question his honor."

Chastened by his stern tone, she studied the pattern in the rug. "I'm sorry, Valamir, but I needed to know." She raised her head, her eyes holding his. "I'm going with you. I'll make sure that you come back unharmed. Attila's plan is sound. It's to our advantage to negotiate and find a common interest, rather than to fight."

Attila smiled broadly. "You learn quickly, Helena."

She ignored his praise. "What do you want from the Persians? Ransom? How would you keep it, even collect it? They are barely a week of hard riding from their border and reinforcements."

Attila stood and paced the length of his small tent, before returning to stand above her. "We travel on the wind. They could never catch us. But the situation requires special handling. First, I must meet with their commander. Valamir and you shall negotiate a time and place between the two armies, preferably closer to our side."

Helena's throat was dry. "I'll help. But I ask that the Shaman be within the ranks, watching when we first engage the Persians. We might have need of his Earth magic."

Attila's face was shuttered, inward. But his nod was unequivocal. "Your words have wisdom. It shall be as you ask."

Helena persevered. "Winter comes and she'll not wait while you are distracted by one more raid, then another. Rhoddinia's caravan has brought us nothing but trouble, costing us precious time. It's time to go back to your homeland."

Attila's eyes were cold, but he laughed. "Don't be such a woman, Helena! Blind to opportunity! Who knows what will come of this encounter? We shall watch and learn."

"As you say, Attila," Valamir said. "But I wouldn't mind seeing my father and how he fares with his new bride. It's been two years. I don't want him to forget his older sons."

Attila chuckled derisively. "You mean, you wonder if he's managed to whelp another heir! Watching out for your crown, are you?"

Valamir shrugged, not looking away from Attila's inquisitive, brown eyes. "My tent's drafty in the winter. A stone hearth would be a welcome change. Besides, I'm tired of not knowing what Rugliva does with the Romans."

Attila's mouth rippled in a snarl, his voice rasped. "We agree on the last point. Like a beggar, he accepts their gold. How many men has he sacrificed, hiring them to be mercenaries for Roman wars?" He cleared his throat, regaining his composure. "But that must wait. Now we resolve the problem of the little girl."

"Before we go, I should see her," Helena said, feeling guilty that in all of the excitement, she had neglected her. She added to Valamir, "I'll need my tack for Passial."

Valamir's eyes crinkled with amusement. "Why did you come without it?"

"Bevion was in a hurry. He wanted to ride double, but I refused."

Valamir smiled, reaching for her. "Maybe you should ride the mare."

"No, I want Passial. He'll bring us luck." She paused, afraid to ask. "Valamir," she said in a low voice, "I'll need my grandfather's sword."

"Why a sword, Helena?" Attila asked.

"I can't explain, but it matters. For me, it's like a talisman. It will give me courage."

Attila chuckled. "Courage is not a quality that you lack, Helena. But when a soldier goes to battle, he should bring what gives him confidence. Let her take it, Valamir."

She found his support patronizing and ignored it. "Before we go, I'll speak with Altiere."

Attila's nod was abrupt. "Valamir, take her to my women. I'll send word to your servants for the sword and tack. Be quick with the brat, Helena. We ride soon."

Though angry at his name-calling, Helena refused to be goaded into an outburst. Attila gained power by inciting others to lose control. Like a puppeteer, he held the strings and made everyone dance to his song, even Valamir.

She met his eyes, not reacting to the disparaging remark. "And what of Rhoddinia? The commander will ask."

Attila's smile was rich with memories. "She lives. But you can say that we prepared her thoroughly for his interrogation."

Shivering imperceptibly, Helena restrained herself from flinching. "I'll see the child now."

He raised an eyebrow, inclining his head regally. "Be quick."

She turned her back on both men, stepping into the clear, fall air. The wind felt like a cleansing breath to her body, sweeping away her gnawing anxiety. Valamir was at her side, issuing rapid instructions in Gothic to a small, dark-haired Breton, another of Attila's numerous slaves. His words flew at the man, who bowed and ran toward a soldier.

As they walked to the women's tent, Helena took his arm. Valamir stopped suddenly. "I've changed my mind. You won't ride with me today."

"But I must."

"No one else is asked to risk his wife! Attila or not, I'm taking Caratipian. You'll wait in my tent."

Tears in her eyes, Helena shook her head adamantly. "But I have to go. If you die, I'll follow. Without you, there's nothing left."

His face softened. Disregarding the curious stares, he pulled her to his chest, cradling her in his arms. "Together, we'll see tomorrow," he whispered in her ear. "We must hurry. By the time that you've finished with Altiere, I'll have Passial ready."

As they approached the tent, a guard intercepted them. Valamir barked an order in Hunnic and the man moved to one side. Before entering, Helena smiled at Valamir. "Be here when I come out. If you leave without me, I'll make you finish what you started on your chest!"

He smiled, but his face was tinged with sadness. "Women should not be called to battle, Helena. But I give you my word: I'll wait."

Her hand lingered in his, comfortable as a nesting bird. "I won't be long." Once in the women's quarters, Helena was greeted with stares. Speaking hesitant Gothic, she tried to communicate. "Attila...told me I could see Altiere."

One of the wives, a beautiful dark-haired woman, gestured toward the sleeping child. Her young face, so innocent, was edged with her black curls, reminding Helena of Mikael. Her heart aching, she knelt beside the child. Altiere's eyes had dark circles under them. Hating to disturb her, Helena whispered her name.

The child sighed in her sleep, only opening her eyes when Helena touched her arm. "Oh, it's you," she said. "I'm glad."

"I didn't want to wake you, but I had to tell you what's happened. Persians have come looking for you. I'm to go talk with them. But Caratipian will come to visit. Would you like that?"

"Oh, yes! He tells me funny stories. He makes me laugh and I forget about things."

With heartfelt sympathy, Helena smiled at the unexpected glimpse of Caratipian's playful side. "That's good, Altiere." She paused, thinking for a moment. "Is there anything that I can show the Persian commander so that he knows that you are really here? He might not believe me."

The child looked anxious. "Will you give it back?"

"I promise, Altiere."

"You may have my necklace. Mama told me to keep it hidden under my dress. She said that it's very valuable."

Helena's eyes widened with surprise. "I'll keep it safe."

Reaching under her clothing, Altiere drew out a golden pendant hanging from a delicately tooled chain. It was an emblem with an eagle, intertwined with two snakes, encrusted with small rubies and emeralds.

As Attila's wives watched, Altiere placed it over Helena's head. "How did you keep this from Rhoddinia?" Helena asked.

The child's chin thrust forward with defiance. "She never thought to search me."

Helena hugged her. "You did well, Altiere. I'm proud of you. Are you hungry?"

The child nodded. Before leaving, Helena asked the wives to see that she was fed. To her relief, they clustered around Altiere with smiles, offering her an assortment of treats. Though Altiere did not understand a word, her face brightened at the attention.

Outside, Valamir and Caratipian waited. Helena grinned at the servant. "She likes your funny stories."

But Caratipian had eyes only for Altiere's necklace, reflecting the morning sun. His voice was hushed. "Where did you get that?"

"From Altiere, as proof to the Persian commander."

"It's the Imperial emblem," he said, awestruck. "This child is closer to the throne than we thought." He frowned with disgust and consternation. "Rhoddinia lied, even to Attila, sticking to her story about the child being only a niece. The bitch!"

Helena remembered how Rhoddinia's words about Valamir had stung. "Did she insult you, too?"

"Yes."

"She's vicious, but only part of the whole," she said. "There's a pattern in all of this, but I can't see it. Even Altiere believes that she's the Emperor's niece. Rhoddinia may not know the entire truth. I believe that Attila's stumbled on a serious threat to the throne. Why else would they go to all this trouble to kidnap a female of the Emperor's blood line?"

Valamir was thoughtful. "Attila must be told. We are out of our depth, leagues from reinforcements. It would be suicide to demand ransom."

Caratipian snorted with derision. "The gods would have to work in harmony to turn Attila from his greed!"

Valamir was abrupt. "Hush, old friend."

Attila appeared suddenly beside them, his approach soundless. He scowled at Caratipian. "What did your servant say?"

"Nothing of consequence. Caratipian, take Helena to Passial, while I speak with our leader."

Not hesitating to escape from Attila's glare, Caratipian hobbled quickly to the horses. As Helena rushed after him, she shouted, "Did you bring my grandfather's sword?"

Out of Attila's hearing, Caratipian slowed his pace. He was panting for breath. "We are of one mind, Helena. Somehow, the sword will matter today. I've fastened its sheath so that it hangs from your saddle, in plain view, but within easy reach. If anyone threatens you, don't be afraid to use it."

Impressed, Helena nodded. "You think of everything, Caratipian."

"Sometimes I'm lucky, other times, not," he said, his smile rueful.

Thinking of his maimed leg, Helena agreed. Her mood became somber. "Spend time with Altiere. The women are kind, but she can't talk to them."

"Don't worry. Today, you stay in the moment, be the moment, and all will be well."

"I pray so, Caratipian. My words have been brave to Valamir and Attila, but I'm filled with uneasiness. Though I ride with Valamir to the Persians, it's as if I guard Valamir instead of the other way around. I don't understand what I'm feeling, but it has nothing to do with dying. I just want this day to be over and tomorrow to have begun."

Attila watched with folded arms as Valamir strode toward them. His face was reflective, even calm; his presence was a balm to Helena's anxiety.

"I told him about the emblem," he said. "Naturally, he was upset that no one thought to search the child. These are his instructions: We're not to mention ransom. Indeed, we're to be eager to turn Altiere over to the proper authorities, but let them understand that a gift of a reward would be appreciated."

"Thank God he's seen reason," Helena said. "We're too close to their border to play games."

"We ride, Helena. Stay close."

She grinned at Caratipian with more bravery than she felt. "'Till tonight."

He smiled back, his eyes bright. Valamir lifted her to horse, then mounted Hassan. The roan snorted, making a show of his excitement. As they joined Attila, astride his black stallion, he stared at the pendant around her neck.

He frowned, extending his hand. "Let me see it."

Reluctantly, Helena obeyed, watching him sharply as he examined it. He muttered, "I'd be satisfied with this as the child's ransom."

"If it's what we suspect, they'd kill us all to get it back," Helena said.

He returned it to her. "We'll have to see, won't we? Come. You two ride with me."

They wove their way through the camp, horsemen swelling the ranks behind them. Once free of the tents, Attila whirled his horse in a tight circle, signaling it to rear. The lines of men were silent, waiting for his words. He spoke in impassioned Hunnic, but Helena did not listen to the incomprehensible sounds. Instead, she watched the affect of his words on the men's rapt faces. They would walk on fire to please their leader.

Accidentally, her gaze found Greillia. As his eyes focussed on Attila, Greillia's mouth was retracted in a wide grin, his teeth snarling like a rabid wolf's. She refused to dwell on him, not wanting the darkness that was certain to follow. She disciplined her thoughts and pictured herself surrounded by golden light.

When Attila pointed at her, she became the object of the men's attention. She kept her outward composure by breathing quietly, concentrating on Passial's mane, silver in the morning sun, denying the urge to push him into a run and take her away from the staring eyes. Though her mind understood that Attila was explaining her presence as a translator, her body's terror was visceral.

Dropping his hand to his side, Attila released her, recapturing the men. Freed from their scrutiny, she exhaled deeply and calmed her pounding heart. As if compelled, she looked up and saw the Shaman in the forefront of the crowd. No one pressed against him, creating an emptiness around his horse. Not understanding how she could have missed seeing him before, she wondered if he had her grandfather's ability to melt into his surroundings, as if invisible.

As their eyes met, Helena felt unclean, his quiet examination penetrating her heart. She waited for him to flinch at the horror of her darkness. But his face was serene, strong, holding no judgment, only compassion.

Attila shouted a war cry, piercing her quiet communion. The men's voices pummeled the sky, erupting with anticipation of battle. Beside her, Valamir was silent, his eyes dark with concern. As the horses surged forward, Helena smiled at him bravely, shielding him from her desperate fear. Down from the foothills of the Ural Mountains, they raced to the steppes and to the destiny that awaited them.

CHAPTER TWENTY-SIX

At a smooth canter, Passial carried Helena across the steppes. His white mane streamed in rhythm to the steady beat of his hooves. Swept forward with the horsemen, Helena was no longer afraid. The moment had crystallized into small fragments: the odor of sweat from Passial's neck, the rumbling of the earth beneath the horses' hooves, and the chill wind at their backs.

Valamir was laughing; his grimness had vanished. He was one with his horse, his shield, and his sword at his side. Attila remained unchanged: intense as ever, remorseless with cunning, and shouldering all responsibility for the tribe. He met Helena's glance with an ironic, if fleeting, smile, but did not break his silence.

The morning sun flirted with mid-day when they saw on the horizon a cloud of dust created from the feet of marching men. Lifting his arm, Attila signaled a halt and scanned for higher ground. But the undulating steppes offered no hills, just numerous crests rising from the plain. With an emphatic motion of his sword, he led his army to the highest one.

As they waited for the Persians on the slight elevation, Helena's stomach churned with fear. Her throat was parched and her thoughts were in turmoil at the prospect of confronting the Persian command.

Less than a league away, an Imperial column formed into lines, one behind the other, and prepared for battle. Their force was greater than Attila's. Helena estimated the number at three thousand which was larger than what was reported by the scouts. Yet, except for a sizable number of horse and chariots, most of the soldiers were on foot. The Huns rode as a cavalry, more than leveling the odds.

Helena whispered to Valamir, her voice cracking, "Where's the Shaman?"

Valamir was composed and his eyes were compassionate when they rested on her face. "He won't be far. Before we ride, he'll speak some words. Listen and trust that we'll survive."

She smiled uncertainly, finding slender comfort in his soldier's creed. Ishyite and two other Huns joined them, their faces carefree and alive with anticipation.

From horseback, the Shaman spoke to their small group, using a mixture of Gothic, Hunnic, and some other tongue. His hands made strange gestures in a precise rhythm. He raised his staff, shaking the fur tassels that hung from its top. "It is done. May the Earth Mother fold you in Her arms when you go forth upon Her."

Finished, his eyes, so vibrant and bright moments ago, became veiled and withdrawn, as if he no longer saw them. Helena felt abandoned: she needed more and did not want him to stop. But when his brown eyes lingered on her, she felt as if a beam of light swept up and down her spine and dissipated her terror. Melting back into the ranks, he vanished as if he had never been.

"Go with the gods, Valamir!" Attila commanded.

Bevion galloped toward them, waving his arm. "Wait for me!"

Attila scowled.

"Please, Lord Attila, let me ride with my brother!"

"No, not today. I won't risk both of Vandalarius' sons."

"Let me take his place. He is the heir."

"I honor your courage. But today requires Valamir's experience. Have patience. Your time will come."

As he accepted the decision, Bevion's face fell. "Valamir, come back. Promise."

Valamir smiled gently at his brother, his evident love at odds with his seasoned soldier's face. "I promise, Bevion."

"The gods protect you, always!" Bevion said, smiling with a show of bravado.

"Until we meet next, Bevion," his brother said. He turned to Helena. "We ride!"

At a trot, the five horses set off toward the Persians. Valamir's approach was in a diagonal, rather than a straight line. Through his teeth, he spoke to Helena. "They'd be blind not to see that we travel with a woman."

When they reached the middle ground, Valamir raised his hand, signaling a halt, and faced the opposition. They waited silently, their heads held high, and ignored their enemy. The Persians shields were raised, in anticipation of an attack, and their swords were thrust forward. Helena felt the prickling of an arrow's aim in her throat. Her heart pounding, she prayed. The Persian commander, astride a magnificent black horse, wheeled his mount in a tight circle. Suddenly, Helena thought of Attila and his penchant for drama. As she recognized the Persian as a human being, not as an evil archetype, she considered the possibility that he might listen to them.

The commander shouted, "Zarakisitiah! See if you can understand these barbarians! Perhaps they know how to signal with their hands!"

Obedience was marked only by the clicking of the chariots' wheels. Three vehicles surrounded a horseman in a triangular formation. At a measured trot, the group approached.

Insulted, Helena set her jaw and watched her grandfather's compatriots with narrowed eyes. The second in command was a lean, elongated man; his style of riding was laconic and loose. But as he pulled out his sword with an expert flourish, Valamir rested his hand on his hilt, quiet with confidence.

Three horse lengths away, the Persians halted. Zarakisitiah surveyed Valamir and Ishyite, his contempt scarcely veiled. But when his eyes rested on Helena, his breath drew inward.

He raised his sword in salute. "Greetings! You have come to surrender?" he asked. His blue eyes were like stones in an angular face.

Helena edged Passial two paces forward, presenting herself in clear view. As she spoke in Persian, her voice was pitched low. "My name is Helena, daughter of Michilieh, granddaughter of Balusistriam. To whom have I the honor of speaking?"

Zarakisitiah's face turned pale. "Impossible!"

"Pray excuse me, but I speak the truth."

The Persian's brow creased with thought. "Your accent is unquestionably noble. I do not understand how you find yourself in such unsavory company. Explain yourself."

"My story is for your commander's ears."

He pursed his lips. "You'd best be certain of your tale, *Helena*." Zarakisitiah jerked his head to a charioteer. "Tell our leader I require his expert judgment."

Silently, Helena watched the chariot's progress back to the Persian line and to its broad-shouldered commander. After conferring a moment, their leader cantered his mount toward them. He was flanked on both sides by two other chariots, each drawn by a pair of sleek, black horses.

Helena's eyes were locked on the horseman. As he approached, she heard a roaring in her ears. She knew it had nothing to do with darkness and runes, but with the man himself: the way he sat his horse, his squared shoulders, his short-cropped black hair gleaming in the sunlight.

Joining Zarakisitiah, the commander acknowledged his subordinate with a curt nod.

"The woman speaks Persian," his aide reported.

Disdaining his guards' protection, the commander reined his horse to the forefront. His gaze rested first on Valamir, who returned the scrutiny in silence. Helena's temples throbbed.

Into the void, Passial nickered, his whinny deep with recognition. The Persian's head jerked to the white stallion and Helena, who stared intently at the man who had her grandfather's face, only younger, and lined with disdain.

"Passial!" he said with disbelief.

The stallion's ears pointed forward and he neighed again.

The Persian's dark blue eyes flashed with pain, but he staunched his distress with hostility. "Where did you get this horse?" he said, not recognizing her.

Helena answered him in Persian, her tone exquisite with contempt. "The same place where I got my sword." She held it up so that the sunlight glinted off its silver sheath.

"He is dead, then. My father's dead."

Helena was vehement. "You are correct, Father. He died as we searched for *you*!"

"No," he said, looking at her closely for the first time. "It cannot be!"

Overwhelmed by anger, she closed the distance between them, her green eyes blazing. Forgetting everything - Attila's mission, the two armies poised for battle - Helena felt alone with him on the windy steppes.

"Look at me! I am the child you left behind in Constantinople. I survived, but no thanks to you!"

"Helena, you could be your mother," he said, his voice hushed.

His grief dampened her fiery outrage. Remembering the circumstances of their meeting, she took a deep breath, steadying herself. "This is my husband, Prince Valamir of the Ostrogoths. The fact that I'm alive, I owe to him." She turned to Valamir, his hand still poised on his sword. "Meet Michilieh, my father," she said in Greek.

Valamir raised his right eyebrow in surprise. With a slight nod of his head, he acknowledged his father-in-law in the same language. "It is an honor to meet you."

Michilieh frowned. "I thank you for protecting Helena. In appreciation of your services, I shall not accuse you of the crime of raptus, though you wed my daughter without my permission. Indeed, you shall have a just reward." Finished with Valamir, he turned to Helena. "A most favorable union awaits you. But don't worry. I am certain your betrothed will be able to forgive your unfortunate loss of virginity. After all, his interest, nay his passion, rests in our ancient and noble bloodlines."

Helena's face tightened. She shifted her weight on Passial, signaling him to step backward. "How dare you! I'm not your chattel," she said in Persian. "*You* are not my father. *He* is dead, dead these five long years. Until his last breath, he tried to keep me safe."

"Do not forget my rights, Helena. Under both Roman and Persian law, you are guilty. Your marriage to this barbarian does not exist. As a woman, you can't understand the magnitude of my arrangements. Come with me quietly and I shall not punish you for your disrespect."

Her cheeks grew hot. She itched to slap him, to wipe the arrogance from his face. Choked with hate, she felt the familiar darkness seeping into her and feeding her rage. The hollow voice was close, nestled within her mind. It craved to be unleashed and sweetened its demands with the promise of invincibility. But she refused its call; she did not want to pay its price with more of her soul.

With quick precision, she drew the Light sign on Passial's neck and breathed deeply, releasing the dark power to the sun. She felt cleansed, as if shedding a loathsome burden.

Michilieh stared with avid intensity.

Deeply unsettled, Helena concentrated on delivering Attila's message and kept her voice flat and neutral. "The Huns have rescued the child, Altiere. She is safe. They have in their possession the woman, Rhoddinia. Their leader, Attila, requires a meeting to discuss terms." She pulled the pendant from beneath her coat. "Altiere lent me this to prove the story."

Michilieh reached for it. Helena shook her head. "I promised to return it to her."

Her father studied the emblem on her chest, then looked into his daughter's face. "Does the Hun ask for ransom?"

"No, but he hopes for a fair reward."

Michilieh nodded his head once. "That is just." He asked, almost as an afterthought, "What of the guards?"

"Regrettably, they are dead. And I must inform you that once Altiere's abduction was uncovered, Rhoddinia was questioned extensively."

"The Huns did our work for us. The moment the child was seized, the traitors were marked for death." Michilieh's eyes glinted. "Rhoddinia has much to confess."

"My leader, Lord Attila, would meet with you," Valamir said in his accented Greek.

Looking down his thin nose, Michilieh examined Valamir. His eyes were the same brilliant blue as her grandfather's, but were remote and almost devoid of humanity. "How is it that you speak Greek as a native of Thrace?"

Valamir's face was expressionless. "My mother was Thracian."

For an instant, she saw pain in Michilieh's aloof eyes. "So was my first wife. Helena's resemblance to her mother is striking."

"Indeed," Valamir said. "From the beginning, she reminded me of my mother. Perhaps the two women were related."

Michilieh's superior expression softened. "In Thrace, the blood lines run together. Unless your mother lives, we'll never know."

Staring at Helena, Michilieh's eyes became wistful with memory. All at once, she remembered how his laughter filled the house in Constantinople and her heart hurt.

Her father's voice was hoarse. "You must stay with me, Helena. We've lost too many years. The marriage I arranged is with Altiere's true father. The honor of being one of the Emperor's wives should take your breath away. Every luxury would be yours. And Altiere's alone now, with no one to protect her in the harem. She needs a woman's love. You can give her that."

"Michilieh," Helena said, finding her voice and pointing to Valamir. "This is my husband, and the Wise Lord willing, I shall grow old with him. Not once have you asked about me or about your father. I have a husband," she repeated. "And I love him."

"Helena," Valamir said. "Let Ishyite take you back. You don't need to translate for us."

"If she leaves," Michilieh said, "there will be no meeting with your leader."

"You will see Helena soon. Do you forget Altiere's importance to your Emperor?"

Michilieh's hand was at his sword, his lips twisted. "You dare to remind me of my duty?"

"I'll stay, Valamir!" Helena interrupted. "It's for the best."

"If that's what you want, Helena," Valamir said. He called Ishyite closer, and spoke to him in rapid Hunnic. The Hun nodded his head once, then wheeled his horse back to Attila.

"Attila should know you are Helena's father," Valamir said.

"As you wish," Michilieh said, then spoke in Persian. "Helena, did my father die at peace?"

"No, he fought death. He died with a curse on his lips and blood on his hands," she said, answering him in Greek.

Michilieh's eyes shone, betraying his fervor. He whispered with repressed excitement, "Did he show you the rune?"

"I saw it," she said nonchalantly, enjoying the look of frustration on his face.

"Show me, show me what he did!" he commanded.

"I will not."

"You are disobedient."

"Perhaps, but if grandfather had trusted you, he would have taught you himself." She hesitated, her chest tight. "Evil comes with the power."

"And how do you know, Helena?" Michilieh asked, his voice reminding her of a snake, hissing softly.

She stared at him, watching the play of emotions cross his face that was dominated by greed. "Once summoned, the power is exquisite. But the wielder of the rune is not the master, but its victim. A presence comes with it, feeding from the one who calls it forth, leeching away the life force. If Grandfather hadn't used his last strength invoking it, hoping to protect me, he might have lived. The curse is two-edged, cutting where you least expect. I survived, as Grandfather commanded, but not my son." She paused. "That surprises you, Father, that you had a grandson? A fine boy? But he's dead now, murdered before my eyes."

Michilieh gasped, his voice a low sob. "Who did this to our family? I demand his head!"

Stung by his method of reprisal, Helena covered her mouth with her hand. "He's a dead man, though his body still fouls the Earth. I cursed him with my own blood, but Father, it was not well done."

"Helena, you're a woman. It needs a man's strength to work the dark magic."

"No, Father. You don't understand. It's foul, evil!"

"You know nothing! Even the priests dared not defy Balusistriam. And why? Because of the heritage that you deny me! It's mine! Tradition demands it be passed from father to son. You can still heal the rift in the pattern. Show me the rune."

"No, it's profane. It will die with me. It twists nature against her will. I deny you knowledge of the Dark Lord, though already he plays you on his web. Be in the Light; remember the essence of your father's teachings, not his mistakes."

Michilieh became still, as if considering her words. But as he spoke, Helena knew he lied. "My daughter, stay with me. You have the best of my father. Share his wisdom with me."

She shook her head. "I named my son for you, calling him Mikael. If you want your father's teachings, ask Balusistriam's spirit for guidance, and pray to the Wise Lord for the strength to keep to the righteous path. Beyond this, I can offer nothing."

Michilieh's lips compressed into a tight line. His eyes shifted to the left. Following them, Helena saw Attila and Ishyite galloping hard toward their small group.

"My Lord approaches," Valamir said.

Attila and Ishyite reined their horses to a sliding halt. Michilieh sneered. But as Attila's eyes probed his face, the Persian's haughty expression changed into one of grudging respect.

"So, Helena," Attila said in Greek, "you've been reunited with your father." Inclining his head, he acknowledged Michilieh. "Your daughter has shown courage and integrity, qualities I look forward to discovering in her father."

"Lord Attila," Valamir said, "this is Michilieh, the Commander of the Imperial Force. Michilieh, Lord Attila, nephew of King Rugliva of the Huns."

Both men studied the other, each seeking signs of weakness.

"I thank you, Lord Attila, for ensuring my daughter's safety. She looks well."

"Indeed, the gods have been generous to Prince Valamir."

Hostility shadowed Michilieh's face, but he suppressed it. "We've much to discuss. The Emperor himself will be pleased by your rescue of his niece and your capture of the traitor. You shall have your reward!"

"You are most generous, Michilieh. But winter nips at our horses' hooves. We travel westward to our domain."

"Stay. Pass the winter in Istakhr, where the weather is warm. It is our holy city; its sacredness guarantees your safety."

"Your offer is noble, but my men long for home. Yet, I'm surprised that your Emperor would send you searching for a child of such importance with empty hands."

"Of course, we have something to offer, but it's not nearly enough." He lowered his voice, as if to a fellow conspirator, glancing pointedly at Helena. "I have another matter that might interest you."

"Follow us back to the hills, Michilieh. You can set up camp near us, but we'll keep enough distance between the men to preserve the peace."

"Why not here? In moments, my men could erect a tent."

"Your offer is kind, but in my quarters you'd be able to see Altiere."

"Agreed!" Michilieh said. "We'll follow you. My daughter is surety of your safety."

"That is noble, but we place our trust in our horses' swift legs and the aim of our arrows. We ride. Command your men."

Without another word, Attila wheeled his horse, signaling their departure. As Helena felt Passial burst under her into a gallop, she did not look back, her heart feeling lighter with each stride away from Michilieh.

Attila shouted to her, "Sad to leave your father?"

The wind pummeled her face, stealing all but the loudest of words. "No!" she said.

He smiled with cynical amusement. "Indeed. We must speak more of this before I meet him again."

As they reached the Hunnic line, their horses stretched out into a run. Not slowing the pace, Attila roared with exultation.

The Huns answered him with chilling cries, once again sending waves of fear down Helena's spine.

Following their Lord, the mounted force galloped toward camp, easily outdistancing the Persians. Helena glanced at Valamir, riding at her side, and longed to be alone with him, wanting to reaffirm their love and to dispel her bitter disappointment with her father. She hoped there would be time.

CHAPTER TWENTY-SEVEN

Raising clouds of dust behind them, the Huns galloped toward their camp. Helena rode alongside Valamir in confusion, feeling with equal passion both hate and love for her father. She remembered his laughter and part of her still longed for his approval.

Her grandfather's judgments about Michilieh had been harsh from disillusionment. Helena had made excuses for him, needing to believe in her father's love. As a child, she had pretended that he *had* written letters and sent gifts, but they had been lost. Her adult mind saw him clearly; but her heart still carried the longings of the inner child.

Well ahead of the Persians, they reached the encampment, filling the rows of tents with hot, lathered horses. Greeted by a welcoming roar, Attila raised his hand for silence. He spoke crisply in Hunnic, issuing commands. Women, slaves, and servants ran to the men, offering refreshment while others brought water for the horses. He shouted commands and the Huns re-deployed their forces within sight of the camp, yet far enough away to be out of range of an enemy's arrow.

Attila organized the men in three separate squares, keeping Helena and Valamir with him at the core. Much time passed before they saw the Persians marching, chariots arrayed at its center like a phalanx, ready for attack.

Suddenly afraid, Helena glanced at Attila. Feeling her gaze, he turned to her, his eyes fierce with confidence. "Do you trust your father?"

"No," she said, realizing her fear had dropped away, its intensity crumbling to dust in face of Attila's self-possession.

"I thought not." He paused, his eyes narrowed. "Valamir, do you think he'll order a charge?"

"Not with his daughter here. He cares nothing for her happiness, but he won't put her person at risk."

Helena looked at Valamir, masking neither her grief nor her need. Attila's eyes sparkled with amusement, but he moved his horse to the right, giving the two lovers an illusion of privacy. She steeled herself against the inevitable sarcasm, but he ignored them and engaged Ishyite in conversation.

Valamir's face was stern and his voice was abrupt. "Do you want to go with your father?"

"Not at all! Perhaps once I would have accepted his life, though with regret. My grandfather reared me to think for myself and to make decisions. It could be that he did me a disservice. My father's world has no tolerance for a woman with opinions. Valamir, each day you give me freedom and in return, you have my heart."

His smile was brilliant. The sun, well past mid-day, was a pale luminescence. The chill wind brushed her face, but she laughed, warm with love.

"Your opinion, Helena," Attila said shortly afterward.

Her brow was etched with thought. "My father has wealth, but it does not satisfy him. He craves power, as much as he can grasp. Through me, he plans a marriage to unite his blood with the Emperor's. My refusal counts for nothing, an inconvenience to surmount. Next he'll negotiate with you."

Attila paused, then shook his head. "For a price, I shall release Altiere and Rhoddinia, but I don't sell my friends."

His words filled her eyes with tears. Momentarily embarrassed, Attila was brusque. "After all, who else insults me with such style? And think of what Valamir would do? First, he would murder me, then get himself killed attempting your rescue. No, we'll keep things the way they are. Michilieh will learn to understand, one way or another."

"Please don't hurt him," she said. "Despite everything, he is my father."

Attila nodded as if he approved, but concentrated on the Persians' advance. Across the empty steppes, Michilieh shouted, commanding his men to halt.

"Bevion!" Attila said. "You come with us this time. And you, Ishyite."

The five proceeded to the middle ground. Once again, Helena felt the prickling of danger along her neck. Two black horses erupted from the Imperial ranks, ridden by Michilieh and another man.

"Your pace was good," her father said to Attila as they met.

"We breed our horses for speed. Less than a league south, another stream comes out of the hills onto the steppes. For obvious reasons, I insist our men not be camped too close. Do you agree, Michilieh?" Attila asked.

"Yes. But I need time with my daughter, alone."

"As we share our meal, she'll be with us. If you need to say anything privately to her, speak in Persian. Neither Valamir nor I will understand."

"That will be adequate. Allow me to introduce Altiere's cousin, my aide, Zarakisitiah." Michilieh gestured toward Attila and spoke in Persian to the thin, younger man. "Their commander, Lord Attila."

With a smile, he fastened his eyes on Helena. "Zarakisitiah, may I introduce you to your cousin's future bride, my daughter, Helena?"

The Persian studied her with proprietary interest. "She's well-formed, Michilieh. Such a woman would be a welcome addition to any man's harem."

"Zarakisitiah," Helena said, a knife in her voice, "my father forgets that I already have a husband."

At a loss for words, the Persian looked at Michilieh for direction before speaking. But her father ignored him and stared at Helena, his face a study in stone.

He snapped, "She wed him without my permission. The marriage is invalid."

"I think not, Father. As a widow and a mother, my life is my own!"

He shouted, "Not under the laws of the Sassian Empire or Rome!"

"But we are not in Persia, and Rome is far away! Should we come together before a Roman magistrate, you may state your objections to him!"

"You are disobedient! A great disappointment as a daughter! A natural woman would be thrilled at the prospect of marriage to the Emperor! What is wrong with you?"

She shouted back, "Absolutely nothing!" Then she quieted her voice, speaking between clenched teeth. "Altiere waits. Did anyone remember to bring one of her dolls?"

Her father was silent. Helena's lips tightened into a frown. "Does she know either of you?"

His nostrils flared. "Yes, Helena! Altiere knows me well. Her mother was my wife's sister."

"I'm sorry for her loss," she said, keeping her tone neutral. "Has your marriage to her been fruitful, Father?"

Zarakisitiah rolled his eyes, indicating a trespass onto a delicate subject. Undaunted by his warning, she persevered. "I have no brothers or sisters?"

"You remain the only one," Michilieh said.

"How sad for you to have no son," she said with the barest hint of compassion. "Does Zarakisitiah understand Greek? It's rude to speak Persian at length in front of Valamir and Attila."

Zarakisitiah shook his head emphatically. "I have no need of such a barbaric tongue."

"Greek? Barbaric?" Helena said, switching to it, thinking of the ancient, but durable hatred of all things Greek by the Persians. "It would seem that some attitudes haven't changed in Persia even after a thousand years!"

Attila coughed, interrupting Helena's and Michilieh's bickering. Both turned to him, startled.

"Would you honor me by accepting my hospitality, Michilieh? As we speak, my slaves prepare a feast," he said.

"That would be excellent," Michilieh said. "But I require two hostages as a guarantee of our safety. A minor formality."

"I understand your concern. In exchange, I need your promise that my men will be well-treated. If they suffer any disrespect, I cannot answer for the consequences."

Michilieh nodded, narrowing his eyes as he glared at Valamir. "I'd be satisfied with Prince Valamir alone, having noted his importance to you."

Helena held her breath.

"That's impossible," Attila said. "In his place, I offer Prince Thiudimir, Valamir's only brother."

Helena felt a wave of relief. Michilieh's problems would be solved too conveniently by Valamir's "accidental" death.

"I accept him. Who will be the other?"

"Ishyite, my cousin."

"Done."

Attila signaled to his force. A horse and rider responded, emerging from the ranks, galloping toward them.

"Bevion and Ishyite," Attila said. "Do you agree to go as hostages to the Persians?"

Bevion did not hesitate. "I'm honored to serve the tribe."

Ishyite seconded him. "My life is yours to command."

His voice like steel across stone, Valamir interrupted. "Michilieh, my brother is close to my heart. Warn your men that should he be mistreated, Zarakisitiah will pay with his life."

Her father smiled, but it was frost on Helena's heart. "Had I a brother, I'd feel the same. But for my daughter, I'm alone. It brings me joy she *had* you as her protector."

She shook her head at his unyielding stubbornness.

"Father, does anyone else speak Greek?" she asked, concerned that Bevion would be unable to communicate his needs.

"Are we barbarians who would travel without a scribe?"

"I don't know what you are. But Bevion and Ishyite will need him to make themselves understood."

Her father shrugged. "It could be arranged."

As Bevion and Ishyite crossed over to Michilieh, Helena ached with foreboding. She stared at Bevion, almost as if she would never see him again.

Listening to her heart, she spoke in earnest Greek. "Father, you expressed great interest in Grandfather's heritage, thinking it was for you. Perhaps he did leave me a power. When I summon it, the cost is great, stealing from my very being. Should Bevion or Ishyite be harmed in any way, I'll use his legacy to curse not only you, but everyone under your command. Do I make myself clear?"

"More than clear, Daughter. Now I remember why I so rarely came home. My father never agreed with me, preferring to meddle in my affairs. You are just like him! I'll keep these two safe, but not because of your threats! The Emperor would never forgive me if Zarakisitiah died."

His words stung, unlocking turmoil. Containing her anger, she stared at his face, so reminiscent of her grandfather's. Instantly, her heart was weighted by sadness. "Then we understand each other. As Grandfather always said, your word is good when it is to your advantage."

Michilieh's eyes blazed and his jaw pinched with suppressed rage. His speech was measured. "You'll not provoke me, Daughter, on this auspicious day. Whatever your feelings, you are of my blood and have obligations to me."

Helena seethed. He turned from her, holding up a hand with fingers extended. In response, five men galloped their horses toward their leader. He spoke to them at length, detailing the care of the two hostages. Helena listened intently with her mouth set in a grim line.

When he had finished, she asked, "Where's the translator?"

"With my men."

"Attila, with your permission," Helena said, "I'd like to see and hear this scribe for myself."

"You disbelieve me?" her father asked, his voice nasal with temper.

"I mean no insult, but it would give me peace of mind to see the man with my own eyes."

"It would please me as well, Michilieh," Attila said.

Nodding curtly, her father spoke to one of his men, succinct in his instructions to bring the scribe. Immediately, the soldier obeyed, urging his horse into a run. While they waited, the silence was pronounced.

Finally, Zarakisitiah pointed to two men on horseback. "See, they come." Expertly, the soldier brought his mount to a smooth halt. But the translator could not bring his horse under control until it had almost reached the Hunnic line.

As the Huns shouted with laughter, Michilieh's face flushed with anger. "He's a scribe," he said, making an obvious statement. At a walk, the man rode his large, black horse on a short rein to his commander, his narrow face ashen with fear.

Attila ignored Michilieh's embarrassment and kept a straight face. "Is he yours to sell?"

"Possibly, if the price agreed with me."

"Excellent! We'll barter," Attila said, smiling.

The translator bowed his head to Michilieh. "How may I serve you?" he asked in Persian.

"Speak to this man in Greek, Alexander," he said. "You should be able to speak your own language despite your evident lack of skill on a horse!"

The man was effusive. "Greetings! It brings me pleasure to speak to you in the most cherished tongue of the Roman Empire!"

"I'm satisfied," Helena said, interrupting the Greek's enthusiastic flow of words. "Please accept my thanks."

"Very well," Michilieh said, frowning. He gave his men further instructions about the hostages, along with orders to set up camp for the night.

As Bevion and Ishyite followed their escort to the Persian line, Valamir shouted, "May Mithras be with you always, Bevion!"

Nonchalantly, his brother glanced back with a wave. Meanwhile, the Greek attached himself to the blond Goth, chatting non-stop and taking full advantage of the opportunity to speak his native language. Bevion ignored him. Soon, they were out of earshot.

Riding alongside Attila, Michilieh voiced his disgust to Helena in Persian. "With his very presence on the earth, the scribe makes a mockery of his namesake!"

She answered in the same language, finding its rhythm seductive and comforting. "What? Alexander?" Helena said. She remembered playing with her father's toy horse and chariot, and creating intricate sagas about her hero, Alexander the Great. Her voice was wistful. "Did Grandfather make him come alive for you, too?"

"He made history magical. I could almost smell the flames after Sikunder the Destroyer set fire to the Great Library."

"He was good to me."

Michilieh's smile was calculated, its warmth forced. "Balusistriam would be proud of you, Helena. But he'd be shamed by your stubborn refusal to honor your duty."

Unblinking, she held his eyes, her heart sore. She switched to Greek. "You care nothing for me except as a commodity for trade. Ambition fills you, stripping away any love you could have felt for the flesh of your flesh, the bone of your bone. But it's your loss, not mine."

He kept to Persian, disregarding her Greek. "I only want what is best for you, Helena. You deserve better than these barbarians."

Valamir's voice cut the air between them. "Michilieh, enjoy the time you have with your daughter before your paths part."

"Nothing has been settled!"

"You are wrong. I stand by Helena's decision. Respect it or dance with my sword."

Mocking the warning, Michilieh raised an eyebrow. His smile was bleak. "We shall see, *Prince* Valamir."

Attila shouted, "Come, Michilieh! Show me how well you Persians breed horses. We ride!"

Pivoting his black stallion, Attila charged the Hunnic line at a run. The waiting horsemen shifted position, creating a narrow pathway. The rest of Attila's small entourage cantered behind him through the channel. As Helena glanced back, it closed as if it had never been. The Hunnic force kept vigil, watching the Persian force move southeast, away from the camp.

When they arrived at Attila's quarters, slaves ran to tend to their horses. Inside, a small feast awaited, set on three low tables. Altiere was nowhere to be seen. Helena understood Attila's strategy: her absence would force Michilieh to inquire about the child and subtly tip the balance of power toward the Hun.

With a smooth, but imperious, gesture, Attila indicated places on the rug before his simple chair. Despite Helena's intentions, her father managed to seat himself beside her and blocked her view of Valamir. Instantly, she remembered his scent. It brought back the memory of the sunlit house in Constantinople, filled with her grandfather's quiet presence.

She turned to her father and spoke in Greek. "It's been a long time since you were so near."

Michilieh's eyes flashed with torment, but he kept his expression impassive. His voice, however, betrayed him. "You remind me of your mother," he replied in Persian.

She answered in Greek. "What was her name? Grandfather would not speak of her."

He was shocked. "I named you for your mother, Helena. I never imagined that you would not know," he said, keeping to Persian.

"He considered her unworthy of your ancient bloodlines. Did he tell you?" she asked in Greek.

"Many times."

"With your intolerance for my marriage, you walk in Grandfather's shadow."

"It's different. You're a woman."

She hated his smug expression and his unyielding belief in the superiority of his male knowledge.

A man poured wine. Helena's gaze followed the serving hand to its owner's face and saw Caratipian. Betraying no hint of recognition, he seemed like just another servant. But when his profile obscured the left side of his face from the Persians, he quickly blinked his eye.

Repressing a smile, Helena glanced at Attila, his face alive with mischief. For a moment, Zarakisitiah studied Caratipian suspiciously, then dismissed him, perhaps unable to imagine a Persian in such low company.

Attila smiled. "We questioned Rhoddinia at length, but despite our persistence, we learned little. I think she's shielding someone, someone at court who knows poisons."

Michilieh nodded. "Your theory has merit. We have the time and the means to discover the truth. Would you be so kind as to present Altiere?"

"But of course! It is my pleasure to offer such a small service to the Sassian Empire!"

"And you shall have your reward. We also require the woman, Rhoddinia."

Attila paused, his eyes deep with regret. "She is another matter."

"Explain yourself."

"The return of the child is a gesture of friendship between two nations. But for Rhoddinia, we need payment."

"And just what do you want?"

"That would depend, Michilieh, on your appreciation for Altiere's safe return."

"Indeed," he said, then fell silent.

Unconcerned, Attila chewed his meal with enjoyment, smacking his lips. Zarakisitiah picked at his food, eyeing the Hun with disgust.

Suddenly, he spoke Persian to Caratipian. "More wine."

Caratipian's face was blank.

Zarakisitiah relaxed, his mouth transformed by a condescending grin. "You!" he said, tossing a chunk of meat at Caratipian's cheek to attract his attention. He gestured to his glass. "Wine!"

Responding to the pantomime, Caratipian obeyed with alacrity.

"I could have sworn that slave was Persian," Zarakisitiah murmured to Michilieh. "But he doesn't understand a word of our language. He appears to be a simpleton."

Helena's father frowned. "The man's no fool. Watch your tongue."

Zarakisitiah blew up with exasperation. "You're too cautious! Looking for spies behind every curtain. Where's Altiere? Why haven't they brought her in?"

Michilieh glared at him. "You talk too much. We wait."

Suddenly, Helena had enough of them. She stood abruptly and repositioned herself on Valamir's right. With him as a shield between Michilieh and herself, she felt safe.

Valamir wrapped his arm around her shoulders and whispered in Gothic. "Don't worry, Helena. All will be well."

Compared to Michilieh and Zarakisitiah's fine garments, Valamir's clothing was coarse and uncivilized. Yet, as she met his eyes, nothing had changed. Their lives were joined, linked in a way that reached beyond words, apart from time and space. She wanted to be alone with him, sequestered in their tent. As if reading her mind, Valamir's breath was a caress to her ear.

"Later," he said.

Her father interrupted, his voice percussive as a drum. "What happened to your hand?"

"It was broken."

"I have training. Let me examine it."

Reluctantly, she extended her arm. Reaching across Valamir, Michilieh unwrapped the bandages carefully and pressed gently on one bone, then another.

"Does this hurt?" he asked. She shook her head, both repelled and fascinated at his expertise.

"Move your fingers."

She obeyed, but found that too much motion brought pain.

"Does that hurt?"

"Just a little."

"Your hand is all but healed." Slowly, he turned it over and saw her palm. "What is this? It looks like a knife wound."

She shook her head. "It doesn't matter."

Still holding her hand, Michilieh's eyes were zealous and insistent. He blinked, as if coming back to himself, and let her go. "Who was your physician? His work was excellent. Worthy of a Persian."

Not wanting to betray Caratipian's masquerade, she was silent.

Valamir cut through her confusion. "Tell him. Caratipian deserves praise."

"Father, this is Caratipian. He was Valamir's tutor."

Michilieh smiled broadly and spoke in Persian. "Thank you for saving my daughter's hand. Because of you, she'll have use of it. But it will stiffen if not encouraged to move. It's time for all wrappings to be removed."

Caratipian brought his palms together and half bowed from the waist, but did not respond in Persian, maintaining the essence of his charade.

"What about Altiere?" Michilieh asked.

"But of course," Attila said. "Nothing would give me more pleasure than to see you two reunited."

He clapped his hands. A Hun entered from behind, his black hair creased with braids, a short sword at his side. A diminutive woman followed, clad in a long blue dress. Her white hand held Altiere's. The child, smiling, prattled happily in Persian to her new friend, who did not understand a word. But the young woman's eyes were warm as she held her finger to her lips, encouraging Altiere to be quiet.

The child stood still, bewildered at her change of surroundings. Then her eyes lit up when she saw Caratipian. "Look! Attila's wives made me my own doll! Isn't she beautiful?" she exclaimed in Persian.

"Altiere," Helena said. "Greet your visitors."

The child stared at Michilieh. Then she gasped, shouting, "Uncle Mischa!" Forgetting Caratipian, she rushed to Helena's father, burrowing her face in his chest. "You came!"

As Helena watched, her heart ached - not for Altiere, but for the years when she had been a child, longing for the comfort of her father's arms. She blinked back tears, and looked away.

Attila bowed his head formally to his wife. Taking her gently by the hand, he spoke softly as he ushered her from the tent. The guard walked a respectful six paces behind them.

Returning to his guests, Attila studied Altiere nestled in Michilieh's lap, but kept his face a blank mask. Despite the child's embrace, Michilieh preserved his dignity; his lips were taut with arrogance and his Greek was clipped, almost strident.

"You've been good to Altiere. I offer my thanks."

"My wives spoiled her. They'll miss her."

"This is my friend, Helena," Altiere said to Michilieh, smiling at Helena. "She's very kind."

"Well, I have a surprise for you," Michilieh said. "She's the daughter I thought I'd lost."

"She's the girl you talk about? But she's all grown up!"

"So it would seem," he said to himself. His voice became harsh. "Lord Attila, I offer all that we carry with us. It's not enough, but unless you wish to travel to Istakhr, I can do no more."

Attila's fists were at his waist. "Send your aide for your gifts of thanks and we shall see. My men will provide him an escort. While we wait for his return, we'll discuss Rhoddinia. I'll allow him re-entry to the camp with no more than ten guards. When our negotiations are complete, we'll exchange hostages."

"Done." Michilieh was curt as he told the other Persian his requirements. Zarakisitiah spoke in a whisper. "Are you mad? You don't plan to give these barbarians everything! They have no appreciation for quality!"

"Do as I command. We're in no danger. And the price is modest. Think of *our* reward for rescuing Altiere. Bring the scribe. Attila has need of him. He'll sweeten the pot."

"Alexander?"

"Zarakisitiah, you tire my patience. Do as I command."

The aide stood, dusting off imaginary specks of dust from his clothes. "Very well. Not having to see his simpering face will almost be worth what we're about to give away."

Michilieh looked at him sternly, his voice sharp with vehemence. "Remember. I remain with Altiere. Don't do anything foolish."

Zarakisitiah swept his brown hair from his face. "I'll not disappoint you."

"Just keep to your orders. Anything less, or more, and I'll have your head, royal connections or not!"

"Yes, Michilieh!" he said, almost sounding like a soldier.

"Excellent!" Michilieh said in Greek to Attila. "Zarakisitiah has his orders."

Attila clapped his broad hands twice, loudly. Two armed Huns answered the summons. When Attila spoke to them in terse Hunnic, they took positions at either side of Zarakisitiah. As one gestured toward the door with his sword, the Persian looked ill.

"I think that they want you to follow them," Michilieh said with a cold smile.

Zarakisitiah glanced nervously at his companions. "Until I return, Michilieh."

"Until then. Walk in the Light."

Once he had departed, Michilieh's eyes met Attila's. "The man's a fool," he said.

The Hun was serious. "I have found that even a fool has his uses, given the correct circumstances."

"Then you have discovered a truth known only to a few," Michilieh said. "But to another matter, one that presses on my heart, Lord Attila. I petition your help. My daughter, Helena, must remain with me. Being a woman, she does not know what is best for her. Through the marriage I have planned, she will create a great alliance between my family and the Emperor himself. But she spurns my offer, refusing to leave the man she wed without my permission. If you command Prince Valamir to release her, I'm certain that he would obey."

"Why would the emperor take as his wife a woman who is no longer a virgin, only half-Persian, and not even royal? This makes no sense, Michilieh."

"They want the blood lines of my father. He always insisted that he was descended from the prophet Zarathushtra himself. This has been confirmed by the Imperial Historians. Balusistriam possessed certain powers. Some have called it a Legacy. The Emperor wants it. Helena, the last of my father's line, can endow their children with the Prophet's Gift."

"Why don't you just father another child? Have you suffered a wound that prevents it?"

"My wife, cousin to the Emperor, has yet to give birth to a live infant."

"You confine yourself to one woman?"

"There have been others, but they've suffered strange illnesses and passed away."

Thinking of Magga and the younger rival who had died mysteriously after catching Kansbar's eye, Helena thought immediately of poison.

Valamir interrupted. "Michilieh forgets. Helena is my wife. To take her, he'll have to go through me first."

Attila laughed. "And that's the crux of the problem. You see, Michilieh, if you draw Valamir's blood, we'll have to kill you. It's our way. Find a way to make another child. Discipline your wife. It's a man's right to share his seed."

"I need Helena. She carries my father's teachings."

"Unless Helena wishes otherwise, she stays," Attila said.

Her father glared at her, not angrily, but with hunger. "In Thrace, the blood ties are complex. Perhaps Valamir has married his cousin unknowingly. I've forgotten the name of my wife's village, but she mentioned it was near the northern border. She came to Constantinople as a girl of ten or twelve. Her father had left his land, wearied by defending it against the Goths. He became a goldsmith of great renown. But the finest jewel in his shop was the woman who became my wife."

He added in a whisper, "Helena, wouldn't you like to learn more about your mother? My father was wrong about Thrace. Even Socrates praised their abilities in medicine and healing. I will teach you what you long to know."

Mutely, Helena shook her head and squeezed Valamir's hand hard.

Attila frowned. "Michilieh, I wonder if you'd relinquish a beloved wife."

Michilieh's body was rigid and his breathing was shallow. "You interfere, Attila," he said in a tense voice.

"It is my right. Valamir is my second-in-command. Can you be reconciled to Helena's choice of husband?"

"Never."

"Unless you want to taint our negotiations about Rhoddinia, the subject is closed."

Michilieh tightened his jaw. "For the moment, but it's not finished." He stared at Helena. "If she comes to regret her chosen life, would you send me word?"

"Yes. But I hope that day never comes. I'd miss her. Few have the courage to speak their hearts before me."

Michilieh glanced at her. "You compliment my daughter's courage."

"Yes."

"You didn't answer Attila. Would you allow *your* wife to return to her family?" Helena asked.

"No. It is not the Persian way."

"Then why do you expect otherwise from my husband?"

"In exchange for your freedom, I offer him a fortune."

"You insult both me and your daughter," Valamir said. "Is she a horse to be traded at market? Show her respect and you may come to visit us. Perhaps we'll present you with a grandchild."

Michilieh's face transformed, reminding Helena of a wild animal, trapped and desperate. Yet, watching him, she was unafraid. Suddenly, she yearned to help him.

"Father, I will always love you, even though our lives keep us apart. And Grandfather, despite his bitter words, searched for you until the end," she said, speaking from her heart.

"If you truly loved me, Helena, you'd obey my wishes. You can't begin to understand your importance to me."

Helena ground her teeth, hating his expediency. Altiere asked, "Why is Uncle Mischa so angry?"

"Because he's not getting his way. Show me your new doll while we wait for your cousin's return."

As Helena admired Altiere's rag doll, dressed in a multitude of colorful fabrics, she felt her father's eyes. But she ignored them. She had offered no conditions for her love. In return, he had demanded her soul.

When Helena placed the Imperial pendant around Altiere's neck, the little girl beamed.

"I knew you wouldn't forget," she whispered.

The tent was quiet as Caratipian cleared away the remains of the meal. The fire burned brightly in the hearth. Altiere yawned.

As the child rubbed her eyes, Helena spoke to her father in Greek. "As I said, once you were a grandfather. Let me tell you about my son."

Without waiting for a reply, she described Mikael in loving detail. For once, her father did not interrupt. With somber eyes, he listened silently. As if to give her privacy, Attila and Valamir spoke quietly to each other, not breaking the soliloquy. Her gentle flow of words did not stop until a slave brought the news that Zarakisitiah had returned.

CHAPTER TWENTY-EIGHT

Zarakisitiah entered Attila's tent. His mouth was a gash of contempt. Two Persian soldiers followed him, carrying a medium-sized, wooden chest suspended between two poles. He pointed his forefinger at Attila, imperiously ordering them to place their heavy burden at the Hun's feet. Zarakisitiah's hands clapped in dismissal and the Persian escort withdrew soundlessly.

He took his position by Michilieh, grumbling audibly under his breath. "It's too much. Half would have been enough."

Attila did not glance at the chest, but signaled a guard to open it. As the Hun flung open the lid, Zarakisitiah gasped at the heap of golden coins, intermixed with sparkling stones. Attila was silent; his face was devoid of expression. Slowly, he leaned down to select a single, gold piece, then a few gems. He bit the coin, testing its quality.

Ignoring Michilieh, he strode to the tent's entrance. A servant leapt to open the flap and held it open uncertainly, unsure of his master's intentions. All watched as Attila methodically raised each jewel toward the declining sun. As he re-entered the tent, the entrance flap dropped behind him with a whisper.

"Michilieh," he said, dropping the valuables into the strongbox, "the gold is pure, bearing the seal of your Empire, but I'm disappointed in the quality of the gems. They are at best semi-precious. Still, I accept your token of thanks. For two small concessions, I'll release Rhoddinia to your care."

Michilieh frowned. "Name your conditions."

"First, I want the scribe. Though he's clumsy as a horseman, he might be useful."

"Agreed. He waits with the two hostages."

"Thank you. The other will be more difficult. If I give you Rhoddinia, you must relinquish any legal claim to your daughter. She's old enough to make her own life."

Michilieh glared at him. "I waive any claims over my daughter under Roman law," he said, his voice low, like a snake hissing.

Attila beamed at him. "Excellent! And what of the laws of Persia, the Sassian Empire?"

"Impossible. The Emperor would never allow me to forfeit my rights over my own flesh."

Attila chuckled and dismissed the argument with a shrug of his shoulders. "We will not travel to Persia. Your claim on your daughter lacks jurisdiction."

Helena studied her father's face and was chilled. His expression was that of a fanatic fixated on his salvation at any price. With abhorrence, she pictured life at the Persian court. They sought to make her into a living mannequin. Her will and her passion would be crushed. Fear of poison or worse, an assassin's blade, would be her reality. She shuddered

Attila clapped his hands. "Bring Rhoddinia!" he shouted. Within moments, the woman was half-escorted, half-dragged into the tent; her heels resisted and pressed the ground. Her cheeks were bruised and her dress was torn. Glancing at Attila, she tossed her head and spat. When she saw Michilieh, her eyes widened and her face abruptly turned ashen. She threw herself to the ground, groveling, and her hands clutched his ankles.

"Get up!" he commanded in Persian.

She obeyed quickly, bowing her head in submission.

With an open palm, he struck her cheek hard. She fell. "Now you may abase yourself before me," he said with a smile.

Zarakisitiah laughed.

Attila breathed deeply, inhaling the violence. Thirsting for revenge, Michilieh had forgotten everything, even Altiere, whimpering with fear.

Helena held the quivering child. She turned to Valamir. "Please, take us from here."

He was indifferent, bored by the prospect of Rhoddinia's interrogation. "As you wish. We are not needed."

"Altiere will be more comfortable with Attila's wives," Helena firmly persisted.

Valamir nodded in agreement. Beside Michilieh, Attila's face shimmered with anticipation. "Tell her I'll have my men skin her alive, slowly, one layer at time, unless she confesses all she knows," the Hun said in Greek, rubbing his hands together.

Michilieh smiled darkly: two conspirators in harmony. As he translated Attila's suggestion to Rhoddinia, Helena carried Altiere outside. Neither man noticed their departure.

The sun hung low in the sky, casting long shadows throughout the camp. The aroma of meat cooking drifted in the cold breeze. Underlying the hum of activity, birds called to each other, signaling the end of the day. Away from her father, Helena felt as if a weight had been lifted from her chest. But breathing hurt, like after running hard. Soft footfalls followed them. She wheeled with alarm, but saw only Caratipian.

She exhaled with relief, loosening the tension in her chest. "Will you stay near, in case Altiere needs you?"

"I'll be just outside."

They walked the few paces to the women's tent behind Attila's headquarters. To the guard stationed outside, Valamir requested the head wife. She answered the summons quickly. A remarkably pretty woman, she was no more than twenty-one. She listened carefully to Valamir's explanation and gestured for Helena to enter. Inside, the light was murky and the fire was low. Helena did not relinquish her grasp on Altiere. But the wives clustered around her, smiling affectionately at the child. Altiere smiled shyly, concealing a yawn behind her hand.

Helena was stern. "You're exhausted, Altiere. Did you have enough to eat?"

She nodded.

"Good. You need sleep. You have a long journey before you. Rest while you can."

"Can you stay with me?"

"For a moment."

Helena placed Altiere on a soft sleeping pallet and carefully nestled her doll beside her. Attila's head wife spoke in rapid Hunnic to the others, mentioning Altiere by name several times. Helena ignored the discussion. She hummed a soft lullaby, her eyes fastened on the child's sweet face, which showed signs of strain from her ordeal.

Once Altiere slept, Helena faced Attila's wives. Words failed her. Suddenly, she was assaulted by the image of Rhoddinia, bleeding and alone with Michilieh and Attila. Both were different, but so alike in their quest to devour their prey. In his passion, her father had not considered that Altiere, the child he professed to love, should not witness his interrogation.

She stammered haltingly in her rudimentary Gothic. "Altiere needs sleep."

The first wife's smile was warm. "We'll watch the child."

"Caratipian waits outside," Helena said.

"It's too cold for him out there!"

"He's old. No threat to Attila's honor."

The woman laughed, waving her hand at the hearth. "He can sit by our fire."

"Thank you," Helena said, the woman's kindness bringing tears to her eyes. With sharp poignancy, she remembered her friend, Arianna, and the way her face had lit up with an impish smile.

As she returned outdoors, her throat ached. She wanted to run to Valamir and be enveloped by him, obliterating her memories.

But she controlled herself and walked to him with measured steps. She reached for his hand and looked down to conceal her tears. "They said Caratipian could wait inside."

Valamir lifted her chin and looked into her eyes. Wordlessly, he pulled her to his chest. Comforted, she relaxed in his arms.

"Caratipian," he said, speaking over her head, "what do you think?"

"I'm too infirm to be a hazard to Attila's wives."

"Warm yourself at their fire, but take care."

"Don't I always?"

Quietly, Caratipian asked permission to enter. The flap closed behind him, dampening the lively sounds of the women's greetings.

Valamir kissed her lips. "We need to be alone," he said.

Rhoddinia's scream shattered the moment as she pleaded desperately for mercy. Trembling, Helena reached for Valamir. "I want to be with you, but I'm so afraid. For now, my father is occupied, but soon it will be my turn. I saw his face. He won't give up. He will have from me what he wants: the worst of my grandfather. I feel so frightened, like a little girl. Do you think the Shaman could help?"

He held her firmly. "I'll take you to him, I promise. But later."

He kissed her forehead, then her lips. His breath stroked her ears. "Come with me."

Her body answered his embrace and soothed her turmoil. "I'll go with you, Valamir."

His smile was broad. "Hassan!" he called.

The roan cantered toward them, whinnying, and reminded Helena of Passial. An attendant ran to catch the animal. Reaching Valamir, the stallion pulled his chin to his neck and halted, as if for inspection. Without a word, the slave gave up the chase and shook his head. Valamir laughed, patting Hassan on the neck and praised his performance. In contrast, Passial, unperturbed, walked quietly alongside his groom.

"Did you think your horse was the only one who could learn a few tricks?" he asked her, his eyes twinkling.

"Did you teach him that?"

"Maybe, maybe not."

She laughed. As they rode back, her body moved in easy rhythm to Passial's smooth canter. Rhys waited outside and stared at the sunset, his face a study in melancholy. Valamir dismounted, but before Helena could follow his example, he had her in his arms.

"Don't take off Hassan's saddle, but unbridle him. I'll need him again," he said to Rhys. "And don't let anyone disturb us. We've much to discuss in private."

Rhys kept his expression neutral, but his eyes were amused. Inside the tent, the fire burned low, but the coals were hot. He lowered her to their bed; his hands were a soft caress. Putting a finger to his lips, he whispered, "Wait."

As he placed sticks on the hearth, the flames rekindled, leaping up in orange and blue. His eyes fixed on her, he took off his tunic and dropped it on the ground.

He lay beside her, his lips a fervent caress on her brow, her cheeks and her mouth. As he removed her clothing, her passion escalated, demanding release. For a fleeting instant, she saw in her mind's eye her father's disapproving face. The image vanished, overwhelmed by waves of ecstatic sensation.

Afterward, she rested in Valamir's arms in comfortable silence. When he kissed her again, she returned his embrace without restraint. They merged together; their motions were delicious with intensity. Finally, their passion complete, Helena met Valamir's eyes. With a chuckle, she smiled.

"Why are you laughing?" he asked, frowning.

"It's hard to explain, but when I'm alone with you, my father becomes absurd. He only hears the thoughts in his head, and forgets to listen to his heart." She set her laughter aside. "But you, Valamir, my husband, remain true to yourself. Perfect for me, a civilized woman. Our worlds are irreconcilable, yet we remain one."

He smiled, his arms drawing her close. "You have my heart, Helena." His face tightened. "But I don't trust your father. He'll not go easily without you. You're more important to his plans than he has revealed."

For Helena, her father was far away, a subject not worth considering. Naked, they rested in each other's arms, drowsily content. Later, when they heard angry voices outside, it was a shock. They sat up, pulling on their clothes with surprising speed.

Rhys shouted, "You're not to enter!"

"Michilieh," Attila said, "I don't know what the custom is among civilized Persians, but we respect a closed tent flap. Wait."

Silence met Attila's injunction. Then her father shouted, "Helena! I've come to speak with you."

"I'll be a moment," she said, combing her hair.

She felt Valamir's eyes and looked up.

"Until tonight," he whispered.

Her father repeated his call, "Helena!"

"I don't want to see him," she said, suddenly weary. "He'll argue, trying to persuade me, and not listen when I say *No*."

"I'll be your translator. I think he understands the point of a sword."

She shook her head. "I won't have him touched. After we've said our farewells, I'll wait for you here during the hostage exchange. The farther away from Michilieh, the safer I feel."

When they emerged together from the tent, the sun was an orange ball, streaking the sky with purple and gold. Her father was astride his black horse; Altiere was in his arms. He surveyed Helena, his face cold with contempt. But behind his arrogant mask, she sensed rage.

"Did Rhoddinia confess?" she asked in Greek.

"She only implicated her husband. I remain dissatisfied," Michilieh said.

"What could they gain from kidnapping Altiere?"

"They planned to poison the entire Royal family. Rhoddinia's husband, Sheavatza, planned to marry Altiere and declare himself Emperor. Since others stand in line before Altiere, she was not adequately guarded. It will not happen again."

"How could they get close enough to the Emperor to poison him?"

"That's what I need to discover. The mystery remains unsolved until we have Sheavatza in our custody."

"Why does Altiere have the royal pendant?"

"Each of the twenty heirs possess the emblem. Your child would be so honored."

"No, Father. Chance has brought us together, choice takes us apart. Despite our differences, I'm pleased to know that you are well. Be gentle with Altiere. She saw things that no child should behold."

"Aren't you coming with us?" Altiere asked.

Helena answered her in Persian. "No. But I wish you joy."

"But why aren't you? Uncle Michilieh promised you would!"

"I can't. My life is with my husband."

"I'll miss you."

"And I'll miss you, too. Grow strong. Remember me. I'm sure that your Aunt, my father's wife, will love you as her own."

"Her? Don't you know anything? She doesn't care about anyone except Uncle. Everyone in the harem knows what happens to the pretty girls who catch Uncle's eye when she tricks them into drinking her special wine."

Helena's eyes narrowed. Even a child knew the truth about Michilieh's wife. She was a murderess, sacrificing her husband's yearning for an heir on an altar of jealousy.

"How long would I last at court? How many murders will you allow your wife? Be careful, Father. You could be next!" Helena said, her voice vibrating with anger.

For the moment, Michilieh's shoulders were slumped and his face was drawn.

"Zarakisitiah," Helena said. "Is it true? Do all my father's young brides die unexpectedly, years before their time?"

Unable to meet her eyes, he shrugged.

Michilieh found his voice, but his Persian was harsh, like rock scraping rock. "I can't believe anyone would dare touch you, Helena. You carry the old blood. Altiere's only a child. She doesn't understand. You must honor your duty to your ancestors. Come home and fulfill your obligation!"

Helena switched back to Greek. "I owe you nothing! I remain with my husband."

"Stop! I won't hear you! You don't understand the magnitude of what you spurn!"

"I owe you nothing," she repeated.

"I gave you life! Your mother died birthing you!"

"And what would she say? Would she tell me to embrace a loveless marriage and to abandon the man I love?"

Michilieh's eye twitched.

"Where would I send you a letter?" asked Helena.

"Do you think I'll settle for letters, Helena? You are my daughter. It's your duty to stay."

"Only a fool fights the inevitable, Michilieh," Valamir said. "And you don't have the look of a stupid man. Instruct your daughter how to reach you."

The veins on Michilieh's neck stood out. "You are impertinent!" He squared his shoulders, asserting self-control. "You may address any correspondence to me at the Emperor's residence. As the seasons change, I follow him from palace to palace." He frowned with distaste. "And how do I write you? In care of the Huns?"

"Rugliva's domain is north of the Danube. Ask Attila for the rest," she answered.

Her father urged his horse closer to her. With a leap, he dismounted before her. He opened his arms. "You'd not deny your father a parting embrace?" he asked.

Helena hesitated before stepping into his arms. As he held her close, he placed his mouth beside her ear and whispered in Persian, "It's not over, Helena. Your barbarian signifies nothing. You are of my flesh, my bone. Until I relinquish you to a lawful husband, you are my property, as is the custom."

"No, Father," she said, unsuccessfully trying to pull away.

"Yes, Daughter," he said, suddenly relinquishing her. Yet, his hands remained on her shoulders. "Farewell," he said, "until we meet under more auspicious circumstances."

Then he lowered his tall frame and kissed her full on the lips. Shocked, Helena recoiled from him. His response was a twisted smile. "It is my right as your father, Helena," he stated.

"Somehow I disagree," she replied coolly. Yet, as she turned from him, her cheeks blazed with shame.

As he remounted his waiting charger, he laughed. Yet, the look he gave Zarakisitiah was far from jovial. He quickly arched his right eyebrow then nodded almost imperceptibly. The next instant, he became remote, even haughty.

Stepping well away from him, Helena said, "Be well, Father," then wiped her lips with the back of her hand.

His answering stare was fervent. "Remember what I said, Daughter," he said. He bowed with a flourish of his hand, almost in a parody, rather than respect. "Until our next meeting," he added.

"Time to leave, Michilieh," Valamir growled as he loomed above him. In a moment, Valamir was astride Hassan, blocking Helena from her father.

"I'll wait here, Valamir," she said.

He smiled. "I won't be long!"

Yet, her father averted his face as he rode forward.

Altiere called out to her. "I won't forget you!"

As Helena waved, her view of Altiere was blocked by the horse following Michilieh. Wrapped in a rough cloth, a long bundle was tied to its back. Flies buzzed around it. Helena stared, her eyes widening as she saw human hair dangling from one end, red with blood. She gagged, covering her mouth with her hand, as she realized that it was Rhoddinia's corpse.

Witnessing her reaction, Attila winked with a smile, as if to trying to lighten her mood. Deep in her bones, Helena understood that her father and the Hun had reached beyond the barriers of civilization to embrace the other as a brother, each sharing a fascination with others' blood.

Alone with Rhys, Helena sat in companionable silence by Valamir's tent. She held her knees to her stomach, trying not to retch. In the distance, she kept her eyes on Valamir and her father surrounded by an armed guard as they moved toward the Hunnic line.

Wanting to see the hostage exchange, she stood to scan the distant Persian ranks, trying to find Bevion. She breathed with relief as she saw his blond hair flash in the sun.

Suddenly, Rhys leapt to attention. Alarmed, Helena followed his gaze, but saw only Caratipian hobbling quickly toward them.

She shouted in Persian, "Caratipian! Slow down. You'll hurt yourself!"

He called back, "Helena!" But his words were muffled as he gasped for breath.

"I can't hear you!" she exclaimed.

Running to meet him, she hastily scanned the forces to the far left. Bevion and Ishyite had reunited with Attila and Valamir in the long corridor between the two lines. Her eyes caught a glimpse of a solitary Persian riding south, his horse galloping in her direction. As he passed within an arrow's shot of the camp, Helena's arms tingled with apprehension. Suddenly, she questioned Valamir's wisdom in placing his tent at the camp's perimeter.

As she neared Caratipian, she heard running footsteps behind her. She whirled to face her pursuer, but saw only Rhys limping after her. Trying to dismiss her feelings of dread, she smiled at him. But as she saw the lone Persian soldier wave a blue cloth with rhythmic precision as a signal, her smile died.

Caratipian shouted to be heard over a gust of wind. "Helena! Call Passial. Something's wrong. You'll be safer mounted."

Not questioning him, she whistled for the white stallion. He answered with a whinny, cantering to her, with his tail raised high and streaming behind him. Her legs turned to lead when she saw a small band of mounted Persians erupt from behind a hill, galloping toward her, their quarry.

In Gothic, Rhys shouted, "To me!"

But the Huns' fighting force was out of earshot, leaving the women and the few children to scurry for cover. Rhys grabbed a long staff leaning against a tent and positioned himself between Helena and the abductors. Passial reached her, his eyes alert and ready.

Without being asked, Rhys gave her a leg up on the horse. "Go on!" he shouted, slapping Passial hard on the rump, urging him in the direction of Valamir and the Hunnic force.

As the white stallion plunged forward, Helena held on for life. She dug her heels into his sides and pushed him into a run to lead the Persians away from Caratipian and Rhys, protecting them.

Behind her, she heard horses thundering in pursuit, but did not look back. The situation ached with bitter familiarity, echoing when she had been Greillia's prey. With her knees, she guided Passial within the camp, away from the Hunnic line, knowing her flight in view of the two armies would act as a catalyst for battle. As she wove through the many tents, she prayed that no small child would dart into the path of the horses' hooves.

Suddenly, a Persian, astride a large black horse, blocked her way. She sat back on Passial, her weight signaling him to stop. Then she touched her right heel to his side, urging him left. They bounded from the soldier's trap and his smile of triumph faded to a grimace.

But the Persians' horses pounded after her, steadily gaining. Suddenly, she saw a small brown horse carrying a Hunnic rider. The animal was stretched out at a run, low to the ground, heading toward her. As Passial brought her near, she recognized Greillia, his face a mask of death. With the Persians at her back, she despaired, having no place else to run but forward.

Greillia's bow was in his hands, an arrow aimed at her heart. Passial galloped steadily, bringing her within range. As Greillia released the shaft, she screamed with terror, but she felt the wind whistle as it passed her ear. Behind her, it met flesh with a dull thud.

Compelled to look, Helena turned to see a Persian soldier with his hand to his throat the end of an arrow protruding through his bloodied fingers. Like a rag doll, he fell limply to the ground and moved no more. Another shaft swept the air. A horse screamed as it took the flint in its neck, dropping to the ground in a heap. Greillia's smile was a grimace.

With practiced smoothness, he pulled out his sword. His eyes scanned her face. He grunted with recognition, but allowed her to pass unharmed. His throat opened in a blood curdling yell, answered by other Huns galloping their horses to his aid.

Behind her, Greillia's sword rang its battle song. Passial carried her onward, into the path of another Persian horseman. His sword was drawn, aimed at the white stallion.

With hate, she shouted, "You won't take me!"

He laughed at her. "I'll kill your horse."

She drew her dagger, urging Passial to leap away from the Persian's blade. But his horse matched her maneuver, keeping position at her side. From his saddle, he extracted a small, coiled whip. He snapped it, knocking her dagger from her hand. As his hands reached for her, his eyes widened with surprise.

An arrow met his throat, followed by another to his eye. Blood spurted from his wounds, spraying Helena with a red haze. Passial snorted and jumped. The Persian fell ignominiously to the ground, dead. Turning left, she looked for her rescuer and saw Valamir, astride Hassan, many strides away. She blinked back tears.

"Valamir," she whispered, her voice hoarse with fear.

Trembling, she forced herself to glance back at Greillia. Though upright, his horse and he were dirty with blood. He was badly wounded, barely able to stay astride. The three Persians who had fought him hand to hand had not survived. One had lost his head, but the other two, judging from the number of jagged openings in their bodies, had taken longer to kill.

Beyond Greillia, she saw another corpse: the Persian who had taken the first arrow. Another black horse lay near, but Helena did not see its rider. She scanned the area with sudden urgency and caught a glimpse of the last Persian, fading behind one tent to the next. With his sword drawn, he made a dash toward Greillia, thirsting for glory instead of life.

Unaware of his danger, Greillia dropped his head to his chest, as if in fulfillment of her curse. But Helena could not keep silent. In her heavily accented Gothic, she shouted, "Greillia! Behind you!"

The warning was enough. With effort, he wheeled his horse from the attacker's sword. Instantly, many arrows rained on the Persian, mortally wounding him.

When Valamir reached her, he leapt from Hassan and pulled her into his arms, kissing her. He whispered, "I thought I'd lost you! Are you all right?"

Returning his embrace, she began to cry. "Greillia saved me!"

"As punishment, Attila had forbidden him to ride with us. By defending you, he upheld the tribe and brought honor instead of shame."

"But for my warning, he'd be dead. I don't know why I didn't hold my tongue," she said with bitterness.

"A man could not have done better."

She shook her head. A deep cry chased the air currents, resonating in her ears. "Helena! Helena!" her father repeated over and over again. She looked at the Persian line and saw him, alone, slightly in front of his men.

"Are you sure?" Valamir asked. "I accept your choice, whatever it is."

"How could you ask? You know who I want."

He smiled, his blue eyes soft as he touched her cheek, then her hair.

A crowd of Huns had gathered around Greillia, prone on the ground. As the Shaman approached, the throng was hushed. Helena wanted to leave and find the sanctuary of open earth and sky, away from prying eyes. Instead, she slid from Valamir's arms and walked slowly toward her enemy.

At the fringes of her vision, she saw Attila, astride his black stallion, watching as the men made room for her to pass. She was aware of Valamir's hand, pressing hers. Silently, she observed the Shaman's administrations to Greillia. From a small leather pouch, he poured liquid down the injured man's throat, then pressed points on his body in a specific pattern.

The Shaman spoke in Hunnic to Valamir.

"He wants us to come near," Valamir translated.

As they approached, the Shaman's eyes were fixed on Helena. She was in the moment - in harmony to its rhythm. Greillia moaned; his suffering transformed him from evil incarnate to a man.

Again, the Shaman spoke. Valamir translated. "He asks you to remove the curse. He is unable to lift it. Without your help, Greillia will die." Valamir paused, listening. "He tells me in the end, the curse will corrupt you, drawing you down the same path as your enemy. The darkness exacts a heavier price from you than its victim. He begs you to save yourself and release Greillia."

Helena's heart burned, but she knew the Shaman spoke the truth. In Persian, she whispered, "Forgive me, Mikael. I must do this or be no better than my father."

She bent down, close enough to touch the Hun. Her throat was constricted, fighting against her words. The Shaman watched her, without judgment, and steadied her with his eyes. She accepted the gift of his strength and turned inward to her soul.

Using ancient Persian, she spoke softly, "I ask the Wise Lord to forgive me. I have been proud and arrogant, not trusting his justice, looking to the Dark One for revenge. I ask the Wise Lord to intercede, to free me from my hate, and from my connection to this Hun, the murderer of my son." She paused. Then she touched Greillia's forehead, no longer aware of the Shaman or even the outside world.

"Greillia, through all time and space, I revoke any and all curses against you, cast by me."

A woman's voice rang out. "No, Helena! Let him die!" Magga screamed in the language of the Arals.

Unperturbed, Helena observed Magga struggling in a soldier's arms and fighting to intervene. The woman's face was contorted, as if she choked. Her eyes bulged.

"Magga, I do what I must," Helena said with quiet authority.

She returned her attention to Greillia. Her voice was soft. "I ask the Wise Lord to forgive me for letting the Darkness flow through me, channeling it to this World."

Greillia's eyes fluttered open. When he saw her, they reflected fear.

"My son's blood is on your hands. Nothing can change that. Justice will find you, but at the Wise Lord's choosing, not mine. I put you in the Light, Greillia, so that you will find your destiny, whatever it is," she finished in Gothic.

She stared at him one last time, knowing that she would never forgive him for his crime. But revenge felt as dry as dust in her mouth. Slowly, she traced the rune of Light above Greillia's chest. For a moment, she closed her eyes. As she stood, she clapped her hands twice, hard.

She spoke to the Shaman, "It is done."

He nodded. "Be at peace."

Feeling cleansed, she turned to Valamir, and was suddenly aware of the silent crowd. Magga was crying, her face swollen from tears. For once, Helena did not mind being the focus of so many stares.

Her heart open, she smiled and reached for Valamir's hands. "Let's go home, my love."

THE END

About the Author

Katherine Gibson Newcomer is a "Renaissance" woman well acclimated to the new millennium. After a year at Ripon Hall, Oxford, England, she graduated from Drew University with a B.A. in Religion and Music. In 1978, she received her J.D. from Rutgers Law School-The State University of New Jersey at Newark and gained admission to the N.J. Bar.

Opting out from law to stay home with her two children, she manages a thriving business as a music teacher and refines her skills as a classical pianist through performance. She has explored a fascination with religion by conducting small workshops in personal growth and self-empowerment. Yet, almost at any time of the day or night, K. Gibson Newcomer can be found writing on her computer. She is hard at work on her second novel, <u>Tatiana and the Hidden Land</u>, a fantasy set in the distant future.

She has been a repeated guest on "Changes," a live radio program on WDVR F.M. Along with other interests, she studies various martial arts and perseveres in her life-long passion for riding horses.

Printed in the United States
16615LVS00001B/178-201